TARGET

Forthcoming by Robert Wangard

MALICE

TARGET

ROBERT WANGARD

Robert Wangard (signature)

AMP&RSAND, INC.
Chicago, Illinois

ISBN 978-098181269-4

Design
David Robson, Robson Design

Published by
Ampersand, Inc.
1050 North State Street
Chicago, Illinois 60610

To Hailey and Caitlin,
both budding young authors.

ACKNOWLEDGEMENTS

When I announced I was leaving the practice of law to write fiction full-time, a friend remarked that now I would be unburdened by the facts and could write whatever entered my mind. Well, not exactly. The reference library in my office includes at least thirty works on subjects ranging from crime scene investigation and forensic science to poisons and how to track down people using computer data bases and other tools. I've consulted those works often and am grateful to the authors.

I'm also indebted to several of my former law partners for unselfishly contributing their knowledge in various areas. They include Jeff Rogers, a former Assistant U.S. Attorney, who advised me on many matters involving criminal procedure, and Tom Spahn who contributed his expertise on the arcane aspects of lawyer-client privilege.

My family — my wife Helen, my son Jon and my daughter Alison — has been unwaveringly supportive as the weeks turned into months and the months into years and the long-rumored "book" had yet to appear. They nevertheless continued to talk up what I was doing, and I'm always amazed at the people who know about it as a result. I'm forever grateful to them.

I'd like to acknowledge the contributions of my former secretary Ruth Zeppetello and her colleague, Lydia Rickert, who typed many of the early chapters of this book and have offered moral support since then. Ruth also continued to be my lifeline while I was learning to fly on my own and master the intricacies of the word processing system.

The folks at Ampersand, Inc. deserve their share of credit as well. David Robson suffered my micro-management of the design process in good humor, and Suzie Isaacs contributed her wisdom to make it all come together.

A final caveat. While I've acknowledged some of the people and sources I've relied on in writing this book, any errors are mine and mine alone.

ONE

I t was a rotten day to die.

That thought kept nagging at Pete Thorsen as he stared out at the flat, gray lake where a search and rescue team had begun to probe for the missing woman's body. All around him, the beach swarmed with people. Most looked miserable in the dog days heat, but followed the action out on the water with a peculiar intensity in their eyes. He'd seen that look before. Usually it was reserved for occasions like a 10-car pileup on the expressway or a high-rise fire. It was always the same, though; human misfortune never failed to draw a crowd.

The source of the anxiety was a stack of clothes on a small sailboat pulled up on the sand where the public beach abutted private property. The clothes had been found early that morning, and when they remained unclaimed a few hours later, someone called the sheriff's office. Now at one in the afternoon, the clothes were still there. The boat had been cordoned off with crime-scene tape strung around orange traffic cones and a uniformed deputy stood guard.

Pete removed his cap, ran a hand through his damp sandy hair, and glanced at his watch. He had a decision to make. He could hang

1

around and wait for something to happen, which meant enduring more of the suffocating heat while he stood there feeling like some damn ghoul, or he could go back home and let Harry fill him in at dinner that night. Going home had a lot of appeal. Still, he hadn't seen anything like the crowd that had gathered at the lakefront in all the years he'd been coming to Clear Lake. He brushed the sweat from his forehead and clamped his cap back on. Maybe he'd give it another half-hour.

Sirens had been the one constant all day, and the sing-song wail of yet another one cut through the dead air. He turned to see what had to be the last police cruiser in the county not already there pull in and join the tangle of official vehicles parked along Shore Road. The siren went quiet with a final whoop, but the cruiser's light bar continued to crank out puffs of red and blue that gave an otherworldly glow to the thin veil of haze hanging over the lake. Every pair of eyes on the beach had shifted to the road, as if the cruiser were a messenger that would clear up the mystery surrounding the unidentified woman who'd abandoned her clothes and just vanished into thin air. Or as Pete suspected they really feared, was lying dead someplace out there at the bottom of the lake.

A police photographer squeezed past him and made her way through the crowd to the boat. Pete watched her for a while and began to wonder again, as he had when he first saw the yellow tape, why they were treating the area as a crime scene. As far as he knew, there was no evidence that a crime had been committed, and they apparently weren't even sure there was a body. The deputy standing guard beckoned to a colleague and together they held back the gawkers as the photographer began to snap pictures of the boat. Slowly she worked her way around the perimeter, ignoring two men who clamored for her attention and kept pointing at the boat's stern. One of the deputies stepped in and moved them back.

Pete watched the side-show for a while and then scanned the crowd. It didn't take him long to spot Bud Stephanopoulis. At six feet seven, Bud stood out even in the throngs of people on the beach. He made his way through the crowd to where Bud was standing and poked him in the shoulder. "Enlighten me, Bud."

Bud's tan, hawk-like face twisted into a smile when he saw Pete and then turned sober again. "Sorry," he replied, shaking his head. "All I know is that they found some woman's clothes over on that boat."

"Even I know that," Pete said, giving his friend a sly grin. "The authorities must know something if they're treating it as a crime scene."

Bud shrugged. "I heard a deputy say they don't want anything disturbed until they figure out what happened. They're not giving out any more information." He eyed Pete sympathetically, looking at his tee-shirt that was still soaked with sweat from the mile jog from his summer home at the west end of the lake. Pete immediately felt a little uncomfortable. Bud never seemed to sweat and wasn't sweating now in spite of the conditions. It reminded him of something he'd learned long ago, which was that Scandinavians didn't handle high heat and humidity very well. Italians and Greeks, they were the hot weather folks. But not Scandinavians. Upper 80s was the limit of his comfort zone and the temperature had blown right through that ceiling and was still climbing. Pete self-consciously mumbled something about how it was a mistake to try to get in a run on a day like this.

Bud seemed to enjoy Pete's discomfort. He glanced at the lake then back at Pete and pointed to his cap that had "Save the Boat" emblazoned on the front. "What boat is Sir Galahad saving now?"

Pete used Bud's question as an excuse to remove the cap and wipe his forehead again. He held the cap at arm's-length and looked at the logo. "Ever hear of the Viking longboat that sailed from Norway to Chicago for the 1893 Columbian Exposition?"

"Actually, I have," said Bud.

"It's bounced around the Chicago area ever since and a bunch of us are trying to raise money to restore the boat and find a permanent home for it."

Bud slapped Pete on the shoulder. "You need some Greeks in your group. We were the real seafarers, you know."

Sparring with Bud never failed to get his competitive juices flowing. He put his cap back on and said, "Maybe, if you stop measuring time at the point when Ulysses sailed that little pond around the Greek city-states. We could use some Greek money, though. I'm going to have our treasurer contact you."

That prompted a full-fledged belly-laugh from Bud. "Send him around," he crowed. "I never pass up an opportunity to see one of you Nordic types grovel."

As they stood there talking, the divers bobbed out of the water and clung to the side of the boat while they conferred with the stocky woman on board. Like everyone else on the beach, Pete strained to hear what they were saying. He saw the woman brush the sheaf of straw-like hair away from her face and point to an adjacent patch of water. Then she coaxed the boat's engine to life and guided it slowly in that direction. After cutting the engine again, she resumed fanning herself with a magazine. Her bright blue life jacket was the only color on the still water.

"That's our local volunteer outfit, right?" Pete asked after the two divers had slipped below the surface.

"Lizzie McCabe's team," Bud said. "This ought to be interesting," he added, shooting Pete a knowing look. "The law enforcement people didn't decide to mount a search until noon and Lizzie has her guys out there already. She likes to get to the scene of a reported drowning first and find the body before the state boys arrive. Then she'll hit the bars and drink Labatt's all night and brag about how they're the real pros and make fun of the drop cameras and scanning sonar and the other fancy equipment the state team has."

"Sounds like a lady who enjoys her work," Pete said, chuckling. "How about that guy who drowned here a dozen years ago? Did she find him? It was right before I started coming up, as I recall."

"Cam Hatley? No way. This is a deep lake, about 175 feet out in the middle. Cam was way down in the trough. It took the state team a full day to find his body even with their equipment. Lizzie did beat them to bodies in Long Lake and Glen Lake, though."

"Hatley was drunk, right?"

"Totally shit-faced," said Bud. "Took his boat out one night with enough beer to sink a freighter and capsized. Someone saw the boat bobbing around on the lake the next morning and went out to check, but no Cam."

Lizzie was conferring with her divers again. There was more gesturing and conversation that couldn't be heard on the beach, then she moved her boat one more time and the divers disappeared beneath the surface. Pete and Bud resumed their conversation and speculated about who the woman might be and why she'd folded her clothes so neatly and placed them on the boat. A bony, older man with pasty skin protected by a floppy tweed hat had been steadily inching closer to them. He'd taken an obvious interest in their conversation while his shih tzu fought its leash and appeared intent on humping every leg in sight. When Pete inadvertently made eye contact with the man, it seemed to encourage him to join them.

"Neatly folded clothes are a sign of suicide," he croaked in a hoarse, conspiratorial whisper. His eyes — the only thing about him that could be remotely described as animated — flicked back and forth between Pete and Bud, seeming to invite dialogue. Pete said nothing, but wondered how someone would be able to just let herself drown. Bud looked at the man and pursed his lips and nodded politely. The man seemed crestfallen when Pete and Bud went back to their conversation.

After more talk about family and politics and the disastrous stock market, Pete decided his neck needed relief. He was six-two himself, but looking up at the former University of Minnesota basketball star for any length of time always made him think of scheduling a visit to a chiropractor. Besides, he wanted to get away from the aggressive little dog that had developed a special affinity for his leg.

He excused himself and made his way through the crowd to the water's edge. The region was in the clutches of the worst stretch of

August weather he could remember. On Saturday mornings when he didn't have a golf game, his usual routine was to sit on his porch, occasionally pecking away at his laptop, and watch the boats in the regatta with their colorful sails and sleek hulls slicing noiselessly through the water. But on this particular Saturday, the dead air had reduced some of the best sailing waters in northwest Michigan to a giant stagnant pond and forced cancellation of the event. He'd read somewhere that the ancient Egyptians believed the mid-summer heat and humidity made their dogs go mad. He thought about how edgy everyone seemed to be and decided that the ancients could have included humans, too.

As Pete watched the underwater team, his mind drifted back to that day 40 years earlier when they'd located his sister Loraine's body snagged in some brush along the side of the river, below a stretch of rapids. Two boys out for a day of fishing had spotted her clothes on the rocks. It was eerily similar to the scene playing out in front of him. That was a long time ago and he rarely thought about it anymore. But as he stood there, the painful memories crawled from the recesses of his mind like a replay of a tragic old film.

The hairy little creature making new sexual advances to his leg rescued him from his dark musings. He edged away from the dog and saw Shih Tzu Man standing a few feet behind him. The man seemed to have materialized out of nowhere, like he'd followed his new friend Pete to the water's edge, and was facing the lake with his eyes closed, swaying each time his dog lunged for another leg. His pale skin looked clammier than it had just a short time earlier. Pete was about to ask the man if he was okay when his eyes snapped open.

"They're searching in the wrong place," he said in his trademark whisper, looking at Pete as though he were a close confidant. "She's over there." His bony finger pointed to an area farther out and 30 or 40 yards east of where the underwater team was operating. Then his lids flopped closed again.

Pete took a deep breath and moved away, not wishing to chance being invited to join in a séance to commune with the woman's soul. He filtered through the crowd to the small sailboat. The name on the boat's stern, which he hadn't been able to see before, was "Destiny." He shook his head. If Shih Tzu Man saw that, he'd surely take it as a sign.

The photographer was gone and the woman's clothes had been placed in a large evidence bag. A sheriff's deputy stood talking to a gangly college-age boy with stringy blond hair, a wispy beard covering his chin, and frayed cargo shorts that ended below his knees. The deputy, at most 10 years older than the kid, could have been from a different planet. He was carefully groomed with a powerful torso that seemed out of proportion to the rest of his body. His uniform looked crisp in spite of the weather; only his flushed cheeks gave away his discomfort.

The kid scuffed at the sand with his green Crocs while the deputy paged through his small spiral notebook.

"Let's go over this again," the deputy said. "You came to the beach about 7:30 this morning to see whether there was enough breeze for windsurfing. That's when you first saw the clothes, right?"

"Yes sir, that's right."

"And when you came back about two hours later to check on the wind again, the clothes were still there."

"Yes sir, and the purse. That was still there, too. I thought that was kind of funny because women usually don't leave their purses, you know?"

Several onlookers had inched closer and did little to conceal their interest in the conversation. The deputy looked their way and led the kid farther down the beach. No longer able to hear what they were saying, Pete made his way back to where Bud was standing.

"I just heard something interesting," he said. "That kid talking to the deputy said the woman's purse was with her clothes. If that's true, they must know who she is."

"I hadn't heard about the purse," Bud said. He appeared to think for a minute, and then added, "If she did drown, maybe they want to keep her identity quiet until they can notify the family."

Pete nodded. "Who's the kid?"

Bud squinted in the direction Pete had motioned. "That's one of the Morrison boys. Adam, I think. Nice family. He goes to Alma College. Or maybe Albion, I don't remember. I always get the two mixed up."

Lizzie's team had moved to an area closer to where Shih Tzu Man had pointed. Pete felt a little foolish when he got the urge to motion them out and over another 25 yards.

"I haven't seen you since you got up," Bud said, never taking his eyes off the lake. "How's your law practice going?"

The missing woman had taken Pete's mind off the memorandum, but Bud's question rekindled the anger he'd felt that morning. His old nemesis, Marty Kral, seemed to dog him even when he put Chicago in his rearview mirror to spend a little time at Clear Lake. He toyed with the idea of flipping out a terse "fine" in response to Bud's question, but felt a need to unburden himself. "Do you remember a guy named Marty Kral?" he asked. "I had him up for a weekend six or seven years ago, right after we brought him into our firm."

"Sure," Bud said, giving him a quick glance, "we played golf, remember? Small, dark guy? Kind of twitchy?"

"That's him. He was on good behavior back then, but now he lobs grenades my way every 10 minutes. Our administrative partner just emailed me his latest memorandum. He's demanding that I ax nine of our partners by year-end. Calls them deadwood."

"Nine. Out of how many?"

"Fifty-two."

Bud whistled through his teeth. "Is he right about them being deadwood?"

"Maybe one. Most of the others are within a year or two of retirement and already have had their compensation reduced. One guy on his list had by-pass surgery and has been out half the year."

Bud gave him a long, hard look. "Why do you put up with him? You're the managing partner. Why don't you find a way to shove his ass out?" Bud had spent his business life in the rough-and-tumble world of investment banking, retiring before age 50, and it wasn't the first time he'd given Pete that advice.

"The day is coming," Pete said, clinching his teeth. He decided not to mention that he'd spent the morning using Kral for target practice with his new longbow.

"We need to get together for some one-on-one so you can take out your frustrations on the court." A grin spread across Bud's face and he nudged Pete. "I've missed seeing those eyes of yours turn black when I stuff one of your shots."

"Sure," Pete said, ignoring the crack about his eyes. "But let's wait until it cools off. I know how tough this heat must be on you seniors."

"Look, pal, who's the one sweating? In a couple of years when you hit the Big Five-O, I'm going to hire an eight-piece band to dress in black and play funeral dirges in front of your cottage 24/7."

Pete waved a hand dismissively. "Never happen. You're too cheap."

The high-pitched *whrrrrr* of a powerboat slapping across the flat water from the other side of the lake interrupted their banter. The man at the controls throttled back when he got close to where the divers were working. He glided alongside Lizzie's boat, and while they talked, the two men with him busied themselves with the equipment on the rear deck.

A man standing near Pete lowered his binoculars. "They have a hoist and some kind of harness. Maybe they've found her."

Conversations on the beach went silent as they usually did when something was happening with the search. One of the men in the second boat threw something — the harness, Pete assumed — into the water. A diver grabbed one end and disappeared below. Fifteen minutes passed, although it seemed like an hour. Finally the men in the boat began to work the hoist and the stern settled in the water as the line tightened. Slowly the body came into view. Pete grimaced at the sight and a murmur rippled through the crowd. They'd not only found the woman, they'd found her eerily close to where Shih Tzu Man had pointed.

The boats soon headed toward shore. Except for the rhythmic chug of engines running at little more than idle speed, the only sounds came from children romping and squealing on the playground, seemingly oblivious to the weather and the tragedy unfolding right in front of them. The poignancy of the moment washed over Pete as he continued to stare at the boats approaching like a small funeral procession. The crowd inched forward as gawkers jockeyed for a better vantage point. Pete could feel a surge of excitement run through the crowd. He grew tired of being pushed and elbowed. He left Bud and circled around the crowd to the water's edge on the left.

Two EMTs began to push a gurney across the beach. Even empty, the wheels cut into the sand and made it a tough go. Then there was the crowd. "Get back!" a sheriff's deputy shouted, trying to help. "Clear a path!" The people packing the beach gave ground, but only grudgingly. Recognizing reality, the EMTs followed Pete's path around the side. They wound up close to where he was standing.

The lead boat changed course to head for the EMTs. The man at the controls cut his engine when they neared shore and the crew splashed into the water. They lifted the blanket-wrapped body from the boat and carried it to the gurney. Lizzie McCabe stood in her boat observing, not exactly smiling, but not doing much to hide her look of triumph either. The EMTs took over and prepared to transfer the body to a heavy blue bag. At the first sight of skin, Pete saw people around him recoil or avert their eyes. One matronly woman wearing a lavender straw hat clasped a hand to her mouth and inched steadily backward, dribbling yellow-green vomit as she went.

That spectacle caused Pete to shift his gaze back to the gurney. When the EMTs peeled away the rest of the blanket, Pete could see that the dead woman was clad only in her underwear. Her gray flesh showed traces of goose-skin, and the unforgiving glare of the afternoon sun, even with the haze, magnified every blemish on her body, every ugly manifestation of death. Pete had been prepared for all of that, unsettling as it was.

He hadn't been prepared for the woman's face. The high cheekbones. The wide-set eyes, recognizable even as they bulged like oversized opaque marbles. The long dark hair. He stood there, stunned, and stared at the lifeless body of Cara Lane.

TWO

Pete was still thinking about that afternoon on the beach when he settled in at his usual table at Rona's Bay Grille to wait for Harry. The place was jumping. That wasn't surprising; it was Saturday night during the height of the season and the restaurant was the best in Millport. Just as important on that particular night, it had good air-conditioning.

The bartender, a broomstick of a man named Adorjan Kovacs but known to all as "Frankie" for reasons no one seemed to remember, waved and sent over a drink. Pete acknowledged the courtesy and took a sip of the vodka and tonic. It was perfect; light on the vodka with extra lime. He let the icy liquid trickle down and felt cool for the first time all day.

Rona's looked out on a bay that was a natural harbor. He could see the outlet to Lake Michigan from his table and watched a pair of fishing boats plow furrows through the leaden water as they powered in toward slips that lined a walkway just outside the restaurant's plate glass windows. Across the bay, the forested bluffs of Elberta turned darker green as the sun settled below the treetops.

He reflected on the day. After the emotional jolt of seeing Cara Lane's body had worn off, he'd tried to look at it analytically. None of the scenarios he could think of made sense. Then he just tried to put it out of his mind, telling himself he barely knew the woman. That hadn't worked either, and he continued to think about the two hours they'd spent together the previous night. What they'd talked about at dinner, her reaction to his questions, even her facial expressions. And most of all, he began to wonder who she was and why she was at Clear Lake.

He glanced at his watch. It was a half-hour past the time Harry had promised to meet him. That meant his old friend should arrive any minute. Knowing Harry, he would have talked to someone in the sheriff's office and everyone else in the county with a scrap of information about the dead woman. Maybe he'd be able to shed some light on things.

Harry lumbered in right on cue. After giving the hostess up front a squeeze, he maneuvered his egg-shaped body between the tables toward where Pete was seated. Pete smiled as he watched him come. There was no way the guy was five-eleven as he claimed. Unless that was his waist measurement. Harry dropped into a chair opposite Pete. The offices of his newspaper, *The Northern Sentinel*, were only a block up Main Street, but he looked like he'd just run the half-marathon.

"What a day," Harry said. He took a deep breath and let it out like a punctured truck tire expelling air. Then he removed his half-glasses and wiped them with a napkin. The glasses were so much a part of his *persona* that Pete assumed they'd been permanently affixed to the bridge of his nose when he pushed out of his mother's womb. Everything about him looked damp, including the fringe of salt and pepper hair that ringed his head. He swiped at his face with the napkin. Looking at Harry, Pete decided it would be wise to let him collect himself before pumping him for information about Cara Lane. That didn't mean a little needling was out of bounds, though.

"Nice of you to wimp out on golf," Pete said, knowing it was easier to lure a bat into bright sunlight than to get Harry McTigue on a golf course when the temperature soared into the 90s and the humidity kept pace. "A lot of people played, you know. And it's nice to see you're right on time as usual."

Harry looked at his watch and his eyebrows, which resembled a pair of gray bristly caterpillars, inched up on his forehead. Then he glanced toward the bar. Frankie seemed to have four eyes when it came to keeping good customers happy and already had a drink coming his way. Harry was a fixture at the Bay Grille and whether he verbalized it or not, everyone knew his drink of choice was single malt scotch with a splash of water. Recently, though, Rona had been doing her best to introduce him to the pleasures of wine with his evening meal.

Harry dabbed at his face again and pointed to Pete's glass. "You want another? Vodka and tonic, right?"

"Thor's Hammer, but I think I'll wait."

Harry frowned. "Do you think that's the best vodka?"

"I do. Besides, I always stick with the family brand."

Harry's face went blank for a minute. "Oh I get it," he finally said, his eyes showing sparkle again, "the 'Thor' connection, right? That's good. But you're Norwegian. That stuff is made in Sweden."

"All Norsemen, my friend, all Norsemen. Plus my mother had some Swedish blood."

Harry ignored the information about Pete's family genealogy and took a sip of his scotch. A satisfied sound gurgled up from his chest after he swallowed.

"And just so you know, I didn't wimp out on golf. We're short-handed at the paper, like I told you, and some stuff came up."

"Umm hmm," Pete said. "I bet that air-conditioning in your car felt good."

Harry shot him a look and took another swallow of his drink.

Pete decided that he'd given Harry enough time. "What have you heard about the dead woman?"

Harry took his time chewing an ice cube and then said, "Well, they know she's dead."

Pete gave him a long look and rolled his eyes. "Damn," he said, "I really love the insights you bring to journalism. I can just see your Tuesday edition headline: 'Dead Woman Confirmed Dead.'"

"Hey, that's not bad. Maybe I'll go with that. You're not claiming copyright or anything, are you?"

Harry had been in line to become managing editor at one of the Chicago dailies when its marquee political reporter fell in love with the bottle and began to fabricate news stories. Harry wound up taking the fall as part of the paper's public relations damage control. Not long after, he moved to Millport and bought the local weekly. The new venue allowed him to indulge his twin passions of fly fishing and reporting the news. In a more modest arena, obviously.

Pete was puzzled. Normally if there was news of any kind, even something as mundane as the crowning of a new Coho Queen to celebrate the fishing season, Harry would be spewing out the details before his double-wide butt hit the chair. Cara Lane's drowning had to be the hottest news to hit the area all year and he just sat there like a sphinx.

Pete tried again. "I'm surprised you weren't at the beach this afternoon."

"Couldn't," Harry said, chomping on another ice cube. "I was busy like I said. I had to do a bunch of interviews for a feature we're planning to run in two weeks."

Pete saw the restaurant's owner, Rona Martin, approaching but not in time to alert Harry.

"What a pleasure, boys," she said, coming up behind Harry and giving him a peck on the cheek. "You know, my tables average two point seven turns on busy nights like this. Except for table five; that averages one turn. How do you think we can explain the difference?"

Harry scrambled to his feet to give her a hug, knocking his silverware to the floor in the process. Pete started to rise as well, but Rona pressed down on his shoulder and slid into an empty chair between them. She scooped up Harry's silverware and waved at a busboy. Then she brushed her thick mane of sun-streaked hair from her face and looked around the room, obviously pleased with the evening's business.

Harry was grinning again like he'd just landed a 17-inch rainbow. "Maybe it's because you need us here at table five to draw in customers," he said. "We're part of the local color."

She smiled at him and stuck out her tongue. "You planning to be up for a while?" she asked, looking at Pete.

"Most of August with any luck."

Rona continued to look at him with those bottomless eyes that had put Harry in a trance from the moment they met. "That has to be a change for you. But it's good. You look like you could use some rest." She rose to her feet. "That was awful over at the lake today, huh?" She shook her head sadly and left to continue her rounds. Harry's eyes followed her like a magnet drawn to iron. Her waistline had filled in a little, but for a woman flirting with 50, she still turned a lot of heads.

Pete rapped on the table with a spoon to get Harry's attention. "I really don't know what she sees in you."

Harry turned back to him, looking indignant. "How many times do I have to tell you? It's my body. She admires my penetrating mind, too, but without this Adonis body, I wouldn't stand a chance."

Pete laughed. He decided to take one more stab at getting Harry to open up about Cara Lane before he reached across the table and choked it out of him.

"I assume you've talked to some people about the drowning by now," he said. "What have you found out?"

Harry peered at him over his half-glasses. "You seem awfully interested in that dead woman. Is there something I should know?"

"In case you haven't heard," Pete said, frustrated with Harry's continuing tap dance, "I had dinner with her last night. When someone you just dined with turns up dead in the lake, it sort of piques your interest."

A hint of triumph showed in Harry's dark eyes. "I heard you two knew each other. I've been waiting for you to tell me about it, but all you seem to want to do is make bad jokes and interrogate me."

Pete would have laughed if he hadn't been so irritated. Round one to Harry on this particular night.

"Sounds like I didn't have to tell you," he mumbled. A minute later, he added, "Just curious, how did you find out?"

"Have you forgotten I'm a newspaperman, counselor? I have sources. You think you can have dinner with a woman in this town without me knowing about it?" An impish smile crept over his face. "I notice you didn't bring her here."

Pete ignored the jab and said, "What else did your sources tell you?"

"I was counting on you to fill me in," Harry said, giving him a sly look. "It sounds like you're the one with the first-hand information."

Pete sighed. "Okay, what do you want to know?"

"For starters, how did you know her? The two of you old friends or something?"

"No, as a matter of fact we weren't old friends. I met her at the art fair on Thursday afternoon and had dinner with her last night. That's it." He caught Frankie's eye and ordered another Thor's Hammer and tonic. It was turning into that kind of night.

Harry's eyes danced. "So you picked her up at the art fair . . ."

"Stop," Pete said, holding up a hand. "I didn't pick her up. I was walking through trying to find a booth with something other than Petoskey stone necklaces or hanging baskets. We just happened to be looking at some watercolors by the same artist. We talked for a while and then agreed to have dinner. I thought we'd try Ship's Cabin as a change of pace."

That was mostly true. When he first suggested dinner, Cara hadn't exactly jumped at the invitation, but he'd talked her into it. And he selected Ship's Cabin for a very practical reason: he knew Harry would be at Rona's and if they went there, he would have been at their table in a nanosecond, babbling on about everything he thought she ought to know about him. He preferred to speak for himself when it came to women.

"Okay," Harry said, making a show of looking thoughtful, "I guess that's not a pickup." He leaned back in his chair and looked like he'd swallowed something from the live bait shop at the marina.

Pete stared at him for a while. "You know, I can think of a lot of people I'd rather be having dinner with right now."

Harry's face sobered. "Jesus, I'm sorry. I didn't realize you were so touchy about it. I was just trying to get you going a little and lighten things up. No question it was a tragic thing. For me, it's a news story, but I don't understand why you're so obsessed by it."

"I'm not obsessed by it. Interested, yes, but hardly obsessed."

"Well I guess I can understand why you'd be interested, having had dinner with her and all."

They sat in silence for a few minutes and Pete bent his swizzle stick into various shapes. Then he said, "She was a strange woman. We spent two hours together and I learned absolutely nothing about her."

"So you're saying she was, what, mysterious? Evasive?"

"Like a well-schooled espionage agent. I didn't even get her serial number."

"Mmm," Harry said, "interesting. Well, to get you off my back, here's what I've been able to find out so far. It's not much. Her name is Cara Lane, which you obviously know, and she lived in Chicago. That's why I asked if you knew her. She rented the Lyman cottage for a week. If you don't know their place, it's on the other side of the public beach from you, off on a side road called Walker's Trail. I talked to the Lymans just before I came here. They said she was polite and gave an address in Chicago, which jibes with what I got from the sheriff's office. The Chicago address was on her check, too, I understand. The Lymans didn't know why she was up here. They assumed she either knew people or had heard about Clear Lake and thought it might be a nice place to spend a few days."

They let conversation take a break and worked on their food. Pete had the parmesan-crusted brook trout, his favorite dish at Rona's. Harry had a rib eye steak. He cut into it with the precision of a surgeon to make sure it was medium rare and forked a chunk into his mouth. He washed it down with a healthy swallow of merlot and a contented look spread across his face. Rona's civilizing influence seemed to be working.

"Getting back to Cara," Pete said, resisting the urge to dig into his twice-baked potato, "I don't know if she was really being evasive." He paused for a moment and thought about it. "No, that's wrong. She was evasive, but she also seemed distracted if that makes any sense."

"What do you make of it?" Harry mumbled through a mouthful of steak.

"Not sure. She seemed touchy about everything. Then after we finished eating, she went to the ladies room and when she came back, she said she had to leave. Didn't even sit down again. We left part of a bottle of a damn nice pinot noir on the table, too. It was like she just remembered she had to be somewhere or meet someone. I chalked up the evening to experience, but after what I saw on the beach this afternoon, I started to think about it again."

"Didn't sit down again, huh?" Harry said, swallowing. "That sounds like unusual behavior even for one of your dates." He choked back a laugh and quickly raised a hand. "Sorry, I didn't mean that."

Pete gave him the most disgusted look he could conjure up and switched his gaze to the bay. Millport was on the western edge of the time zone and it was nine and the light was fading. Ever the optimist, Harry agreed that there did seem to be a few tiny ripples on the water. Maybe the weather was finally changing.

"For what it's worth," Harry said, "here's what I think happened. She went swimming alone and drowned. Maybe when she got back to her cottage, she couldn't sleep because of this friggin' heat and humidity. She could have gone for a walk down to the beach and you know, kind of a spur of the moment thing decided to go for a swim to cool off. That would fit because she wasn't wearing a bathing suit. It was dark as hell last night and maybe she got too far out and lost her bearings or something."

"Possible," Pete said, thinking about it. "But that doesn't explain her strange behavior at dinner or why she left so abruptly."

Harry shrugged. "True. I'll see if I learn anything else when I talk to the sheriff's office again on Monday. I'm going to try to see the Medical Examiner, too."

"Will you let me know what they say?"

"Sure, as long as it doesn't require me to breach any confidences."

"Oh for crissakes, Harry, it's not like I'm asking you to compromise your journalistic integrity or something. I'd just like to know what happened to the woman."

He regretted the tone as soon as the words left his mouth and could feel Harry's eyes on him. But damned if he was going to apologize, not after the way Harry had played games with him all evening.

"You seem edgy," Harry said softly, giving him a long look. "This reminds you of your sister, doesn't it?"

Harry knew him better than anyone else. Too well, maybe. Loraine had remained on his mind after he left the beach. He remembered how much it hurt when his mother told him she wasn't coming back. Her death had been quickly branded a swimming accident, and only later in life did he find out that many people in the community believed there should have been more of an investigation. The kind of investigation there would have been if the drowning victim had been a child of George Ferguson, who owned half the town, instead of the wayward stepdaughter of that loser Lars Thorsen. But he wasn't in the mood to talk about demons from his past, even with Harry.

"You're playing amateur psychologist again," he said.

Harry shrugged and continued to study the dessert menu. Pete wasn't a big dessert man, but agreed to join him for a piece of key lime pie. The best outside Florida, Harry liked to boast. Pete enjoyed every bite of the pie, but thought about the softness around his waist and vowed to get in a good run on Sunday, heat or not.

After scraping his plate to capture the last morsel of pie, Harry looked at Pete and said, "I'm a little disappointed in you. I thought a crackerjack lawyer like you would do a better job of grilling me about how I found out you knew Cara Lane."

Pete forced another grin, which he'd been doing a lot of that night. "You told me it was one of your sources. I knew that pumping you for details would be like trying to get a priest to disclose dark secrets told to him in a confessional."

"It was my contact in the sheriff's office," Harry said. "They found your business card in her purse. They're going to want to talk to you."

THREE

When Pete arrived at the County Government Center, there were only a few cars in the visitors' parking lot. That didn't surprise him. The place was never a bee hive of activity and it *was* a Monday morning in August.

He walked into the sheriff's office five minutes early. The woman behind the counter stopped working on her crossword puzzle and gave him a *Why are you here?* look. From what he could see, she had four or five words filled in. He gave his name and said he had an appointment to see the sheriff.

The woman scooted her chair to the left and hunched over a large month-at-a-glance appointment calendar. As Pete waited, he was treated to an intimate view of the battle raging between the dark roots sprouting aggressively from her head and the rest of her peroxide blonde hair. Had he been a betting man, his money would have been on the roots.

She finally looked up. "Are you the man who called early this morning about the Cara Lane case?"

"Yes."

"Okay, that explains it." She shook her head and he could see the tension drain from her body. "Sheriff Haskins isn't available today. You're scheduled to see Deputy Richter. That's what threw me off."

Pete just looked at her, not having the faintest idea what he could do to ease her trauma.

"This way," she said, exiting her barricaded workspace through a swinging half-door. "I'll take you down."

Pete followed her along an inner hall that branched off the main corridor. She opened a door and extended her arm in a theatrical sweep. Then she turned and headed back down the hall with a purposeful stride, like she'd just thought of a three-letter word for nine-across and wanted to get back to her desk to pencil it in.

"Where's the sheriff?" Pete asked. His voice brought her up short and she looked back with an annoyed expression.

"He's not in the office, sir. I'll tell Deputy Richter you're here." This time she was off before he could fire a follow-up question at her.

The cold front had come through on Sunday night, but this lovely windowless room seemed to have missed out. Eighty degrees would be a good guess. He squeezed between the wall and the laminated fake wood-grain table and slid into a molded plastic chair. Then he waited. After 30 minutes, his mood was hotter than the room. He had zero tolerance for being kept waiting. Okay, he made an exception for Harry, but with him being late came with the gene pool.

Just as he was about to walk down the hall and kick in someone's door, two men walked in. The one in uniform was the deputy he'd seen interviewing the college kid on the beach the day they found Cara Lane's body. His name tag read "Franklin Richter." In close quarters, his upper body looked even more formidable than it had outside. His shirt fit like Lycra on a cyclist, and his brushed-back hair looked like it had just been given an extra dollop of styling gel.

The deputy's plain clothes companion was reed-thin with longish dark hair that swept across his forehead like a crow's wing. With his neatly trimmed moustache, he would have looked almost rakish but for his pale skin. Apparently not all of the locals enjoyed the great outdoors.

"Thanks for coming in Mr. Thorsen. I'm First Deputy Richter and this is Detective Tessler."

They settled into chairs across from him. No handshakes. No apologies for keeping him waiting. And if Pete's hearing was still good, Franklin Richter had just introduced himself as "First Deputy." So much for the informality of a small community. Pete had expected to be on his way out of the building by now, hopefully with some insights into Cara Lane and what had happened to her. Instead, First Deputy Richter and his sidekick were just revving their engines.

"Bill not around?" Pete asked.

"Bill," Richter said, chewing on the name like it was some strange word out of a foreign dictionary.

"Bill Haskins," Pete said, helping him along. "The sheriff."

Richter stared at him with flat eyes, like cops do on television shows. "You know Sheriff Haskins, I take it?" he asked.

"We've met."

Richter paused for a moment and continued to stare at him. "You mind telling me how?" From his tone, Richter seemed to be hoping he was sitting across from a man the sheriff had once booked for some serious offense.

"Bill was the county liaison to a citizens committee I served on a few years ago," Pete said, using that foreign word again.

Richter gave him a final stare. "Sheriff Haskins is out of town," he said. "I'm in charge of this investigation. Shall we get started?" He opened his spiral notebook with a snap.

"That's why I'm here," Pete said genially.

Richter placed a small recording device on the table. "Do you mind?" he said. "It's just for convenience so Detective Tessler and I won't have to spend all our time taking notes."

Pete raised an eyebrow. He had nothing to hide, but instinctively didn't like the recording business. "Is that really necessary? I can't believe this will take us very long."

"Are you objecting?"

"I'm not saying I'm objecting. I just don't understand why it's necessary. I'll be happy to give you a written statement so you don't have to take notes."

"Since we're all here together, that doesn't make much sense," Richter said. "Let's do it this way. We'll record, but if at any time you become uncomfortable with that, you can tell us and we'll turn it off. Fair enough? As a lawyer, I'm sure you're not bashful." He slicked back one side of his hair with an open palm.

"Fine," Pete said, not wanting to make too big of a stink about it. "But I want to go on record that I believe it's unnecessary."

"Noted," Richter said. He clicked on the machine and had Pete state his name. Then Richter asked him where he lived.

"Chicago, but I have a place on Clear Lake." He gave both addresses.

A smirk crept over Richter's face and he glanced at Tessler. "Have you been in our community long, Mr. Thorsen?"

Ah, Pete thought, maybe that was what the wait was about. Locals versus lakies. Show him who ran things.

"Ten years," Pete said, trying to sound like a very appreciative guest.

"Good," Richter said, "You must enjoy it up here." He fiddled with his notebook. "To get things started, why did you call us?" He leaned forward and drummed on the table with the end of his oversized pen that had a lot of flashy gold trim.

"I explained that when I called this morning. I had dinner with Cara Lane on Friday night and thought I should offer to provide any information I have that might help you piece together what happened."

Tessler had been quiet, but now he jumped in. "Mr. Thorsen, if you have material information about the vic, why did you wait to contact us?"

"I didn't say I have material information," Pete said, trying not to take offense at the question. "I have no idea whether what little information I have is material or not. But I thought I should offer to provide what I do have for what it might be worth."

"You didn't answer my question," Tessler said. "Why did you wait until today to call us?"

"Until today," Pete said slowly. "There was, what, one day — a Sunday — between the time they found her body and when I called? If I'd had some hot information about what happened, I would have been in your office Saturday afternoon. But I don't. I called first thing this morning, but I guess I was off a little on the time of our appointment."

Richter and Tessler exchanged glances again and Tessler shifted in his chair and looked uncomfortable. Richter ignored Pete's comment and paged through his notebook. "Please tell us about your relationship with Cara Lane," he said, shifting gears. He slicked back the other side of his hair.

"There was no relationship."

When Pete didn't continue, the deputy said, "You must have had some relationship with her. You took her out on a dinner date."

"To me, relationship means romantic involvement. I had no romantic involvement with Cara Lane, or any other involvement for that matter. I took her to dinner once. That's it."

After sparring over the meaning of "relationship" and other semantics, Pete told them how he'd met Cara at the art fair and then had dinner with her on Friday night. They questioned him about the details for close to an hour. About the only thing they didn't ask was the kind of dressing he'd had on his salad.

Just when Pete's patience was being tested by Richter's repetitious questions, Tessler jumped in again and took them in a different direction. "You and the vic are both from Chicago, but you're telling us you didn't know her from there, is that right?"

"Right," Pete said, "Like I said, I never met her before Thursday."

"Are you married, Mr. Thorsen?"

"Was. My wife died a couple of years ago."

"I'm sorry to hear that," Tessler said. "What did she die of?"

Pete locked eyes with him. "What does that have to do with Cara Lane?" He knew there was an edge to his voice, but he didn't give a damn. The question was ridiculous.

"Do you have some reason for not wanting to tell us how she died?"

"Only that it's completely irrelevant to your investigation," Pete said, continuing to stare at Tessler. "But if it's that important, it was an aneurysm, okay?"

Tessler seemed unsure of whether to ask a follow-up question or move on to something else.

The First Deputy bailed him out. "So you've been widowed for two years, but you never ran into the vic at a singles bar or something?"

"I'm going to say this one more time. I met Cara Lane for the first time ever at the Millport art fair on Thursday. The only other time I saw her alive was at dinner on Friday night."

Richter continued the annoying ratatat with his flashy pen. "What was the vic wearing the night you had dinner with her?"

There it was again. That phony cop-speak, referring to her as the "vic." Why couldn't they just say Cara or the dead woman like everyone else?

"I don't remember exactly," Pete said. "A sleeveless blouse, I think, and some kind of shorts."

"What color?"

"What color? What does that . . ."

"We're just trying to determine whether she might have gone home after she left you," Tessler interjected. "If we knew she changed clothes, that would help us trace her movements that night."

Finally something that made sense. Pete tried to remember.

"Her shorts were dark blue, as I recall, and she had on a light-colored jersey top — white or cream — with trim that matched her shorts. Are those the clothes you found at the beach?"

Richter looked irritated at Pete's question and gave him that flat-eyed stare again. "We're just gathering facts today, not giving reports on the details of our investigation, Mr. Thorsen."

Pete smiled.

Richter checked his notebook again. "Now, did the vic tell you why she was up here?"

"Not really. She just said she wanted to get out of Chicago for a few days."

"Did she say anything about having friends or relatives in this area?"

"No," Pete said, thinking back, "she didn't seem to want to talk about personal things." He recalled how sensitive she'd been to some of his questions.

Richter flipped through his notebook one more time. Apparently finding the prompt he was looking for, he asked, "What time did you leave the restaurant?"

"About nine. She went to the ladies room, and when she came back, she said she had to leave. I remember looking at my watch."

"Did you take her home?"

"No, we met at the restaurant. I asked if she needed a ride home and she said no. I was parked a half-block down the street. She was going in the same direction so she walked with me that far. Then we said goodnight and she continued on. That's the last time I saw her." As a lawyer, he knew he should just answer the question that was asked, but he wanted to get the damned inquisition over with.

"So she could have been picked up by someone after you left her."

"Could have," Pete said, "I really don't know."

"But you didn't see her get in a car?"

"No."

"What did you do after the two of you separated?"

"I went home."

Richter paged through his notebook for about the ninth time. "Is there anything else about the night you had dinner with the vic you think might of use to our investigation?" he asked.

Pete thought back to that night at dinner. After thinking it over for a moment, he said, "There is one thing. I don't want to make too much of this, but she seemed edgy that night. Maybe it was just her personality, I don't know."

Richter's eyes narrowed. "What do you mean, edgy?"

"Nervous maybe, or distracted? Like I said, I don't want to make a big deal out of it because maybe it was nothing."

Tessler broke in. "This could be important. What you seem to be saying is that she acted afraid or fearful."

"That's not what I said."

"Maybe not in those exact words," Tessler replied, "but that's what you seemed to imply."

"No, that wasn't what I was implying. I said she seemed nervous or distracted. That's different than fear. Fear would be too strong of a term, I think."

Richter exchanged glances with Tessler again, then said, "Anything else you can think of?"

"Not really. I was only with her for two hours, like I said, and never really got to know her."

"Are you planning to be up here for a while, Mr. Thorsen?"

"I'm leaving tomorrow afternoon for a one-day business meeting in Chicago and coming back Wednesday night. Otherwise I hope to be up for the rest of the month. Maybe another short trip or two back to Chicago."

"Good. So we can reach you at one of the numbers you gave us if necessary?"

"Yes," Pete said, wondering why that would be necessary.

Richter looked at Tessler. "It looks like we're done, Detective." He rose to his feet.

Pete remained seated and looked at Tessler and then Richter. "I have a question," he said. "Have you come up with any background information on Cara Lane? Apart from what we talked about, that is."

Richter looked at him. "Like I said before, we're just gathering facts today. It would be premature for us to get into details like that."

Pete smiled again. "Okay, last question. From some of the things you asked, it sounds like you haven't classified her death yet. Am I right?"

Richter continued to look at him and folded his arms across his chest. His tight-fitting shirt bulged with his muscles. "This case is like any other unexplained death," he said. "We look into all of the possibilities."

FOUR

Pete had spent too much of the first good day of his vacation indoors dealing with the Cara Lane affair and decided to go for a run to clear his head. First, though, he needed to satisfy his curiosity about something. He logged on his computer and Googled "Cara Lane — Chicago." He got 65,000 hits. After close to an hour of scrolling through the entries, none of which remotely related to the Cara Lane in whom he was interested, he laced up his Nikes and headed out.

The shadows were lengthening as he loped along M-22. He swung east on Shore Road and followed it along the lake. A gentle breeze out of the west ruffled the water and the evening was so clear he could almost count the leaves on the birches on the other side of Clear Lake over two miles away. A few other runners were getting their exercise in at the close of the day and as always, the dog walkers were out in force.

He thought about what Harry had to report when he stopped to see him at the offices of *The Northern Sentinel* late that afternoon. According to the M.E., they'd established the cause of death was drowning in Clear Lake because only lake water was found in Cara's lungs. They also found a cut on her head and some scrapes and bruises on her body. They were still evaluating the cause of those injuries, but a theory being considered was that she swam out to the far raft, tried to dive, and hit her head on the edge. They were testing to see whether blood found on the raft was a match with hers. So far, they'd found no evidence of sexual molestation. Time of death was estimated to have occurred between 11:00 p.m. and five the following morning

The thing that bothered him the most about Harry's report was the alcohol. The M.E. said they found a high level of alcohol in Cara's system. Harry also said that his contact in the sheriff's office, a deputy by the name of Ernie Capwell, told him that a near-empty wine bottle with Cara's fingerprints on it was found by the boat where her clothes were left. That seemed odd. He thought back to their dinner and knew Cara didn't have much more than a glass of wine that night. In fact, he had the impression she wasn't much of a drinker. Somehow it didn't quite ring true to believe she would take a bottle of wine to the beach by herself and sit there and get drunk.

When he reached the public beach, he saw that the crime-scene tape was gone and a senior couple was sitting on folding chairs and holding hands and looking out at the water. Over on the playground, a college-aged girl, probably a babysitter, watched her young charges as they cavorted on slides and an assortment of horses and lions and alligators. A wind surfer — it looked like the Morrison kid, but he couldn't be sure — caught the breeze and glided over the water, apparently determined to milk the last minute out of a splendid day. He was struck by how everything seemed to get back to normal so fast.

Pete continued on, breathing harder but enjoying the cool evening. He glanced at Walker's Trail where it branched off to his right, away from the lake, but kept running east on Shore Road and thinking about his conversation with Harry.

The other interesting thing to come out of that conversation dealt with the internal politics at the sheriff's office. Apparently Capwell had his nose out of joint over Sheriff Haskins' decision to make Richter and not him responsible for the investigation when Haskins was out of town, which was a good part of the time since the sheriff was shamelessly pursuing his political ambitions. Capwell had 15 years seniority over anyone else in the office and according to Harry, lost no opportunity to snipe at Richter for the way he was handling the investigation. He accused Richter of being out of control and eager to build his reputation so when Haskins ran for higher office, he'd be the logical replacement. Based on his own experience with Richter, Pete found it hard to argue with Capwell's assessment.

All in all, it had been an interesting day. On the surface, most of the signs pointed to a swimming accident, which is what Capwell told Harry he thought it was. But some things kept gnawing at him. At the top of the list was the way Cara had acted at dinner that night. The alcohol bothered him, too. And he wondered once again who she was and why she was at Clear Lake.

He turned and headed back toward his cottage. When he came to Walker's Trail this time, he veered left and took the narrow road up a hill through stands of oak and maple and the occasional pine. He'd been through this area before and particularly enjoyed it in the spring when the trillium coated the forest floor in white like a blanket of fresh snow.

A quarter mile in, he came to the Lyman cottage. No cars were parked outside, and everything looked dark and quiet. He assumed someone from the sheriff's department had checked the place out after Cara's body had been found in the lake. Maybe not, though; it wouldn't be the first time details like that had fallen through the cracks. He wondered about the car. She must have driven up from Chicago, or at least would have needed wheels to get around the local area. Unless she was with a friend or family member who had a car. Of course someone might have picked up her car and driven it away after she drowned. Someone from the sheriff's office, possibly.

The Lyman cottage was nestled back in the woods, visible from the road, but with the summer foliage, only if a person were looking. On impulse Pete did something he immediately knew was a little stupid;

he looked around to make sure no one was in sight and then walked swiftly up the wood-chip path that served as a driveway, went around to the back, and peered in a window. The interior was barely visible in the fading light. He could make out an open kitchen separated from the living room by a breakfast bar. Two doors opened off a short hall. Bedrooms, he assumed.

Pete stood there for a few moments, thinking. If someone had collected Cara's belongings, maybe they'd missed something. Books, possibly, or a journal. But he quickly got a grip on himself. Tempting as it was, he wasn't about to do something truly idiotic like go in and look around. He tore himself away from the window and headed out the driveway.

Twenty-five yards down Walker's Trail his pulse jumped when he saw a couple walking up the road toward him. *Damn*, he hoped they hadn't seen him come out of the Lyman's driveway. He pulled his cap lower on his forehead and hugged the opposite side of the narrow road to give them room. They stared at him as he passed. He muttered a soft hello and raised a hand to his cap. It looked like an old-fashioned gesture of politeness, but really was intended to block the cap's logo from view. He exhaled deeply when he got back on Shore Road.

He stopped when he reached the beach and found an empty bench. The older couple and the babysitter were still there. They'd been joined by a group of teens who were roughhousing and climbing on the jungle gym. The windsurfer had just packed up his gear and was trudging through the sand toward Shore Road.

"Hey, Adam," he called.

The kid looked Pete's way. "Hi," he replied slowly, eyeing Pete cautiously and obviously trying to figure out whether he should know him.

"The wind is a little better than Saturday, huh?"

"Yeah, man," he said slowly, "that was the worst."

"My name is Pete Thorsen, by the way. I saw you on the beach Saturday afternoon. Bud Stephanopoulis told me who you are. That was a very responsible thing you did, calling the sheriff when you found the clothes."

"Thanks, man," he said, looking pleased with himself. "Are you a friend of Mr. S?"

"Yes."

"He's a cool dude," Adam said, giggling. "I let him try my board once. It was so funny. He couldn't stay up and was like a total klutz."

Pete laughed. "I know what you mean," he said, having a little fun at Bud's expense. "Let me ask you a question, Adam. Did you see anyone else around the beach that morning when you found the clothes and purse?"

Adam pushed his long hair away from his face. "Only a few people walking on Shore Road like they always do in the morning. That's it."

"How about the woman who drowned? Did you ever see her on the beach or swimming or walking on the road before that day?"

"No, man, I never saw her before and I'm down here a lot. Look, man, I've got to go. My old lady is waiting dinner on me."

Pete looked at him. "You mean your mother?"

He looked embarrassed. "Yeah, man, my mother."

Adam continued toward Shore Road and then turned and said, "If you're down here sometime, you want to see if you can do better than Mr. S on my board?"

"Sure," Pete said, making a mental note to give Adam Morrison a wide berth if he should see him near water with his surfing equipment.

He gazed out at the far raft. Even in the twilight, it was little more than a dark blob out in the water. He thought back to Friday night when there was no moon and the hazy sky cloaked the stars and wondered how Cara Lane would have been able to see the raft to swim out there. He added that fact to the list of reasons he was suspicious about the theory that everyone seemed to accept except him and, it appeared, First Deputy Richter.

• • •

The package the UPS man had left while he was out contained what he'd been waiting for: three CDs he'd ordered late one night while surfing through every cable television station on the planet. He scanned the Patsy Cline numbers listed on one case and grunted in satisfaction. For $14.95 plus shipping, it was a helluva bargain. Harry liked to kid him about his music, but he didn't give a damn. He liked the old stuff.

He grabbed a carton of yogurt from the refrigerator, slipped the disc into the CD player on his porch, and settled down to enjoy the music. He grinned when Patsy swung easily into "Why Can't He Be You." *Damn, that woman could sing.*

Darkness had crept in and it felt good to just sit and gaze out. Pinpoints of light blinked on across the water as cottages around the lake shifted into evening mode. It was going to be a clear night with a lot of stars visible. There were many things from his Wisconsin childhood that he preferred to forget, but the nights free of urban smog weren't one of them. He remembered lying on his back outside, looking up at the sky and feeling lonely, wondering about everything.

Patsy moved on to "Back in Baby's Arms." He closed his eyes and let the lyrics wash over him. The telephone's shrill ring halfway through the song jarred him back to reality.

"Dad? Where have you been? I've been trying to reach you."

He smiled at the sound of her voice. "Hi, Sweetie. How *are* you?"

"I'm great, Dad, but why haven't you called back? I called three times."

"Sorry, I haven't checked my messages. I've been out all day."

There was a brief silence at the other end of the line. "What's that music? That's not another one of those old things, is it?"

"That's Patsy Cline. I just got a new CD with her greatest hits."

More silence. "Patsy Cline. I've never heard of her."

"I'll get one of the CDs for you. She had one of the best voices of her time. She was 'hot,' as you like to say."

"Dad, that word sounds so lame when you use it. You should stick to groovy and stuff like that from the old days. And when I come up to see you, we're going to go shopping and get you some tunes that are at least from this century."

He smiled again. "Are you planning to come up?"

"Is it okay? I'm finished with summer school and I'm almost done with my workout program for cross country this fall."

"I'd love to have you up. When would you like to come?"

"In a week or two. I'll let you know."

"Great," Pete said, pausing, "but you know we'll have to check with Wayne."

Another silence, and then, "Why do we have to do that?"

"You know why," Pete said, trying to be as gentle as possible and thinking about how everything in their lives had changed when Doris died suddenly and Wayne Sable, Julie's biological father, managed to regain legal custody of her.

"I don't care. You're my dad, not him."

"I am your dad, Sweetie, but things are more complicated than that."

"Then you ask him. But I'm coming regardless of what he says. Just a minute, Dad." She put him on hold and came back on a minute later. "Sorry, I have another call waiting and have to run. Love you. And Dad — start checking your messages, okay?"

After Julie hung up, Pete's eyes drifted to the framed photographs on the fireplace mantle: Julie — five at the time — standing triumphantly on top of Sleeping Bear dune; Doris casting for trout on the AuSable; the three of them canoeing down the Platte River. He stared at the photographs for a long time and then turned up the sound on Patsy.

FIVE

The call from First Deputy Richter was less welcome than the one from Julie the night before. Richter asked him to come in again before he left for Chicago to, as he put it, "fill in a few details." After sparring with Richter over why they couldn't handle it on the telephone, he finally relented. He consoled himself with the thought that it would give him another crack at pumping Richter and his sidekick for information.

Ms. Dark Roots was sitting alertly behind the counter working on a stack of papers when he walked in. It was heartening to see the corner of a crossword puzzle peeking out from the bottom of the stack, though. She greeted him by name this time and escorted him down to the same cozy interview room. Richter walked in with Tessler a few minutes later. Maybe it was just Mondays when things were in slow motion around the County Government Center.

"Thanks for coming in, Mr. Thorsen," Richter said. "We appreciate your cooperation." He pointed to his recording device and Pete just shrugged. Richter clicked on the machine and fussed with his spiral notebook. Pete wondered again what the guy would do if that little notebook should go missing sometime.

"Has the cause of death been determined yet?" Pete asked innocently as Richter continued to try to find his cue in the notebook.

Richter looked up with narrowed eyes. "Why do you ask that?"

"Just curious. Is it a secret?"

"Our investigation is ongoing, like we told you yesterday."

"Down in Chicago, the authorities routinely release information about the cause of death. Is there some reason you're not doing that in this case?" This was turning out to be fun after all, he thought.

Richter looked peeved. "When the cause of death is established, I'm sure we will announce it. Should we get to our questions? You said you're driving back to Chicago this afternoon. We certainly wouldn't want to hold you up."

Pete ignored the sarcasm. He also resisted the temptation to tell Richter he knew from Harry that the sheriff and M.E. were planning to hold a news conference that very afternoon to announce the information he'd just requested, and more. He shrugged again and waved a hand, signaling that he was ready.

They didn't exactly get right to their questions. Richter retraced just about everything they'd covered on Monday. Tessler jumped in whenever the First Deputy appeared unable to come up with another repetitious question. It was close to an hour before they finally broke new ground.

"One thing we do know," Richter said, "is that tests showed a certain alcohol level in the vic's system. Could you tell us what the two of you had to drink that night?"

"Less than a bottle of wine between us."

"How much less?"

Pete thought about it for a moment. "There was maybe a quarter of the bottle left. In that range."

"Of the other three-quarters, how much did the vic drink?"

"A glass, not much more."

Richter and Tessler exchanged their usual glances. "Was there any sign the vic had been drinking before she met you?"

"If she had, I didn't notice it."

"Now you told us yesterday that you didn't learn much about the vic when you had dinner with her that night. But thinking back, did she say anything at all that might be of help to us? Jobs she held, what she'd done with her life, where she went to school, things like that?"

"Nothing I remember," Pete said, shaking his head.

Tessler jumped in. "How about friends and people she associated with? Did she tell you anything about them?"

Pete shook his head again. "Not a word. Like I told you, she seemed very private and didn't talk about those things."

Richter studied his notebook again. "I understand you went to college at the University of Wisconsin in Madison, right?"

Pete wondered how he knew that, but quickly realized it was public information that was readily obtainable from lawyer directories like Martindale-Hubbell. It also meant they'd been checking him out. He nodded in response to Richter's question.

"How long have you worked for your law firm, Mr. Thorsen?"

"Twenty years."

"That's a long time," Richter said, glancing at Tessler. "Did you take any time off after you graduated from law school?"

"No, I graduated one day and started to work the next."

"So you didn't travel for a while. Europe or other parts of this country? Out West, say."

Pete wondered where they were going with these questions, but replied, "I just told you. I started to work at my law firm as soon as I got out of school. I was a poor boy and one step away from debtor's prison."

Richter shot him a disbelieving look and drummed on the table with his oversized pen. Then he leaned forward and gave Pete his favorite flat-eyed stare. "What was the fight all about?"

Pete looked at him and then at Tessler. "What fight?"

"The fight you and the vic had in the restaurant."

"We didn't have a fight."

"People who were there told us you did."

Pete thought back to that night. They hadn't had a *fight,* although she must have raised her voice once because he remembered other diners staring at them. But it wasn't a *fight.*

"I'm telling you again," Pete said, "we didn't have a fight. As I recall, she got irritated once when I kidded her about something, but it certainly wasn't a fight."

Richter stared at him for a long time, then asked, "What were you kidding her about that caused her to react that way?"

Pete let the implication in his last question pass and said, "You know, I don't even remember. I was trying to get to know her and I must have pressed her about something she didn't want to talk about. Her family or something. But we never had a fight."

Richter stared at him again. "Well, I guess we have a conflict in the statements because eyewitnesses tell us you did."

"That's bullshit. Who are these so-called eyewitnesses?"

"That will all come out in due course," Richter said. "We told you we can't disclose that kind of information at this time."

"I'm a lawyer and I know you can disclose anything you want to disclose. Is there some reason for this cat-and-mouse game?"

"Cat-and-mouse game," Richter said slowly. "That's your term. We call it conducting our investigation in a responsible manner."

Pete looked at his watch. "Is there anything else?" he said, doing nothing to conceal his irritation. "I've been here well over an hour already."

The deputy scowled and continued to search his notebook. Then he looked up. "Now you told us yesterday that you've been coming up here for 10 years. Have you gotten to know other people in the area?"

"I know a lot of people up here."

"No, I think you misunderstood," said Richter, "I mean the broader area, outside Clear Lake and Millport."

Pete thought about Richter's question for a few moments. "I have a client over in Cadillac. A company named Colcorp."

"Have you met any people over that way?"

Pete shook his head. "Only a few associated with the company."

Richter studied his notebook one more time. "Now you told us before that after you left the vic outside the restaurant about nine o'clock, you went home, is that right?"

"Yes," Pete said, deliberately trying to sound weary, "that's right."

"What did you do after you got home?"

Pete felt his temper flaring and he locked eyes with Richter. "What's this all about? Do you think I had something to do with Cara Lane's death?"

"No one is accusing you of anything, Mr. Thorsen," Richter said. "All we're trying to do is establish the facts."

"Well the facts as they relate to me ought to be well established by now. I've told you everything I know about Cara Lane. Your question implies that I need to establish an alibi for that night. That's nuts. If I'm a suspect or a person of interest, as you like to say, I want to know right now."

He continued to glare at Richter. For the first time the deputy seemed unsure of himself and color showed in his cherubic face.

"I'm sorry if you took our questions the wrong way," Richter said, regaining his composure. "Like I just said, no one is accusing you of anything, and you're not a suspect. We're just investigating. Everyone who had any contact with the vic is a person of interest, but that's just routine." He flipped through his notebook again. "Now if you'll tell us what you did after you got home, we can wrap this up."

Pete was tempted to tell them to go to hell, but held his temper in check. Maybe he'd let things go further than he should have earlier, but if he tried to avoid answering questions now, he might only make things appear worse.

"Okay," he said, "I got back to my place about nine-thirty. I turned on the television to check the weather report and then I read for a while. It was too hot to sleep, so I went for a walk and then came home and took a shower and went to bed. That's it. And before you ask, no I didn't talk to anyone."

Tessler had been shifting around in his chair during Pete's confrontation with Richter but now asked, "Would you mind telling us where you went on your walk?"

Pete saw what was coming before the words were out of Tessler's mouth. No use dancing around it.

"I walked east on Shore Road, past the public beach a ways, and then came back home."

Tessler's eyes darted toward Richter. "Did you stop at the beach?" he said.

"No."

Richter was looking at his notebook again. He looked up at Pete. "So you stayed on Shore Road then?"

"Yes. Except for the short time I was on M-22."

"Now while you were on your walk," Richter said, "did you see anyone else?"

Pete thought about it for a minute. "Not Cara Lane if that's what you mean," he said. "I did run into some guy on Shore Road, but I didn't talk to him."

"Any idea who it was?" Richter asked.

"It was dark and he was on the other side of the road, but it might have been the guy who's always hanging around town collecting cans and stuff like that. What's his name, Willie? I've seen him walking along the lake at night before."

Richter wrote something in his notebook. "How about the beach?" he asked. "Did you see or hear anyone on the beach? People sitting around talking? Someone swimming?"

"Not a soul. It was quiet as a graveyard, if you'll excuse a tasteless joke."

"What time was it when you passed the beach?" Richter said.

"I don't know. Before midnight, maybe a half-hour before."

Richter stared at him. "Do you have a habit of going for walks late at night?" he asked.

Pete wanted to hit the smug prick right in the face, but just stood up and said icily, "Are we finished?"

They continued to stare at him as he walked out.

• • •

Pete was driving south toward Chicago and still seething over his latest session with Richter and Tessler when his cell phone rang. It was Harry.

"I just came from the press conference. Haskins was masterful as usual. He ran the show like he's been personally involved in every detail of the investigation from the moment they fished Cara Lane from the lake. Overall, it was pretty much like I told you yesterday. The only thing new is that the deceased was originally from a small town called Hawkins just west of Cadillac. Her maiden name — I assume she was married at some point — was Janicek." He spelled the name.

"Does she still have family there?"

"No idea."

"Anything else?"

"Not from the press conference, but I talked to Cap afterwards. He told me something interesting. He said the woman had a 'sheet'."

"A 'sheet.' What does that mean?"

"A rap sheet, I assume. I asked him a couple of questions, but it was clear he didn't want to tell me more so I backed off."

After Pete got off the phone with Harry, he began to wonder about Cara Lane's northwest Michigan roots. Maybe that explained why she was at Clear Lake. But why had she gone there and not to her parents' house? Then he thought about some of the questions Richter had asked. Maybe the First Deputy knew a lot more about the dead woman than he did.

SIX

After his meeting with long-time client, Clarence Abbot, finally ended, Pete closed his office door, took a few deep breaths to relax, and got on the Internet. He Googled "Cara Janicek — Hawkins, Michigan" and got no hits. Then he tried "Cara Janicek — Chicago" and got 221 hits. He scrolled through the list; none of the entries seemed to relate to the woman he knew as Cara Lane. He considered asking one of his partners, a former prosecutor, to have her contacts at the Chicago Police Department run Cara through their computer, but decided to try LexisNexis first. He logged on to the firm's account and entered his personal charge number. He didn't do much computer research anymore and had lost his touch, but after going down several blind alleys for the better part of an hour, he finally hit pay dirt.

He stared at his computer screen as he skimmed the old news stories. One from *The Register-Guard*, a Eugene, Oregon paper, laid it all out. Twenty years earlier, Cara Janicek, then a student at the University of Oregon, had been a member of a radical group led by an on-again, off-again graduate student named Allen Weisner. According to the article, Weisner had a history of political activism dating back to the anti-war movement of the 1960s and 1970s. Following that, he'd gradually seg-ued into anti-globalization. The article pointed out something Pete already knew, which was that anti-globalization activists opposed free trade agreements between the United States and developing countries on the grounds such agreements fostered the exploitation of workers in those countries, lacked proper environmental and labor safeguards, and shipped American jobs overseas.

Weisner's group engaged in the usual activities. They organized ral-lies, cranked out literature, and on at least one occasion, tried to orga-nize a boycott of Nike. Then, according to the articles, they decided to go for the big strike to publicize their cause, and bombed a campus building occupied in part by a think tank that consulted with the federal government on free trade issues. The only people in the building at the time of the bombing were several members of the night cleaning crew. No one was killed, but two workers were seriously injured.

He shook his head and read on. Federal and local law enforcement authorities quickly zeroed in on the Weisner cell. Six members including Weisner and Cara Janicek were arrested. The seventh, a freshman stu-dent named Ted Corrigan, fled and was never apprehended. According to a later news story, Corrigan was still on the FBI's wanted list. Weisner was convicted on a variety of charges and sentenced to 20 years in prison. Cara and most of the others entered into plea agreements and were given sentences of varying lengths. Cara got five years and, according to one follow-up story, was out in three.

Pete propped up his feet and gazed out at Millennium Park along Chicago's lakefront. He was always struck by how peaceful the world looked from 30 floors up. People thronged the park paths, taking in the sights and enjoying the August sunshine. It was as though there were no Cara Lanes and no Allen Weisners and no political bombings. He thought back to dinner that night. No wonder Cara wasn't anxious to talk about her past. He wondered how she'd gotten involved with the Weisner group and whether she still clung to her old views. He hadn't detected any sign of that at dinner, but as guarded as she was, it was impossible to judge. He also wondered whether there was any connection between her death and her past. His musings were interrupted by a knock, followed by his door easing open.

"Couldn't stay away from us, huh?"

He smiled at the sound of the familiar throaty voice and swiveled around to see Angie DeMarco looking at him. "Yeah, right," he said. "More to the point, Clarence Abbot couldn't do without me for more than a week."

"How is Clarence?"

"The same. There are no small problems. Everything quiet around here?"

"Like a tomb. Marty Kral is at his place in Door County and a lot of his cronies are away, too. Probably busy making Molotov cocktails for a post-Labor Day offensive."

Pete laughed. "I can hardly wait."

They made small talk about the firm for a few minutes and then Angie asked, "How are you going to respond to Marty's memorandum?"

Just thinking about the memorandum with the nine names made his blood boil again. "I'm not," he replied tersely.

"You're going to ignore it?"

Pete looked at her. "You saw the memorandum. We can put lawyer productivity on the agenda for the October meeting if he wants, but without a vote by the full partnership, I'm not going to sack a bunch of partners who've been with the firm their entire careers and are a year or two away from retirement. I'm not even sure I have the authority. Kral is the one who needs to go."

It must have been a court day in spite of the August lull because Angie wore a tailored navy blue suit that complemented her dark curls. Like most of her clothes, the suit was snug but in the right places. A lot of people misjudged her because of the way she dressed and learned the hard way that she could be tough as nails when the chips were down. Pete had recruited her out of the Cook County State's

Attorney's office eight years earlier and they'd since become staunch allies within the firm.

"How long are you planning to be with us?" Angie asked.

"Not long. I'm driving back to the lake tonight."

"That's a shame. You were looking so dreamy-eyed when I came in that I was sure you were planning to spring for dinner at Gibson's."

"I'm not sure dreamy-eyed is the right description. Thoughtful, maybe." He hit the "print" button on his computer and handed her the *Register-Guard* piece. "Here, read this."

"Interesting," she said when she finished. "Is there some reason you're showing me a news clipping about an old campus bombing?"

"That woman Cara Janicek mentioned in the story? I had dinner with her at the lake last week."

"Really? Did she hire you to represent her in connection with some new bomb charge? Or do you just find bad girls exciting these days?"

"Neither, I'm afraid."

Angie flashed her Colgate smile. "I told you before, you should take up with me instead of these bimbos you come up with. At least you'd know what you were getting."

"I do know. A true partner and a great friend."

"And . . .?" She twirled her index finger.

"And a helluva woman."

"There you go. That wasn't so hard, was it?"

They both laughed. It wasn't hard at all. Angie had a way of connecting to his inner wiring, but getting involved romantically with one of his law partners could make life a little too complicated. Particularly when that partner was already married.

"She's dead."

"You mean this," Angie glanced at the article again, "Janicek woman? This *femme fatale* you had dinner with?"

"Yes, that one."

After a brief silence, she said, "I have a feeling there's more to this story."

Pete got up and walked to the window and stared down at the park. "Keep this quiet for obvious reasons," he said, "but I've been questioned a couple of times in connection with her death. They found her body in Clear Lake last Saturday, the day after I had dinner with her."

Angie's expression went blank. "You're kidding."

"No, I'm not." He told her the story, beginning with the afternoon he met Cara Lane at the art fair and ending with a summary of his two sessions with Richter and Tessler.

"If I understand everything you just said, you called the sheriff and volunteered to go in and give a statement."

"Right. Harry McTigue — you've met him — told me they found my business card in her purse. I thought it was better to call rather than wait to be called. I know the sheriff up there, a guy named Bill Haskins, and expected to meet with him. But when I arrived, I was told Haskins was out of the office and I was hooked up with a pompous young deputy. He kept me waiting in an over-heated room for more than a half hour and then . . ."

Angie put her hand over her mouth to stifle a laugh. "He did that?"

"What's so funny?"

"When I was a prosecutor, that's what cops I worked with did all the time. They'd let suspects stew for a while to put them on edge. But why would they do that with you?"

"No idea, except that First Deputy Richter, as he calls himself, seems to view this as a career-making case."

"Your first session with them doesn't sound so bad."

"It wasn't; it was just annoying since the whole thing shouldn't have taken more than a half-hour if they knew what they were doing. What got me was when they called me in again the next day and raised that fight bullshit and grilled me about my alibi."

Angie looked at him. "You could have called me, you know."

"I didn't see any need," Pete protested. "I expected it to be routine. Then when they started to raise all that crap, I didn't want to say 'Stop, I need to talk to my lawyer.' Anyway, what was I going to do? Lie or refuse to answer? I did get Richter to state on the record that I wasn't a suspect, although I think he just said that to squirm out of my question."

"Have they established that she was killed?"

"Not yet, at least that I know of, but it's clear that Richter believes she was. That's what bothers me."

"How about her past?" Angie asked. "Do you think there's some connection between that and her death?"

Pete looked thoughtful. "I don't know. Maybe she wasn't even killed. But there are some suspicious circumstances."

"How about your sessions with Richter? Did you get along with him? Were things civil?"

"Mostly," Pete said. "I walked out on him at the end of the second session."

Angie gave him that motherly look he always found annoying. "I've told you enough stories that you should know it's best to be deferential to those guys regardless of how much they grate on you. They hold the cards at that stage and it never helps if things become confrontational."

"I know, I know," Pete said, waving a hand. "But you know me. I can't stand self-important people, particularly when they try to jack me around."

"I do know you, which is exactly why I asked. I'm not trying to be preachy, but if you'll remember, I worked with cops on a regular basis for a long time. Some are decent guys, but a lot of them are pricks who will try to get you if you don't genuflect in their direction every five minutes. Hell, a lot of them will try to get you even if you do genuflect."

"Okay," Pete said, "I get the point. But why would Richter treat me like a serial murder suspect? I barely knew the woman and sure as hell had nothing to do with her death, assuming she was killed."

"You're probably right about him being pompous and overzealous and all that," Angie said. "But let's look at the facts. A woman died in mysterious circumstances. You'd gone out with her. Eyewitnesses in the restaurant said the two of you had a fight. You were the last person known to have been with her the night she died. You've admitted to being in the area where she died. You have no alibi. I'll tell you, we used to push investigations on a lot less than that."

• • •

Pete mulled over Angie's sermon as he maneuvered his old Range Rover through a residential section of Chicago's North Side, looking for the address Harry had given him. He thought about his MP days and how they dealt with suspects. He was just a driver, but had seen enough to know that what Angie said was true. He also bristled again at the thought of the way he'd been treated by Richter. And the more he found out about Cara Janicek a/k/a Lane, the harder it was to shake his feeling that there might be more to her death than appeared on the surface. Like it or not, he was smack dab in the middle of things. At least until he got the Richter/Tessler tag team off his back.

The traffic congestion made him yearn to be back in Millport. Cars clogged both sides of the street; many looked like they hadn't been moved in weeks. They sat there like metallic front yard ornaments for the Victorian and gray stone houses and reduced the street to a one-lane chute. He waited for a double-parked SUV to move on and finally tapped his horn out of frustration.

Pete found the 2200 block of Bissell and located a parking spot a few blocks away under the "El" tracks. As he walked back toward Bissell, he wondered what he hoped to accomplish by paying a visit to Cara Lane's old building. Get lucky, he supposed, and maybe run into someone who knew Cara and might be able to shed light on a person who was shaping up to be a very mysterious woman with an interesting past.

A steely screech that was trademark Chicago pierced the evening air as the wheel flanges of an elevated train ground against the rails on a curve just to the south. The sound reminded him more of a mournful wail than the everyday clatter of urban life. He chuckled. And he'd suspected Richter of watching too many crime shows.

Lane wasn't listed on the board in the vestibule at 2243 Bissell. The name shown for unit 2D, the apartment Cara reportedly occupied, was M. Vrba. That's strange, Pete thought. It seemed unlikely that the apartment would have been rented to someone else that soon. He considered punching the intercom button, but found the inside door open and decided just to go up. He knocked on 2D. No answer. He knocked again. Still no answer. As he was about to leave, a slight young woman with mousy hair that looked like she'd cut it herself and a complexion that screamed for extreme makeover came up the stairs and turned the other way toward 2C. She stood in front of her door and fumbled around in her backpack.

"Hi," Pete said. "Do you know if Cara is around?"

The woman's body jerked upright and she swiveled her head and peered at him through small wire-rimmed glasses. She clutched her keys in a white-knuckles grip. "Are you a friend of Cara's?" she finally asked in a weak voice.

"Yes," Pete said, not entirely without some basis. He was glad he'd changed into shorts and a worn polo shirt before leaving his office. If he'd appeared behind her in the dimly-lit hallway still dressed in his dark business suit, she probably would have gone directly into cardiac arrest.

"Marcus was around early this morning," she said. "I haven't seen Cara for over a week." She turned back to her door. Her eyes flicked toward him a couple of times as she fumbled around trying to fit her key in the lock.

"I bet you go to DePaul," he said, deciding it was time for a charm offensive.

She looked at him again and hesitated. "Yes, grad school."

"Let me guess." He rubbed his chin for effect. "Elizabethan literature."

"Philosophy," she said, sounding downright haughty. "I'm doing my dissertation on Hegel."

"Hegel," Pete said, nodding like he should have known all along. "I always preferred him to Kant. *Philosophy of Right* was his best work, don't you think? Better than *Science of Logic*."

Her eyes widened. "Are you a Hegel scholar?"

He shook his head. "Just took a few courses. I do like to re-read the great works now and again, though." He prayed she wouldn't ask any follow-up questions because he'd exhausted his razor-thin knowledge of the dreary Georg Wilhelm Friedrich Hegel.

Pete pursed his lips. "I was really hoping to catch Cara and Marcus. Have you gotten to know them?"

"Some. They're both very committed and have their own lives. Look, I really have to go."

He smiled. She closed the door behind her and he could hear the deadbolt slide into place.

Pete decided to wait an hour and then try Vrba again. He wandered around the neighborhood for old times' sake and stopped at John Barleycorn's Pub on Belden and ordered a cheeseburger. The place had been an institution in the neighborhood for as long as he could remember. He watched the Cubs score three runs in the seventh to take the lead over the Reds, and was pleased that the burgers were as good as ever. When he finished, he headed back toward Bissell. If Vrba hadn't returned, he was going to hit the road and try him some other time. He'd be driving half the night as it was.

The inner door was locked when he got back to the building. He pressed the intercom button for 2D.

"Yes?" a nasal voice answered after a minute or two.

"Is this Marcus Vrba?"

There was a brief silence at the other end, then, "I believe that's the name on the board if you have the right apartment. If you're soliciting for something, I'm not interested." His speech pattern was precise, but as whiny as a three-year-old demanding dinner.

"My name is Pete Thorsen. I'm not soliciting. I'd just like to talk to you for a few minutes about Cara Lane, please."

Another silence, then, "Are you with the police?"

"No."

He laughed a curious sort of cackle. "Tell me, why would I talk to you, a person I don't even know, about someone who may or may not be a friend or acquaintance of mine. Now goodbye whatever your name is." The intercom went dead.

Pete pressed the buzzer again. No response. He pressed it a second time.

Vrba's voice came on again, this time sounding angrier. "Look, mister, if you don't stop harassing me, I'm going to call the building manager and have him get one of those clowns in blue uniforms over here."

"I'm sorry, sir, I don't mean to harass you," Pete said. "I just want to talk to you for a few minutes. I assume you know that Cara drowned up in Michigan last week. I'm trying to figure out what happened to her. I was hoping you might be able to help."

Silence again, then, "I know nothing about it. I already told your Inspector Clouseau that. Now I'm going to make those calls and suggest you be gone before they arrive." The intercom went dead again.

Inspector Clouseau. That could only mean that Richter had beaten him to the punch. The guy was nothing if not thorough.

Pete thought about pressing the buzzer again, but reconsidered. He'd been spending a lot of time with law enforcement people recently and wasn't eager to branch out to the Chicago Police Department, even with a friend like Angie DeMarco to fall back on. He decided to leave and made a mental note to add the charming Marcus Vrba to his list of people to check out.

SEVEN

Getting back to the lake at four in the morning didn't exactly make Pete anxious to bound out of bed at first light, so when the telephone rang, he just burrowed deeper under the covers and let his voicemail earn its keep. When he did get up, he ignored the flashing message light and went for a run to get his system back into equilibrium.

The weather was as spectacular as the day he left. Fluffy clouds drifted overhead and painted the aqua water with patches of darker blue. Sailboats with billowing spinnakers added a touch of color chiseled straight from the celestial palette. Everything looked right with the world. Everything that is except for Cara Lane who continued to prey on his mind.

He checked his refrigerator when he returned to his cottage. The only food was some left-over whitefish wrapped in foil, a bag of carrot sticks, dry cereal, and a near-empty carton of milk that was well past its "sell by" date. He crunched on a carrot stick and decided to go into town for one of Ebba Holm's tasty breakfast sandwiches. Never mind that it was already past noon.

First, though, he forced himself to check those messages. One was from Harry, reminding him they were supposed to have dinner that night. Angie had called just to check in. Her story about a case she'd once handled for Clarence Abbot made him hoot with laughter. Three calls were from a local area code; he didn't recognize the number and the caller hadn't left any messages. There were several other messages, including one from Bud Stephanopoulis about getting together for basketball, but nothing from Wayne Sable in response to the two messages he'd left for him about Julie. That irritated him. He dialed Sable's number, got his voicemail again, and left another message. He was thinking about Angie's stand-up comic routine again when the phone rang.

"Is this Mr. Thorsen?" It sounded like an older woman. Her voice was shy and tentative.

"Yes, this is Pete Thorsen."

"Mr. Thorsen," she said in the same weak voice, "my name is Marian Janicek. I tried to call you a few times before, but I guess you weren't home. Do you have time to talk to me now?"

He almost dropped the phone. Why would Cara Lane's mother be calling him, or how would she even know his name?

"No, I can talk," he said.

"I'm Cara's mother, Mr. Thorsen. I know you two met before she died."

Now he was really puzzled. "Yes, we did meet," he said slowly. "I'm very sorry about what happened to your daughter."

"Thank you." He could hear sniffling at the other end of the line. "You probably wonder why I'm calling you."

"Please tell me, Mrs. Janicek," he said, not knowing quite what to say. "I know this must be a difficult time for you."

There was an awkward silence and more sniffling. "Cara said such nice things about you," she finally said. "She felt real bad she had to leave right after dinner that night. She was afraid you might be mad at her or something."

"I enjoyed her, too," Pete said, stretching the truth. "It sounds like you spoke to her after we had dinner."

"Yes, we always talk on Friday nights. She didn't have much time that night, though. We couldn't talk like we usually do. She said nothing was wrong, but I could tell there was. A mother can feel those things, you know Mr. Thorsen?"

That's interesting, he thought. Apparently Mrs. Janicek had sensed the same thing that kept gnawing at him.

"Mrs. Janicek, I'm curious. How did you get my telephone number at Clear Lake?" He'd had an unlisted number for the past year after a series of crank calls.

"Cara told me your name and said you were a lawyer in Chicago. I called the telephone people and they gave me your office number. Your secretary told me you were at your home at Clear Lake and gave me that number. Everyone was real helpful."

Pete grimaced. His long-time secretary, Ruth, was on vacation for two weeks and her replacement, a woman from one of the temp agencies, had given out his local number without telling him. He wondered what other calls might have come in that he didn't know about.

"Mrs. Janicek, you still haven't told me why you called."

Silence again and then in a voice so quiet he could barely hear it she said, "One of my friends in my quilting group said I should talk to a lawyer about Cara."

"You mean about Cara's estate?"

"That and other things," she said in her weak voice.

"I agree you should talk to a lawyer, but it might make sense for you to talk to someone local. Someone who specializes in estate matters. If you like, I can get you the name of a lawyer in Cadillac. It'll be closer."

More silence. "I thought you might be willing to meet with me since you knew Cara and everything," she said. When he didn't answer right away, she blurted out, "I know it wasn't an accident, Mr. Thorsen."

Mrs. Janicek's comment left a cold feeling in his gut. "The sheriff is investigating," he said slowly. "Did you speak to him?"

"Sheriff Haskins and one of his people came to see me. They were real nice and everything, but the sheriff kept saying it might have been a swimming accident." Her sobs were more audible now.

"Was the person with him a deputy named Richter?"

"I really don't remember. It could have been. He looked real young and he didn't talk much except at the end. The sheriff was the one who kept saying it looks like a swimming accident. He did tell me how sorry he was."

He found it hard to believe that Mrs. Janicek would have called him if she knew he was being eyed by Richter as a suspect. "Are you aware that I've already talked to the sheriff's office twice and told them about my dinner with Cara?" he said.

"The sheriff told me they had talked to some people Cara knew. I thought one of them might be you. I wish you could have heard the nice things Cara said about you, Mr. Thorsen."

Pete resisted the temptation to make a flippant comment and said, "Mrs. Janicek, please don't take this the wrong way, but why do you think Cara's death wasn't a swimming accident?"

"I just know it wasn't. Will you meet with me Mr. Thorsen? I need somebody who can help me. I can tell you everything if we can meet."

Pete mulled it over. He was anxious to hear what Mrs. Janicek had to say, but getting involved with a distraught mother was something entirely different than checking out the dead woman's past. He thought of a dozen reasons to gently tell Mrs. Janicek no, but that wasn't what came out of his mouth.

"I don't think there's much I can do to help, Mrs. Janicek, but I'm willing to listen to what you have to say. No promises, though. Where would you like to meet?"

"Could you come to my home, Mr. Thorsen? I don't drive."

He paused. He'd prefer another venue, but there didn't seem to be many choices if she didn't drive. "Maybe I could stop and see you sometime tomorrow."

"Could you come early in the afternoon? That way Hank will be finished with lunch and have gone back to work."

Finished with lunch and gone back to work. When he heard those words, all he could think was that dumb had become his new middle name.

• • •

Harry listened as Pete vented about his second session with Richter and told him, off the record, about the background he'd managed to dig up on Cara Lane.

"Do you think there may be some connection between the Lane woman's past and her death?"

Angie had asked the same question. He sloshed his drink around in his glass and said, "I don't know."

"Any hunches?" Harry persisted, peering at him over his glasses.

"Not really."

Harry studied him. "Are you planning to share this stuff with your friend, the First Deputy?"

Pete shrugged. "I have a feeling they already know. Some of the questions they asked didn't make any sense to me at the time, but they do now that I know about her past. Besides, what would I do — march into Richter's office, tell him that Cara did hard time for some terrorist act, and suggest we team up and try to get to the bottom of this mess?"

"Yeah, I see what you mean," Harry said, looking thoughtful. "He'd probably use anything you tell him to try to establish that you really did know her from before. Jesus, I can't figure out why the guy has such a hard-on for you."

"I don't know. But I'm thinking about going to see Bill Haskins and complain."

"Bill's a decent guy," Harry said, peering at him over his glasses. "Too politically ambitious for my taste, but not a bad guy. What would you say to him if you do go in?"

Pete shrugged again. "Maybe tell him about the way Richter has been jacking me around and ask him to get the guy to back off."

"Might work," Harry said, looking thoughtful. "Haskins knows you're a lawyer and all."

"The only flaw in what you just said is that lawyers don't seem to scare people these days," Pete said with a sigh. "Not the way they used to."

He scanned the menu and broke with his pattern and ordered Lake Superior whitefish, grilled, with extra asparagus instead of a potato. Harry, apparently feeling that one deviant at the table was sufficient, had his usual rib eye.

"Well," Pete said, "you're up to date from my end. Have you heard anything new?"

"A little. The M.E. tells me they've determined there was no sexual assault."

"How about the cut on her head?"

"Like we talked about before, they're still thinking she might have struck her head when she tried to dive."

"That's a bunch of bull, Harry. It was so dark that night that *I* couldn't have found that raft and I know where it is."

Pete looked across the room. Rona was talking to a tall woman, maybe five-eight or five-nine, with long honey-brown hair held back with a red scrunchy. He'd seen her sitting at the bar earlier writing on a pad.

"Who's that talking to Rona?"

Harry craned his neck around. "That's our accountant, Lynn Hawke," he mumbled through a mouthful of crackers and smoked trout. "Rona wants to fix you two up."

"She new up here?"

"Lynn? Naw, she's been around for a couple of years. She just broke up with some guy." He slapped more trout on a cracker and shoveled it into his mouth. "You want to meet her?"

Before Pete could respond, Harry had leveraged his body out of his chair and was on his way over to where Rona and the other woman were standing, chewing on the way. After a couple of minutes, he headed back to the table with the woman in tow.

"Lynn, this is Pete Thorsen." He looked at Pete. "Lynn's going to join us for a glass of wine."

"We can get you something to eat, too," Pete said, rising to his feet. "We just put our order in."

She looked at her watch. "I was on my way home to make a salad and then curl up with a book."

"They have salads here," Pete said. "The seafood salad is great. I like the chicken Caesar, too."

Harry speared another piece of smoked trout and jabbed his fork in their direction. "I've been thinking of having that seafood salad myself one of these nights."

Pete and Lynn exchanged amused glances.

"Thanks," she said, "but I'll settle for the wine. If I won't be interrupting any boy talk, that is."

Harry grunted. "No chance of that. We're tired of talking to each other anyway." He winked at Pete and caught Frankie's eye and pointed at Lynn.

"Rona tells me you're from Chicago," she said to Pete, sliding into an empty chair.

Pete nodded. "Not a native, but I've practiced law there for 20 years." He tried not to linger on her eyes that sparkled like twin emeralds.

"I lived in Chicago until a couple of years ago. I was a forensic accountant with Ernst & Young and then had my own practice."

"Then you got smart and moved up here."

She didn't laugh at his joke. "I enjoy it here," she said. "I'm a jill-of-all-trades for people like Harry and Rona." Then a mischievous expression crept over her face. "I'm looking for some more high net worth individuals, though. You're a prime candidate from what Harry tells me."

Pete smiled. "Only if you specialize in restructuring debt." He tapped the pad she'd laid on the corner of the table. "I saw you working at the bar earlier. I hope those aren't Harry's ledgers."

"This? No, I'm off duty. I was just sketching."

"Can I see?"

"Sure." She opened the pad and showed him pen-and-ink sketches of Frankie and Harry and a couple of other patrons of the restaurant.

"Very nice," Pete said, taking the pad from her and examining the sketches more carefully. "I like the way you've captured Harry's classic good looks."

Harry sat there with a smug look and continued to munch on a cracker while he stole a glance at the sketches.

Lynn watched them play off each other, obviously enjoying it. "What's your firm's name?"

"Sears & Whitney."

"Pete's too modest to tell you," Harry chimed in, dragging a napkin across his mouth to wipe off the cracker crumbs, "but he's the managing partner of that firm. It's one of the most prosperous law firms in Chicago."

"Not according to some of my partners," Pete said, sounding disgusted.

Lynn blew a wisp of hair away from her face and seemed to instantly pick up on his sarcasm. "Aren't professional firms great? I didn't stay at E & Y long enough to make partner, but my friends told me about what goes on behind the scenes."

"Multiply that by ten and you have a law firm. Harry said I was the managing partner. Managing fire hydrant would be a better way of putting it. Everyone in the place wants to relieve himself on my leg."

Pete liked her laugh and snuck another look at her eyes.

"How many lawyers do you have?"

"One-seventy. We're at the lower end of mid-size by today's standards."

Harry, who was munching on another cracker, said, "You two have something in common besides being successful professionals. You're both archers."

"Are you into competitive archery?" Lynn asked, looking at him with new interest. "Or are you a hunter?" She asked the last question with a slight letdown in her voice.

"Neither," Harry said, answering for him. "He just likes to pretend he's a Viking warrior from the old days."

Pete jerked his head in Harry's direction and rolled his eyes. "I just do it for fun," he said, deciding it was best not to put a damper on the conversation by mentioning his penchant for using his law partners for target practice. "How about you?"

"That's what I do these days, too."

"Tell Pete about your Olympic experience," Harry said.

Pete raised his eyebrows. "Olympics. That's impressive."

"I tried to find a way to bump one of the people ahead of me — like that skater a few years back? — but was unsuccessful. We should get together and practice some time."

"Sure," Pete said, "as long as you don't tease me about my old wooden bow."

"Old bow," Harry said, snorting. "He has this thing that's about 10 feet long. Had it made for him by some old guy in Norway named Ulf who lives on the side of a mountain and meditates while he looks out at the fjords."

She smiled. "A longbow?"

Pete nodded. "Just got it a few weeks ago."

"I can't wait to see it. Well, boys, thanks for the wine. I'm going to be on my way. I have a busy day tomorrow." She gave Pete a warm smile and let those eyes linger on him. "Let's find a time when we can sit down together and you can transfer your personal business to my firm."

Pete watched her cross the room to say goodnight to Rona. There was an athlete's grace to her walk, but enough sway to make things interesting.

"She's something, huh?"

"Very nice," Pete said. "Now getting back to Cara Lane, did you learn anything else?"

"Very nice," Harry said. "I almost puked when I saw those eyes of yours pop out of their sockets. They have excellent salads here, Lynn. How about a glass of that fine pinot grigio? You know, you'd do better with women if you were more like me and played hard to get."

"Umm hmm."

"Here's a tip for you," Harry continued. "If you make a date with Lynn, don't talk about other women in front of her. Not even dead ones. Women don't like that."

"Thanks for the advice, Harry. Now how about the investigation?"

Harry looked at him and shook his head in disgust. "Okay, I found out from Cap that Richter has been questioning another guy here in town who was seen with Cara Lane a couple of times. His name is Kurt Romer. He works for your buddy Arne Breit on one of his charter boats. I guess she was out on his boat or something."

"Is he a suspect?"

"Don't know. Cap didn't volunteer any details."

Pete nodded and looked thoughtful. "Here's something I forgot to mention earlier. When I was in Chicago, I stopped at Cara's old apartment out of curiosity. A guy named Marcus Vrba is living there. I don't know if he was Cara's boyfriend or what. I tried to ask him about Cara and he turned hostile on me. Said something about having already talked to 'Inspector Clouseau'."

Harry arched his bristly eyebrows. "Who's that?"

"I have a hunch it's Richter."

"Ummm. Well like Cap said, he's approaching this like a career case."

"Something else happened this afternoon that will blow your mind."

When Pete didn't continue, Harry said impatiently, "Well?"

"Cara's mother called me," he said. "She wants to meet with me."

Harry sat with a blank look on his face. "You're kidding."

"Nope. She said Haskins and one of his deputies — I assume Richter again — came to see her. She said Haskins kept saying he thinks it was a swimming accident."

"That fits with what I heard Haskins has been saying about the case," Harry said. "How did the mother sound?"

"Devastated."

Harry looked at him with narrowed eyes. "You're not going to meet with her, are you?"

"I am."

Harry continued to look at him. "You're nuts, you know that? I can understand your wanting to find out what's going on because of the way Richter is on your ass. But getting involved with the mother? That I don't understand."

"Harry, if you'd heard her, you would have agreed to listen to what she has to say, too."

Harry shook his head. "This reminds me of those cleaning ladies in your building down in Chicago a few years ago. They cry on your shoulder about getting screwed out of overtime, and the next thing we know you're representing them *pro bono* for two years and getting your partners pissed at you for wasting firm resources. You just can't keep your nose out of things."

He grinned and pushed back from the table. "What time should I pick you up on Sunday?"

Harry got a puzzled look on his face. "Sunday."

"The Colonel's chili festival?"

"Damn, I almost forgot," Harry said, slapping the table.

"We've got to go. The Colonel would never forgive us if we didn't."

"I know, I know," Harry said. "It's supposed to be a nice day, too." He looked thoughtful for a few moments and then his face brightened. "Look, I've got a perfect excuse for us to make a cameo at the festival and then split. I'll have Rona see if your new friend Lynn is available and we'll all meet at your place and go for a swim and have a couple of drinks and grill some steaks. How does that sound?"

"You're a man with no end of good ideas," Pete said, grinning again.

EIGHT

Pete found the Janicek house on the outskirts of Hawkins. It was a two-story clapboard structure with faded yellow paint that was peeling from age and the ravages of northern winters. That fit with the rest of Hawkins. The two taverns in the block-long business district looked like the most prosperous establishments in town.

He parked on the side of the road near the driveway and felt the gravel crunch under his feet as he walked toward the house, briefcase in hand, trying to look as professional as possible. As he got close, a curtain dropped back into place and the front door edged open. Marian Janicek stood in the opening. She could have been one of a hundred women from his own rural youth. Mid-sixties, he guessed, with a faded blue gingham dress that hung well on her full figure and a kind face that tilted toward sorrow.

"Thank you for coming, Mr. Thorsen."

He waited for her to open the door wider so he could enter, but her eyes flicked back and forth between his face and his green Range Rover.

"Could you move your car up by that tree, Mr. Thorsen?" she said. She pointed toward a large maple 30 feet up from where he was parked. "The mailman hasn't come yet."

Pete did as she asked, but had a hunch it wasn't the mailman she was concerned about. As he walked back toward her house, an old pickup that was either badly in need of a new muffler or just rigged for big sound rattled past. The men in the cab stared at him.

The Janicek living room was orderly and free of clutter. Frayed corners on the fabric sofa and matching wing chairs apparently were the price Marian was willing to pay for having the good taste not to use clear plastic covers. A collection of ceramic rabbits, geese and raccoons cavorted on a glass wall shelf, and two prints of pheasants taking flight in an autumn corn field adorned one wall. He had yet to spot a speck of dust.

She thrust a glass of iced tea into his hands. Two healthy wedges of lemon hung on the rim and she presented a tray with a spoon and packs of sweetener. Either she'd done her homework on him or she was a woman of naturally good taste.

Mrs. Janicek sat back on the couch and smiled at him while he doctored up his tea. While she waited, she refolded a rust and tan afghan. He wouldn't exactly say she was beaming, but it seemed clear he'd made her a happier woman just by coming.

He broke the awkward silence by engaging in small talk. She told him they'd lived in the house for almost 35 years and had four sets of neighbors during that time. He eased into the subject uppermost on both of their minds. "Why don't you tell me about Cara."

"Let me show you her room," Marian said, bouncing off the couch like a woman half her age. She led him up the stairs to one of the bedrooms. Dolls and stuffed animals rested against stacks of pillows on the neatly made twin bed. Rock music posters from an earlier era that showed their age were taped to the walls. The room looked like Marian had just tidied up in anticipation of her daughter's return from a day at school.

"Here's her school yearbook," she said. She stood beside him with a proud smile as he leafed through it. After a few minutes, he noticed that the yearbook was from Cara's sophomore year. He found the page with her class picture. Cara was young, but there was no mistaking the pretty dark-haired girl. No world weariness in her eyes, just sparkle and spunk. A variety of school activities were listed under her name: sophomore class treasurer, junior varsity soccer team, swim team, hall monitor.

"It looks like she was very active in school."

"Yes," Marian said, beaming, "she was a popular girl."

Pete flipped through the rest of the yearbook and found pictures of Cara working on the homecoming float and playing in a soccer game and dancing at some school event. "She went to college in Oregon, I understand," he said, looking up at Marian.

She searched his eyes, apparently wondering how he knew that. "Yes," she said, smoothing the stiff hair of a Barbie doll.

"That's a long way from here," he said, trying to draw her out. "How did she happen to go to school out there?"

Marian held the doll at arm's length and studied it. "My sister lives in Oregon," she said softly. "We thought it would be a good place for Cara to go to school. Everyone says it's a real nice state."

He stood there and looked at Marian. Her eyes avoided his, and he waited for her to open up. It took a while. She rearranged the stuffed animals and dolls on the bed, then retied a bow around a teddy bear's neck. Finally she said, "Of course, Cara didn't get along so good with her father in those days, either. That was part of it."

"What was the problem?" Pete asked. "The teen years? I know how that goes. I have a daughter of my own."

She finally made eye contact with him. "Is she pretty?"

"Very," Pete said, "and a real handful."

She smiled weakly. "Hank and Cara used to get along. He would take her fishing and things. Once he made a swing for her. It's still out back, Pete. You can see it from this window." She held a curtain back and pointed to a rope swing with a broken seat that hung from an old oak.

"He was real nice to her at Christmas, too. He would go outside on Christmas Eve and throw tin cans on the roof so she would think it was Santa and his reindeer. But then they just stopped getting along. I don't know." She shook her head several times as though baffled by it all.

"So Cara lived with her aunt while she finished high school. How about college?"

"You know how it was with colleges in them days," Marian said. "They made students live in the dorm the first year."

"And after that?"

Marian was fussing with one of the dolls again. "She got an apartment with some other students," she said softly.

"But she still got along with her aunt."

"Oh, yes, but she wanted to be independent. Young people are just so independent." She shook her head several times again.

They returned to the living room and Marian folded and refolded the afghan about nine times. Pete thought back to their telephone conversation and how she had wanted to meet with him when Hank wasn't around. The family dynamics were coming into focus. Still, there were some things he didn't quite understand.

"I don't want to pry, Marian, but did something else happen between Cara and her father?"

She continued to finger the afghan as though counting the loops. Then, without looking up, she said, "I suppose I should have told you before. Cara got pregnant when she was a junior in high school. That had something to do with it, too."

Jesus, he thought. Julie flashed through his mind and he got a lump in his throat.

"What happened?" he asked gently. "When Hank found out she was pregnant, I mean."

Marian's eyes grew moist. "He went kind of crazy. He went off somewhere for three days and when he came back, he said Cara had to have the baby and then give it up for adoption. He said a slut like her could never be a good mother." She choked on the s-word and was unable to hold back the tears.

He waited for her to compose herself and then asked as gently as he could, "Do you know who the father is?"

Marian shook her head slowly and got a faraway look in her eyes. "She wouldn't tell." She paused for a minute or two. "I think I might know, though."

"Who?" Pete asked.

She shook her head again. "I don't want to say, Pete. It was a long time ago and it wouldn't do any good. It's so sad, those adoption agencies don't even let you see the baby. They just took her away."

"So Cara's pregnancy was the real reason she went to Oregon to live with her aunt."

She sniffled and continued to look down. "Things got so bad between her and Hank that they just couldn't live in the same house anymore. He was already mad at the world because he'd lost his job and everything."

"What happened with his job?"

"Some company bought the plant where he worked. They wanted to make more money, I guess, so they closed it and moved the work to some other country. I don't remember where. Someplace. Hank worked for them 17 years and all they did was give him two months notice. They didn't help him find a new job or nothing."

"He eventually found something, though."

"He found a new job, but it don't pay as good and there are no benefits."

Pete didn't want to add to Marian's emotional turmoil but there was another question he knew he had to ask. "How did Cara get mixed up with those people at the university?"

She studied his face for an uncomfortably long time and then her shoulders slumped like the very will to live was slipping away. She tried to speak a couple of times, but was unable to force out the words. Finally she said in a wavering voice, "She was a good girl, Pete. I know it may not seem that way, but she was a good girl."

Pete looked at her and felt empty inside.

"Weisner was a bad man," she continued, her eyes glistening with tears. "I know he must have lied and tricked her into getting involved in those bad things they were doing." There was anger in her voice now.

"How did Hank react when he found out Cara was going to prison?"

"He said she was just bad, that's all there was to it." She shook her head several times again to convey her puzzlement. "He didn't want to hear any more about her."

"So there was no contact with her while she was in prison."

"She tried to stay in contact. She would write letters but if Hank saw them before me, he would tear them up. Once I tried to tape a letter back together again and he grabbed it from me and burned it. I just ached, Pete. I wanted to hear from her so bad. That's why we started to talk on the telephone on Friday nights after she moved to Chicago. Hank comes home from work to eat and then goes out with the crazies, so it was safe for us to talk."

Pete thought about what she'd just said. "Maybe that's why she had to leave dinner with me that night. She wanted to call you."

"I don't know, Pete. Like I said, she couldn't talk to me very long either. She wouldn't tell me what it was, but I think she had to meet someone."

"But you don't know who it might have been?"

She shook her head and looked sorrowful. "No."

"So you don't know if it was someone from her past?"

She shook her head again. "She didn't even say she was meeting someone. It was just something a mother can feel."

"I see. Did Hank ever speak to Cara after she got out of prison?"

"Never. I think he still liked her deep down and everything, but he was hurt and embarrassed because everyone around here knew about all of the things that happened. We never talk about it. He just wants it all to go away."

"Who are the 'crazies' you mentioned?"

"Those men who are always mad about the government and things. All they want to do is go hunting and shoot their guns and stuff. They go to Kelties and the Whitetail all the time."

"Those are bars?"

She sniffled and nodded her head.

He thought back to their conversation on the phone. "When you called me, you said you knew Cara didn't die in a swimming accident. What did you mean?"

He heard a quick intake of breath as she looked away. Her eyes grew moist again. He waited for her to collect herself.

"Something was bothering her, Pete. I know that. She was a good swimmer, too. She was on the swim team in high school and she would swim at the "Y" in Chicago almost every day. I know she wouldn't drown by herself like the sheriff kept saying. She didn't drink like he said either."

After a brief pause, she continued. "The other thing the sheriff said was maybe she took her own life, but I know my Cara. I know she would never do that. She had problems and everything, but she had lots to live for, too. Like that soup kitchen and everything."

"Soup kitchen?"

"She worked at the soup kitchen at her church in Chicago. You know, feeding poor people? They were going to put her in charge of it. She was so excited. That's the first thing she told me when I talked to her that night. I think she hoped she might see you, too."

"You mentioned suicide. Why did the sheriff say that?"

Marian dabbed at her eyes again. "I guess they found her clothes folded real neat on that boat. He said that's often a sign of suicide. He used the words 'very deliberate.'"

He remembered Shih Tzu Man saying the same thing at the beach. "Did the sheriff ask you any other questions about Cara?" he said.

"That young deputy did. He asked why Cara was in Millport and stuff."

"What did you tell him?"

"I said I didn't even know she was there until she called me that night. I told him she never comes home anymore."

"Did he ask why?"

She nodded. "I said she doesn't get along with her father."

"How about her pregnancy? Did you tell them about that?"

"No, Pete," she said sternly, shaking her head, "I don't like to talk about that with strangers."

"Did they ask you anything else?"

"The deputy wanted to know if Cara still had friends up here. That and whether she was friendly with any of those militia people." She dabbed at her eyes. "I told him I didn't think so."

Pete thought about it for a minute. "Do you know if she had any contact with the people out in Oregon after she got out of prison?"

"I don't know, Pete. She could have. She would never talk much about those days, but she seemed so depressed sometimes."

"Recently?"

"Yes, mainly."

Pete felt a need to bring their conversation to an end. "I know this has been difficult for you, Marian, but I still don't understand what you'd like me to do."

"You're a lawyer," she said haltingly. "Could you help me find out what happened to Cara? I think the sheriff just wants it to go away like everyone else. I'm the only one who really cares."

Pete looked at her and said gently, "Marian, this is really a job for the law enforcement people. I'm very sorry about what happened, but I'm not an investigator or even a criminal lawyer. I just help companies with their legal problems."

Her tears began to flow again. "I need help, Pete. I'm sorry I can't pay you very much."

Pete looked at Marian and couldn't help but think about the grief his mother must have felt when Loraine's body was found. He remembered how he would see her quietly sobbing years later when she thought no one was around. They were so alike, Marian and his mother, quietly suffering through the blows life had inflicted on them. He knew he had to do something.

"I'll tell you what I'll do, Marian. I'll talk to the sheriff and go over the things you've told me. Maybe he'll listen."

As soon as he said that, he wondered what kind of reception he'd receive when he told Haskins his suspicions about Cara Lane's death and, minor matter, then asked him to get Richter off his back.

She clasped his hand in hers. "Thank you."

He picked up his briefcase and started to leave. Marian touched his arm and asked him to wait. A few minutes later she returned and pressed a bag into his hands.

"These are made with real oatmeal. They're very healthy."

NINE

Pete Thorsen, old soft heart, saw the sign for the Whitetail just ahead on the right as he headed toward M-115. He'd missed lunch and had a choice to make: scarf down Marian's cookies on his drive back to the lake or stop for a bite to eat at the place that advertised the world's best burgers. The lure of seeing some of the local crazies in their native habitat tipped the scales in favor of a burger. He'd save the cookies for later.

It wasn't difficult to figure out how the place got its name. At least 20 whitetail deer mounts, all with trophy antlers, filled the knotty-pine walls. In a token gesture toward species diversity, two wolves stood on a stand near the pool table and peered at the players with yellow eyes and exposed fangs as they lined up their shots.

It reminded him of a place called Ma Kasik's from his youth. Ma ran a tight ship with one notable exception: she was a little lax about carding her young male customers. She would scowl at them and size them up and after grilling them about their age, finally allow any boy who looked like he was at least 15 enjoy a beer or two, but nothing else. But not the girls. If a girl showed up Ma would demand to see her driver's license and two other pieces of ID by the time she was a foot inside the door and bounce her out on her ear if she was one day under the legal age. The girls, knowing this, would hang around outside and peer in the windows and try to catch the boys' eyes and persuade them to buy a six-pack or two of Leinies and join them in the parking lot.

Ma's was a rough place, too, and fights were almost a nightly occurrence. A man named Darryl, who was once a Golden Gloves boxer, was usually in the thick of things. He had one glass eye as a result of serving in the Viet Nam War and later in the evening, when the demon rum had a chance to work on his brain, he would take the eye out and place it on the bar and offer to take on all comers. Pete smiled and shook his head as he thought about those days.

The Whitetail's menu featured beef, beef and beef, with buffalo and one chicken item tossed in as a change of pace. Twelve ounces was the house standard, but down at the bottom of the menu, in letters requiring a magnifying glass to read, an eight-ouncer was listed as available for diners with puny appetites. No salads, though. Apparently the Whitetail didn't cater to the kind of clientele once dubbed effete snobs by a disgraced politician. Pete ordered the under-sized buffalo burger, medium rare, on sourdough bread with a slab of cheddar cheese. Lettuce wasn't entirely banned from the premises because he was able to have a leaf or two with his burger.

He took a sip of iced tea and watched SportsCenter on a large-screen television over the bar. Some things took getting used to. One was having both the Cubs and the Tigers still in contention in their respective divisions in August. Apparently word hadn't trickled down that it was time to fade.

It was just past four and the after-work crowd was trickling in. The patrons looked ordinary enough. Most sported baggy tee-shirts that hung loose over jeans or work pants. An occasional chambray or plaid shirt was mixed in for variety. Caps in one style or the other topped off the standard-issue uniform. Not a single man wore camouflage fatigues and there wasn't an AK-47 in sight. Disappointing after the way Marian had built up his expectations.

Pete munched his buffalo burger and thought about his conversation with her that afternoon. There was no way to get around the fact that Cara's life had been a mess. In hindsight it seemed almost inevitable she would come to a bad end, but he knew that didn't lessen the pain for a mother who had little else in her life. It also didn't explain her death.

He took another bite of his burger and thought about what he knew. It still wasn't much. The woman who now called herself Cara Lane had a record and acted jittery at dinner with him. He was sure she was meeting someone else that night, as her mother had speculated too, and then she turned up dead the next day. Who, and about what, those were the questions. That was about it. If she were murdered, who would have had a motive and how had he done it? The cut on her head might have come from a blow used to disable her, but that seemed awfully clumsy. And how then to explain the blood on the raft? Another possible scenario was that a person she knew had slipped her something and the empty wine bottle was a plant. That would fit with his own observation, and Marian's comments, that she didn't drink much.

A cacophony of cheers from the bar interrupted his thoughts. He looked up to see two newcomers walk in like a pair of conquering heroes. One was a bear of a man, maybe six-three or six-four, with a neatly trimmed reddish beard that wrapped around a fleshy face. He wore a dirty yellow cap with an Arctic Cat logo. His companion was short and wiry with the annoying habit of removing his cap and scratching his head every ten seconds. For Itchy's sake, Pete hoped it was just a nervous affectation and not some more serious condition.

Pete took another bite of his burger and turned back to SportsCenter. He tried to tune-out the raucous behavior at the bar. It wasn't easy; the decibel level had been ratcheted up with the arrival of the two men. Then he heard the booming voice directed his way and the noise in the bar quieted down.

"I couldn't help but notice when I come in that we have us a visitor from Illinois." His pronounced it with "noise" at the end. "Saw that foreign luxury vehicle of his around town earlier this afternoon, too."

Pete glanced over and saw Big Red standing with his back to the bar, thumbs hooked in his belt and looking in his direction, a smirk on his face. His drinking companions grinned and waited with thinly-veiled anticipation. Probably wondering if Pete would take the bait.

"That can't be," one of Big Red's adoring fans chimed in. "Them idiots from Chicago don't come up here until the November season. Of course, then they blast away at every cow in sight. Got to get me one of them two-point black-and-white bucks, you know." Laughter exploded and bottles clinked.

So much for first appearances, Pete thought. The crazies were here after all.

"Hey, buddy," Big Red called, "You belong to them Illinois plates?"

Pete smiled and tried to act casual. "Are you talking to me?"

"I sure don't see no other person sitting at that table with you." More laughs.

"Well, I don't understand the reason for your question, but if you mean that old green beater out front, yeah, that's mine."

Big Red turned to his fans. "You hear that boys? He calls that foreign luxury vehicle of his a beater." This time there were hisses instead of laughs.

He turned back to Pete. "Why don't you big city people buy American so folks around here can get jobs?"

"If that's what you're concerned about," Pete said, "I'm holding up my end of the bargain. Land Rover made my vehicle and it's owned by Ford right here in Michigan." He felt no need to explain that Ford hadn't acquired Land Rover until 2000 or that it had the company on the block for sale again.

Big Red looked at him as though uncertain of how to respond. "That vehicle ain't made here," he finally said.

"Well, if it's not, your beef is with Ford and not me. These days vehicles are assembled from parts made all over the world. That's the global economy."

He realized he'd just served Big Red a slab of red meat. "That's the goddamn problem. Them chickenshits in Washington let them foreigners dump their crap here and don't do nothin' about it. They sure as hell get after the little guy, though. We got the Second Amendment, but you can't hardly buy a gun in this country no more."

Pete wasn't about to get into a debate on the Second Amendment with this group, but did decide, maybe foolishly, to take one more jab at Big Red.

"Would you mind taking off your cap for a minute?" he said.

Big Red's face darkened. "What's the matter? My cap offend you or somethin'?" The bar became quiet again.

"No, it doesn't offend me. I was just wondering what the label says."

He glared at Pete for a while and then took off his cap and examined the label.

"Well," Pete said, "what's it say? China? Bangladesh? Maybe Korea if that's an expensive cap?"

Big Red stood there with a sour look on his face. "You can't compare a cap with that piece of foreign crap you're driving."

"Maybe, but my point is that we all buy goods from other countries these days. Even you."

Big Red grabbed a fresh bottle of beer and walked toward Pete's table. *Shit*, Pete thought, maybe he should have just let the guy have his fun rather than one-up him in front of his buddies. When Big Red reached his table, he spun a chair around and dropped into it like a sack of grain. He rested his arms on the back and thrust his face toward Pete.

"What the hell are you doing here?" His voice was low now, like the growl of an agitated animal.

"Look," Pete said, "no offense, but isn't that my business?"

"You're in our community, now. That makes it our business. We look out for each other around here."

Pete just stared at him.

Big Red's eyes were like slits over his fleshy red cheeks. "That was you we saw parked in front of the Janicek house this afternoon, wasn't it?"

"Well, if it was, that's my business like I said."

Big Red glared at him. "What do you do back in Illinois?" His voice was louder now, as though he wanted to get his fan base with him again.

"I'm a lawyer," Pete said, locking eyes with him.

"You hear that boys?" he said, turning toward the crowd at the bar. "This here gentleman from Illinois who drives a foreign luxury vehicle is a lawyer." He turned back to Pete and said in the same loud voice, "I thought it might be somethin' like that. You don't exactly look like you work for the railroad or Jiffy Lube or nothin'. What's the matter, you run out of ambulances to chase down there so you need to open up new territory?" More laughter from the bar.

Pete decided he'd had enough. He fished out some money, dropped it on the table to pay his bill, and stood up to leave. Big Red rose with him and blocked his way. His voice returned to a growl.

"You leave the Janiceks alone, you hear me? They've just gone through a terrible thing and want to grieve in peace. You stay away from them or you'll have us to deal with." He jerked his head toward his buddies at the bar.

"Would you mind moving out of my way?" Pete asked.

Big Red just stood there taking up half the county.

"Red, let the man pass." It was the bartender. He'd stayed out of the confrontation, but clearly didn't want a ruckus in his establishment. "Besides," he added, "he's a good customer. He pays cash, unlike some people I know."

The group at the bar tittered as Big Red shot the bartender a withering look. Before taking a step to one side, he jabbed Pete in the chest with a finger and said, "You remember what I said about the Janiceks."

Pete started toward the door and didn't worry about it when he bumped Big Red as he passed. He waved at the bartender and walked out.

The air felt good. He walked to his Range Rover and was about to get in when he noticed that his left front tire looked as though it had dissolved into the gravel. He squatted down to examine it; there was a long gash in the tire wall.

"It looks like them foreign tires don't stand up so good," a voice called. "Probably got punctured by a pine needle or somethin'."

Pete turned and saw Big Red and some of the other men from the bar standing in the Whitetail's door. Wide grins were plastered on their faces.

Pete walked back to within 20 feet of the group. His anger churned close to the surface as he stared at Big Red. "Did you do this?" he demanded.

"Me?" Big Red asked, pointing to his chest in feigned surprise. "Golly no. I was inside with you." He turned to his friends. "Hey boys, did I touch the lawyer's foreign luxury vehicle?"

"Nope," Itchy said right on cue. "You was with us."

Big Red continued to smirk. "Look, we don't want you to think we're not hospitable or nothin'. Could we give you a lift somewhere?"

Pete ignored him and walked back to his Range Rover. He pulled out his cell phone and angrily punched at the keys. His first call was to roadside service. The second was to Marian Janicek to tell her he'd just expanded his range of services.

TEN

After returning from his morning run, he called Angie DeMarco to see whether she'd found out anything more about Cara Lane. Angie picked up on the first ring; he was never completely sure whether her penchant for spending most Saturdays in the office reflected her workload or a desire to avoid spending time with her husband. She had been out of the public sector for over eight years, but maintained her network of contacts in the Chicago Police Department. He'd asked her to have one of them run Cara's name through the databases to which only law enforcement personnel have access.

"Your girlfriend's story keeps getting more interesting," she said after they exchanged the usual pleasantries.

"She wasn't my girlfriend."

"Yeah, yeah, that's what they all say."

"I take it you uncovered something new?" he asked, still feeling irritable over the incident at the Whitetail the previous day and wanting to get to the point.

"My, aren't we touchy today," she said picking up on his impatient tone. "Okay, here's what I came up with. Remember the Detroit federal building bombing?"

Pete thought for a few moments. "That was back in the mid-1990s, wasn't it? Just after Oklahoma City."

"Right. Well Cara Lane — or Cara Janicek or whatever name she was using back then — was questioned in connection with that bombing, too."

He thought back to his meeting with Marian Janicek and what she had said about the questions Richter had asked her. Maybe that was what he had in mind when he asked if Cara kept in contact with people in the area and if she knew any of the militia people.

"As I recall," he said, "no one was ever arrested and indicted in connection with the Detroit bombing. Did they suspect Cara of having something to do with it?"

"Apparently. I guess the guy who trained her in the use of explosives lived in Idaho at the time, but was originally from her hometown."

"Was he a militia guy?"

"I don't know, but he clearly harbored anti-government views. He also learned explosives in the military. I guess he landed on the FBI's list because he fit their profile."

"So Cara was questioned because of her past and the connection to him."

"Yes, as I understand it."

Pete mulled over what she had just said. "How about the other guy I asked you about? Kurt Romer. I sent you an email. Anything on him?"

Angie sighed deeply. "Am I your law partner or personal investigator?" she said. "You're up north playing detective and seem to think all I've got to do down here is spend time on your requests."

"Sorry," Pete said, feeling sheepish about his brusque question.

"I've only got so many favors I can call in, you know."

"I know," he said. "Just do this one more for me. I promise to buy you dinner when I'm back in Chicago. You can bring along your friend if you want."

"Okay," she said, the resignation clear from her voice, "I'll talk to Marc first thing Monday morning."

He thanked her one more time, told her to get out of the office and enjoy the rest of the weekend, and hung up.

The Saturday morning regatta was in full bloom out on the lake. He watched for a while, and then found his mind drifting back to the incident at the Whitetail. How did Big Red fit into all of this? The guy had zeroed right in on him and warned him to stay away from the Janiceks. Was he just being territorial, shielding members of the community, or was there more to it? Did he have a history with Cara?

He glanced at his watch. He knew that the charter fishing boats went out early in the morning and then again about five in the afternoon. Maybe he'd try to catch Romer and size him up even without some advance intelligence from Angie.

• • •

The Eagles' 1970s hit "Take It Easy" blared from a boom box on the 32-foot craft with "CohoBandit" emblazoned on its stern.

"Hey Arne," Pete called, "doesn't all this noise scare away the fish?"

Arne Breit looked up. If fishing hadn't been in his blood, he would have made the perfect proprietor of a bierstube in his ancestral Bavarian homeland. Fleshy red cheeks gave him a genial appearance, and a loose gray tee-shirt did little to conceal an expansive midsection that bore testament to his fondness for barley and hops.

He pushed his worn blue nautical cap back on his head. "I've got news for you, counselor. When I take a party out, we don't just troll around the bay playing music. Plus the fish love this stuff. When I really want to drive them crazy, I put on some Led Zeppelin."

Pete laughed. "Led Zeppelin would drive me nuts, too."

"To what do I owe this honor, Mr. Thorsen? You finally going to give me some business?"

"Might. My luck with trout hasn't been very good lately."

Arne squinted at him. "I never could figure out why guys like you crawl around in creeks casting for minnows when you could be out on the big lake catching real fish."

"Artistry, my friend. Could I talk to you for a minute?"

"Sure, as long as we can do it while I work. I'm getting ready to take a group out."

"It's about a guy who works for you," Pete said. "Kurt Romer."

Arne stopped swabbing the deck and looked at Pete. "What's your interest in Kurt?"

"Off the record?" Pete asked.

Arne nodded slowly.

"He knew Cara Lane from what I hear. That's the woman who drowned. I've been appointed the attorney for her estate — I'm really doing it as kind of a favor to the family — and I'd like to see what he can tell me about her."

Arne continued to look at him with narrowed eyes. "The sheriff has already talked to him, you know."

"I know that. But part of my job is to locate Cara's assets to file a report with the probate court. I was hoping Kurt might be able to help me fill in the picture." Pete felt bad being deceptive with a friend, but didn't want to come right out and tell Arne the real reason he wanted to talk to Romer.

"Well, to get back to your question, I don't know a lot about him. He's from Cleveland. This is the second season he's worked for me. He's pretty damn good."

"Any problems with him?"

"Nothing serious. He can be hotheaded and I've had to straighten him out once or twice. Sometimes he's late getting down to the boat. He's single and spends time in the bars. Real ladies man. Customers seem to like him, which is the important thing."

Pete grinned. "Gets along with them better than you, huh?"

Arne's face turned a deeper shade of crimson. "That was a bullshit charge and you know it."

Pete chuckled at Arne's discomfort. He didn't look like a guy who'd rough up a member of his fishing party just because the guy refused to release an undersized fish.

"That's what they all claim," Pete said. "You just had a good lawyer who got you off."

"Oh sure," Arne said, feigning a look of disgust that would do Harry proud. "You'd been admitted to practice in Michigan for what, three days when that happened? Hell. I told you everything to say."

Pete grinned again. "We kicked butt, though, didn't we? Where can I find your man Kurt?"

"Fifth slip down. Don't take up much of his time. He's scheduled to take a group out about the same time as me."

● ● ●

Pete walked down the dock and saw a man working on the deck of a boat that was a clone of CohoBandit except it had some Second Amendment signs stenciled on the stern.

"Kurt?"

Romer looked up, then removed his cap and ran a hand through jet-black hair that curled over the collar of his chambray work shirt. "You're a little early," he said. "We're not scheduled to go out for another hour."

"I'm not part of your charter group. My name is Pete Thorsen. I'm a friend of Arne's. Can I talk to you for a minute?"

Romer stared at Pete. "About what? I'm kind of busy right now."

"This shouldn't take long. It involves that woman who drowned. Cara Lane."

Romer slipped the butt of the fishing rod he was holding into a clamp on the side of the boat and walked over to the stern. He was about Pete's height, but standing on the deck of the boat, loomed over him. "Why do you want to talk to me about Cara Lane?"

"I'm a lawyer," Pete said. "Her family retained me to handle her estate and one of my duties is to marshal her assets. I was hoping you'd be able to help me."

His eyes continued to bore into Pete. "I don't understand, what makes you think that?"

"You knew her, I heard. She was out on your boat."

"A lot of people go out on my boat. That doesn't mean I know anything about them."

"Granted," Pete said, "but I hear you spent some time with her around town, too, and I thought this might be different."

Romer looked at him through narrowed eyes. "What kind of information are you looking for?"

"Well, for one thing, did she have a car up here?"

Romer stared at Pete. "I have no idea."

"Did you pick her up the night you were at the Car Ferry? She was staying over on Clear Lake. I doubt if she walked all the way to town."

"Do you think I check with every broad I meet whether she has wheels? I met her at the bar."

Pete laughed. "No, I'm sure you don't check on the transportation needs of every woman you meet. That's just an example."

"What else would you like to know? Whether she was a good lay or something?" A smirk replaced his steely stare.

"No," Pete said, not taking the bait, "that's not what I had in mind. I'm just trying to get a handle on her assets."

"I'm sorry I can't help you, Pete. I don't know anything about her 'assets' as you call them. Oh, wait, she did have a pair of assets that were pretty nice now that I think about it." The smirk widened. "Now if you'll excuse me, I need to get back to work before Arne is all over my ass." He picked up another rod and began to check it over.

"Here's my card," Pete said. "I'd appreciate it if you'd call me if you think of anything that might be useful."

Romer reached over the rail, took the card, and shoved it in his pocket without looking at it.

Pete glanced over his shoulder as he was walking off the pier and saw Romer watching him. A real asshole, he thought.

• • •

When Pete got back to his cottage, he emailed Angie telling her that Romer was originally from Cleveland. He was sitting on his porch reading the latest C. J. Box mystery when the phone rang.

"Is this Peter Thorsen, the hotshot lawyer?"

Pete recognized the voice. It was Wayne Sable and he sounded drunk.

"Thanks for calling back, Wayne. I assume you got my messages."

"I got your messages, Peter, and the answer is 'no.'"

Pete thought he heard the slosh of liquid over ice cubes. "You must be kidding. Julie wants to come up for a few days. Why would you object to that?"

"Peter, Peter, Peter, and you're supposed to be a lawyer. I'm her father. I have a responsibility for the welfare of my child. You should understand that." Pete heard the ice cubes rattle again. "Or maybe you don't. You don't have any children of your own, do you, Peter. I'm sorry. I almost forgot."

Pete held his temper in check and said, "Wayne, I think you're forgetting something. The court order gives me regular visitation rights. That includes three weeks during the summer. I don't need your permission. I just called you as a courtesy." Pete knew he was pushing the envelope, but maybe a shot across the guy's bow wasn't the worst thing.

"Peter, I'm disappointed in you. You're supposed to be such a good lawyer, too. I just came from my own counsel's office and he explained quite clearly that your visitation rights are limited to your home and at times convenient to me. Unless something has changed, Peter, that little cabin of yours in Michigan isn't your home. I don't even know if it's safe and I certainly won't have any time in August to check it out and discharge my parental responsibilities."

"Responsibilities?"

"That's what I said. Responsibilities."

Pete tightened his grip on the handset. "Well, you're getting very bad advice if that's really what your lawyer told you. Why don't you just have another drink, Wayne, and I'll talk to Larry on Monday. If we have to take this before the judge, I think he'll be very interested to hear the recording I've made of this telephone conversation."

There was a pause at the other end. "You can't record . . ."

Pete slammed down the handset and smiled in spite of his irritation.

ELEVEN

They could smell chili a quarter-mile away. When they arrived at the Colcorp facility, it was easy to see why. Booths filled the parking lot and were laid out with military precision. All had signs of some kind and a dozen banners flew high overhead. It looked like a medieval fair.

Chili simmered on grills and cooks proudly ladled out samples of their finest creations. Without exception, they claimed to use some special recipe passed down through the ages and guarded like a sensitive military secret. They boasted of using the hottest peppers or the freshest ingredients or some herb so special that no one else was even aware of it. There was Dog Breath Chili and 24 Carat Chili and Road Kill Chili. Chili aficionados strolled from booth to booth eating bits of French bread and tasting samples of chili from small paper cups and forming their own judgments. Harry was mopping his brow by the time he'd been there five minutes.

Pete saw the Colonel across the parking lot wearing a soft cap with his old tank unit insignia. He watched him attend to his official duties with gusto, introducing the festival queen one minute and the head of some local charity the next. All the while he kept a watchful eye on the judges as they went from booth to booth to discharge their solemn responsibilities. The Colonel played the gracious host, but he also liked to win. He spotted them and made his way over.

"Jesus," he said, "this is something, huh? You get some of mine?"

"I got some of your beer," Pete said. "Couldn't you find a way to make this place any hotter?"

"Its only 85 degrees," the Colonel said with a surprised look. "I guess it's hotter here in the parking lot. The heat doesn't bother me, though."

Harry gulped down the last of his chili and took a deep swig of beer. He wiped his mouth on his sleeve and said, "That's because you're used to racing across deserts in a friggin' tank."

The Colonel laughed and poked him in the ribs. "Pete," he said, "I've got good news. I think we have a deal with RyTech. Let's go inside and I'll fill you in. You, too, Harry. Just don't print anything we talk about in that rag of yours."

"Who's minding your booth?" Harry asked.

"My son-in-law." The Colonel grinned. "He's my chili-master-in-training."

They went into the Colcorp headquarters building and walked down to the Colonel's office. He fumbled with the lock and clicked on the lights. Pete had been in the Colonel's office a dozen times, but never failed to marvel at it. It was like a museum. Military artifacts were everywhere, and one wall was covered by a floor-to-ceiling blow-up of a tank unit racing across southern Iraq. A red arrow pointed to the Colonel's tank. The one in the lead, naturally.

"See what I mean?" Harry said, pointing at the blow-up.

The Colonel's eyes flicked toward the wall and he stood motionless for a while, staring at the huge photograph. "That was Desert Storm, you know. Damn, it was really something. Tanks were spread out across the desert as far as you could see." His square face turned serious and he ran a hand across his copper brush-cut hair and clamped his cap on again. "Too bad the politicians screwed things up after we kicked their butts that time. There's a struggle for civilization going on, gentlemen. A lot of people just don't realize it."

"You're not the only one who believes that," Pete said. "Well, what's the story on RyTech?"

"Typical friggin' lawyer," the Colonel said, shaking his head. "Always has his mind on business. Anyway, I talked with the RyTech CEO twice yesterday. The first time was around nine in the morning. He said they had a big board meeting on Friday and blah, blah, blah. Bottom line is they came up to 47 million — I keep the debt — but couldn't go beyond that."

"That was at the upper end of our price range," Pete said.

"I know, I know. But I was feeling a little cranky that morning. Too much celebrating the night before, I guess, so I told him I needed five more or I pull the company off the market. He sputters and blusters and says that's unacceptable. I say, 'Okay, it's been nice knowing you.' Pretty soon I get a call from Frank Callahan who wants to know what's going on. He was sure I'd take $47 million, he says, and clearly was worried about his fee on the deal. I told him that RyTech had dicked around for three months and July's numbers looked like they would come in 30 percent higher than we assumed and the price was now $52 million, take it or leave it. He said someone would get back to me."

The Colonel was in a storytelling mood and obviously relishing every detail. Pete let him take his time.

"Anyway, about three I get another call from the RyTech CEO. He blusters again for a while and says they'll go up another five but it has to be contingent on revenue and earnings going forward. I say 'okay' and by the time we're done I had the numbers set so low that Harry here could run the business and we'd meet the targets."

"Hey," said Harry, looking hurt. "I'm a businessman, too. I do pretty well in a business where the margins are a lot lower than yours."

The Colonel laughed. "Just wanted to see if you were still awake."

"Lets see," Pete said. "In effect, they'd be absorbing the debt and you'd net $47 million, give or take, less Callahan's fee. Not bad."

The Colonel wore a wide grin. "The company was worth less than two million when I took over after leaving the service." He turned serious after a minute. "I need to get this deal closed so I can buy out the rest of Madelaine's family and then invest in my other businesses. That night vision technology we're developing is going to be damned important to our troops in the future."

Pete nodded.

"Can you bang out a draft of a letter of intent and meet with me on Wednesday to go over it?" he asked Pete. "They wanted to do the drafting — I know that's customary — but I convinced the CEO that you're a real pro and completely fair in these things." He winked at Pete.

"Sure, no problem."

"Good, good." The Colonel cracked a riding crop into the palm of his left hand, and stalked around the office, flicking specks of dust off the saddle used by his great-grandfather when he rode with Black Jack Pershing and rearranging other artifacts. He was one of those men who had left the army, but never really left it behind. His real name was Walter Shelhorn but everyone called him Colonel, something he encouraged, and he was descended from four generations of military men. All had attended the Military Academy and three had gone on to reach the rank of brigadier general or higher. The Colonel had to settle for Virginia Military Institute — he blamed politics for not getting into West Point — but rose to full bird colonel before he was retired along with a slew of other officers in the 1990s. He was very sensitive about that, feeling it deprived him of his opportunity to make brigadier general and uphold the family tradition. Harry had introduced Pete to the Colonel three years earlier and he'd taken over all of his legal business shortly after that. They'd also become good friends.

"Well, I've got to get back outside," the Colonel said. "Got to keep an eye on those judges." He gave Harry a slap on the back.

As they walked down the hall, the Colonel pulled Pete aside. "Excuse us for a minute, Harry. Pete," he said, lowering his voice, "I know you're on vacation, but I need your undivided attention on this deal. We've got to close by September 30."

"You'll have it."

"Okay, tell your team to start cracking. It's pedal-to-the-metal time."

They rejoined Harry and the Colonel slung an arm around his shoulders as they continued down the hall. The Colonel was an inch or two taller, but that's where the comparison ended. Harry had an impressive girth, but the Colonel was solidly built with a flat stomach that showed his penchant for staying fit. After a little banter, Harry said, "Have you heard about the excitement over our way last weekend?"

The Colonel stared at him for a few moments. "You mean that woman who drowned?"

"Yeah."

"Some guys I played golf with were talking about it. I guess she got loaded and decided to go for a midnight swim."

Harry looked like he was going to say something just as they left the air-conditioned comfort of the building and the heat and chili aromas hit them like a slap in the face. Two of the judges spotted the Colonel as soon as he walked out the door and beckoned him over. He excused himself and huddled with them.

Pete breathed a sigh of relief. He was wondering how he was going to rationalize his involvement in the Cara Lane affair in view of the Colonel's deal and the urgency he placed on getting it closed on a tight timetable. Now it looked like the Colonel's attention was fixed on other matters. Pete was also thinking about the price. Forty-seven million net. He'd been shaving the firm's recent bills to Colcorp and the deal was his opportunity to recoup the write-offs. There'd be plenty of gravy to go around at that price. He made a mental note to talk to the Colonel about fees on the deal.

Harry's mind, too, seemed to have shifted to other matters. He cupped a hand and said to Pete in a low voice, "When he gets back, let's say our goodbyes and hit the road. We can call the ladies from the car and have them meet us at your place."

"They've narrowed it down to the top five," the Colonel said when he returned. "They wouldn't tell me who they are." From his grin, it was just a question of who would come in second.

After more small talk, Harry said, "Colonel, we've got a couple of beautiful women waiting for us at Pete's. We have to get going. This has been a blast."

"Glad you could come," the Colonel said. "The three of us need to get together for some golf or fishing." He winked at Pete. "I never realized what a big businessman Harry has become, so I guess we'll have to work around his schedule." He turned back to Harry. "Call us with a couple of dates and let's set something up."

Harry just gave him a dirty look.

• • •

"You know what that event makes for local charities every year?" Harry asked. "Over 80 grand. Biggest fundraiser in the area."

Pete grunted and shook his head. He looked down at his speedometer and eased up on the accelerator. He was anxious to get back to his place before Rona and Lynn arrived, but didn't want to risk getting stopped by the police who seemed to make it their life's mission to nab motorists on M-115.

"I noticed you clammed up when the Colonel said Cara Lane's death was a swimming accident," Harry said, "and you didn't say a word about having had dinner with her."

Pete glanced over at him. "We were interrupted, remember? Plus I learned early on in the practice of law not to share too much with clients, even those I'm close to personally. Every client likes to think he's the only one his lawyer represents, and if disabused of that notion, inevitably begins to wonder if his lawyer is really paying attention to his affairs when he's out of sight."

That was doubly true when he had a deal going for the client like the one for Colcorp. He had another reason for keeping his personal investigation quiet from the Colonel, too. Much as he liked him, the old soldier sucked up information like a Hoover in search of dirt, and he'd just as soon not have it spread around that he'd been questioned by Richter.

"Do me a favor, will you?" asked Pete.

"If I can."

"Don't say anything to the Colonel about my suspicions. I'll tell him myself in due course, but no sense getting him riled up in the middle of our deal."

"Sure, no problem. I assume that includes your meeting with Mrs. Janicek and your rumble with Big Red."

"Everything."

Pete passed through Benzonia and hung a left at the only stoplight in the county. He turned to Harry again and said, "Do you think the M.E. would talk to me?"

Harry frowned. "You mean about the dead woman?"

"Yes."

"Depends. What do you want to talk to him about?"

Pete thought about it. "Get a little more detail about what they found. And maybe just hypothetically, if she was killed and someone dressed it up to look like an accident, how he might have done it."

"Jesus, I don't know. You'd be asking him to speculate."

"All off the record," Pete said. "I wouldn't try to hold him to it."

"I don't know . . ."

"Maybe you could call him and make the introduction."

Harry looked at him

"You could say I'm the attorney for the Janiceks and would like to ask him a few questions."

"Since when are you the attorney for the Janiceks?"

"Since Friday afternoon."

He could feel Harry's eyes on him as he swung into his driveway. Rona's car was there and he saw the two women on his porch. Cara Lane faded from his mind. He killed the engine and stepped out of his Range Rover. He smiled when he heard Johnny Cash's voice fill the air.

TWELVE

Dr. Ethan Pennington, the M.E. for the unified three-county area that included the adjacent Grand Traverse and Leelanau Counties, looked about 60, maybe a year or two older. He was trim, of medium height, and had thinning gray hair. With his white lab coat and round tortoise-shell glasses, he looked like the prototypical physician.

"Nice to meet you, Mr. Thorsen. Right this way please."

Pete followed him down the corridor to his office. The wall behind his desk was covered with diplomas, certificates, and pictures of his family. An adjacent wall must have contained 20 photographs of the Doc tying flies, casting for trout on various streams, and holding fish aloft for everyone to admire.

"That's a nice one," Pete said, pointing to the fish in the top photograph. "Where was that taken?"

Dr. Pennington glanced over at the wall and a wistful look crept over his face. "The AuSable," he said. "Seventeen and a half inches. Are you a fly-fisherman, Mr. Thorsen?"

"I try."

"Harry tells me you're also the attorney for the Janicek family."

"Yes," Mrs. Janicek hired me last week. I'm co-executor and attorney for Cara Lane's estate as well."

"I assume you have evidence of your appointment?"

Pete opened his briefcase and pulled out the letter he had Marian Janicek sign. He handed it to Dr. Pennington. The M.E. studied it and handed it back to him, then looked at him over his glasses. "Were you at the press conference Sheriff Haskins and I held last week?"

"No, I was in Chicago at the time."

"But you read about it in the papers."

"Yes."

Dr. Pennington continued to study Pete. "Well, like I told Harry when he called, I don't know if there's much I can add to what we announced at that time."

"I understand that, Dr. Pennington, but I'd like to hear it from you first hand and in a little more detail. My client, Mrs. Janicek, is very distraught and doesn't believe Cara's death was an accident."

Dr. Pennington arched his eyebrows. "Oh? What does she base that on?"

"Between you and me, I think it's partly the mother coming out, but I promised her I'd look into it. To be fair, though, she does have some good points."

"Such as?"

"Well, for one thing, Cara called her the night she died. Mrs. Janicek is convinced Cara was meeting someone that night and said she acted funny. Cara also didn't drink much, according to Mrs. Janicek, and the notion that she got drunk and went for a swim and drowned seems a little far-fetched."

Dr. Pennington studied Pete again for a long time. "Are you aware of what the Medical Examiner's office does, Mr. Thorsen?"

"A little. You examine the body, perform toxicological tests where required, determine the cause of death, estimate the time of death, things like that."

"That's essentially right, although we do much more than that. But taking what we do and melding it with motive and opportunity and things, that's the work of the police."

"I understand that. Let's start from the beginning, if we may. You concluded that Cara Lane died from drowning, right?"

"Yes," Dr Pennington said, "that's right. In lay terms."

"And it all occurred in Clear Lake, I understand."

"That's what we concluded. Water and other elements from the lake were found in her stomach and lungs."

So far, it was consistent with what Harry had told him. "Have you reached any judgment as to whether she was dead or alive when she entered the water?"

A faint smile crossed Dr. Pennington's lips. "Are you a criminal lawyer, Mr. Thorsen?"

"No."

"I was wondering because that's a question someone not familiar with forensic science normally wouldn't ask." He paused for a few moments and appeared to be gathering his thoughts. "Our preliminary conclusion is that she was alive when she entered the water, which supports our drowning conclusion."

"What do you base that on?"

"We found a large number of diatoms in her system. Do you know what those are?"

"No idea," said Pete, shaking his head.

"They're microscopic organisms. There were a lot of diatoms in her lungs and blood. That may not be absolutely conclusive, but it's a pretty good indication that she was alive when she entered the water."

"I see," Pete said. "Is that a firm conclusion or are you still evaluating it?"

"Everything is preliminary at this point, but that's the way we're trending. We've been very busy this past week."

"I understand the body hasn't been released to the family yet. Is it still in the morgue at Munson?"

"Yes, it's still in the morgue. We hope to release the body to the family by the end of this week."

Pete nodded. "How about the head injury and the scrapes and bruises you found on the body? Have you formed any conclusions about what caused them?"

Dr. Pennington paused again and looked at him in a deliberate way. "We found some blood on the edge of the raft. One possible explanation is that the deceased swam out to the raft, tried to dive, hit her head on the edge, and it disoriented her enough that she drowned. That would explain the location of her body when she was found."

"Cara Lane was an excellent swimmer."

Dr. Pennington shrugged his shoulders. "Even a good swimmer can lose her bearings when she has as much alcohol in her system as we found in the deceased. It looks to us that she swam away from the shore rather than toward it."

"How about the blood on the raft. Was it a match with Cara's?"

"Yes. That hasn't been announced yet, but it was a match."

"In your medical judgment," Pete said, "would a blow to the head like the one Cara suffered be likely to disable her long enough for someone to get her out beyond the raft and let her drown?"

Dr. Pennington thought about the question. "It depends, I suppose, but I think it's unlikely. Assuming she was knocked out by the blow, it would have been only temporary and it wouldn't have given a perpetrator sufficient time to get her out to deep water. It's not like in the movies where the hero lays one on the bad guy's chin and he's out for a half hour."

Pete laughed. "I see your point. She was a big woman, too, and in good shape. There would have been a struggle when she came to. Question: were there other marks on Cara's body? Like from a tazer gun, for example."

"Not that we found."

"They'd be pretty obvious, wouldn't they?"

"They should be. We went over the body very carefully."

Pete thought about what the M.E. had told him and decided to air something that continued to fester in his mind. "One thing that bothers me," Pete said, "is how she would have been able to even see the raft to swim out there. There was no moon and clouds covered the stars. It was pitch black that night."

"I'm afraid I can't help you there. That's for the sheriff to analyze, not us." He appeared to think about it for a while. "Of course, your darkness point cuts two ways. It might also explain how she slipped and hit her head on the raft and then swam away from the shore."

"Possible," Pete said. Then he added, "Getting back to the alcohol, you said you found a heavy concentration in her system."

Dr. Pennington nodded. "Yes. Put in layman's terms, she was well over the limit allowed for motorists."

"I understand the sheriff's office found a wine bottle near Cara's clothes that was nearly empty. Doesn't it strike you as odd that the bottle only had Cara's prints on it?"

"Again, that's a matter for the sheriff to evaluate. That isn't something that we get into here at our office."

"I understand that," Pete said. "But speaking as a layman, don't you find that unusual?"

"I hadn't thought about it before and really don't care to venture an opinion."

"Okay," Pete said, "last question. When you ran the blood tests, did you test for other substances? Drugs, things like that?"

"We performed a basic screen, which is how we detected the alcohol level. We found no evidence of other toxins."

"But you didn't test specifically for date rape drugs, things like that."

"There are so many drugs. We saw no need to test for them in the circumstances."

"Do you know if the sheriff shipped the wine bottle off to the state crime lab for testing?"

"I really don't know, Mr. Thorsen. The drowning occurred in a poor county, remember. They simply don't have the budget to test for everything in a case like this where all the signs point to an accident."

"So what you're telling me is that Cara Lane's death was a swimming accident."

Dr. Pennington seemed to be uncomfortable with his question. "It looks that way, but I'm not prepared to say that conclusively at this time. We'll issue a public statement when we finish our evaluation."

• • •

Driving home, Pete reviewed in his mind the location of the far raft off the beach. There was a lifeline that ran to the close-in raft, but not to the far one as he remembered. But if she were killed, how would whoever did it get her body out there to stage the accident? The blow to the head likely wouldn't have done it, as Dr. Pennington pointed out. The only thing he could think of was some drug that wasn't easily detectable and normally wouldn't be tested for in what appeared to be a garden-variety drowning.

He could see how this was a win-win situation for a politically-ambitious sheriff. He had nothing to lose by letting his aggressive young deputy continue the investigation in the short-run and then pull the plug after a reasonable period of time if he came up dry. On the other hand, if his deputy got lucky, he could turn events to his advantage and take credit. Maybe Haskins letting his deputy run wild wasn't such a contradiction after all.

THIRTEEN

When Pete walked into the Car Ferry, the place was already jammed. Tuesday was ladies night, and while the half-price drinks for females attracted a lot of them, it drew in even more hungry-eyed males who were happy to pay full price in return for the improved odds that particular night offered.

He slid onto a stool just vacated by a hulk of a man, who had to go 300 pounds, with greasy hair pulled back in a ponytail and ordered a Miller Lite. He looked around the room. He'd only been in there twice before, when the owner he was representing in a liquor license violation charge gave him tours and explained the operations. An old mahogany bar stretched along most of one side of the dimly-lit room. Framed black and white photographs of car ferries that had plied Lake Michigan for the past century covered the walls. The pungent odor of beer mixed with cigarette smoke hung in the air, and the edgy sounds of a three-piece band had just cranked up and made normal conversation nearly impossible.

After getting back from the M.E.'s office, he'd spent the afternoon playing Bud Stephanopoulis to a standstill in one-on-one basketball.

Okay, technically not a standstill since Bud won three of five games, but the final game went right down to the wire. Bud told him he was taking it easy on him, but he didn't care; wins were wins. And he really didn't believe Bud either. He saw the look on the former collegiate star's face when Pete, who had struggled to make his high school team, got within a point of tying the final game.

But he wasn't there to celebrate his near-victory over Bud Stephanopoulis. He was there because he understood the Car Ferry was Kurt Romer's favorite hangout and he hoped to run into him. Angie DeMarco's report that afternoon had whetted his appetite and he found it hard to wait for nightfall. After playing cat-and-mouse games with him for a while, Angie reported that her contact at the Chicago Police Department told her that Kurt Romer had worked on a fishing charter boat in Chicago for a season after leaving Cleveland. His address was only a few blocks from where Cara Lane lived. Angie liked to save the good stuff for last, but it was usually worth the wait. This was no exception. Romer had a history of domestic assault charges against him in Cleveland and in fact was still subject to a protective order secured by his ex-girlfriend. That wasn't all. The feds had booked Romer twice on meth charges but both charges had been dropped for lack of evidence. The last arrest was right before he left Cleveland and the DEA folks kept an eye on him while he was in Chicago. In short, while there was nothing to link Romer directly to Cara's past, the facts seemed to suggest more than a coincidence.

He scanned the crowd, looking for Romer, and sipped his beer. The men were a lot like the bunch in the Whitetail. Younger on average, but with plenty of exceptions. One group at the upper end of the age scale had staked out a table near the small dance floor and were yukking it up. They had that hungry look of men free from the watchful eyes of their wives for a few days and were on the lookout for action.

The women ranged from barely legal on up. The uniform of the evening was snug-fitting black pants or short denim skirts combined with skimpy tops that showed off the bounty of the right genes, or at least the illusion created by the latest device from Victoria's Secret.

As he waited, he let his mind drift between his meeting with Dr. Pennington and Lynn Hawke. Out of the corner of his eye, he saw a woman with dark hair and a hot pink top winding her way through the crowd. She'd aged five years by the time she made it to the bar. She wedged her way between Pete and the man sitting on the next stool and asked Pete for a light. He filched a book of matches from a bowl behind the bar and got her fired up on the second try. Still Mister Smooth.

She whispered questions in his ear, quickly getting to what he did for gainful employment. When he told her he was a trust fund child, she looked puzzled, but must have concluded that was okay because she nuzzled closer. Her eyes flicked around the room as she talked to him. When they settled on the front door, he looked over and saw the man of the evening. Kurt Romer already had two women draped all over him. Pink Top, apparently determined not to be left out, raked her fingernails across Pete's ribs and eased through the crowd in that direction.

Pete watched Romer operate. He took turns squeezing the hopeful women and periodically would glance at the mirror behind the bar, no doubt admiring the fashionable two-day stubble and soul patch under his lower lip. Just a little vain, Pete thought. Like the old Carly Simon song.

It took a little while for Romer to spot him. When he did, his eyes locked on Pete's and stayed there. Pete smiled and raised his bottle. Romer just continued to stare. Then he disengaged from his female companions and made his way across the room toward Pete.

"What a surprise," he said, "it's the lawyer."

"Hello, Kurt. I heard this was the place to be on Tuesday nights. I thought I'd give it a try. You seem to be a regular."

"I come in once in a while." His eyes still hadn't wavered from Pete's.

Pink Top slid in between them. "How was your day, Kurt?" She stroked his back.

He gave her the standard squeeze. "Sugar, can I catch up with you later? I have to talk to Pete about something."

Her lips curled in a pout and she slithered away, glancing over her shoulder like a jilted ingenue. She didn't go far, though. Not with her competition lurking.

"Boy," Pete said, "it looks like every single woman in town is here."

A little smirk appeared on Romer's face. "And some that aren't single."

"I think Pink Top likes you."

"Bunnie?"

"That her name? Yeah."

Romer gave a little grunt that obviously was meant to be derisive.

"I don't know, Kurt. It looks like she has the hots for you. She live around here?"

Romer's smirk had faded and his eyes were glued on Pete's again. "I assume so. Probably in the back of an old Chevy parked behind the 7-Eleven or something."

"That's good." Pete said, grinning. "In the back of an old Chevy."

Romer didn't laugh. "Are you following me around, Pete?"

"Following you around? Now why would I do that?"

"It's not an accident you're here tonight, is it?"

"Well I admit I thought that I might bump into you, but that's not the same as following you around."

Romer's eyes bore holes in him. "You're the guy the sheriff questioned, aren't you? I heard he was a lawyer."

"I don't know if 'questioned' is the right word. I did call the sheriff's office and go in and give a statement if that's what you mean."

Romer continued as though he hadn't heard him. "You had dinner with her that night, right? It sounds like I'm the one who should be following you around, asking you questions."

Pete smiled at him. "You're forgetting one key point, Kurt. It's pretty well established that she met someone else that night after she left me. I'm thinking that was you."

"Me? I don't think so."

For all the bravado, Pete detected an aura of concern. "You knew her from Chicago, right?" he said.

Romer stiffened and his eyes turned flinty. "Where did you hear that?"

"You're not denying you lived in Chicago for a year, are you?"

"It's none of your damned business where I lived."

"No need to get hostile about it," Pete said. "I just assumed that's where you met her."

Suddenly the bar noise faded into the background and it was just Pete and Romer.

"What kind of bullshit is this?" asked Romer.

"She lived at 2243 Bissell, just a few blocks from where you lived."

Romer just stared at him. He didn't look like a guy who normally suffered from a loss of words, but he seemed to be wondering how Pete knew so much about him.

"What do you think happened to her, Kurt?"

"How the hell should I know? If you didn't have anything to do with it — and I guess we don't know that, do we Pete? — I assume she went swimming and drowned."

Pete continued to bore in, not knowing exactly where he was going but sensing weakness. "I'm curious, Kurt, why did you move to Chicago? You found Cleveland — how shall we say — a little confining?"

"Confining? What the hell are you talking about?"

"I heard you had trouble with your old girlfriend back in Cleveland. I'm sure those restraining orders can be annoying after a while." Pete knew he was pushing it because Romer looked like he was wound like a coiled spring.

"You sonofabitch, I . . ."

"I know a lot about you, Kurt," Pete said, cutting him off. "Restraining orders. Arrests on meth charges. There are probably a lot of opportunities up here, huh? I understand the market is more open. Not as many big boys to worry about. Was Cara involved too? Is that why she was up here?"

Pete winced as Romer's fingers dug into his arm. "I'm getting tired of this, asshole. I'm about to smash your friggin' head in. There are a dozen people in here who will say you started it."

"Let go of my arm, Kurt. *Now.* And before you start smashing anything, you better take a look down at the end of the bar. That's the owner of this place. I saved his liquor license two years ago."

Romer looked down the bar and then back at Pete. "You stay away from me, you sonofabitch." His face was six inches away and Pete could smell beer and sweat. Romer released his arm and shoved him into the bar, then turned and headed for the door. A couple of women moved in on him as he passed but he brushed them aside and yanked the door open and left.

He'd baited the hook. Now let's see what he caught. Romer didn't look like a man with a lot of patience.

"What was that all about?" a man standing next to Pete asked.

"Beats me. I guess he was in a hurry to leave." He felt the wetness under his arms and took another sip of his warm beer.

FOURTEEN

Pete put the final touches on the draft RyTech letter of intent and then went for a run. The sun was still low in the sky, and as he looked east, it cast a sheen on the water that sparkled like a million bits of tinsel. He enjoyed the scene and increased his distance to four miles. He labored at the end, but it felt good.

Ebba was happy to see him when he walked into her shop an hour later, but she looked disappointed when he ordered his breakfast sandwich made with eggbeaters and only two strips of bacon. She told him Harry had been in earlier for his morning muffin fix, and brought Pete up to date on the controversial proposal to expand the local airport.

He walked down the street and found a bench near the marina and ate his sandwich while he looked out at the bay. He loved the history of the place. Pere Jacques Marquette and his fellow voyageurs had paddled their canoes through the bay in the 17th century and later, during the logging boom in Michigan, thousands of logs had floated through en route to the sawmills. Much of the lumber used to rebuild Chicago after the Great Fire had passed right through these waters. It reminded him to finish the second part of his series on those days.

Arne's boat was gone from its slip. Romer's was there, but he didn't see him around. He ate his sandwich and reflected. Few things were clear when it came to Cara Lane's death, but he had very little doubt that Mr. Romer, for all of his success with the ladies, was one very bad hombre. He was into drugs, too, which fit nicely with his theory about Cara Lane's death.

Then as if on cue Romer strolled down the dock toward his boat. He stopped to talk to another man for a few minutes. His ears must have been burning because suddenly he looked in Pete's direction. Pete raised what was left of his sandwich in a mock salute. Romer's eyes were like lasers. After a minute or two, he continued on to his boat without looking back.

Be careful with this guy, Pete told himself.

• • •

Terri Mattingly came out of her office and was all smiles when Pete walked into the Colcorp building later that morning. With her crimped red hair and band of freckles across her nose, she looked like the All-American soccer mom.

"The Colonel isn't back yet," she said. Her eyes danced as she shifted into her flirtation mode. "You're going to have to talk to me for a while."

"Meeting?"

She pursed her lips and shook her head. "Cemetery," she said softly. "He goes almost every morning. His son."

Pete knew that the Colonel's son had been killed in Afghanistan a few years earlier, but he never seemed to want to talk about it and Pete hadn't pried. He passed time with Terri exchanging gossip and comparing notes about their children. He wasn't sure how a single mom did it; just keeping one teen on an even keel was hard enough.

There was some history associated with Terri's position with the company that said a lot about the Colonel. When her husband walked out on her and their three young children and just disappeared — presumably with another woman — she'd struggled to make ends meet. The Colonel found out and with compassion for her situation promoted her to his administrative assistant and gave her a fat raise that busted Colcorp's pay scale. Some actions carry unintended blessings and this was one of them. The Colonel never tired of boasting that it was one of the smartest decisions he'd ever made.

The Colonel finally walked in looking tense and drawn. He apologized to Pete for being late and took him down to his office. Then he excused himself and disappeared down the hall. While Pete waited he looked around and thought about the narrow window he had to see Marian Janicek between the time Hank left after lunch and when her quilting group was scheduled to pick her up. His eyes drifted over to the familiar family pictures covering the credenza behind the Colonel's desk. Front and center was a large framed photograph of Madelaine, his wife of 35 years, looking like the saint Pete knew her to be. She was flanked on one side by pictures of their son in combat fatigues and a beret and in full-dress army uniform. He had the same steely look as his father. On the other side of Madelaine was their daughter riding her prize horse in show competition and another in which she posed with her three children as they petted a colt.

The Colonel returned. "Sorry, Pete, I had to attend to something. My life's not my own these days."

"No problem," Pete said, trying not to show his anxiety to get started.

"Do you mind if I ask Mike Boehm to join us? He's my right hand man these days and he's going to be involved in the deal from our side."

Pete shrugged. "No, I'd like to meet him anyway. I've seen his name on a lot of stuff the last year or two."

Five minutes later Boehm walked in with a file under his arm. He was a compact man with a well-toned body, close-cropped hair, and a man's handshake. Early 40s, Pete guessed. Based on his crisp dress — starched blue shirt and khakis with a knife's-edge press — he probably had a military background himself. Pete shook hands and exchanged the usual pleasantries.

"Okay men," the Colonel said, suddenly sounding like a general addressing his troops on the eve of a pivotal battle, "we have work to do. I want to have a letter of intent signed by next week this time. We close by September 30."

They began to review the draft Pete had prepared. Boehm occasionally made a comment or asked a question, but mostly deferred to Pete as he led them through the various provisions. Pete could sense Boehm sizing him up, though. That didn't bother him. His relationship with the Colonel was solid and he'd gotten to be pretty good at handling corporate lieutenants who might try to curry favor with the boss by making him look bad. They discussed a few changes to the draft and agreed to get a revised version out to RyTech the next day.

The Colonel and Boehm discussed some operational issues at the Bridgeview, Illinois plant that was to be included in the deal and Pete's mind drifted off again to his meeting with Marian Janicek early that afternoon. He'd decided to push her harder on who Cara might have met after dinner with him that night and, in particular, whether Cara had ever mentioned Kurt Romer.

"You know that environmental issue is going to come up in RyTech's due diligence," the Colonel said, switching back to the deal. "I think both of you should be there when our consultant goes out to the plant." He stopped and stared at Pete. "Pete, are you with us?"

"Yes, sorry," Pete said, shaking himself out of his reverie. "I agree."

The Colonel continued to look at him for a moment and said, "Bridgeview's in your neck of the woods, Pete. Why don't you give Mike a couple of days when you're available to go out there."

Pete nodded his agreement.

"I'll be glad to get rid of the damn place," the Colonel muttered.

Neither Pete nor Mike Boehm commented.

After they finished, Pete hung around to chat with the Colonel even though he was eager to get going. The old soldier seemed to perk up when they talked about fishing the Manistee and where he'd played golf lately. They again talked about getting together with Harry.

The Colonel checked his watch. "How about grabbing some lunch?"

"I'd love to," said Pete, "but I have to make a stop on the way back. I'm going to have to pass. Sorry."

The Colonel gazed at him with steady eyes. "I thought you were supposed to be on vacation. Except for my deal, that is," he said, flashing a grin.

"Supposed to be is right. But as the old saw goes, the law is a jealous mistress."

The Colonel gave what was supposed to pass for a chuckle. "How has your office adjusted to you being away for a month?"

"I've been telling my partners since May that I was planning to take August off this year. Not one of them remembers."

"Not much happens in August anyway, does it?"

Pete smiled. "Oh no, just clients selling their businesses, stuff like that."

The Colonel looked at him with a serious expression. "I hate to screw up your vacation, but like I said, we've got to push on this deal."

"No need to apologize. I expected it to be a working vacation anyway."

"I'm counting on you. You seem a little distracted these days."

"Distracted. How so?"

The Colonel looked at him. "Maybe it's just my imagination." He paused for a moment. "What else do you have going in this area?"

Pete was tempted to tell the Colonel what he was doing on the Cara Lane affair, but then caught himself. "Just a minor matter I got myself roped into. It won't interfere with your deal, I promise."

"After we close," the Colonel said, "we'll find a few days to go look at a company I've had my eye on in Palm Springs. We'll take our sticks along and see how many holes we can get in. It's all tax deductible, of course." He winked at Pete.

They wrapped things up and Pete took his leave. He couldn't help notice the look on the Colonel's face when he left. Probably back to thinking about his son.

• • •

Pete parked discreetly up by the maple this time. No use giving Marian Janicek something else to worry about. She was scheduled to be picked up by her quilting group in an hour, and sat on the couch and shuffled though the papers he gave her to sign as co-executor of Cara's estate. Mostly she just looked at Pete with forlorn eyes.

"I'm sorry," he said, "I don't have much new to tell you. The sheriff is continuing to investigate. He's out of town a lot; I hope to see him early next week. I'm trying to check out some other things, too, but it all takes time." He deliberately didn't get into his meeting with the M.E.

"How about that man Cara was living with in Chicago?" He could tell from her voice that the thought pained her.

"His name is Marcus Vrba. I ran a search on him. He's a professor at Roosevelt University in downtown Chicago. Teaches labor history. You know, the union movement and stuff like that."

Her face brightened. "That sounds like a good job. Do you think Cara and him had a relationship?"

"I don't know," he said, thinking about his conversation with Vrba and how uncommunicative he'd been. "Maybe they were just sharing an apartment for money reasons."

"Oh," Marian said, not meeting his gaze.

"When I'm in Chicago next time, I'm going to stop and see Vrba again and pick up Cara's things."

She looked wistful and just nodded.

They sat quietly for a few moments and then he said, "Marian, if you want me to help you, I need to know everything you know. Do you have any idea — even a guess — who Cara might have met after she left me that night?"

She shook her head. "Like I said before, Pete, she didn't tell me anything. I just felt it, you know?"

"Think about it, Marian. She must have been up in this area for a reason. Is there anyone from her past that you can think of she might have met? Anyone she mentioned in your Friday night calls, for example?"

She appeared to think some more, then shook her head again. "I'm sorry, Pete, I guess I'm not being much help."

He decided to float a name that was very much on his mind. "How about a man named Kurt Romer? Did she ever mention him?" He spelled the name for her.

"No," she said slowly, "I don't remember that name."

"I think she knew Romer," he said. "From what I can tell, Cara met him in Chicago and she was seen with him while she was in Millport. She probably knew him for the past two or three years."

Her eyes appeared to search Pete's face. "Do you suspect this Mr. Romer of having something to do with Cara's death?"

Pete hesitated for a moment, not wanting to get her hopes up. "I don't know at this point," he lied.

"I'm sorry, I don't remember Cara mentioning him," she said.

Pete decided to press her on something else that had been on his mind since their first meeting. "You told me when we met the first time that you believe you know who fathered Cara's child. I'd like you to tell me who it was."

She looked sorrowful and tears welled up in her eyes. "I don't want to say, Pete. It wouldn't do any good."

"Let me be the judge of that."

He waited while she wiped away her tears. Then he heard the sound of a vehicle that was too close to be on the street. It skidded to a stop in the gravel driveway. Seconds later, the front door flew open and a man who had to be Hank Janicek stepped in. He stood there with a slight stoop to his shoulders and a very angry look on his pinched face. He glared at Pete and then at Marian and then at Pete again. "I heard you was here again." His voice sounded like a sack of gravel being ground together.

Pete rose and stuck out a hand. "Hank, I'm Pete Thorsen."

Hank ignored his hand. "What are you doing in my home, mister?"

Marian hurried to her feet. "Hank, Pete brought some papers for me to sign. He's a lawyer. He's trying to help us find out what happened to Cara." Her voice broke a couple of times in her eagerness to explain.

"I heard he was here before but didn't say nothin'. Then someone saw his vehicle out front again and called me." He turned to Pete. "You get out of my house right now. I don't want you here."

"Look," Pete said, "if you'll give me a minute, I'll explain everything."

"I don't want your friggin' explanation! Get out of my house! Now!"

"Okay," Pete said. He picked up his briefcase and began to move toward the door. "But if it was my daughter who died, I'd want to listen."

"You lousy bastard!" he screamed. "It's none of your business!" He lunged forward and threw a roundhouse right that just missed as Pete whirled out of the way. Hank tripped over the coffee table and fell to the floor, cursing loudly. He kicked at the table, sending a stack of magazines scattering around the room. Pete readied himself for another bull rush.

"Don't!" Marian screamed. "He's trying to help us!" She stood over him, fists clinched, her face flushed and thrust forward.

Hank was on his hands and knees, eyeing Marian warily. He seemed stunned by Marian's outburst. "We don't need his help." His gravelly voice was softer and halting.

"You're always so mad about everything!" she screamed, jabbing a finger in his direction. "It's just like with Cara!"

Pete stood back and let the scene play out, realizing he'd just stepped into a very ugly family donnybrook.

Hank finished getting to his feet and picked up his striped cap with a puffed top, the kind that was popular before men turned to baseball-style headgear. He looked at Marian, appearing uncertain of how to regain control of the situation. Then he turned to Pete. "You get out of here!" he said, waving his cap. "This don't concern you!"

"He's our lawyer!" Marian said, her voice rising again.

"Marian," Hank said in a softer voice again, "me and you can talk this out later, but I want him gone." He turned to Pete. "You get out now, mister, or I'll put a load of buckshot in your ass!"

Pete snapped. "Let me explain a few things to you, Hank. I came here both times at you wife's request. You've asked me to leave. That's fine. That's what I'm going to do. But if you ever come at me again, or if you ever threaten me again, I'm going to have you locked up on assault and battery charges."

Hank glared at him, looking sullen. "You can't do nothin' to me. I'm just protecting my home."

"Bullshit," Pete said. "Why don't you try it again and test me. You're already guilty of assault. You want to go for more?"

Hank's jaw twitched as he continued to glare at Pete.

"You two need to talk things over," Pete said. "And I mean *talk*." He looked squarely at Hank. "I better not hear anything else, either. And just so you know, Marian is my client and I intend to continue to represent her as long as she wants me to."

Pete turned to leave and then stopped and said to Hank, "I'd like to talk to you, too, if you'll just start acting civilized," he said. "I think there's a better than even chance that your daughter was murdered. All I'm doing is trying to get to the bottom of it."

Hank just looked at Pete with hate in his eyes.

As Pete walked out the Janicek driveway, he wondered who had tipped off Hank he was there. Big Red was the logical explanation. If he'd been the one, though, his personality was such that he would have been right behind Hank when he burst in to confront Pete. But Big Red was nowhere in sight.

FIFTEEN

The Manitou is on M-22 where the two-lane road snakes north through dense woods on the edge of Sleeping Bear National Lakeshore. Pete had agreed to meet Lynn Hawke there because it was on her route back from Traverse City where she'd had a meeting with a potential new client that afternoon. When he suggested it, he discovered that it was also her favorite restaurant after Rona's. That gave them another thing in common.

The familiar black bear glowered at them from his high perch as they passed by on their way to the back dining room. Pete sometimes had dinner with Harry in the Deep in the Woods section off to the right, with its bar and knotty-pine walls and model pontoon plane suspended from the ceiling, but on this particular night he preferred a quieter atmosphere.

"How did your meeting go?" he asked as they gave their menus a preliminary scan.

"New client pitch," she said, wrinkling her nose. "Do you get tired of those, too?"

"God, yes."

"That's what Rona said, that you're getting tired of the practice."

Pete looked up at her with a playful smile tugging at the corners of his mouth. "It's nice of you women to sit around and gossip about me."

"Not much sitting around or gossiping. Rona and I were together for two hours and the conversation involving you lasted all of 30 seconds."

"I guess that's not too bad," Pete said, feigning hurt. "Maybe I can work my way up to two or three minutes next time. I'll take what I can get, though. As Oscar Wilde once said, 'The only thing worse than being talked about is not being talked about.'"

"Oooh, literate too."

He grinned. "No, I just have a couple of favorite lines I trot out when someone is good enough to set me up."

He ordered the best bottle of pinot noir on the wine list. They agreed not to worry about matching wine and food. They'd deal with that later.

An instrumental was playing softly on the sound system. Lynn raised a finger for quiet while she listened for a few moments. "Do you know what this is?"

"Sure," he said. "It's a version of the old Drifters song."

She gave him a flirtatious look over her wine glass. "Now I know why you like this place. It plays your kind of music."

He just smiled.

"What's with you and all those oldies anyway," she persisted. "I bet there's a story there."

"A short story," he said. "A guy I was friendly with in the army had his heart set on becoming a DJ when he got out. He played that stuff over and over. I got to like it."

She cradled her wine glass with both hands. "What else did you do in the army?"

"At the beginning or end?"

"Both."

"Almost all of my friends went into airborne after basic training," he said. "I volunteered, too. That was before I learned you have to jump out of airplanes." That was his stock answer. He refused to be serious about it, preferring to joke instead, and never told anyone except his late-wife, Doris, about the gut-wrenching fear he'd felt as he stood on the training tower platform and waited his turn to jump. It was a fear that didn't go away. Finally he requested a transfer out of jump school.

Lynn laughed at his self-deprecating humor. "So what did you wind up doing?"

"Drove a Jeep. Through circumstances I won't bore you with, I drove a major around. He was in special investigations with the MPs."

"So you were a sleuth even back then."

Pete let the jab pass. He poured more wine and they compared notes on their children. Lynn had a son, Richard, who was in Hollywood trying to break into screenwriting and in the meantime was supporting himself by writing ad copy. Her daughter, Claire, just graduated from college and was living in Seattle while she decided what to do with her life. He told her about Julie and how her biological father had regained custody of her after Doris died.

"How does Julie feel about that?"

Pete laughed. "She's stoic about it, but calls me Dad and him Wayne, if that tells you anything."

"It tells me a lot. Do you see her during the school year?"

"Quite a bit, actually. I'm the trustee of the trust Doris and I set up for her. There's really not much in the trust, but I indulge the fiction and quietly pay most of her expenses out of my own pocket. It lets us keep in touch on a regular basis. Wayne thinks there are millions in the trust and he's more than happy to have her in private school as long as its being paid for by those funds."

The waiter brought their food. Lynn had the lamb chops and he'd ordered the Trawler, a seafood combination. She cut into a lamb chop, took another sip of wine, and murmured contentedly.

"Have you worked it out so Julie can come to the lake?"

"We're doing battle," he said, sighing.

Lynn eyed his plate. "Can I taste some of your Trawler?"

He slid his plate over and she took a forkful of whitefish. "Mmm, that's delicious." She helped herself to more, this time one of the scallops.

He reclaimed his plate and asked, "You said Claire is trying to find herself. What does she do?"

"Gets depressed, mainly." She said it in a flip tone, but it wasn't hard to detect the motherly concern.

"Is it serious?"

"I hope not, but how do you know for sure with those things?"

Yeah, he thought, how do you know. "Do you get out to see her very often?"

She adjusted the scrunchy holding back her hair. "When she'll let me. She blames me for messing up her life. I wasn't a stay-at-home mom."

"That's tough. All you can do is keep trying and be there when she lets you."

Lynn just nodded.

"I'm going to hold you to your promise to get together for some practice with our bows," he said, trying to lighten her mood.

"Any time. I haven't been out in a month."

"You've really got things covered," Pete said, giving her a sly look. "If your clients pay on time, you can paint a nice little daisy for them or something. If they don't, you can go after them with your bow and arrow."

She gave him a long, searching look. "Are you one of those men who's threatened by a woman who does something that's a little different?"

Pete laughed. "If I was, I got over it when I married Doris. She was a black belt in Tae Kwon Do."

"Did she teach you?"

"Some. I got all the way up to green belt."

"Is that good?"

"Not exactly. It's basically one step up from defenseless."

"So what do you do when clients get confrontational with you?"

"Run, mostly."

And bluff his way through. In the past week, he'd had more ugly confrontations than in the past 20 years combined. Standing in the Car Ferry nose-to-nose with Kurt Romer that night, he wondered how he'd react if Romer took a swing at him. They were about the same size, but that's where it ended. Romer didn't have the softness that comes from sitting behind a desk all day. He'd been able to handle himself back in the day, but that was a long time ago. It was one thing to fend off bitter old Hank Janicek, but guys like Romer or Big Red were something altogether different.

Pete poured the remaining wine. Since they'd both driven, he knew that ordering another bottle was out of the question, so he asked the waiter to bring one glass of the best by-the-glass red on the card and split it two ways.

"I've had an interesting few days," he said, changing subject. "I met with the M.E., Cara Lane's father went after me when he showed up unexpectedly while I was meeting with his wife, and a guy on one of the fishing boats threatened to kick my ass when I asked him about Cara."

She looked at him without smiling and said, "So what did you learn?"

"Not much that was new, but my meeting with the M.E. did solidify my view about what could have happened to Cara."

"You've thought she was killed all along. Did that change?" Her manner was still dead serious.

"No proof," he said, "but I did get a better handle on how it might have been done if she were killed. Remember I said that she acted strange that night and I couldn't figure out how she could see the raft to swim out there and the wine bottle looked like a plant?"

"Yes."

"Well the thing that bothered me most was how the killer — assuming she was killed — got her out to deep water to let her drown. Cara Lane was a tall woman and in good shape and the M.E. said that the blow to her head was unlikely to have knocked her out long enough. He also said there was no evidence she was disabled with a tazer gun. That leaves the possibility that the killer slipped her something. It was very useful to talk it through with him."

"How about those two guys who tested your green belt skills?"

He laughed. "Cara's father was no problem. He's just a bitter old fool who wants all of the fuss about his daughter to go away. The guy from the fishing boat is a different story."

"Does this guy have a name?"

Pete thought about it for a while, then said, "His name is Kurt Romer, but please keep it quiet. He has a history of violence against women and a string of arrests on meth charges. I'm convinced he knew Cara from Chicago and he was seen with her up here. I haven't figured out his motive yet, but it could have something to do with his meth operations."

Lynn studied him for a long time and then said, still without the hint of a smile, "Don't you think it's time you took all of this to the sheriff and let him handle things?"

"I can't," he said softly.

"Why not?"

"Partly it's self-defense. I'm still the target of that zealot, Deputy Richter, for some reason. Plus everything I have is circumstantial. I believe the law enforcement people are looking in the wrong direction, too. They know about Romer, but don't seem to be focusing on him like they should."

"So Pete Thorsen has to ride to the rescue."

Her comment was larded up with sarcasm. He thought back to Sunday at his cottage and remembered that she hadn't joined in when Harry and Rona ribbed him about his investigation. "You think I'm nuts, don't you?" he said slowly.

"No, I don't think you're nuts. But I am concerned that you're going to get yourself into a situation you can't handle if you're right about how she died."

"That's not going to happen," he said, "but I've got to play it out a little longer for reasons I mentioned." He thought about it for a while. "There are just so many ends to this thing. What I need is someone to bounce things off of, to test my theories. Like I did with the M.E. that day."

"You've got Harry."

"I know and he's a smart guy. But I was thinking of someone with expertise that's closer to what I need. A former forensic accountant, for example." He smiled weakly.

Her face lost its color and her mouth became a tight line. "No thanks, Pete. I don't want to get involved."

He continued to look at her. "Don't worry, I'll do all the leg work, all of the heavy lifting. I just need someone who has a feeling for these things. Someone I can try things out on."

"I said no."

Her voice was sharp and had the ring of finality. She looked at her watch and suddenly seemed fidgety. Oh great, he thought, I've really blown this one. He'd planned to invite her back to his place to listen to oldies, but now that seemed dead.

"I'm tired," she said, patting his hand. "Shall we call it a night?"

• • •

When Pete got home, he rummaged through his CD collection and put on a Fats Domino disc, poured himself a glass of wine, and settled in on his porch to listen. He thought about Lynn and wondered what he'd said to set her off like that. He replayed the evening in his mind as Fats worked his way through "Blueberry Hill" and "I'm Walkin."

Through the open French doors, he studied the photographs on the fireplace mantle and remembered what his life was like when he first met Doris. As Fats moved into "It's You I Love" he thought about the first time they'd gone trout fishing shortly after they met. Her casts were so effortless, dropping flies under branches and other hard to reach places. Only later did he learn that she'd been trout fishing with her father since she was seven years old. It was the same with Tae Kwon Do. She moved with speed and grace and then, *pow!* One time after a workout, when they were making love, they tried to emulate the positions of the martial arts until they fell into a heap on the bed, laughing. It was all so natural, so honest.

After they married, they took Julie canoeing and attended her soccer games and did a dozen other things together. Julie was theirs. It was just a accident of nature that she was the biological offspring of a drunk and n'er-do-well. The time spent with Julie also provided an excuse for him to decline the invitations to charity and other events that came with being managing partner of one of Chicago's oldest law firms. He hated those things; they were filled with self-important people who flaunted their wealth and pretended to be philanthropic, but were really in it for their own egos.

Work continued to be his balm even then. He worked brutal hours at Sears & Whitney and rapidly climbed the ladder to management. He'd had opportunities to move to larger firms for more money over the years, but always stayed put. Sears & Whitney gave his life purpose and meaning, and made him forget his childhood and the memories of all the indignities that came with being at the bottom of the barrel.

The life he had built for himself came crashing down when Doris died and he lost custody of Julie. But that wasn't the end of it. That came when he was out to dinner with a client one night and got a call from his old mentor, Sam Lawrence. It wasn't like Sam to call him in the evening much less when he was entertaining a client. After he disengaged from the client, he hurried back to the office and found Sam hunched over a stack of documents, clad in his customary three-piece navy suit with a gold watch fob stretched across his expansive girth. They shared some of Sam's vintage port and traded small talk. Throughout the conversation, Pete kept glancing at the Colt Frontier Six-Shooter on Sam's desk and thought he smelled cordite. As an Old West aficionado, Sam had a stock of weapons that, if they could still safely be fired, he liked to take to a nearby range on occasion. That had to be it, Pete assumed. He delicately steered the conversation around to what was really on Sam's mind. Sam confided that Larry Serini, a young partner in the firm who had taken over Sam's major client when he was forced into retirement, was screwing up a deal for the client. He asked Pete to use his authority as managing partner to add Sam to the team to straighten it out. When Pete balked, Sam said that the firm really had no choice. He'd just shot Serini.

Pete was stunned and as soon as word spread through the firm, everything was in an uproar. He personally took over and finished the deal, but in the end was unable to salvage the client relationship. Sam suffered a stroke while in jail awaiting trial and died. For Pete, it was the final crushing blow. The furor gradually subsided and he clawed his way back, but Marty Kral and his allies within the firm used the Sam Lawrence affair against him at every turn. Larry Serini's office had been re-carpeted and re-painted, and even though it was one of the more desirable offices in the firm, it remained unoccupied. Sam's corner office remained empty as well. The two offices stood there as permanent reminders of the horror that had taken place at the firm that night.

He got up and stalked around the porch. Lights were blinking off around the lake, but he wasn't tired. He changed into his running clothes and headed right on M-22. It was unfamiliar territory; usually he ran the other way and picked up Shore Road and went toward the public beach. It felt good to just go. He ran faster than he normally did and tried not to think. He was all alone, running free, the trees hulking dark shapes along the sides of the road. He ran faster.

After a mile, he turned around and headed back. He passed his driveway and kept going, then veered left on Shore Road. He was sweating now even though the night was cool. His footsteps rang in his ears. Everything else was quiet. When he did encounter a car, he got irritated. Shore Road was his.

He came to the public beach and stopped, breathing heavily. It was two weeks ago that Cara Lane had died. It was dark that night, but now the moon bathed the lake in a silvery glow. He sat on a bench and looked out over the water. If Cara Lane had died on a night like this, it would all make sense. But it wasn't a night like this. And who did she meet that night after she left him? There was no evidence that it was someone from her distant past, the father of her child or someone from that tragic incident in Oregon. It had to be Romer, he thought. Nothing else made sense.

Lynn took over his thoughts again. He'd just met her, but when he reached over and took her hand at the Manitou, his skin tingled and he felt an electricity he hadn't felt since Doris died. He was pretty sure that she liked him, too. Then she'd turned on him with stunning suddenness.

He tried to decide what to do next in the Cara Lane affair and it looked like he'd have to continue to do it alone. He'd baited Kurt Romer as much as he could. He thought of Deputy Richter and how he always seemed to be a step ahead of him: Marian Janicek, Marcus Vrba, Kurt Romer. Richter had beaten him to the punch each time, and he had the resources of law enforcement to draw upon. He wondered again what Richter knew that he didn't know. And he wondered why he wasn't focusing more on who Cara had met that night after dinner and less on him. He thought about Marian Janicek, too, and the grief she so obviously felt over the death of her daughter.

The only loose end he could think of was Big Red. He thought about how the guy had zeroed in on him at the Whitetail and about the call tipping off Hank Janicek that he was at the Janicek house a second time. Was Big Red just being territorial and protective of the Janiceks as Harry had said? He needed to find out more about him. Maybe he should make a trip to Hawkins and ask around. What could it hurt?

Suddenly he felt like running again. He started to trot back toward his cottage, but being on his feet reenergized him. He quickened his pace and tried to cleanse his mind of all thoughts. It was just him and Shore Road again. He lengthened his stride and kept running. The night air felt cool on his face.

SIXTEEN

He got back to his cottage about one and didn't have much to show for the morning he'd spent checking out Big Red. Everyone in the area seemed to know him. His name was Les Murton and he worked at a lumber store that catered to local builders. He had a reputation as a bit of a bully, and was stridently pro-gun with Second Amendment stickers all over the bumpers on his truck. That was pretty much it. Most people didn't want to talk about him beyond those basic facts. That included the bartender at the Whitetail.

The light on his phone was blinking; he checked his messages. Julie had called. The other calls were from Angie and his firm's administrative partner, Steve Johnson. They asked that he call back as soon as possible. He checked his watch. It was one o'clock, Michigan time. He dialed Julie's number, keeping his priorities straight.

"Dad, what's with you? I called your cell twice and got no answer and then called the cottage. Don't you *ever* answer your phone?"

"Sorry, Sweetie. I had to go to Cadillac and forgot to charge my cell phone last night."

"Well jeez . . ."

"Sorry."

"Have you worked things out with Wayne yet?"

Pete explained that he'd had a hard time reaching him and that he hoped to have a resolution next week. He decided not to tell her about the unpleasant call he'd had from Sable on Saturday.

"Well I don't care what he says! I'm coming!"

That ended what to his recollection was their shortest telephone conversation ever. He sighed and dialed Kyle Cummings' number. Kyle was the partner in his law firm who'd been dealing with Wayne Sable's lawyer. He got his voicemail, and asked him to call back on Monday.

He wondered what Angie and Steve wanted to talk to him about on the weekend. He looked at his watch again and dialed Angie's number.

"Have you talked to anyone?" she asked after picking up on the first ring.

"I talk to people all the time."

"No, wise guy," she said, "I mean at the firm. Haven't you checked your email?"

Apparently it was the day to be lectured about his communications skills. "Just a minute," he said. He walked over to his laptop and logged on. Tucked among the usual mish-mash of firm communications and outside world spam was an email sent late on Friday by three partners calling a special meeting of the firm's equity partners for Monday at noon.

"What's this all about?"

"Read the attachment. Marty Kral claims he received an anonymous call on Friday saying that you're a suspect in a murder case. According to him, the caller claimed to be a firm client."

Pete opened the attachment and scanned the memorandum while he listened. It was essentially as Angie had described. He read the email again. It stated that the partners who'd called the meeting intended to present a motion calling for Pete to step aside as the firm's managing partner.

"This is bullshit!" Pete exploded. "Kral is behind this."

"Probably. He was clever enough not to include his name on the call for a meeting. Steve and I caught him in the office this morning. He was almost in tears, saying how bad he feels for you, but that the interests of the firm have to come first and blah, blah, blah."

"I thought he was at his place in Door County."

"He came back for a few days. Says he had some client emergency."

"And he just happened to get this anonymous call while he was here on the emergency, right? How do you think he really found out about Cara Lane?"

"No clue," Angie said. "I didn't even tell Steve about our conversation until he saw the memorandum. Marty said the caller told him you'd already been questioned by the sheriff twice. He had a copy of the *Sentinel* article — the one attached to the memorandum — but that doesn't mention your name."

"If there really was a caller, his Caller ID should have told him who it was."

"We asked Marty about that. He said it just showed 'unknown caller.'"

Pete thought about it for a moment. "They have to give 10 days notice, don't they?"

"They're relying on the emergency exception to the 10-day rule. They say that if word gets out the firm's managing partner is a suspect in a murder case before we take protective action, it could have a potentially disastrous effect on our business. They might have a case on the notice issue."

"What's the reaction of the other partners?"

"It's the weekend, but most of the ones I talked to on the phone seem a little shell-shocked. However, they're willing to listen to your side of things. I heard Marty's allies have been raising the Sam Lawrence thing again."

"That sonofabitch. Nothing is below him. For him to . . ."

"The fact you're away from the office for the month of August is fueling the rumor mill, too," Angie interjected.

He gritted his teeth. "Look, I'm in touch on a regular basis and I've already been back to Chicago once. I also spend half my time up here working on a deal for Colcorp. I thought even Pete Thorsen was entitled to a few days off now and then."

"I know."

"This is all being orchestrated by Kral to get me out of the way so he can pursue his own selfish agenda for the firm. The guy would sell everyone down the river in a nanosecond if he thought it would put an extra dime in his pocket. Can't he wait until October? We've already agreed to have a partners meeting to discuss the issues he's always harping on."

"He says this is unrelated and changes everything. I think we're boxed in, Pete. Steve and I have already started to work the partners. You need to get down here as soon as possible and start doing the same."

"I intend to. Could you ask Steve to get someone we can trust to check the phone records and see if we can identify the call Kral claims he received?"

"Okay."

"I've been going over a list of the equity partners while we've been talking and there's no way I won't have a majority with me on this. I intend to stick this thing right up his ass on Monday and send him a message."

"We don't need to stick anything up anyone's ass or send anyone a message. All we need to do is defuse the situation until things in Millport clear up."

"No," Pete said, "I want to send him a message. For him to drag Sam Lawrence's name into this is the final straw. And that memorandum . . ."

"Okay," Angie said. She sounded weary. "We can talk about it when you get here."

"Thanks, Angie, your husband is one lucky man."

"Oh, yeah, right," she said in a resigned tone.

When they were off the phone and he'd settled down, Pete began to think about who might have tipped off Kral that he'd been questioned in connection with Cara Lane's death. He could think of only a couple of possibilities. Kral had been at the lake. Maybe he'd become friendly with someone he'd met and that person might have passed on the information about Pete. But who? Only a few people knew that he'd been questioned by Richter. It just didn't compute.

The other possibility was Romer. He'd lived in Chicago for a year. As much of a ladies man as he was, maybe he'd met somebody — a secretary or paralegal, or even a female associate — who had told him of the internal politics at Sears & Whitney. Maybe he knew that Pete and Marty Kral were rivals at the firm. Clearly he knew that Pete had been questioned by Richter, and it would not have taken much to plant the seed. His money was on Romer. It was the only thing that made sense.

Whatever the source, Marty Kral was trying to seize the opportunity to marginalize him at his own firm. To get rid of him as managing partner. He thought about the aggravations of the job, all the times he'd told himself he was going to quit. The fact was, though, that he liked being the head of Sears & Whitney. If he were ever going to leave his position, it wasn't going to be because that prick Kral had forced him out.

• • •

Taking his place at the head of the conference table had become second nature to Pete. Like shaving in the morning or shutting down his computer when he left the office at night. Today was different. Steve Johnson served as chair because of the subject of the meeting. Pete sat on the long side of the table, near but not at the head. It felt strange. He recalled a conversation he'd once had with Sam Lawrence. Sam told him when the day came that someone else occupied his place at the head of the table, he'd never feel quite the same. Pete expected his new seat to be temporary, but for the first time he truly understood what Sam had meant.

As usual, Marty Kral sat at the far end of the table surrounded by his allies. There was a certain symbolism to that which escaped no one. Kral had run against Pete in the firm's most recent managing partner election and lost by a comfortable margin, but that hadn't stopped him from acting like a firm leader who was every bit Pete's equal.

Several of Kral's supporters addressed the issue of the day in solemn tones, as though gathered reverentially at Pete's bedside. Two of them told of receiving calls from clients over the weekend, which neither named, asking about rumors that the firm's managing partner was the subject of a criminal investigation. One said his client had expressed particular concern in light of the Sam Lawrence episode two years earlier.

Pete seethed but kept a grip on himself.

Kral was the last of his group to speak. He shuffled his papers in a showy way, as though what he was about to say pained him so deeply it was difficult to even know where to begin. Pete looked around the table. Many partners just stared straight ahead. How different from the past when they would look into his eyes and somehow know he was going to lead them through the tough challenge of the moment.

"This is very difficult for me," Kral began. "Pete brought me into the firm a little over six years ago, and while we haven't always seen things the same way, no one has admired his leadership more. My practice has flourished here. Hopefully I've served the firm well, too. I was surprised to see from the June management reports that I had the highest fee collections of any partner for the first six months of the year. But this isn't about Pete or me or any individual partner. It's about the firm and what we have to do to protect the interests of all the partners."

Pete stared at Kral, feeling only contempt and seeing callousness and greed and everything he despised. Spoiled rich kid whose only goal in life was to become richer. He wore it as a badge of honor, too.

If it meant shoving out partners who'd devoted their entire lives to the firm or recklessly cutting staff, well that was just the reality of running a law firm in the 21st century. Pete blamed himself. In his zeal to build Sears & Whitney to compete with the larger law firms, he'd added partners from competitors and probably paid too much attention to economics and not enough to character.

Kral summarized what was in the *Sentinel* story and then added that the anonymous caller had told him Pete and the dead woman had had a fight in the restaurant and that Pete had no alibi for the night she died. Pete was puzzled again over Kral's knowledge of facts that hadn't been reported in the press.

"I believe it's the sense of the partners," Kral continued, "that Pete should step aside until this cloud over his head disappears, as I'm sure it will. I emphasize this would be just a temporary measure; I'm not proposing that he be permanently removed as managing partner."

"So move," one of the partners who'd called the meeting said. "Second," chirped another.

Steve Johnson looked around the table. "Any discussion?"

Several partners delicately asked whether there might be a better way to handle the situation. One suggested that Pete agree to keep the partners closely advised on the progress of the investigation. Another said they might wish to get the firm's public relations agency to spin matters to the media.

"Marty," Angie said, "I have a question. Actually two questions. Who do you think the caller might have been and why did he call you rather than Steve, for example?"

Kral cleared his throat. "As I told you in my office, I don't know who the caller was. He said he was a client and clearly was very concerned. I don't know why he called me, either. What I do know is that I had an obligation to take the information seriously. No, let me correct that. *We* have an obligation to take it seriously. The firm's reputation is at stake."

"I'm sure we do need to take it seriously," Angie said. "We also need to act responsibly and remember we're partners. And I must say, except for a couple of vague comments at the beginning of this meeting, no one I've spoken to has been contacted by anyone about this matter, client or otherwise."

Kral's tanned face turned a shade darker. "What are you saying, Angie? That I made this up? Why would I do that?"

"I'm not accusing you of anything. I'm just saying that the action you're proposing seems awfully draconian in the circumstances. At very best, it's premature."

"It's not just me," Kral protested. "I've talked to a majority of the partners. They agree with me even if they prefer not to stand up and say so at this meeting."

"Maybe," Angie said, "but that's not what I've been hearing."

The room went silent. Kral glared at Angie and two of his henchmen exchanged glances.

"Any other comments?" Steve Johnson asked. "Pete, you're the one who knows the most about what's going on. Would you like to say something?"

"Yes," Pete said, "I would."

He rose to his feet and gazed around the table. "I've practiced law with many of you since the day I joined Sears & Whitney 20 years ago. Some of you were already here when I arrived. Others, like Marty," he said, gesturing in his direction, "joined us more recently. I try not to make a distinction. If you're my partner, you're my partner."

He paused and looked around the room. "That's something I learned from Henry Thornburgh and Mary Crimmons and, yes, Sam Lawrence," he said. "They taught those of us who were privileged to practice with them a lot about what makes a law firm truly great. What creates a bond among partners that holds the place together when things get tough. Topping the list is a willingness to give each other the benefit of the doubt. That's always been our hallmark."

Pete walked slowly around the room as he spoke, looking at each partner. He stopped when he passed behind Kral. "Until now, anyway. This is the first time in the history of this firm that a partner has been called to the dock based on rumor and innuendo and shadowy alleged phone calls from undisclosed sources. I know for a fact I'm not the only one who's concerned about what's taking place here today."

Kral craned his neck around and said, "Pete, are you denying you're a suspect in that woman's death?"

"Yes, I'm absolutely denying it. First of all, the authorities haven't even concluded that Cara Lane was murdered. Second, I did go down to the sheriff's office to volunteer a statement and they asked me questions like any responsible law enforcement officials would do. That doesn't mean I'm a suspect. I just happened to have had dinner with the woman the night before she died." He continued to walk around the table.

"Sorry to interrupt again," Kral said. "Weren't you questioned a second time?"

"Yes I was. I was asked to come in and clarify some things, and during that session I was specifically told I wasn't a suspect. If anyone doesn't believe that, I'll call the sheriff right now and put him on the speaker so you can hear it directly from him."

"He not going to say anything with a bunch of lawyers listening," a partner sitting near Kral grumbled.

Pete ignored him. "Anyone want me to call?"

There was silence in the room.

Pete resumed walking and when he reached the head of the table, his rightful place, his eyes locked on Kral. "I have a question for the group at the other end of this table: why didn't one of you call me and get my side of things before you convened this kangaroo court? Unfortunately, I believe most of us know the answer."

The room was so quiet the blink of an eye would have sounded like a thunderclap.

"And for the information of those who brought this motion," Pete continued, "there is no procedure in our partnership agreement for requiring a managing partner to step aside, temporarily or otherwise. There is a removal procedure. If you truly believe I've committed some heinous act, that's the route you'll have to follow because I have no intention of stepping aside voluntarily. Just make sure you give the required notice next time."

"Now just a minute," Kral said, scowling. "We gave more notice than actually required in an emergency situation. We could have demanded a meeting on Saturday, but waited until today."

"There is no emergency, Marty, and everyone in this room knows it. And I wasn't going to say anything, but I was thinking about your claim that you're the firm's biggest revenue producer. If you'll look at who brought various clients into the firm, not just who sends out the bills, I think you'll find that I accounted for twice as much revenue as you. We just have different philosophies. I believe in pushing billing and other responsibilities down to younger partners and you apparently don't. That's something else I learned from Henry Thornburgh and the other firm leaders I mentioned earlier." He refrained from pointing out that half of Kral's collections came from his daddy's companies and said, "I have nothing else, Steve."

A couple of partners at the far end of the table huddled. Then the one who'd made the motion said, "Steve, could we have a short recess?" Johnson signaled his approval and Kral and a half-dozen partners left the room. The group, minus Kral, returned 10 minutes later. The partner who'd assumed the role of spokesman said, "Mr. Chairman, in the interest of avoiding divisiveness, we're withdrawing our motion, but we reserve the right to bring it again at a later date. We want everyone to understand that we view this as an extremely serious matter and further action may well be required."

"Any objections?" Steve Johnson asked.

There were none.

SEVENTEEN

Pete sat with his feet propped up on his desk. Angie and Steve sprawled on a couch across the room. They looked like they'd been the ones on trial.

"Well?" Pete said.

Angie rolled her eyes. "Thanks for taking our advice and just quietly defusing this thing."

Pete looked surprised. "I just laid out the facts."

"You certainly did." Steve said. "I haven't heard that 'I am Sears & Whitney' speech of yours in a long time."

"That and his 'Everyman' speech," Angie said. She adjusted her imaginary tie and pretended to look around at the assembled group. Then she said in an artificially low voice, "Fellow partners, at least once in every man's life he will experience a situation in which a woman with whom he's just had dinner shows up dead in mysterious circumstances. A man is measured by how he comports himself when that time comes." Angie and Steve howled with laughter.

Pete suppressed a chuckle. "I never said that."

"You were in such a zone you don't even remember," Angie said, continuing to laugh. "I did think you were a little cruel when you stared at Marty for about 15 minutes straight and lectured him on firm tradition, the partnership agreement, and your respective economic contributions to the firm. He looked like you'd just hit him in the head with that Viking battle ax on your wall."

"Actually, I was aiming for a target lower on his body, but was afraid it might be so small that I'd miss."

"Oooh," Angie said, "that was cruel."

When the laughter subsided, Steve said, "Pete, you have a reservoir of goodwill among the partners, but don't misread things. The fact that Marty's personal agenda might have played a role in this doesn't mean the other partners aren't concerned about the allegations and about profitability and things like that."

"I know," Pete said, "and they've done damn well on my watch. I just don't want this to turn into a place where we cut the cleaning crew's wages so we can make 10 bucks more for ourselves."

Steve looked at him and said, "I think the key will be to present a first-rate strategic plan at our meeting in October."

"I agree," Pete said. "By the way, I know you didn't find anything the first time around, but could you have someone who won't blab about it take a closer look and see if he can trace the telephone call Marty claims he received? It's clear he used this incident to attack me. I just can't figure out how he knows the details."

Steve nodded his agreement.

Pete looked at his watch. "Well, I've got to run," he said. "John Fisher is waiting for me." He turned to Angie. "We're stopping at Cara Lane's old apartment to collect her things."

She looked at him and said sarcastically, "Back to the important stuff, huh?"

• • •

John Fisher attended law school at night and worked for Sears & Whitney as a paralegal during the days. Pete liked the idea of having the former Notre Dame linebacker with him when he paid his second visit to the genial Marcus Vrba. Maybe it would encourage him to cooperate.

"Who is this guy?" John asked as they walked toward 2243 Bissell.

"Cara Lane's former roommate. I checked him out. He's a labor history professor at Roosevelt University. Based on his writings, he's to the left of Trotsky."

"I had a professor like that."

Pete looked at him and frowned. "At Notre Dame?"

He nodded and rolled his eyes. "The only way you could get a good grade in his course was to parrot back everything he told you."

"You were a jock. You were protected, right?"

John laughed as they entered the vestibule. "Yeah, right. He hated jocks."

Pete punched the intercom button and after a minute or two heard the familiar nasal voice respond. "Professor, this is Pete Thorsen," he said. "You may recall that I stopped to see you a week ago. I'm the attorney and co-administrator for Cara Lane's estate. I'm here to collect her things. I'd like to come up, please."

Silence at the other end, then, "What did you say your name was?"

"Pete Thorsen."

More silence. "I'm sorry, I don't know you," the voice said. "I'm on the phone and don't have time to talk." The intercom went dead.

Pete punched the intercom button twice but there was no response. "What's the guy's phone number?" he asked John Fisher, snapping his fingers impatiently.

Pete waited 10 minutes and then dialed Vrba's number. When he answered Pete said, "Professor, before you hang up you should know that I'm standing down here in the lobby with a court order that directs you to turn over all of Cara's possessions to me. Now you can do the smart thing and let me come up or you can deal with the police when they knock on your door in half an hour. If you decide to wait for the police, I'd advise you to spend the time looking for a lawyer to defend yourself on contempt of court charges." He grinned at John. In Cook County, he knew it could take weeks to enforce an order like the one in his hand, but he was counting on Vrba not knowing that.

There was a long silence at the other end of the line. "Well, what's it going to be?" Pete asked.

After more silence, Vrba said in his whiney voice, "I'm going to let you up, mister, but if you don't have what you say you do, I'm going to be the one calling the police."

John Fisher choked back his laughter as they climbed the stairs. "This guy is going to go ballistic when he finds you don't have a court order."

"What do you mean?" Pete said "What do you think this is?" He waved the Letters of Appointment at him. "Don't they teach you anything in law school? Plus I've got you."

Marcus Vrba was waiting for them outside his apartment with his arms folded across his chest. He looked like an angry young man who no longer was young. His stringy gray hair was pulled back in a ponytail and his high cheekbones accented small dark eyes and a beak-like nose. Pete reckoned that he was in his 50s and looked fit for his age. Probably wanted to be in shape for when the revolution starts.

Pete offered his hand but Vrba drew back as though afraid of contracting some contagious disease. Pete handed the Letters of Appointment to him and he reluctantly took them and studied them carefully.

"Where does it say I have to turn over Cara's things to you?" he asked.

"It's in the statute. It's inherent in my appointment as co-administrator of Cara's estate." He pointed to the document. "As you can see, Cara's mother is the other co-administrator. Her signature gives me the power to act alone."

"This isn't a court order." He handed the Letters of Appointment back to Pete and folded his arms again.

"Marcus, I'm getting tired of this. See that signature?" he said, holding up the document and pointing to it. "That's Judge Kosinski's signature. He's a judge of the Cook County Probate Court. If I have to call him I will. I brought along his cell phone number just in case." Pete looked at his watch. "On a nice August afternoon like this, he's probably on the golf course. I'm sure he'll be real happy to hear from us and have you question whether what he signed is a court order."

Vrba alternated between glaring at Pete and looking at the document in his hand.

Pete pulled out his cell phone.

Vrba continued to stand there looking defiant. Pete began to punch in his direct dial number at the firm, hoping that Vrba wouldn't call his bluff.

"Well I want a receipt for everything you take," Vrba said, jabbing a finger at Pete and looking like an angry bird of prey.

Pete snapped his cell phone closed and ignored the demand. "Show us her room so we can get started."

They followed Vrba into the apartment and he pointed toward one of the bedrooms. They looked around briefly and then began to stuff Cara's possessions into heavy plastic bags. Periodically Vrba would appear in the doorway and throw books or other items on the bed. John Fisher looked like a man who just wanted to finish the job and get out of there, but Pete didn't want to let the opportunity go to waste. He walked into the living room where Vrba was pecking away on his laptop.

"How long did you know Cara?" he asked.

Vrba continued to work at his keyboard and ignored him.

"Excuse me," Pete said after a minute or two. "I said how long did you know Cara Lane?"

Vrba looked up and his scowl hardened. "You might have the right to collect Cara's things, but I don't have to talk to you."

"No you don't," Pete said, "but we're on the same side." He paused for a few moments and rephrased his question. "Do you know why Cara was in Millport?"

He thought he detected uneasiness in Vrba. He waited for a response, but there was none.

Pete returned to the bedroom and helped John. Fifteen minutes later he walked into the living room again. Vrba still had his laptop on his knees, but was staring off into space.

"You never did answer my question about why Cara was in Millport."

Vrba did everything but jump at Pete's face. "I don't know why she was in Millport!" he screamed. "Now finish your work and get out of here!"

Pete let Vrba settle down, then shifted gears. "When I stopped to see you before, you said that the police had already contacted you. Was the man's name Deputy Richter?"

Vrba shrugged sullenly. "I don't waste my time remembering people like that."

Pete waited for a few minutes and then said, "Most of the people up in Michigan think Cara's death was a swimming accident, but I'm not so sure. What do you think?"

He laughed, if a bitter cackle can be considered a laugh. "That woman could swim across Lake Michigan if she had to."

Ah, Pete thought, now we're getting somewhere. He snuck in another question. "Does Cara still have friends in northwest Michigan?"

"That's enough! No more questions!"

Somehow Pete had the same feeling as the first time he talked to Vrba. The genial Marcus Vrba knew more that he was willing to disclose.

EIGHTEEN

"**W**hat are these things on the ends?" Lynn asked.

Pete chuckled. "Ulf, the old guy who made the bow for me, had never been out of Norway but he had heard of Al Capone, so when he found out I was from Chicago, he added that little touch so I could protect myself in the urban jungle. Back in the Viking Age, many of the bows had fittings of some sort on the ends. They were sharpened so the bows could be used in close combat if necessary."

"This is yew, right?" she asked, testing the pull weight and running her fingers over the grain.

"Yes."

She raised the bow in perfect form and drilled an arrow in the middle of one of the army surplus targets he'd set up in back of his cottage. He watched as she prepared to launch another arrow, and thought of their conversation when he'd returned her calls after getting back to the lake. She'd apologized for her behavior that night at the Manitou, but didn't say what had set her off. He was more than a little curious, but said nothing.

For the next hour, they fired arrow after arrow into the dummies. He could see why she was an Olympic-caliber archer. She had perfect posture when she set up, pulling the string of her compound bow back to her right jaw and letting the arrow fly with deadly accuracy. She seemed to elevate his performance, too. He was not in her league, but his adrenaline kicked in and all but one of his arrows hit the dummies. Not the same tight pattern as Lynn's, but what the heck. He was just relieved he didn't embarrass himself.

They retired to his porch when they were finished. She declined his offer of a drink, saying she had to have dinner with a client that night. He was disappointed to hear that because he'd planned to ask her to dinner himself.

"I think I owe you a further explanation for the other night."

"No explanation necessary," he said, trying to be gracious but still very curious.

"No, I want you to know why I reacted the way I did."

He just looked at her. Something obviously had been eating away at her because she'd left two messages for him while he was in Chicago, asking that he call.

"Did Harry ever tell you why I got out of forensic accounting?"

"No," Pete said, "I just assumed you got tired of it and wanted a change."

She shook her head. "I loved what I did. Until the day someone tried to kill my partner and me."

Pete felt a jolt run through his body. "You're kidding," he said.

"Maybe I should start from the beginning. I left E & Y to start my own forensic accounting practice with my father. He used to be with the FBI in the financial crimes unit. Things went well and soon we were able to pick and choose among engagements we were willing to take on.

"We were working on this one job when we began to uncover some suspicious things. It appeared to us that a party the client dealt with was funneling money through them. We told our contact at the client and he said he'd take it up with his boss. We never heard back from him, and soon we uncovered more and were positive we had stumbled onto a major plot of some kind."

"Money laundering," Pete said.

"Yes. We tried to get in touch with our contact again, but still didn't hear from him. We left more messages, explaining our concern. Then one morning as I was getting ready to go to work, my father called. His voice was weak and wavering. He told me not to get in my car and then faded out. I panicked and called the police and then found out that his SUV had been bombed and he was badly injured."

Pete looked at her in amazement. "Was he okay?"

"Yes, eventually. He likely saved my life because a bomb had been planted in my car, too."

He continued to stare at her.

"We still aren't completely sure of what happened, but suspect our contact was in cahoots with the bad guys. Ownership probably didn't know, although we're not sure of that either."

Pete just shook his head.

"Later we heard there was a fire in the offices of the company we were auditing and all of the records were destroyed. When my father got out of the hospital, we talked about it and decided to fold our business."

"That's when you moved up here," Pete said.

"Yes." She paused for a few moments. "When you asked for my help that night, it all came rushing back. It was such a traumatic experience."

"I'm sorry for putting you in that position," he said.

"No, it was silly of me. I overreacted. All you did was ask me to be a sounding board for you."

They talked about it some more and then he changed the subject and asked whether there were any developments with her daughter. Melissa still hadn't returned her calls, she said. What little information she had she got through her son. She was worried. They talked about what she was painting and how she felt when a spot hadn't opened up for her on the Olympic team. They talked about touring the Leelanau wineries and asking Harry and Rona to join them. They talked about how they missed the Shakespeare Theater at Navy Pier in Chicago and how the local productions in Elberta and at Interlochen were at least something. She looked at him in amazement as he recited from memory the St. Crispin's Day speech from *Henry V.*

"Anything new with your investigation?" she asked, shifting the conversation back to the subject uppermost on his mind the past few weeks.

"Maybe we shouldn't get into that."

"No, I want to know."

He thought about telling her of his problems at his law firm, but thought better of it. He did tell her about his visit to Vrba's apartment to collect Cara's things and his reluctance to talk. "He knows something," he said, "I'm sure of it."

"What, do you know?"

"I think he knows why Cara was in Millport."

"If she came to see someone," Lynn said, "you think it's that man who works on the fishing boat, right?"

"Yes. As I told you the other night, I'm convinced he knew her from Chicago. I just can't figure out why she came up here to see him and what might have happened."

"You need to be careful," she said, placing her hand on his.

He waved off her concern. "I know," he said.

She looked at him like she didn't quite believe him.

• • •

Pete was checking his email the next morning when he heard the gravel crunch in his driveway. He looked up and saw two vehicles pull in. One was a sheriff's department SUV, the other an unmarked van. First Deputy Richter got out of the SUV followed by Joe Tessler.

What the hell could this be? he wondered.

"We have a warrant to search your vehicle, Mr. Thorsen." Richter waved a document in the air.

Pete looked down from his porch. "What do you mean you have a warrant to search my vehicle."

"See for yourself." He waved the document again.

Pete walked outside. He took the warrant and glared at Richter before looking at it. Richter had a "gotcha" look stamped all over his face.

The warrant had been signed by one of the county judges on Monday morning. Objects of the search included hair, fibers, personal articles and other trace evidence that Cara Lane had been in his vehicle, plus instruments that might have been used to cause the cut on her head.

"What's this about?" Pete asked, looking up and staring at Richter again.

"I think you know. The Cara Lane investigation."

"Well I don't consent to the search. You have no reason to search my vehicle. No probable cause." He reached in his pocket and clicked the automatic door locks on his Range Rover.

"The judge found that there was probable cause. Since we talked to you, eyewitnesses told us they saw the two of you walk down the street together and get in your vehicle. Their statements directly contradict what you told us."

"That's absolutely false," Pete said, resisting the impulse to use more colorful language.

"Please unlock your vehicle, Mr. Thorsen."

"No," Pete said, "I'm not unlocking it. I just told you, there's no probable cause for a search."

"We don't need you consent, you know. This warrant permits us to enter the vehicle through whatever means required in the circumstances. Are you refusing to unlock the doors?"

Pete weighed his options, none of which were good. It galled him to admit it, but Richter was right about what the warrant permitted them to do. Then, too, he knew he might be able to challenge any evidence they did come up with on the grounds there was never any probable cause for the search. But what evidence could there be? Cara Lane had never been in his Range Rover.

"I want to make a couple of phone calls," Pete said. "Then I'll let you know what I'm going to do."

Richter put on his flat eyes look. "How long?"

"Ten minutes."

"Okay, but then we're entering the vehicle with or without your permission."

Pete went back to his porch and punched in Bill Haskins' office number. The woman who answered told him the sheriff was out of town. *For crissakes*, Pete thought as he hit the red button, *doesn't that guy ever work?*

Then he dialed Angie. "Hi, this is Pete."

"Gee, I never would have recognized your voice."

"No cute stuff right now, okay? I have half the law enforcement officials in the county here with a warrant to search my vehicle and I need your advice." He described the warrant and told her about his conversation with Richter.

"Unbelievable," she said. "He says he has eyewitnesses who saw her get into your car?"

"That's what he claims. What are my options?"

She thought about it for a few moments. "Well, I could try calling the judge and ask for a hearing on probable cause. That's a real long shot. Even if I reached him in time, which is doubtful, he'd probably just tell me my remedy would be to move to suppress any evidence they come up with. The other option is to let them search and if necessary challenge the basis for the warrant. First, though, I need to ask you a question: was she ever in your vehicle?"

"I know you can't read my lips from there, but no, she-was-never-in-my-vehicle."

"Well I think letting them search is your best option then."

"That galls the hell out of me. I'm being railroaded by this guy."

"I know," Angie said. "Call me after they leave."

Pete went back outside, hit the "unlock" button, and told Richter he was objecting to the search on the grounds there was no probable cause to support the warrant. Richter shrugged and waved to the evidence technicians to commence the search.

He watched as they combed through every inch of his Range Rover for well over an hour. While they did their work, Richter and Tessler sat in their SUV laughing and playing music that should be banned in any civilized society. The technicians took with them a half-dozen bags of material they'd collected, but no large objects. He was glad they hadn't searched his cottage. They would have seized his longbow for sure.

• • •

Pete called Angie to fill her in and vent. When he cooled down, he began to worry about the broader consequences of the search. If Kral found out, he'd have new ammunition to mount another attack against him. After flatly denying he was a suspect, he'd have a difficult time rationalizing the search to his partners. He also knew he'd humiliated Kral at the meeting, and even if the guy hadn't been out to get him before, he would be now.

He thought back to that night and how he'd walked down the street with Cara to his Range Rover. He remembered standing by his vehicle and saying goodnight to her before she continued on. He also remembered opening the passenger-side door and tossing a file he had with him onto the front seat. That had to be what the so-called witnesses on the street saw; they assumed he was opening the door for Cara.

He shook his head. About the only thing he knew for sure was that the Cara Lane affair had become a quagmire. He was in squarely in Richter's gun sights, plus he was being attacked within his own law firm by a guy he hated. But just dropping his investigation wouldn't solve his problem.

Short-term, he could see only two options. He could try to preempt the issue by circulating a memorandum to the partners telling them about the search. If he did that, he could spin it as just a routine part of an ongoing investigation. That would show he had nothing to hide and undercut Kral's ability to go public with a new bombshell.

The other option would be to do nothing and take a chance that word wouldn't leak out before the search results came back. That was dicey, but it might work, particularly if the results came back relatively soon and were negative as he knew they would be. That would drive a stake into the heart of this albatross once and for all. If he followed option two, he knew he would have to strictly limit those he told about the search. Maybe Angie and no one else.

He decided to sleep on it. He picked up the telephone, dialed the sheriff's office, and left a message for Haskins to call him after he got back in town. It might be fruitless, but he had nothing to lose by taking a stab at getting Richter off his back.

Then he thought of something. He'd driven from Chicago to the lake with plastic bags of Cara's possessions crammed into the back of his Range Rover. What if trace evidence of Cara's presence — hair, for example, or fibers — clung to the bags from when they were on her bed and were now in his vehicle? He wasn't sure that was possible, but it gave him something new to worry about.

NINETEEN

The receptionist had gotten her hair touched up since Pete's last visit. He'd obviously become a fixture around the place because she greeted him by name again and escorted him down to the sheriff's office.

Bill Haskins looked like a lawman. Tall and lean, probably in his mid-50s. He had a neatly-trimmed moustache, slicked-back hair with flecks of gray, and weathered skin that seemed to retain its healthy glow year-around. When he donned his favorite broad-brimmed hat he looked like the old Marlboro Man. He'd been sheriff for 17 years and made little secret of his interest in higher office.

"Pete," he said, "come in."

They traded small talk for a while and Haskins told him about some of the things the sheriff's department had been doing to implement the recommendations of Pete's citizen's committee. He acted friendly, like a politician.

"Well, what can I do for you?" Haskins finally asked.

"Two things," Pete said. "I have a complaint and then would like some information."

Haskins nodded and motioned for him to continue.

Pete got right to it. "First of all, I have a complaint about your deputy, Frank Richter. He barged into my place the other day and searched my vehicle. There was no legitimate basis for that search. You know it, I know it and your deputy certainly knows it. The guy is out of control and I'm tired of his harassment."

Haskins' eyes narrowed and he steepled his hands. "Pete, I agreed to meet with you out of courtesy because we know each other. But we have to have an understanding up front. I can't get into the details of our investigation of Cara Lane's death, including as it relates to you. You're a lawyer so I'm sure you understand that."

Haskins spilled a couple of drops of coffee on his shirt. "Damn," he said, reaching for a glass of water and a napkin. After dabbing a few times he said, "As for the search, Frank was just following standard procedure. I can't fault him for that. And don't forget, the judge who signed the warrant found probable cause."

"What probable cause? The fact I'd had dinner with a woman and she later drowned?"

"It was more than that, Pete." He laid out essentially the same story Angie had that day in his office, with the added twist about the two eyewitnesses who reportedly had seen Cara get in his Range Rover that night.

Pete stared at him. "How many times can I say this, Cara Lane was never in my vehicle."

Haskins shrugged. "Then the search results will come back negative."

"They will come back negative," Pete said, "but that's not the point. It's the principle of the thing. The last time I checked, the rule of law still governed in this country. Richter has it in for me for some reason and he's using this as an excuse to jack me around. I don't like it, Bill."

Haskins looked at him and shook his head. "Oh, I don't think that's the case. Deputy Richter is a fine young lawman. I can understand why you're uncomfortable with all of this, but that doesn't mean he's jacking you around."

Pete saw he was getting nowhere with his complaint about Richter and switched gears. "I understand the dead woman's mother has spoken to you."

Haskins' eyebrows moved up on his forehead. "Where did you hear that?"

"She called me, too, and told me so. She talked to Cara after she left me that night and is positive Cara was meeting someone else later on. She's afraid your department isn't following up on leads."

"With you sitting here complaining about Frank, doesn't that sound a little farfetched?"

Pete knew that was coming. "No," he said, "it doesn't. Richter is treating me as an ax murderer when he should be trying to find out who Cara met after she left me. That guy Willie was walking along the road that night. Does he know anything?"

Haskins laughed. "That I can tell you. We talked to Willie twice. Got the usual gibberish about how we'd be surprised at some of the things he sees and other conspiratorial nonsense like that. We're sure he didn't see anything, and even if he had, he'd be useless as a witness."

"How about Cara's cell phone? Have you checked to see if she made or received any calls after she left me?"

Haskins looked surprised. "She didn't have a cell phone, at least that we found."

That's strange, Pete thought. He was positive she had a cell phone at the restaurant because he remembered seeing it in an outside pocket of her purse. Plus, she'd called her mother after she left Rona's and there weren't exactly a lot of pay phones on Main Street.

"I'm convinced she met someone else that night. Her mother is, too."

Haskins shrugged again. "Give me a name."

Pete thought about it and decided he had nothing to lose.

"Do you know a guy named Kurt Romer? He works on one of the charter boats in Millport."

"We know about Mr. Romer. If you're going to tell me that he and the deceased were seen around town together, we already know that."

Pete paused. "Are you aware that Romer has a history of violence against women and he lived within a few blocks of Cara Lane while he was in Chicago?"

Haskins' eyes narrowed again. "This conversation is beginning to get into areas I said we couldn't get into and I'm going to cut it off. But I will say that we know about Mr. Romer's past. That's not enough to label him a murderer. If it was, we'd all be in trouble, including you."

Pete stared at him. "What do you mean?"

"The assault charges in Madison?"

Pete felt like he'd been kicked in the gut. He couldn't believe they'd dredged that up. It was all so long ago — over 25 years — that it didn't even rank as a distant memory anymore. He'd punched another student in a campus bar one night and knocked out some teeth. The casualty was a kid from Pete's hometown. He kept referring to Pete as Lars, the name of Pete's father, trying to tar him with the old family image Pete had been desperate to escape. Finally Pete snapped and hit him. The fight resulted in misdemeanor criminal as well as civil charges against Pete, both of which were eventually dropped. Because he was 21 at the time, the charges remained on his record.

"That's bullshit!" Pete said. "That was nothing more than a tussle in a college bar with a guy who'd been harassing me all night. I disclosed the incident to the bar examiners when I applied for admission to the bar in Illinois and again when I applied here in Michigan. Neither had any problem with it."

"You're not denying it happened?"

"No, I'm not denying it happened. But it was nothing like Romer beating up his girlfriend and having a protective order issued against him."

Haskins just stared at him with baleful eyes, looking like he'd attended the same class as Richter.

"So you're using a minor incident from my college days to cast suspicion on me in connection with the death of a woman I had dinner with exactly once."

"That's not what I said. My point was that a lot of people have things in their past that they probably wish didn't exist."

• • •

"Sorry," Harry said. He dropped into a chair and wiped his brow. "My dad called just as I was about to leave the office."

"How's the professor?"

"The same. The entire journalistic world is going to hell in a handbasket."

Harry's father was professor *emeritus* of journalistic ethics at Northwestern University. The scandal at Harry's old paper, in which Harry had been the fall guy, had unfolded right there in the professor's backyard and he'd taken it very hard. He lost no opportunity to let his son know that he'd been personally and professionally embarrassed.

"Give him my best the next time you talk to him."

Harry muttered something unintelligible, then said, "I haven't seen you since we all had dinner at your place that night," he said. "I thought you'd fallen off the face of the earth. Anything new?"

Pete grunted. "Where to start." He hit the highlights: his confrontation with Romer, the anonymous telephone call to Kral and the partners meeting to get him to step aside as managing partner, his second visit to Vrba's apartment, his meeting with the sheriff to complain. He broke his vow and told Harry about the search of his Range Rover. He did leave out a few things, notably what happened at the Janicek house, lest he put Harry into information overload.

"Jesus," Harry said, focusing on Pete's problems at Sears & Whitney. "You can't let that guy Kral railroad you at your own law firm."

"I know." He told Harry the options he was considering in view of Richter's search.

"Tough choice."

"I'm leaning toward letting things play out."

Harry looked thoughtful. "It's risky either way. Do you know when the forensics results will be back?"

"No. If I did, it would make the choice easier."

Harry eyed Pete's iced tea. "You want a real drink?"

"Sure, I just didn't want to sit here and get schnozzled, not knowing when you were going to wander in."

Harry shot him a look. "I was just going to say that your other priority has to be to get rid of this cloud hanging over you personally, but after that cheap shot, maybe I should keep my concerns to myself."

"Sorry," Pete said. "And I do appreciate your concern."

"Apology accepted," said Harry. He took another sip of his drink and said, "It looks like you can forget about relying on Haskins to get Richter off your back."

"I guess so," Pete said, sighing. "I went in thinking he would at least pretend to be sympathetic and he hits me with something that happened when I was three."

"Richter's obviously been checking you out."

"What a prick," Pete said, shaking his head. After a few moments of silence, he added, "You know, even though I'm a lawyer, I never thought much about it before, but when you're the target of a guy like Richter . . ." His voice trailed off.

"Well," Harry said, looking at him, "I keep telling you what Cap has been saying all along. The guy is out of control."

Or tenacious as hell, Pete thought. He stared out at the bay for a while and then said, "I wish you'd warned me about why Lynn got out of the forensic accounting business."

"Jesus, did that come up?" he said, arching his eyebrows.

"It not only came up, but it ruined a nice dinner at the Manitou."

"I'm sorry," Harry said, shaking his head. "It's still bothering her, huh?"

"I'd say."

"You patched things up though?"

"I think so. She called a couple of times while I was in Chicago. Then we got together and shot arrows when I got back and she told me all about it."

"I guess having your car bombed tends to stay with you," Harry mused.

"It has with her."

They talked about what was happening at his paper. "By the way," Harry said, "I read the draft of your piece on the old logging days. Not bad."

"You going to run it?"

"Might. I have to admit that you really grabbed me with your hook about the old Finn who had to have his leg amputated right there in camp. Course it wasn't as good as if you'd had some training in writing stuff."

"I'll tell you what," Pete said, "give me a couple of weeks and I think I can make it a lot better. Maybe add some legal analysis that everyone loves to read. For example, I could include a technical discussion of the logging company's negligence and then maybe a page or two about the Finn's contributory negligence and how . . ."

"Wait!" Harry said, holding up his hands. "Maybe I can whip it into shape. It shouldn't take long for an old pro like me."

"Speaking of the old pro," Pete said, "has he found out anything new from the sheriff's office?"

"Not a lot, but I did hear that Richter searched Romer's vehicle, too, if it's any consolation. It was sometime early this week, Monday or Tuesday."

"Not surprised. Romer is mixed up in this, Harry, I can feel it. This is not your average solid citizen."

Harry peered at him over his glasses. "Do you want me to continue or do you just want to sit there and go off on Kurt Romer?"

Pete gestured with his hand. "Continue, please."

"I learned something else that's really interesting. We saw it coming, but now it's clear there's a split over what to do with the case. Richter and Tessler are convinced Cara Lane was murdered and want to press on with their investigation. On the other side is Sheriff Haskins and Roz Wentworth, the county prosecuting attorney. They're leaning toward a swimming accident explanation. Kind of like the scenario I've laid out a couple of times."

Pete looked out over the bay and watched a fishing boat come in. He turned back to Harry. "How do you see it playing out?" he asked.

"I understand that Haskins has given Richter and Tessler a couple of weeks to come up with something more concrete — a motive on someone's part, evidence placing someone at the scene of the crime, the instrument used to hit her on the head, something like that — or he and Roz are going to kill the investigation and move on."

"What's the hurry?"

Harry eyed him with a disgusted look. "How have you become such a successful lawyer when you're so naïve? What's next year?"

"I don't know," Pete said, "the Chinese Year of the Pig?"

"No, genius, election year. Ever hear of that?"

"Actually I have. So you're implying that Bill and Roz, if they're shooting for higher office, might find it a tad inconvenient to have an unsolved crime in their backyard."

"Bingo."

"But until they pull the plug, Richter and his boy Tessler continue on the trail."

"You're sharp tonight. Haskins is apparently letting them do the routine things. Interview witnesses, having basic forensics work done, going to the judge to ask for search warrants, stuff like that, but he's balking at running additional toxicological tests. That's expensive and as Ethan probably told you, they didn't come up with anything the first time around except alcohol. If I had to guess, I'd say we're looking at a swimming accident announcement by mid-September."

"And whoever killed Cara walks."

Harry looked at him and shook his head disgustedly. "You're too much. I outline a scenario that gets you off the hook and you complain. If you've got your dander up and feel you need to win something, let it be against that scumbag Kral."

"How about you? Do you still believe it was a swimming accident?"

Harry's eyes narrowed over his half-glasses. "It pains me to admit this, but I'm beginning to think you could be right. When I put together everything I've learned with the stuff you've dug up, it doesn't compute, as you like to say."

"Harry, do you feel okay?"

Harry looked at him and didn't smile or come back with one of his patented one-liners. He stared at the bay for a long time.

"By the way," Harry finally said, "The Colonel has been pestering me for a day when the three of us can play golf. What looks good for you?"

"I'll check my calendar and get back to you. Maybe we can play 36 so I can get my mind off this Cara Lane crap."

· · ·

Pete said his goodbyes after Rona threatened to turn off the lights on them. Except for his Range Rover, which was parked a half-block away, there were no vehicles on Main Street near the restaurant. Two blocks up, though, cars and SUVs and pickups lined both sides of the street. The Car Ferry was going strong. He considered walking up to join Kurt Romer for a beer and another heart-to-heart. Not seriously, though; he hadn't completely lost his mind. Besides, he was tired.

He took Prentice Road back to the lake. It branched off the highway near one of the churches on the outskirts of town and dead-ended at Shore Road three miles away. The hilly, wooded terrain along the road was broken by meadows with an occasional decaying farm house or barn. He liked Prentice Road because when he came over the last rise, he could see Clear Lake spread out before him. There wouldn't be much of a scene tonight because of the cloud cover, but maybe he'd see a deer or two feeding in the meadows.

Pete drove at a leisurely pace and watched for reflective red eyes that would signal the presence of deer. A set of headlights appeared in his rearview mirror, but otherwise the road was dark and quiet. He noticed the driver behind him closing fast. Obviously the guy wasn't interested in observing wildlife. He hugged the side of the narrow road to let him pass.

The vehicle was right behind him now. Not a car; the lights were too high. A truck, maybe, or a jumbo SUV. The lights were intense, blinding. He flipped up his rearview mirror so·he could see. *Idiot.* Another one of those guys who thought he owned the road and could care less about the common courtesy of dimming his lights.

Pete continued to hug the shoulder. Gravel pinged against the underside of his Range Rover as he ran on and off the edge of the asphalt. *Why didn't the guy pass?* Then the vehicle slammed into his rear. His head snapped back and pain shot through his upper body. He lost control for a moment and swerved into the ditch on the right. Tree branches slapped his windshield.

You stupid sonofabitch! He fought to regain control. The vehicle moved alongside him on the left. He got a quick look at it as he swerved back onto the road. It was a dark pickup with an oversized chassis. The vehicle loomed over his Range Rover.

He stomped on the accelerator. The Range Rover surged forward. Gravel spun from his tires and clanged against metal as he tried to pull away. The pickup accelerated and kept pace. It drew alongside him again and swerved right. Metal crunched against metal as the pickup slammed into the left side of his vehicle. He could feel the door panel press into his left side.

The pickup slammed into him again. *What the hell are you doing?* Pete hit the brakes and tried to move in behind the pickup. It didn't work. The other driver hit his brakes too. Pete considered just stopping and heading through the woods on foot, but immediately abandoned that idea. He didn't know how many men were in the truck or who they were or what they might do. He hit the accelerator again and surged forward. The pickup quickly caught up and every 50 feet or so slammed into his side.

They came to the top of another hill and Pete floored it. The pickup kept pace and continued to slam into him. Pete swerved right again. The ditch was deeper here and his Range Rover lurched wildly, almost tipping on its side. The door was crushed against his body now and he felt pinned to the driver's seat. His arms were numb and his head hurt from the banging and the roar of the pickup's big engine through his open window.

They started down the hill and the pickup moved away from him. Maybe that's it, he thought. But no. A better angle, that's all. The pickup accelerated into his Range Rover. He lurched right again on impact and hit the ditch. Pain shot through his body once more and he could feel himself going into a roll. He tried to regain control but his muscles wouldn't respond. His head struck something hard and everything went dark.

TWENTY

Pete heard voices. There were people around him. And lights. Pulsing lights that pierced his brain like hot steel rods. He put a hand over his eyes to make them go away. Someone was close to him. He flailed at the blurred image. *"You sonofabitch!"*

"Take it easy, sir," a voice said.

"Get away from me!" The words sounded like they came from outside his body. His head throbbed. *"Get those lights away!"* Distant sounds again.

"You had an accident, sir," the voice said. "You're going to be okay."

His eyes were beginning to focus but pain wracked his head and made it difficult to concentrate. *"That pickup,"* he mumbled.

"Take it easy," the voice said again. "There is no pickup. This is an ambulance. We're taking you to the hospital."

"No!" Pete said, flailing away again at the figures hovering over him. *"There was a pickup! Get that pickup!"*

He felt drowsy and was aware of being moved. Everything hurt and he couldn't think. *He had to get that man in the pickup!*

"How you feeling?"

Pete blinked a few times and a figure slowly came into focus. He blinked again. It was Harry. He looked around and raised a hand to block the light streaming through the window. A hospital room. He gingerly touched the lump on his head.

"Like shit," he finally mumbled. "Would you pull that shade?"

Harry walked to the window and did as Pete asked. "The nurses told me you have a concussion," he said. "What happened? You doze off?"

It took a full minute for Pete to focus on the question. His head throbbed and he felt groggy. Slowly it came back. Dinner with Harry. Driving home on Prentice Road.

"You ran off the road," Harry said. "Remember? You're damn lucky to be alive."

And the lights behind him. Blinding lights. Then the pickup pulling alongside him and smashing into his Range Rover. And smashing into him again. And again.

"I didn't doze off," he finally said. "Someone ran me off the road."

Harry studied his face for a long time. "Did you tell the police? They think you fell asleep at the wheel."

"Harry, you're the first person I've talked to. At least that I remember."

A nurse stepped into the room. "He needs to rest, Mr. McTigue."

Harry looked at her and raised two fingers.

"Are you sure you remember everything? One of the Millport cops said you'd been running on and off the road for at least a half-mile before you hit the ditch and went into a roll. They said they could see the skid marks in the gravel and dirt along the side."

"Look, my head is killing me, but I remember exactly what happened. Somebody came up behind me and deliberately ran me off the road. Dark pickup truck. One of those things with an oversized chassis."

Harry shook his head. "Thank God for airbags."

"What do you mean?"

"They said the airbags saved your life."

Pete felt his head again. He didn't remember the air bags inflating. It must have happened when he hit the ditch the last time and went into a roll.

Harry continued to stare at him. "I'm being chased out. I'll stop back tonight."

• • •

Pete was picking at a tray of dry roast turkey, dressing and mushy canned green beans that seemed to be reserved for the hospital market when Sheriff William Haskins and his prize deputy, Franklin Richter, walked in.

Haskins studied his face for a few moments. "You don't look as bad as I thought you would. The doc says you're lucky to be alive, though."

Pete grunted. "That's what people keep telling me."

"Harry called me," Haskins said. "He says you claim someone ran you off the road."

"I'm not just claiming it. That's what happened."

Haskins glanced at Richter and then back at Pete. "You feel up to giving us a statement?"

Pete felt like telling them to come back in a month, but spent the next 10 minutes describing what had happened.

"You said it was a dark pickup with an oversized chassis," Richter said. "Did you get a look at the driver, by any chance?"

"No," Pete said, giving him a sarcastic stare. "And I didn't exactly have time to pull out pen and paper and write down his plate number either. I was a little busy trying to avoid being killed."

Richter looked at him but ignored his sarcasm. He checked his faithful companion the spiral notebook again and said, "Now you claim this pickup ran you off the road by repeatedly ramming into the side of your vehicle. How many times would you say he rammed you?"

"How many times? Christ, I don't know. Five times, 10 times, what's the difference? He banged into me and sent me into a roll, that's the important thing."

He was still glaring at Richter when Haskins said, "Pete, we're just trying to get the facts."

"All right, nine times," Pete said, flipping out a number and looking away.

After paging through his notebook again, Richter asked another question that in Pete's mind indicated how seriously he was taking his story.

"Mr. Thorsen, would you tell us what you had to drink last night at the Bay Grille?"

Pete's head snapped in Richter's direction, causing pain to shoot down his back. "I was wondering when you'd get around to that," he said. "Let's see, and you might want to take notes on this if you don't have your little recording machine with you. I started out with a large iced tea that was laced with some very strong lemon while I waited for Harry McTigue to show up. Then I had a vodka and tonic, light on the vodka as usual to live up to my reputation as a wuss when it comes to alcohol. I topped all of that off with a glass of pinot grigio during dinner. That was over a three-hour period. I figure it must have put me at about a third of the allowable blood alcohol level for drivers."

The only sound in the room came from a nurse padding down the hall in her soft-soled shoes.

"Frank, give us a minute, will you?" Haskins asked.

Richter snapped his notebook shut and stalked out.

"Pete," Haskins said, "you're not doing yourself any favors by being so hostile about everything. Frank is just doing his job."

Pete looked out the window. "Yeah, well I'm feeling like crap and he's asking me a lot of stupid questions."

"You need to remember he's a law enforcement official and treat him with more respect. I know you feel like he's been railroading you, but that's no excuse."

Pete didn't reply, but he took advantage of his time alone with Haskins to air something that had been gnawing at him since Harry came to visit.

"I think Kurt Romer is the one who ran me off the road."

Haskins fixed him with one of his steely stares. "You've really got a thing about Mr. Romer, don't you?"

"There's no other explanation," Pete muttered.

Haskins continued to look at him. "What makes you think it was Romer?"

"Two reasons," Pete said. "First, he drives a dark pickup. And second, I bumped into him at the Car Ferry a few days ago. I didn't mention it when I was in your office, but things became a little ugly when we got into a conversation about Cara Lane. I asked him some questions out of curiosity and he threatened to kick my ass. He wasn't kidding either."

"What kind of questions?"

Pete thought back to that night when he'd confronted Romer in the bar. He didn't want to tell Haskins all of the details, but said, "It was a free-flowing conversation. Basically I asked whether he knew Cara from Chicago, whether he'd met her after she left me that night, that kind of thing. You should check his pickup. I bet you'll find damage to the right side."

"We'll check it out," Haskins said, "but I suggest you stay away from Mr. Romer and leave things to us."

Pete looked out the window again and didn't reply.

Haskins stared at him for a long time. "You seem different than when I dealt with you on that committee," he said. "Is something bothering you these days?"

Pete locked eyes with him. "Yeah, I don't like being treated like a criminal."

Between visits from Rona and Lynn and Bud Stephanopoulis, and a call from the Colonel, he had plenty of time to think. And the more he thought, the madder he became. Big Red's threats, the anonymous call to his law firm, being run off the road. It was all too much of a coincidence. He was being targeted and it had to be because he'd been poking around into Cara Lane's death. Nothing else made sense.

He made some notes on a legal pad. That always helped him think, to see things more clearly. He listed the bad things that had happened to him in one column and some names in another. Then he looked for a logical overall connection between events and individuals. After an hour of trying, it didn't seem to be there, much as he tried to force the possibilities.

Maybe all of the dots didn't connect because there was no connection. Maybe he was making things too complicated. Maybe the incident with Big Red was unrelated to Cara Lane's death. Maybe he was just a guy who'd had a few beers and was being protective of someone in the community. Maybe Kral really had received a call and it, too, was unrelated. One of the firm's clients could have been in Millport for some reason, fishing or something, and heard about Cara Lane's death and that Pete had been questioned by the sheriff.

A lot of maybes. In his mind, though, a couple of things weren't maybes. One was his strong belief that Cara's death wasn't an accident. He listed the reasons: her past, strong swimmer, likely met someone else after she left him, acted nervous that night both with him and on the telephone with her mother, cell phone was missing.

And the more he thought about it, the more the empty wine bottle smelled like a plant. Her prints were the only ones found on the bottle, but at some point — certainly at the store where it was purchased — others would have handled the bottle and their prints should have been found as well. The only logical explanation was that the bottle had been wiped clean and Cara's hands placed on it to leave her prints and set up the drowned-while-drunk explanation.

The other thing that wasn't a maybe was his conviction he'd been run off the road deliberately. It wasn't a random act of road rage. There was nothing random about it; he'd been followed out of town by someone. There might have been rage, too, but it was because he was coming too close to the truth, not because he gave the other driver the finger or cut him off in traffic.

Everything kept pointing to Kurt Romer. He clearly knew Cara and must have met her in Chicago while he was there. At the north side bar where she worked, possibly. He had to be the one she'd come to see in Millport, too. Something could have gone wrong between them. Maybe she'd discovered something — his meth operation was one possibility — and he was worried about it. Maybe she'd even been blackmailing him over his drug activities. Romer had a history of violence against women, that much was clear. He'd seen the guy's explosive temper firsthand. There probably wasn't much he wasn't capable of in the right circumstances. And he had it in for Pete after that night at the bar. Pete wanted to make him pay.

TWENTY-ONE

Two nights in the hospital felt like a month. He'd had his fill of nurses poking at him and taking tests and asking him how he felt and giving him pills. The plus side was that his head felt clear again. His body was better too, although his left side still hurt like hell when he even twitched.

After the hospital fare, he was happy to get back to some edible food again. He was a creature of habit and his favorite breakfast when he didn't permit himself the luxury of one of Ebba's tasty sandwiches was original large-biscuit shredded wheat with sliced bananas and skim milk. Basic but good. He finished off the bowl and stared at his targets among the trees. He thought about how nice it would be to take his longbow out for some practice. Maybe plunk Marty Kral a few more times. He knew better, though. No way his body was going to allow that for a few days.

He walked over to his CD player and picked up the case for Dion's greatest hits It was one of the purchases the UPS man had delivered that evening a couple of weeks ago. He'd been so busy he hadn't even listened to it. He broke the seal and slipped the disc into the player. The first number, "The Wanderer," came on. He turned up the volume. It might not heal his body, but did a lot for his spirits.

He moved his chair to a patch of sunlight on the far side of the porch. Then he grabbed one of the boxes containing Cara's books and other possessions and placed it by the chair. He stripped off his shirt and examined his left side; a mass of scrapes and bruises and scabs ran from his rib cage to his hip. It was a sickly collage of black, green and yellow. He positioned himself so the sun's rays hit that side of his body and opened the box. He made a quick survey of the contents. Books. Magazines. Church bulletins. A shoe box with receipts and other financial minutia. The stuff of everyday life.

Then he began a more careful review, starting with Cara's month-at-a-glance calendar, looking for some connection between Cara and Kurt Romer. The recurring entries were "work" several nights a week and "sk" at four in the afternoon on Wednesdays and Saturdays. He assumed that referred to the church soup kitchen Marian had mentioned. The other entries were a potpourri of social and other events: Dinner with so-and-so, party, M's lecture, concert. There were nine entries at random dates and times for "Father Joseph" or "Father J" or sometimes just "FJ." He knew the Janiceks were Catholic and assumed Father Joseph was a priest at Cara's church in Chicago. On July 29th, the entry "Mich" appeared. He knew what that referred to.

The books were an eclectic collection. Four on the evils of globalization, including one co-authored by Professor Marcus Vrba. Those books didn't surprise him given Cara's past. Thomas Friedman's *The World is Flat* was in the collection, as were *Jihad Incorporated: A Guide to Militant Islam in the U.S.* by Steven Emerson and two other books on terrorism. There was a batch of chemistry and other college textbooks. He was surprised to see some paperbacks with Janet Evanovich's trademark pastel covers. Somehow he had a hard time visualizing Cara as a Stephanie Plum fan.

The shoebox contained a mishmash of receipts, pay stubs from a bar on Halsted Street in Chicago called Christopher's, and bank statements. He sorted through the credit card receipts. Nothing for gas or anything else automobile-related.

He flipped through a manila folder containing a collection of maps of the city and area shopping centers and some tourist brochures. Many of the brochures were for Millennium Park. Pete had watched the park take shape and, playing the wag, liked to tell visitors the name came from how long it took to complete construction rather than marking the beginning of a new thousand-year period. A stack of photographs secured by a rubber band was in the folder. They seemed to have been taken by someone who was either an inept photographer or wasn't all that interested in capturing artistic shots of one of the park's highly-publicized attractions.

There were flyers from this year's May Day rally at Haymarket Square and for programs at nearby DePaul University. Most of the newspaper clippings meant nothing to him, but several old ones from the *Traverse City Record-Eagle* did. They chronicled the closing of the plant where Hank Janicek once worked. The buyer was Gulf Investco; he wasn't familiar with the company but made a note of it.

The magazines ran the gamut from *Time* to low-circulation political journals. There were a couple of issues of *Cosmopolitan* as well, proving once again that Cara hadn't been a one-dimensional woman.

He was about to tackle a second box when his telephone rang. It was Angie and Steve. After asking him how he felt and probing him about his accident, Steve said, "I'm sure this is just what you want to hear right now, but there are rumors that Marty and friends are plotting something else."

"Like what?" Pete had a sinking feeling word had gotten out that his vehicle had been searched.

"It's not clear, but it sounds financial. Our collections have been soft so far in August despite our efforts. It might have something to do with that."

Pete hoped that they didn't hear him expelling air in a sigh of relief. Financial concerns he could deal with.

"We were ahead of budget through the end of July," he said.

"I know," Steve said. "But it's like politics. The economy can be humming along like a Rolls Royce, but if unemployment ticks up a tenth of a point some month, the party out of power is all over it like it's Armageddon."

"What do you suggest?"

"When are you planning to come back from the lake?" Steve asked.

Pete thought for a moment. "I don't know yet. Maybe after Labor Day. A lot depends on the RyTech deal and where negotiations are held."

"I think that's a little too long," Steve said. "Can you come down some day next week? We need to show the colors with partners."

He grimaced at the thought of another drive to Chicago and back, but knew he had little choice. They discussed dates. Maybe he could at least combine the trip with getting together with Boehm at the Bridgeview plant.

• • •

He'd finished looking through the second box and was enjoying a ham and Swiss on rye when he heard a vehicle pull in his driveway. He twisted around in his chair, feeling his side protest.

Richter got out of his SUV. He was alone this time.

"Mr. Thorsen," he called, "could I talk to you for a minute?"

Pete slipped on his shirt and went down the stairs. Ugly thoughts suddenly began to swirl through his head as soon as he saw Richter standing by his vehicle.

"How are you feeling?" Richter said.

Pete studied his face. Unless he missed his guess, the deputy looked almost concerned. Or maybe he'd just gotten so used to seeing the guy's smirk that he misinterpreted its absence as a sign of normal human feelings.

"Okay," Pete said curtly. "What can I do for you?"

"I want to give you a report on our investigation of what happened to you the other night on Prentice Road."

"And?"

"We looked at Mr. Romer's truck. There was no sign of damage like there would have to be if he'd been the one who ran you off the road."

Pete stared at him.

"We also questioned Mr. Romer. He denies having anything to do with it. He says he was at the Car Ferry that night, but left about eight and went straight home. Claims he was exhausted and went right to bed."

"Did you try to corroborate that?"

"As much as we could. He claims people in the Car Ferry will back him up about his departure time. We checked with the bartender and he confirms his story. You said you didn't leave Rona's until 10:00 p.m. or a little after."

"What did you do to confirm that he actually went home? He could have been waiting for me."

"We pretty much had to take his word for it. Just like you want us to do the night Cara Lane died."

Pete gave him a long, hard look. "When are you going to get off my ass? You know I didn't have anything to do with Cara Lane's death."

"I told you before, no one is accusing you of anything."

"I know what you said, but I also see what you've been doing. Grilling me about things that never happened, giving me that look just because I didn't have seven people with me at all times after I left the restaurant that night, barging in to search my vehicle. I'd have to be a fool to not understand where you're coming from."

Richter scuffed at the gravel with one shoe. "I had an interesting conversation with Mr. Romer when I talked to him about his truck. He says you've been harassing him. Claims you confronted him in the Car Ferry one night and that you sit down at the marina and watch him."

Pete wanted to smile, but held it back. Maybe a little pressure was just what Romer needed to goad the guy into doing something stupid. "I haven't been harassing him," Pete said. "I think he's overly sensitive."

Richter just stared at him.

"I know you don't like to take advice," Pete said, "but I'll bet that if you look into it more, you'll find that Cara Lane met him that night after she left me. That's the key to your investigation."

"We have looked into it," Richter said.

"And?"

"And we haven't found any evidence that the vic met him that night."

Pete thought about his conversation with Bill Haskins. "You didn't find a cell phone in her purse or on the beach, I understand."

Richter tensed up like the conversation had crossed over into forbidden territory. "If that's a question and you're looking for a response, I'm not going there."

"Oh for crissakes, Deputy, Bill Haskins already told me you didn't find her cell phone. What's the big secret?"

Richter remained silent.

"She had a cell phone with her when we had dinner; I saw it in an outside pocket of her purse. I'm willing to wager that Cara made at least two calls after nine that night. One was to her mother and I'm betting the other was to Kurt Romer. You should try to track down her phone. Check with the service providers."

Richter didn't say anything again. Then as he walked back to his SUV, he turned to face Pete. "Between you and me, your accident doesn't change anything."

TWENTY-TWO

For the third night in a row, Pete sat in his rental car, a gray Ford Taurus, and watched the comings and goings at the Car Ferry. Kurt Romer had been there the past two nights and left before midnight with the lucky lady of the evening in tow. Pete had tailed him to a house in Benzonia both times, parked a block away, and waited. At two in the morning, fighting to stay awake and his body aching from his bumps and bruises, he'd given it up and gone home.

He wondered again what he hoped to accomplish by staking out Romer. The answer was always the same: something that would tie him to Cara Lane. What that would be he didn't know because he'd found no connection between the two in Cara's things. But at least he now knew where Romer lived. The day after his first stakeout, he'd waited for him to leave the dock with his fishing party and then drove to Benzonia and swung past his house. He was tempted to go in and look around, but in the end didn't. It was too much of a risk that someone would see him.

Pete ducked out of his car to buy an ice cream cone. He got lucky and didn't see anyone he knew even though Main Street was bustling.

He enjoyed the cone and thought about Richter's report that Romer's pickup showed no sign of damage. He'd been disappointed, but after thinking about it, he decided that didn't prove a thing. Romer might have been smart enough to use another truck, or he could have ridden shotgun with someone who did the dirty work. He also could care less that Romer had complained about him to Richter. As a matter of fact, Pete *wanted* Romer to think he was watching him.

He was daydreaming about Lynn when he saw a tall man come out of the Car Ferry. He blinked and checked his watch. It was barely 10:00 p.m. and that was Kurt Romer. Alone this time. Maybe three nights in a row was too much even for the town's number one stud. He shoved the rest of the cone into his mouth and fired up his engine. After letting several cars pass, he eased into the street.

Romer took his familiar route toward Benzonia. That was a letdown. The last thing he wanted was to sit in his Taurus again until all hours while Romer snoozed happily in his bed or did whatever he did behind closed doors. In Benzonia, Romer turned onto the residential street where he lived. He parked his pickup at the end of the block rather than at his door, which Pete thought was odd, and walked down the street to his house. Lights went on and a short time later they went off. It was a repetition of the previous two nights. Pete sat there for a while and thought about going home. After a half hour, a figure appeared at the side of the house and looked up and down the street. Apparently finding everything clear, Romer hurried down the street to his pickup and headed for M-115. Well that's interesting, Pete thought.

He stayed discreetly back from Romer. The traffic was heavy despite the time of night and several cars passed him. That was a concern because if too many vehicles separated them, he might not see it if Romer should turn off the highway. He accelerated and passed three of the cars that had been so eager to get by him and then just settled in to go with the flow.

Romer's pickup was comfortably in view again. It was a stroke of luck, too, because just minutes later, Romer's left signal light started blinking. He turned on M-137 toward Thompsonville. Pete followed and half expected to see Romer parked in someone's driveway waiting for him.

He wasn't, but as Pete drove north on M-137, he did see taillights. That had to be Romer. He accelerated and closed the distance. An oncoming car provided enough illumination for him to see that the vehicle just ahead was a pickup. It continued on toward Thompsonville. Pete slowed down when he got close to town. If Romer stopped at a bar or something, he didn't want him to get a look at his Taurus and then become suspicious if he saw the same vehicle behind him later on. Pete pulled into a gas station to wait. He knew he risked losing Romer, but it was a chance he'd have to take.

He was about to pull back onto the road when he saw headlights. It looked like a truck. Could Romer be doubling back? The pickup passed the station and Pete saw the oversized chassis and concluded that's exactly what he was doing. Pete let him get well down the road and then eased out himself. A short time later, he saw the pickup turn right.

Pete passed several driveways he hadn't noticed on his way in. He peered into the yards. Nothing, at least that he could see. He continued on. Then he saw a gravel road coming up on the right. That had to be where Romer had turned. He peered down the road as he drove past. He saw no taillights or other sign of activity, but thought he saw dust hanging over the road.

Pete continued on for a couple hundred yards, watching to see if a vehicle came out of the side road. None did. He made a u-turn and when he came to the side road again, turned onto it. Nothing was in front of him, at least that he could see, but now he was certain there was dust in the air. He drove slowly, peering into the darkness, watching for Romer's pickup. Nothing. He stopped and turned off his engine and lights. He heard no sounds of another vehicle.

He hit the ignition and continued on. He passed a long driveway on the right. Lights burned dimly inside the house at the end, but there was no sign of Romer's pickup that he could see. He came to a two-track branching off to the left. It was overgrown with weeds and had a chain stretched across it with a rusty "No Trespassing" sign dangling from the links. He came to another driveway on the right with a mobile home and a couple of vehicles parked outside. But no dark pickup.

Pete cursed under his breath. He'd lost him. But then he began to think about the two-track. Could Romer have gone in there? He turned around and headed back for a closer look. He wished the damn dust he'd kicked up on the way in would settle down; it was like a beacon telegraphing his location. When he got close to the two-track, he cut his engine and listened. There were no sounds. He started the Taurus again and swung around so his headlights were on the entrance to the old road. He could see a padlock securing the chain at one end. It also looked like the tall grass and weeds had been crushed down. Like someone had just driven through. That had to be where Romer had gone.

He made another u-turn and drove back down the road, going slowly now to avoid kicking up more dust. When he was a quarter mile past the two-track, he pulled the Taurus off to the side into the tall grass and parked. He closed the door as quietly as he could and got a navy windbreaker from his trunk. It was too warm for a jacket, but he didn't want to stand out like a neon sign in his white golf shirt. He walked back toward the two-track, pausing often to listen. Again, he heard nothing. When he came to the chain stretched across the old road, he looked in but saw no lights, no sign of activity.

He ducked under the chain and made his way down the two-track. The tall grass swished against his thighs. He tried to remember what he'd been taught long ago about night patrols. Get his visual purple, be careful where he stepped, stop often to listen. A hundred yards in, he thought he saw something. He stopped and peered into the darkness. It looked like a sliver of light ahead. He moved forward again, continuing to pause and listen. Another hundred yards and he could make out the faint hulking shape of a building.

He inched closer, straining to identify his surroundings. He seemed to be in an overgrown meadow. It might be an abandoned farm, but he couldn't see any other buildings. Then he saw the truck and caught a whiff of something in the warm summer air. It wasn't fresh-mown hay or manure or some other odor common to the countryside. It was chemical. Ammonia, maybe, he couldn't quite tell. But it was definitely chemical. His heart pounded. *Kurt Romer's meth lab?*

Another vehicle was parked close to Romer's pickup. He crept along, keeping an eye on the building and the sliver of light. It was too dark to see much. He searched through his pockets. The key chain for his Range Rover had a penlight, but thanks to Mr. Romer, that was in the body shop. He checked his pockets and felt a book of paper matches. *Thank you Pink Top!* He must have put on the same pair of jeans he'd worn to the Car Ferry that night.

He stood and stared at the building for a couple of minutes. He heard no sounds and saw nothing except the sliver of light. He squatted behind the second vehicle and struck a match. Despite his cupped hand, the flare seemed to illuminate half the meadow. His heart jumped and his hands shook. But he saw what he'd wanted to see and quickly snuffed out the match. It was a Subaru Outback, silver or light gray in color, with Kentucky plates.

He stood there for a few minutes, waiting for his eyes to become readjusted to the darkness and praying that no one would come out of the house. He checked his pockets again. No pen or pencil and no paper. He felt through the contents of his billfold. Credit cards, driver's license, currency. Then in back of the currency he felt a piece of paper. Probably an ATM receipt based on the size. But nothing to write with.

He needed to record the plate number of the second vehicle because no way in hell he was going to trust his memory. He stared at the building again. Everything was still quiet. He crouched behind the Outback and cringed as another match flared in the darkness. He stared at the license plate number for a few moments, trying to program it into his memory, then carefully blew out the match. After his eyes readjusted to the dark, he held the slip of paper against the rear of the vehicle and used the burnt end of the match to scrawl the number. He folded the paper and placed it inside a zippered pocket of his windbreaker. He had to trust it would be readable.

Now he had a decision to make. He could get out of there and call the sheriff and hope the law would arrive in time to bust Romer and his companion. Or he could try to get a look inside. As he pondered his choices, he thought about a story the Colonel had told him about a member of a meth ring who was found dead in a ditch near Traverse City. He'd been chopped up pretty bad. The hardcore meth people don't mess around, the Colonel had said. Pete shuddered at the thought, but he owed Romer and wasn't about to let this opportunity pass.

He edged toward the house, stepping carefully and listening for sounds. The chemical odor grew stronger. The sliver of light came from the edge of a drawn shade just as he'd assumed. But he had a problem. The window was only a few feet from the front door. If someone were to come out while he was peering through the crack, he'd be dead meat. There were at least two of them and he had to assume they had weapons of some kind.

Pete decided to go around the side. He inched along, being careful where he stepped. There were no windows on the side of the house. He reached the rear corner and looked around. A small patch of light faintly illuminated the tall grass behind the old house. Another window. He slid around the corner and saw the source of the light. There was a small tear, an inch or two at most, near the bottom of the shade. He didn't see a back door.

He edged toward the window, continuing to pause and listen after each step. Then he crouched and slid his head to the right so his eye centered on the tear in the shade. The room was lit by a pair of Coleman lanterns. He ducked back. He was pretty sure a person inside wouldn't be able to see him unless he had his own eye right on the tear from inside. That seemed unlikely.

He slid his head to the right again and peered in a second time. Romer was there with another man who had a full beard that looked like it hadn't been trimmed in five years. Both men wore white surgical masks and were busy at a long table filled with glass containers and funnels and hoses and other paraphernalia. Camp stoves rested on the table and several gas canisters lay nearby. Containers of various sizes lined one side of the room. Pete had never seen a meth operation before, but had absolutely no doubt he was within a few feet of one.

Then in one blinding moment everything came unhinged. The dog that had been lying on the floor, apparently asleep, went nuts and began to bark and snarl and race around the room. The last thing he saw as he jumped back from the window was the dog's bared fangs and Romer and the other man whipping off their masks and looking frantically around.

Pete knew he had to get out of there! He was on the opposite side of the house from the two-track out to the road where his car was parked so that was out. He turned and ran as hard as he could in the opposite direction away from the house. He heard a door slam open behind him. Romer and his companion were outside! He glanced over his shoulder and saw flashlight beams rake the darkness. He continued to run flat out, hoping he wouldn't stumble over something in the darkness. Reach the woods, he told himself. He could hear the dog bark and snarl behind him.

Trees loomed ahead like dark shadows. Safety, or at least cover! Run faster! The flashlight beams swept the meadow behind the house. Then one beam centered on his back. He'd been spotted! A few seconds later both beams were on him and he heard angry shouts. He kept running, willing his legs to move faster. Brush slapped his face when he finally reached the woods. He heard the dog again. Closer now. Keep running! He slammed into a tree and went sprawling. Pain shot through his shoulder and he felt dazed. He scrambled to his feet and began to run again. His left side felt sticky. Fear clutched his gut with icy tentacles and his heart pounded.

Suddenly he pitched headlong into the darkness. He grabbed wildly, reaching for something — anything — to break his fall. Then he hit water. *Get up!* he told himself. He struggled to his feet, water pouring off him. It was shallow and he began to run. He could hear the dog close behind, snarling, frenzied. He stepped into a deep hole and went sprawling again. He started to swim, then reached shallow water and resumed running. His legs ached and his left side throbbed and his lungs were ready to explode. Suddenly the dog sounded farther away. Were they giving up? Or were his senses just dulled by fright and exhaustion. He glanced toward the bank but saw nothing. Maybe the dog had lost his scent in the water.

He kept wading. He could feel the current and continued to follow it downstream. He tried to run again, but was too exhausted. He willed himself to continue. Fifty steps more, he told himself. Then he would rest. He counted. *Seven, eight, nine* . . . He made it to 32, then his body sank into the water and he was unable to move. The gentle ripples flowed over him. It felt so cool, so comforting.

He had no idea how long he'd been lying in the water, but suddenly his brain reengaged and he knew he had to push on. He struggled to his feet. It was no use. His body wouldn't function. But he realized that if he stayed in the water, sooner or later he could end up like Cara. And Loraine.

He angled for the opposite side. Reach the bank, he told himself, then he would rest. One foot in front of the other. The water got deeper. He went under and flailed like a man who couldn't swim a stroke. His feet touched bottom again and he continued toward shore. He fell into the bank. His fingers dug into the mud and he lay there, gasping for breath. Then he mustered the strength to pull himself up the incline, inch by inch, and crawl until he was away from the stream.

He fell into a heap, chest heaving from exhaustion, too tired to even brush off the mosquitoes feeding on his neck and hands. Everything was quiet. No dog barking. No angry voices. Only silence and darkness. He rolled over on his back. The soft earth felt good. He needed to rest.

Then he saw it.

TWENTY-THREE

Angry tongues of orange and yellow licked the sky. Then an explosion rocked the night like a thunderclap, sending the flames higher. A string of new explosions followed. Like the grand finale of the July 4th fireworks display at the Millport beach, only louder, like sonic booms. Flames snaked upward with each blast and cascades of glowing embers lit up the night. The flames slowly settled below the treetops, but the fire continued to illuminate the night like some spectacular evening sunset. Only it was two in the morning.

Pete lay in the woods and watched. He continued to gasp for air and every part of his body ached and he felt light-headed. Not so light-headed he didn't realize what had happened, though. Romer and his partner had torched the building. Either that or something had accidentally ignited the chemicals.

He had to gather himself and move on. His first thought was not to go back past the house; if Romer and his partner were still alive, they could be searching for him or waiting near the scene of the fire for him to come out. But then he thought about it and realized that was unlikely because of the attention the fire would draw. Even so, he wanted to stay away from the fire for another reason. If he were to be seen in the area in his present condition, looking like a deranged madman, he might be courting other problems. Particularly if Deputy Richter happened to show up.

He continued to follow the flow of the water and slogged along the bank, hour after hour, fighting his way through brush and tripping over fallen trees. Finally after what seemed like half a day, he came to a highway. He couldn't see any signs but figured it had to be M-115. He was pleasantly surprised to find that his cell phone still worked. Harry sounded shocked to receive his call but agreed to pick him up even though it was nearly five in the morning. It was the kind of request that would have doomed lesser friendships.

$$\bullet \; \bullet \; \bullet$$

The expression on Harry's face said it all. He seemed unable to speak for a full minute and just stared at Pete after he dropped into the front seat like a 200 pound sack of grain and leaned back motionless except for his heaving chest.

"For the holy love of God, what happened to you?" Harry finally asked.

Pete could only imagine what he must look like. Clothes still wet and caked with mud, matted-down hair askew, scratches on his face. He closed his eyes again. If he'd been sure Harry wouldn't take it the wrong way, he would have leaned over and kissed him and told him he loved him.

"Where's your car?" Harry asked, apparently feeling a need to talk because Pete had yet to utter a word.

Pete forced out an answer. "Someplace near Thompsonville."

Harry studied him. "There was a big fire over that way. Did you see it?"

Pete nodded. He was exhausted, but he knew he owed his friend an explanation. He took three or four deep breaths and laid it all out in a halting voice, beginning with his stakeout of Kurt Romer and ending with the run for his life through the woods and then seeing the fireball rise over the trees.

Harry was silent for a long time after Pete finished. Then he reached over and placed a hand on Pete's shoulder. "Pete," he said softly, "when we get out of here, we need to have a serious talk. You're going to get yourself killed if you keep this up."

Pete continued to lean back with his eyes closed. He just wanted to sleep. He knew Harry was right, though. He'd never intended things to go this far. It had been a challenge at first, but now he realized that everything could have ended that night on the road or, worse, if Romer and his friend and their killer dog had caught up with him. What would happen to Julie if he were gone?

"You're right," he said, just wanting to get past the moment. "But first, I have a couple more favors to ask. Could you take me back to my car? Then we need to find a way to get word of this to Bill Haskins without involving me."

Harry stared at him again. "You really shouldn't be driving around at this time of the morning looking the way you do. If you get stopped by the state police or even one of the locals you'll get run in for sure."

Pete forced a faint grin. "Do you have a change of clothes for me?"

"Actually, I might have something. But first we need to get off the highway."

Harry exited M-115 about two miles up and parked on a side road. Then he dug around in his trunk and came up with a golf shirt and an old towel. Pete slapped the towel in the dewy grass to moisten it and wiped the mud and dried blood from his face. Then he did his best to scrub his filthy jeans. He winced when he peeled off his soggy shirt; the scabs on his left side had reopened and blood stained his shirt. He used several BandAids fished from Harry's golf bag to tape some paper napkins over the worst of his wounds and slipped on the XXXL shirt. The sleeves ended below his elbows and he sported a pleated look around his waist, but no garment had ever felt better. Harry even came up with a comb. That was a miracle in itself since he hadn't needed one in years. When Pete finished, he was looking almost good enough to greet royalty.

• • •

The Taurus was still there, but Pete could tell someone had been inside the vehicle since he parked it in the tall grass. One corner of his rental contract stuck out from the closed glove box. It hadn't been that way earlier. Either Romer and his partner had spotted the car when they fled the scene and rifled through it, or one of the cops who'd been called in had checked it out. Neither scenario was good news, but Pete's money was on Romer because it looked like the glove box had been closed in haste. That meant they knew he was the one outside the house.

A fire truck was just leaving when they passed the two-track leading to the burned-out house. Even from the road, they could see there were a lot of vehicles still at the scene. Firefighters, Pete assumed, or cops. Or both. Pete pulled over and walked back to Harry's car. He explained why he didn't want to be seen near the fire even in his current pristine condition. They agreed that Harry would go in with his newsman's hat and they would rendezvous later in Thompsonville.

• • •

Pete found a diner and sat in the Taurus until the cook flipped the sign to "Open." Two grizzled men who didn't look like they had a big day ahead of them beat him to the door and took seats at the counter. They snuck looks at him when he walked in. He grabbed a booth in the rear and ignored the stares. Hopefully Harry would have something to tell him that they wouldn't want others to overhear. He'd tried to call Harry on his cell phone to tell him where he was, but got no signal. He'd have to rely on Harry finding him.

He went to the men's room and a glance in the mirror told him he didn't look quite as good as he thought he did. That explained the looks by the two men at the counter. Some water and a handful of towels helped. He returned to his booth and perused the menu. It was another one of those places that catered to healthy appetites. The All-American Breakfast consisted of a four-egg omelette, hash browns, a side order of ham or bacon, and a choice of Texas toast or two English muffins. All for $5.95, no extra charge for the grease. For another buck, you could get a steak as your breakfast meat.

Suddenly Pete was hungry and he was considering placing his order when Harry rolled in. He dropped into the booth opposite Pete, grabbed his menu, and placed his order after getting assurance from the waitress that he would still get four eggs if he had them scrambled rather than in an omelette. Pete ordered the same except when he asked the waitress if the cook could use Eggbeaters, she looked as though she were about to call the local authorities and have him hauled away for dementia.

"Well?" Pete asked.

"This looks like a decent place at reasonable prices," Harry said, eyeing the two men at the counter who were working on their pancakes. A short stack, Pete assumed, with only four pancakes, each a foot in diameter.

"I meant 'well' as with the fire. What did you learn?"

"Not a lot. They're planning to examine the scene more carefully when the light is better. One guy told me he doesn't think it was arson unless it was wanton vandalism. The place was ready to fall down anyway. They found a bunch of cans but they were still too hot to examine. One theory they're considering is that something flammable was stored in the house and it somehow ignited."

"It was flammable all right. Chemicals to produce meth. Propane or something, too. I must have been over a half-mile away when it blew. It sounded like a war zone."

"You think Romer and that other guy torched it, huh?"

"Either that or they accidentally kicked over a lantern or a stove and that set it off. I take it they didn't find any bodies." Pete didn't feel the least bit ashamed if his voice sounded hopeful.

Harry shook his head. "And no vehicles either. Romer and his partner obviously got away unscathed since they both would have had to drive."

"Did the cops pick up any signs that someone had been there that night? Like matted grass, that sort of thing?"

"No, because as you might expect, this wasn't exactly a pristine crime scene. When someone called in the fire, the first truck was on the scene in 30 minutes. They came roaring in and that took care of any bent grass or similar evidence. The driver told me he busted right through that chain across the entrance. Didn't even stop. He was real proud of himself and grinning like hell."

"That's good," Pete muttered, thinking about the combination padlock.

Harry was tearing into his eggs and side dishes like he hadn't eaten in a week and had just poured a third cup of coffee. Pete had to admit the food tasted good to him, too. Maybe it was the grease, but the breakfast seemed to recharge his batteries,

"We can't let him get away with it, Harry. Romer is the one who killed Cara, I'm sure of it. Now we've got him on meth charges, too. Plus he may be the one who ran me off the road that night."

"The two are not the same, you realize that don't you?"

"I do realize that. I'm hoping that once Haskins sees Romer is a very bad guy, he'll pull out all the stops to pin him to Cara Lane. I bet they'll find Romer knew her from Chicago. He has no alibi for that night, and a search of his house probably will reveal he had some kind of drugs he used to disable her. That ought to be enough to justify running additional toxicological tests on the body."

Harry shoveled another load of eggs into his mouth and pointed his fork at Pete. "What do you suggest? You don't want to step forward because of your own situation and I can't blame you for that."

Pete looked at him for a while. "But you can."

His eyebrows inched up on his forehead and a strip of bacon disappeared into his mouth. "How so?"

"An anonymous tip. You news guys get them all the time. Or at least you claim they're anonymous."

"Yeah? I still don't see your point."

"How about if you call Haskins and tell him you received an anonymous call this morning. That's why you came out here. Tell him the caller identified Romer as one of the guys running the meth lab. The tipster didn't know the other guy's name, but he gave you a description of the man and his vehicle, plus his plate number."

"So you want me to lie to the sheriff."

"It's not a lie. I saw everything. You're just not going to identify me."

Harry's eyes narrowed. "So this anonymous tipster saw everything. How about Romer's partner? You don't have much on him except that he has a scraggly beard."

"Not true. Do you have a pencil?"

Pete folded a corner of his paper placemat over and sat with Harry's pen poised over it for a few moments. Then he wrote down a number.

"Can I get in your trunk?"

Harry handed Pete the keys and in a few minutes he was back with his messy windbreaker. He unzipped the pocket and removed the piece of paper. It was soggy and he carefully unfolded it. He stared at the charcoal scrawl. It wasn't exactly a model of penmanship, but four of the numbers matched what he'd written on the placemat. Moisture had rendered the rest of it illegible.

Pete handed the pen back to Harry. "Write this down in your notebook: late model Subaru Outback, silver or light gray in color, Kentucky plates." Then he gave him the plate number he'd written down. He wasn't positive about the number, but had a high level of confidence as his investment banker friends liked to say.

"You never cease to amaze me," Harry said, grinning, as he wrote down the information. "How did you get the number?"

Pete fished the pack of Car Ferry matches from the zippered pocket and waved them in the air. Harry saw the bar's name on the matchbook cover and his grin this time was like the smiley face a first-grade teacher might put on one of her student's papers.

"One other thing," Pete said. "You might suggest to Haskins that he have his people check the lock on the chain for prints. That's one part of the crime scene that should have integrity if the firefighters busted through like the driver said and they didn't try to open the lock. I'll bet Romer's prints pop right out of the national database."

TWENTY-FOUR

A shrill sound grated on Pete's eardrums and roused him from his deep sleep. He fumbled around on his night stand to find his clock. The glowing red digits that stared back at him read 3:15. He shook his head, feeling disoriented. Then he realized that had to be afternoon time. The phone stopped ringing. He lay back for a few minutes and finally forced himself to get out of bed. Every part of his body ached.

He turned the dial all the way to red and stepped into the shower. He jumped away as the hot water hit his left side and repositioned his body to baby that side as much as possible. Twenty minutes later, he got out of the shower and checked his face in the mirror. It wasn't as bad as he'd expected. Some scratches and a scrape on one side of his forehead. He shaved, brushed his hair into place, taped some gauze to his left side, and got dressed.

He used the remainder of the ham to make himself a sandwich and grabbed a carton of raspberry yogurt. As he ate his late lunch, he wondered where Romer and his partner were and whether his ruse had worked. The authorities had time to check the prints on the lock. If everything worked according to plan, they would have an APB out for Romer and his partner. And if it didn't work, well he didn't want to think about that just then.

It was going on five o'clock and he had no idea what to do with himself for the rest of the day. Harry and Rona had tickets to a performance at Interlochen, and Lynn had plans of her own. She hadn't said what, and while he was more than a little curious, he kept his cool and didn't ask. He stared out at the lake and thought about the previous night again. And he wondered when his life was going to get back to normal.

He put on the Patsy Cline CD and settled in with his laptop and worked on the second part of his series on the old logging days in Michigan. After 20 years of writing nothing but legalese, it was nice to produce something people might actually enjoy reading. As he was tapping away at the keyboard, he heard laughter and giggles and looked up to see two girls park their bicycles against a birch and head for his back stairs.

"Hi, Dad," the one with the dark ponytail yelled as they scrambled up the stairs. "Surprised to see me?"

He got up and met them at the door. "A little," he said, trying to regain his composure, "but I'm also very happy to see you. You look great."

They hugged and held on to each other for a long time. He closed his eyes to fight back the tears.

When Julie stepped away, she looked at him and frowned. "What happened to your face?"

He was puzzled for a moment and then remembered. "You mean the scratches? I went fishing yesterday and slipped down the bank. Nothing serious."

"Geez, Dad," she said touching his face lightly, "you need to be more careful." She motioned toward her friend. "Do you remember Sarah Cranston?"

"Sure, it's been a while, though. God, you both look so grown up."

Julie looked at Sarah and did a little wiggle. They both laughed. Pete couldn't help but smile. If ever there was someone who felt she had the world by the tail, it had to be a teenage girl.

"What did I tell you about the music," Julie said, giving Sarah a sly look and giggling. "Is that the woman we talked about on the phone the other night, Dad?"

"It is. Patsy Cline. This is my second time through this CD. Do you like it?"

Julie looked at Sarah again. "Could we put on something else?"

"Sure," he said, walking over to his collection and flipping through the CDs. "How about Buddy Holly?" He handed her the case.

She stared at the picture of the man with the large black-rimmed glasses and wrinkled her nose. "This guy looks like a total super geek."

"Put it on and you'll change your mind."

She looked skeptical but slid the disc into the player. Her eyes widened when she heard the sounds.

"Wow!" she said, going into her moves. "C'mon, Dad, let's dance."

They jitterbugged through "Peggy Sue" and "Ready Teddy" and "That'll Be The Day." He barely felt his side. On a day when he'd been feeling sorry for himself, it felt very good to have his daughter home.

"Can we go swimming?" Julie said, blowing a strand of hair away from her face.

"Sure."

She grabbed him by the arm and whispered in his ear. "First you have to call Sarah's parents and tell them it's okay if I stay with them."

Yes, Pete thought, he'd been wondering about that little detail. She'd obviously decided to work around the technicality of clearing her stay with Wayne. The girl had skills. He thought back to a school program when Julie was in the fourth grade. She stood in front of the audience, dressed in what was supposed to pass for a pinstripe suit, and said, "I want to be a lawyer and fight like a warrior." And, like her dad, she wasn't afraid to get a little creative when circumstances required. Pete dialed the Cranston's number and made a mental note to have a heart-to-heart conversation with Miss Julie when Sarah wasn't around.

He sat on the beach and watched the girls cavort in the water and shriek and bat a ball back and forth. He didn't join them for the very good reason that he didn't want to expose his battered body and invite more questions.

They were hungry when they got out of the water. That was a problem because he didn't have much in the house after his own late-afternoon lunch. Some grapes and a few bags of potato chips were about it. They roared through those in no time flat and chased it all down with half a case of Fuze.

Reenergized, Julie rummaged through Pete's CD collection and went into a pantomime to express her feelings. She clutched her heart and clapped her hands and played air guitar and blew kisses. The best was when she slid a Julie London CD into the player and propped herself up on the floor in front of the fireplace and looked at her audience with half-lidded eyes while she sang along with the old torch singer in a sultry voice, using her Fuze bottle as a mike. Pete just smiled and shook his head.

He asked the girls to join him for dinner, but Sarah's parents had beaten him to it. Julie did tell him exactly what they wanted to do the next day.

He felt a void after they left, but bucked up, drove into town, and bought the best steak he could find. He slapped it on the grill and then wolfed it down while watching part of a baseball game on television. When he was finished, he walked down to the water and stared into the gathering darkness. He thought about Julie and how much he missed her when she wasn't around. And he thought about Loraine. He remembered the bright lipstick she always wore and how she would take him for long walks and talk to him about life. He didn't understand a lot of it, but he would sit close to her and nod his head and pretend he did. He knew he wanted a girlfriend just like her when he grew up.

• • •

Ebba was excited to see Julie for the first time in two years. She fussed over her for five minutes, to the irritation of a gang of tourists waiting for service. Pete finally regained control of the situation and herded the girls back into line to wait their turn.

They sat on a bench at the marina and ate their breakfast. Arne's boat was gone, but Kurt Romer's, not surprisingly, was in its slip. The girls amused themselves by feeding grain Ebba had given them to a family of mallards. He watched Julie and shuddered when he thought about the fear that had gripped him as he fled through the woods that night.

The next stop on Julie's itinerary was Sleeping Bear. He took a lot of good natured ribbing from the girls for not climbing the dune with them, but eventually they relented and set off by themselves. He sat in the warm sunshine and watched as they worked their way up, one step forward, a half-step back. They slipped in the sand and knocked each other over and laughed.

His cell phone vibrated.

"We're a couple of heroes!" Harry crowed, not bothering with social pleasantries.

"I never expected less."

"The information we provided led directly to the apprehension of that guy Romer and his partner."

Pete had been feeling pretty good that day, but suddenly he could have bounded right up the giant dune in front of him. "Did Haskins call you?"

"I touched base with his office this morning to see if there was any news," Harry said. "Haskins wasn't in, but he called me back from home. He said the state police picked up Romer and friend in southern Indiana. They found a shit load of meth in their car. Street value of over a hundred grand I understand."

Pete couldn't help but smile. "No kidding."

"Yeah, no kidding. Haskins was so giddy he was about to blow a happy valve. He's planning to hold a press conference first thing in the morning to announce the arrests. Reading between the lines, he wants to go public before the feds grab credit."

"It sounds like they bought your story."

"Hook, line and sinker."

"Okay," Pete said, "I know the destination. Tell me about the journey."

"You mean tell you what went down. If you're going to play detective, Pete, you have to learn to speak the lingo."

"Umm hmm."

"Anyway," Harry continued, "when I called the sheriff's office that morning, I insisted on speaking to Haskins and no one else. I laid it all out for him just like we discussed. He tried to grill me about the tipster, but I didn't have any trouble handling that. It was like an amateur dealing with an old pro.

"According to Haskins, they took the tip seriously and involved the DEA right away. This big team of law enforcement people then arrives at the crime scene. They were able to lift the prints of both guys from the lock. You know how they did that? From the sides," he said, answering his own question. "When a guy opens a combination lock, he usually grips the sides with the thumb and first finger while he works the combination with the other hand. With the technology they have these days, they were able to run the prints through the national databases right away and got hits on both guys."

"I'm not surprised that Romer was in the database, but it sounds like his partner has a record, too."

"He does. His name is Geron. He has at least two prior meth offenses."

"Did they find anything useful at the scene? There couldn't have been much left after that fire."

"They found pieces of equipment I understand. Stoves, metal containers. That sort of thing. They also found a burn pit out back with residues of chemicals used for making meth."

"Interesting. Were Romer and his partner caught together?"

"Yeah, after the fire, they hit the road in Geron's vehicle. They ditched Romer's truck behind a trailer park outside Thompsonville."

"I guess I did a good job of getting a description of Geron's vehicle and his plate number, huh?"

Pete could hear Harry grunt. "I wasn't going to say anything, but since you raised it, honesty compels me to say that you almost screwed up the entire operation. The plate number you gave me was wrong. One of the digits in your number was a two when it should have been a three. Fortunately, when they got Geron's prints, they knew his name and were able to get the correct information from the Kentucky DMV or whatever they call it down there."

"Good."

"You know, I was embarrassed when all of this came out because by passing on the information I was kind of vouching for the tipster. Next time we do this, you need to make sure you provide accurate information."

"I'll tell you what. I'm going to start carrying pen and paper and a waterproof pouch so I'll have them handy next time I bust a meth ring."

"That's a good idea, but no sweat on this one. I managed to cover for you."

"You're the most considerate man I know. How about Cara Lane?"

"Haskins didn't say anything about that. I'll ask him in the morning."

The girls were flush with adrenaline when they got down from Sleeping Bear and prodded him to drive faster as they headed for the launch point of the last leg of their day of adventure — a canoe trip down the Platte River.

Julie took the stern and Sarah scrambled into the bow. That left the middle for him. He wondered how long it would be before they all got dunked as the girls paddled furiously and jerked around in their seats and giggled and shouted instructions to each other. It didn't take long. They jerked at the same time and they were all in the water before he knew it.

TWENTY-FIVE

His hopes for a neat, clean end to the Cara Lane affair that had dogged him for weeks were dashed the following morning. Harry called again to report that he'd just gotten off the phone with Haskins and learned that Geron had confessed to everything and given up his pal Romer. Geron was on probation for his prior drug offenses and had decided to cooperate in the hope of gaining leniency or at least a reduced prison term for his latest transgression. That was the good news.

The bad news was that Geron had indicated in his sworn statement that he and Romer had both been at another abandoned house near Traverse City on the night Cara Lane died. He said they'd been doing a big drug deal with a Detroit street gang. The meeting was set for midnight, but the gang representatives didn't show until well after two. It was past four when Romer got back to his house in Benzonia. He was going down, as Harry liked to say, but it wouldn't be for the murder of Cara Lane

Pete felt like he'd been kicked in the gut. He replayed everything in his mind and realized that he must have misread Romer that night in the bar. He thought Romer had reacted the way he did because of

Pete's insinuation he was behind Cara Lane's death. In hindsight, he must have feared that Pete was onto his meth activities.

He'd been so sure, convinced even, that Romer was responsible for Cara's death. And whether there was damage to his truck or not, Pete had absolutely no doubt that Romer was responsible for running him off the road that night. That still might be the case, but Romer now had an alibi for the night Cara died. Unless of course Geron were lying, but why would he do that? If he were going to give up his partner in an effort to save his own ass, why would he lie about that particular drug deal on that particular night? It made no sense.

. . .

Pete didn't want to talk to anybody and got in his rental Taurus and just drove. He put on the Johnny Cash CD Lynn had played at his cottage that night when they got together with Harry and Rona and turned up the sound. The Man in Black crooned about shooting a man in Reno just to watch him die and walking the line and falling into a ring of fire. When the CD ended, he played it again.

There was a line when he got to Art's Tavern in Glen Arbor. He wandered up the street and browsed around The Cottage Book Shop for a while. He bought a couple of books by Michigan authors and then returned to Art's and ordered a whitefish burger. Normally it was one of his favorite sandwiches, but today it tasted flat and unappealing.

He left half of the sandwich on his plate, settled his bill, and continued north on M-22 to the tip of the Leelanau Peninsula and then south to Sutton's Bay. There he found a place to park and looked out over Grand Traverse Bay. A stiff breeze ruffled the water and the sailboats tacked against the wind and skimmed over the surface when the wind was with them. As he sat there, he thought about Lynn's selection of music again and slipped an Eagles CD into the player. He listened as they sang about runnin' down the road and when they got to "Desperado," he turned up the sound, lost in thought. The lyrics wailed through the open windows of the Taurus and people looked at him as they passed. He was barely aware of the stares.

• • •

It was almost five when he got back to his cottage. He sat on his porch and looked out at Clear Lake. As he'd thought about it that afternoon, the only thing that had changed since Harry's call was that Romer was off the board as a suspect in Cara's death. He was still convinced that Cara had been killed; he just didn't know why or by whom. He also knew that the cloud over his own head was still there. In fact, it was arguably darker than ever with Romer off the hook. And he knew the search of his vehicle continued to be a ticking time bomb back at his law firm where Kral would pounce like a cat after a ball of string if he should get wind of it.

He knew something else, too. Despite Harry's concern, he couldn't just walk away even if he were out of the woods personally. He'd seen the grief on Marian Janicek's face both times he met with her. It was the same look he'd seen on his mother's face after they found Loraine's body in the river. He knew there was nothing he could do about Loraine after all those years, but he had to find out the truth about what happened to Cara.

The question that kept pounding away in his head like a drummer trying to claw his way into a garage band was, if not Kurt Romer, then who? He thought about Marian's lament that Cara seemed depressed recently and how it might have been linked to her past. He came back to the two possibilities that had stuck in his mind since the first time he met Marian. Cara's death might be linked in some way to her pregnancy as a teen that set her life on a slippery slope. Or, moving along the spectrum, it might be connected to the people involved in the bomb plot at the University of Oregon. He couldn't think of anything else that made sense.

It was half past four in Chicago. His law firm's librarian was still there when he called and he asked her to come up with every scrap of information she could find on the Oregon bomb plot and email it to him. Then he dialed Marian's number. She was a nice lady and he felt very sorry for her, but it was time to take the gloves off with his client. He just hoped that Hank wasn't home.

He wasn't, but Marian spent five minutes apologizing for his nasty behavior the day he'd appeared unexpectedly. Then she pressed Pete for information about what he'd learned. What did the sheriff have to say? Were they really investigating Cara's death? Had he talked to Cara's Chicago roommate again? How about that man Romer he'd mentioned before?

He told her about Romer's arrest on drug charges and did his best to answer her other questions. Then before she could go off on some new tangent, he hit her with the reason for his call.

"When Hank interrupted us the other day," he said "I'd just asked who you believe fathered Cara's child. You didn't have a chance to answer, but you need to tell me now. It could be important."

There was a long silence at the other end of the line. "Like I said, it was so long ago, Pete," she finally said in a tone that was barely more than a whisper. "I really don't want to say. It wouldn't do any good."

"Let me be the judge of that."

More silence.

"Look," he finally said, "if you won't level with me about everything, I'm going to resign as your attorney. You'll leave me no choice."

He could hear sniffling and felt like a shit to lay it on the line like that, but he didn't care. He'd been run off the road by someone who probably intended to kill him and narrowly escaped God knows what when he tailed Romer to his meth operation. It was all because he'd been poking around, trying to find out what had happened to her daughter. There could be some link to the problems at his law firm, too. Dammit, it was time for her to stop feeling sorry for herself and step up.

"It was one of her teachers," she finally said in a voice that was weak and wavering.

Her words hit him like a slap in the face. Could this whole affair get any sleazier?

"What's his name, Marian?"

More sniffling. "Mr. Diener," she said in the same weak voice. "Frank Diener."

"And this Frank Diener," Pete said, "do you know where he is now?"

Having broken through the psychological barrier, Marian answered without hesitation. "He's the principal at the high school."

Pete shook his head and anger welled up inside him. He thought about Julie and how vulnerable teenage girls could be. That scumbag had not only ruined the life of a young girl, but now he was in the ultimate power position over others just like her. How many young girls had he screwed or fondled on his way to the top?

"Is there anything else you can tell me about him?"

"He was Cara's soccer coach, too. He looks like a nice man when you see him, but . . ."

"Are you sure Diener was the father?" As a lawyer, he knew the hazards of falsely accusing someone of a crime, particularly one as inflammatory as statutory rape.

"Yes, Cara told me after she got out of prison."

That might be hearsay in a courtroom, but it was enough to put Frank Diener near if not at the top of his new suspect list.

"Do you know whether Cara kept in contact with Diener?"

"Cara said they would meet in secret after she got pregnant and he would tell her everything was going to be okay and that he loved her. He said they could be together after he worked things out with his wife."

"How about after she moved to Oregon?"

"Cara would write him letters and everything, but he never wrote back and never called her."

Pete thought about what she'd just told him and shook his head again. Lucky him that Cara had a judgmental father who drove away his only daughter.

"Did Cara ever talk about trying to find her child?" he asked.

"Sometimes. We both wanted to see that baby so bad. Course she's not a baby anymore. She's a grown woman now, but she's never even known her real mother or her grandparents. It's so sad, Pete."

"How about Hank? Does he know about this?"

"No! He doesn't know anything except that Cara got pregnant and wouldn't tell who the father was! You can't say anything to Hank! He'd kill Mr. Diener!"

Pete wanted to kill Diener himself.

• • •

The email traffic from his librarian had begun to flow in. Each had one or more news clippings about the Oregon bomb plot attached. Some were duplicates of the stories he'd pulled off the computer himself; others were new. He printed out the attachments and stared at the stack of paper in front of him. He'd made a mistake with Romer and concentrated his investigation on him because of his intense dislike for the guy. That had cost him valuable time and in the end he'd come up empty. He wasn't going to repeat that mistake. He'd go after Diener, but at the same time not ignore the other obvious possibility.

The Oregon bomb plot hadn't received as much coverage as the 1970 bombing on the University of Wisconsin-Madison campus. Still, a lot had been written about it, including articles in *The New York Times*. The local papers, not surprisingly, provided the most sustained coverage.

He poured over the articles, learning little that was new to him. A recent "where are they now" article chronicled the present whereabouts of the cell members. Weisner, who was now out of prison, and a woman named Cynthia Brotman, reportedly were in Berkeley. Arnold Frasor was living in New Orleans and Kelley Dotson had returned to his hometown in West Virginia. Cara, as he already knew, had been living in Chicago. George Matkov had died of cancer five years earlier. Corrigan remained on the FBI's most wanted list.

According to several news accounts, Cara had been represented by a lawyer in the Eugene Public Defender's office named John Stump. Pete thought about it for a couple of minutes and then Googled the office and came up with the telephone number.

He checked his watch; it was nearly four in Oregon. He dialed the Public Defender's number and asked for Stump. His call was transferred a couple of times and he was finally patched through to the office chief who was still there. She remembered the case but wasn't involved herself, and said Stump had retired several years earlier. She told him she wasn't authorized to give out his number, but that it was listed and Pete shouldn't have any trouble getting it from directory assistance.

Pete jumped through that hoop and dialed Stump's home number.

"John Stump," a hearty voice answered.

"John, my name is Pete Thorsen. I'm a lawyer in Chicago, but I'm calling from my summer place up in Michigan. Do you have a few minutes to talk?"

"Sure, Pete. What can I do for you?"

"Do you remember a woman named Cara Lane? I understand you represented her about 20 years ago. Her name was Janicek back then."

"Janicek. Remember her? Christ, that was the highest profile case we had in the office. What's your interest in Cara?"

"I'm the lawyer for her estate. I'd like to ask you a few questions about the criminal case if I could."

"Estate," he said and then paused. "Does that mean she's dead?"

"She drowned up here in Michigan a few weeks ago."

"I'll be damned," he said. "What happened?"

"It's not clear yet. On the surface, it looks like a swimming accident, but there's at least an outside chance she was murdered. That's why I'd like to talk to you and see what you remember."

There was another brief silence at his end of the line and then he continued, "Professionally, I'm not sure how much I can get into my representation of her. I have client confidentiality obligations, as you know." After a few moments he added, "Maybe the fact she's dead changes things, I'm not quite sure."

"I think it does change things," Pete said. He knew that was just a stab in the dark because he seemed to remember — he didn't recall the source — that death of a client doesn't relieve a lawyer of his confidentiality obligations.

Another pause. "I don't know, Pete. I'm not real comfortable with this."

Pete thought about it and then tried a different tack. "Look, even if your obligations didn't terminate with her death, the fact I'm the lawyer for her estate should effectively make us co-counsel and alleviate your concerns. If you like, I can fax you my Letters of Appointment from the probate court in Chicago."

Stump asked him to do that and a half-hour later they were back on the telephone.

"Okay," Stump said, "now I'm more comfortable. Go ahead, Pete. I'll see what I remember."

"You had her enter a plea, right?"

"Yeah, as I recall the evidence was pretty overwhelming. The feds found bomb-making materials under the floorboards of the house they were living in. Cara's prints were all over those materials. They also matched a typewriter found in the house to threatening messages that had been sent to the think tank. A lot of other evidence, too. It was a very tough case. We tried to challenge the search, but really didn't have any grounds."

"I read in one of the news accounts that Cara and several of the other defendants testified against Weisner. That got her a better deal I assume."

"That's right. He's the one the feds were really after. They already had his nuts in a vice, but I guess they wanted to make the case as much of a lock as they could. To be honest, I was surprised at the deal we were able to cut for Cara."

"How did she get mixed up with Weisner?"

"I really don't remember, but you know how it is with college kids," Stump said. "A lot of them tilt to the left. That's just the reality with their idealism and a lot of the influences on campus. I seem to recall that Weisner latched onto Cara early on, made her his woman and all of that bullshit. She seemed to be having problems with her family at the time so she was an easy mark."

"I understand that Cara and a couple of the others were seen around the building a few times before it was bombed. Did Cara help Weisner set the bomb?"

"It's not clear who actually planted the bomb, but Cara might have been involved. Weisner was the kind of guy who let others do the dirty work and set up alibis for himself. He controlled the operation with an iron hand, though. According to the other members of his cell, he kept control of the detonation device."

"I'm puzzled, John. It's one thing to be involved in radical politics, but only the extreme hardcore resort to that kind of violence."

"Did you ever meet Cara? She wasn't exactly an angel, at least in those days. There was a lot of anger that ran pretty damn deep. No question she had a big role in the whole affair, but the government was after Weisner like I said. He was one of the campus radicals they were determined to bring down. If that meant going easy on some of the others to buy their cooperation, they were more than willing to do it."

"Who actually made the bomb?"

"You want my opinion? It might have been Cara. At least she had a hand in it."

"Look," Pete said, "I was in the army for a few years and was exposed to a lot of military hardware. Even with my background, I couldn't rig a bomb unless maybe it was a stick of dynamite with a long fuse. I'd probably blow my hands off even then. How would someone like Cara learn about explosives?"

"It wasn't dynamite they used, I can tell you that. It was plastic explosives of some kind and a remote detonator. Pretty sophisticated stuff. Where did Cara learn? She wouldn't talk about it, but one of the prosecutors told me he believed she got her training from a guy up in Idaho. Remember Ruby Ridge? Well even before those days Idaho was a magnet for antigovernment types. In their minds, it was a refuge where they could set up their own little isolated state or something. I understand what tipped off the feds was a bus ticket stub they found in Cara's stuff."

"Any idea who the Idaho connection was?"

There was a brief silence at the other end of the line. "I'm not sure I ever knew. I guess the feds knew, though, because I heard they raided a couple of places up there. The people they were targeting had already moved on. I understand at least one of them might have been from the area in Michigan where Cara grew up."

"That's right, I heard the same thing. In case you aren't aware of it, John, Cara was questioned some years back in connection with the federal building bombing in Detroit. The Michigan militias were suspects. The guy in Idaho seems to have been the link that caused the FBI to question her."

"Could be. I never spoke to Cara again after she went to prison."

"Earlier in our conversation, you mentioned the hate she carried around. Anything you can add?"

"Not a lot," Stump said. "Radicals like Weisner always dress things up in terms of the oppression of workers, stuff like that. With Cara, though, I had the impression there was a personal element to it. I guess she didn't get along with her dad very well. She seemed to connect things with him losing his job."

"I know a little about the family situation," Pete said. "Her dad worked at a plant that made parts for GM. He lost his job when another company bought the business and moved production outside the country to cut labor costs. Maybe that's what attracted her to Weisner."

"That squares with what I recall. But whatever the reason, there was a lot of hate there. You could sense it."

"John, I really appreciate your taking time to talk to me. I have one last question and then I'll let you go. Looking back, do you think someone from the old days could be mixed up in her death?"

"Gosh, I have no idea. That was so long ago. Maybe that guy Weisner. I guess he's out of prison now. She gave evidence against him, but he was going away for a long time anyway. I just don't know, Pete."

TWENTY-SIX

The next morning, Pete was still thinking about his conversation with John Stump. Weisner didn't make much sense as a suspect, he decided. He had no connection to northwest Michigan that Pete knew of and there would be no reason for Cara to meet him at Clear Lake. If Weisner were hell bent on revenge, he would have done something in Chicago where she lived.

That left Diener, who did live in the area and had a history with Cara, or someone else. And he began to wonder whether that someone else could be the seventh member of Weisner's cell. Ted Corrigan. The fugitive. It was just a hunch, but all of the other members of the cell were accounted for according to the news story. Corrigan wasn't from this area, but that didn't mean anything. If a man were going to run, he wouldn't return to his home town where people knew him. He would go someplace where no one knew him. A place like Millport, maybe. He called John Stump again and asked him to fax what he had on Corrigan, including anything with his picture or physical description.

He sat on his porch, feet propped up, and thought of how to check out his theory about Corrigan. Only one way occurred to him, and he knew it was a long shot. He got on the phone with Harry and asked for the name of someone in the area who might have a handle on people who'd moved to Millport during the past 20 years. Harry thought for a minute and then gave him the name of a self-styled local historian named Art Norman. Harry was probing for the reason for his interest when another call came in that he had to take.

• • •

Art Norman met Pete at the door. He was a small-boned man, maybe five-ten, with thinning white hair and watery eyes. When Pete shook his hand, he quickly eased up on his grip because it was like grabbing the hand of a skeleton.

"I was excited to receive your call, Pete. Are you a historian, too?"

"Strictly amateur. I have a two-part series on the old logging days that will appear in the *Sentinel* in a couple of weeks. For my next project, I'm planning a piece on the recent development of Millport. That's what I'd like to talk to you about."

"I'll watch for your series. That sounds very exciting." He looked at Pete with a shy smile. "I assume you want to interview me for the Millport piece."

"I'll definitely want to do that, but first I need to gather some raw material so I can decide how to position my story."

"Ummm," Art murmured. His eyes continued to dart around, looking more animated now. "Have you seen this?" he said. He pressed a coffee table-sized tome into Pete's hands. It was grandly titled *The Homes of Millport* and chronicled the history of every house in town. His eyes darted between the book and Pete's face, seeming to look for signs of appreciation of his masterpiece.

"Very impressive," Pete said, looking up. "So if I needed a list of people who've moved to or from the Millport area in the past 20 years, you'd be able to help with that?"

"I think I could help," Norman said, flashing an indulgent smile. It was as though Pete had foolishly asked whether he could list all of the families that had lived in a certain gingerbread Victorian on Forest since it was built in 1890.

"Let me show you, Pete." He led him into a room off the kitchen. It had once been a walk-in pantry, but now the shelves were lined with files. He selected at random an accordion folder labeled "1997" and went to pocket "J." Norman had to be over 70, but his bony fingers looked as dexterous as those of a blackjack dealer as he sorted through the collection of photographs, news clippings, church bulletins, welcome wagon stories, and obituaries in the folder. It was clear Pete had found the right man.

"Where will you publish your piece, Pete? The *Sentinel*?"

"Maybe. I haven't decided yet. I might try to interest *Traverse Magazine*."

Art Norman's eyes jumped around in their sockets like ping pong balls at a lottery drawing. He rubbed his hands together.

"I think we'll be able to come up with a very nice piece," he said, adding himself to the authorial team. "You know, people make up a community, Pete. That's what it's all about."

"I agree."

"When do you need my list?"

"I'm going to be gone a couple of days. Could you have something by, say, next Wednesday? I'd like to start fleshing out some possible story angles as soon as I get back from Chicago."

Art shot him that indulgent smile again. "That's very doable, Pete. I thought you might need it over the weekend and I was prepared to work through the night so we could meet our schedule."

Pete assured him that wouldn't be necessary.

• • •

It was noon and Pete was already running on fumes. He'd taken Julie and Sarah to dinner Sunday night and stayed out later than he'd planned. Then he'd gotten up at four to drive to Chicago. He stopped at the office briefly, following which he'd met Mike Boehm for lunch at a place on Michigan Avenue. Boehm was dressed for business, but when he saw that Pete was in casual clothes, he took off his coat and tie, folded them carefully, and placed them in the back seat of his company Hummer before turning the vehicle over to the valet.

Boehm was cordial but his normal reserved self on the drive to Colcorp's plant in Bridgeview, a southern suburb of the city. They drove down Harlem Avenue and Pete amused himself by looking at all of the Arabic signs as they approached the plant. On the way, he gave Boehm a brief tutorial on the legal aspects of modern environmental law. Boehm asked good questions, he thought. Pete then outlined what happens in the due diligence phase of a corporate deal.

When they arrived, Pete discovered that the environmental problems were more serious than he originally assumed. The consultant described various remediation alternatives, none of which had a remote chance of being accomplished before the closing date the Colonel had in mind. Pete asked the consultant to come up with cost estimates and a timetable for each alternative. Any way you looked at it, however, it was going to be a problem.

Boehm periodically ducked out of the meeting and got on his cell phone while Pete and the consultant continued their conversation. Talking to the Colonel, Pete assumed. On their way back to the Loop, Boehm seemed even more distracted than he had been earlier. He weaved in and out of traffic at well over the speed limit. Once Pete had to cry out when he was headed directly toward two men in the crosswalk. They skittered out of the way and screamed at Boehm in a foreign language. Boehm neither flinched nor slowed down. Pete had a hunch he was feeling pressure from the Colonel to come up with a solution to the environmental problem that would let the deal proceed without taking a haircut on the financial side.

When Boehm dropped him off at his office building, Pete wasn't sorry to say goodbye. He checked his watch; it was close to four. If he went up to the office, he risked becoming mired in conversations and wouldn't get to the church until early evening when Father Joseph was having dinner or doing whatever priests did at that time of the day. He hailed a taxi and gave the driver an address on the north side.

St. Catherine's looked like it had been built early in the last century. Pete entered the sanctuary and looked around. He didn't see anyone and wasn't sure what to do. Churches didn't have receptionists. You couldn't just walk in and ask for one of the priests. He went back outside and followed a walk around to the rear. He saw a courtyard with a fountain in the center and a priest in a simple black robe kneeling before a statue of the Virgin Mary. He rattled the wrought iron gate gently to get the priest's attention. The priest didn't move. Pete rattled the gate again. After a few minutes, the priest crossed himself and rose to his feet.

"May I help you?" he asked.

"I'm looking for Father Joseph."

The priest eyed Pete for a few moments and then said, "I'm Father Joseph."

"My name is Pete Thorsen, Father. I'm sorry if I interrupted your prayers. Could I speak to your for a few minutes?"

"Are you here for confession?"

"No, I'd like to talk to you about Cara Lane. May I come in?"

Pete saw a flicker of sadness cross the priest's eyes when he mentioned Cara's name.

"Please, come in."

Pete opened the gate and stepped into the courtyard.

"Why do you wish to speak to me about Cara?"

"Are you aware she died a couple of weeks ago?"

"Yes," the priest said, crossing himself. "I was deeply saddened to hear the news. Were you a friend of hers?"

"I didn't know her very well, but, yes, I'd call her a friend. I'm also the co-executor and attorney for her estate."

"We will miss Cara. She was a very special woman. She's with our Lord now."

Pete looked the old priest. "Are you aware of how she died?"

The priest gazed into Pete's eyes and studied him for an uncomfortably long time. "We called her apartment when she didn't show up for our meals program. Her friend told us she drowned in Clear Lake." He shook his head. "Tragic, tragic."

"That's why I'm here, Father," Pete said slowly. "I don't think her death was an accident."

Father Joseph pursed his lips and shook his head again. "This is all so sad."

"How long did she attend your church, Father?"

He thought for a few moments. "Six, maybe seven years."

"Did you get to know her on a personal level? I mean apart from her attending services."

"Yes, I knew Cara quite well." Father Joseph told him about Cara's participation in church life and his association with her.

Pete listened and then said, "Cara left for Michigan at the end of July. Did she tell you why?"

The old priest hesitated, appearing to think about his answer. "No, she didn't tell me. She just said she was going to be away for a few days and we arranged to substitute for her."

"You mean at the soup kitchen?"

He smiled benevolently. "We prefer to call it our meals program."

"Father, just to be completely open with you, I had dinner with Cara the night before she died. I could tell something was bothering her. Did you sense that in her before she left?"

The old priest fumbled with his prayer beads. "Are you Catholic, Mr. Thorsen?"

"No, I'm not."

"But you are a lawyer, you said."

"Yes."

"We have similar confidentiality obligations, Mr. Thorsen. I'm sorry, but I'm unable to discuss what Cara might have told me in confession or when she sought my counsel on spiritual matters."

"Look," Pete said, "I know a lot about Cara's personal background. The child she had as a teen, her involvement in that bomb plot out in Oregon, the time she spent in prison. I'm not asking you about intimate details of those events. All I want to know is whether she had some concerns recently, whether she was afraid of something or someone. Things that might shed light on what happened to her that night at Clear Lake."

Father Joseph gave him a long look. Compassion was stamped all over his face. "I'm sorry, Mr. Thorsen," he said, shaking his head.

Pete stared back at him. "I'm not familiar with all of your priestly obligations, Father, but I believe you're carrying your interpretation of them to an extreme. I don't see how telling me your impressions would breach any confidences."

His sad eyes never left Pete's. "How would you know, Mr. Thorsen?"

Pete stood there and thought about Father Joseph's last comment. He was right; how would he know, but that was the point of his question.

"I'm very sorry, but I must leave now for evening prayers."

Pete looked at him again. "Father, I believe Cara was murdered. I also believe you could have information that might shed light on who did it and why. You obviously cared deeply for her. This is your opportunity to help see that justice is done. I'm going to come back tomorrow afternoon. I hope you'll reconsider by then."

He watched as Father Joseph shuffled across the courtyard.

• • •

Pete arrived at his office the following morning at seven-thirty, feeling more rested. No one else was on his floor. That concerned him.

Either the firm's business was down or lawyers were coasting through the Labor Day holiday. He hoped it was the latter.

Some newspaper clippings with a cover note from Angie lay on the center of his desk. The first item under the note was the obituary of Marcus Vrba. Pete stared at it in disbelief. According to the obituary, Vrba had died in an "El" train accident over the weekend. A companion piece quoted eyewitnesses as saying that Vrba either jumped or stumbled into the path of an oncoming train. Police were investigating, the story said, but the preliminary conclusion was suicide.

He leaned back in his chair and stared out the window and cursed his bad luck. Deaths on the "El" tracks were hardly a daily occurrence, but they did happen now and then. He recalled an incident when he'd just moved to Chicago. A man standing close to him committed suicide in that same manner. He shook his head. He'd planned to take another run at Vrba to see if he could get more information out of him about Cara Lane, but now that was out.

Angie walked in. "That's a shock, huh?"

Pete looked up at her. "I guess."

"It's a good thing you talked to him when you did."

"Yeah, but I didn't get much out of him. I was hoping to talk to him again. I'm convinced he knew why Cara Lane was in Millport," he said, thinking back to his efforts to get Vrba to open up. "I guess we'll never know now." He paused for a minute or two and then said, "Funny, he didn't strike me as the type to commit suicide."

Angie shrugged. "You never know about people."

Pete brought her up to date on his investigation. He told her about Kurt Romer's arrest on meth charges, skipping the details about his involvement because he wasn't interested in another lecture, and his latest conclusion that Cara was at Clear Lake to see someone who was connected to her past in some way. She shook her head when he told her about Diener.

When they finished talking, they moved to a conference room with a glass wall so Pete could be seen in the office attending to firm business.

Steve Johnson joined them and they poured over financial reports and developed a plan to improve collections to deflect criticism by the Kral group. Sears & Whitney, like most law firms, used a cash basis of accounting and it was greenbacks in the door rather than just accounts receivable that mattered. They called key clients about their receivables and met with partners and asked them to do the same with other clients. They also emailed partners who were traveling or on vacation and reminded them of their obligations to the firm. The latter was Angie's suggestion; she had an uncanny knack for sticking in the stiletto.

When they finished four hours later, Pete spent time with Angie again and discussed the search of his Range Rover. They decided the passing of time had pretty much eliminated his option of circulating a memorandum to the partners to co-opt the issue. He'd just have to take his chances that word of the search didn't leak out.

• • •

At two that afternoon, Pete walked into the courtyard at St. Catherine's. Father Joseph was there again, this time sitting on a bench. He wasn't sure whether he was waiting for him or just liked to spend time outside enjoying the sun while he prayed and meditated.

"May I come in, Father?"

Father Joseph waved a hand.

Pete took a seat on an adjacent bench and looked at the old priest. "Have you thought any more about our conversation?" he asked.

Father Joseph searched Pete's face with those sad eyes, like he'd done the day before. Pete waited for him to speak.

"Why are you investigating Cara's death, Mr. Thorsen? Isn't that a matter for the police?"

"The police are investigating," Pete said. "I'm the lawyer for the family. They asked me to look into things, too, because they're concerned the authorities will just brand Cara's death a swimming accident and move on." He chose not to get into the Janicek family dynamics or his personal reasons.

"May I ask why you believe it wasn't a swimming accident?"

Pete covered the main points, including his belief that the wine bottle might have been planted.

"Cara rarely drank these days," Father Joseph said, looking across the courtyard. "Maybe a glass of wine at dinner to be polite." He paused. "Are you aware she had an alcohol problem after she got out of prison?"

Pete raised an eyebrow. "No, I didn't know that." Suddenly he had a sickening feeling. Maybe she'd been so stressed out by whatever was troubling her that she'd gone on a binge that night. But that didn't square with his observations at dinner.

"Did she ever talk about her child, Father?"

The priest seemed to struggle with his question. "Yes, sometimes," he finally said.

Encouraged by Father Joseph's response, he asked a follow-up question. "Do you think that could have been the reason she went up to Michigan?"

He looked compassionate again in a way Pete never knew quite how to interpret. "Perhaps," he said. "Her child was always on her mind."

The priest seemed to be choosing his words carefully and Pete was trying to read between the lines. "How about other things in her past? Did she mention anything recently?" he asked.

Again Father Joseph was careful, like he was picking his way through a mine field. "I counseled her spiritually on some of the things she'd done in her life, if that's what you mean."

"Like her involvement in the Oregon bomb plot?"

The priest just looked at him.

"Let me ask my question another way," Pete said. "Had her past resurfaced in some way?"

There was a long silence as the priest gently touched the petals of some flowers. "Cara was never able to put her past completely behind her, Mr. Thorsen."

"That's why she went up to Clear Lake wasn't it?"

The old priest stood up. "I really can't say for sure. Most of us are prisoners of our past. Cara was no exception."

He looked at Father Joseph for a long time. "Did Cara ever talk about a student named Ted Corrigan? He was the only member of that group in Oregon who was never caught."

"She mentioned him once or twice."

"Is he living up in Michigan? Is that who she went to see?"

"She didn't say. Cara didn't open up very much, even with me. I always had the feeling that chapter of her life was never completely closed."

The old priest rose, looked Pete in the eye, and adjusted his robe. It was clear that the conversation was over. As he walked across the courtyard, he turned and said, "I hope you're successful in your investigation, Mr. Thorsen."

• • •

On the drive back north, Pete thought more about Vrba's untimely death. When he and John Fisher picked up Cara Lane's possessions, he had the impression that Vrba knew something. What, that was the question. He also thought about the police reports that had tentatively branded Vrba's death a suicide. Was there more to it than that? He quickly put the thought aside. There was no indication that the police were wrong, and he was beginning to see evil in everything that occurred.

A while later his mind drifted back to his conversation with Father Joseph and his comment that most people were prisoners of their pasts. His answer to Pete's last question, whether Cara had gone to Millport to see Corrigan, was telling, too. It was the best confirmation yet that he was on the right track with his analysis. He felt a surge of excitement as he drove and kicked himself again for becoming so fixated on Romer that he'd ignored other possibilities.

TWENTY-SEVEN

Art Norman popped out his front door while Pete was still coming up the walk. He clasped Pete's hand in his bony fingers.

"Exactly on time, Pete," he said with a satisfied smile. "You're just like me. You don't like to be late." He sounded out of breath and as excited as if someone had just handed him a tintype of the oldest home in Millport.

He led Pete into the dining room where a long mahogany table was covered with neatly printed lists. Pete couldn't help but stare. The two-color lists reminded him of ledgers that might have been compiled by some fastidious bookkeeper in the green eye-shade days. Ten names to a page, maybe 300 in all based on a quick count, with information about each person in a contrasting color.

Art stood by the table, beaming.

Pete smiled appreciatively. "This is perfect. You've been a busy man." He began to scoop up the lists but felt Art's hand on his arm. The look in his eyes showed he wasn't about to let the moment pass so unceremoniously.

"Maybe I should explain some of this," he said. It was more of a command than a suggestion.

He began to take Pete through the lists, name by name. As some snippet of additional information occurred to him, he would pause to tell Pete and then carefully note it on the appropriate sheet. He repeatedly reminded Pete that visualizing people was essential to getting a true sense of the community. To drive home his point, he might fish out a photograph of some house or maybe one of a family enjoying teriyaki chicken at the July 4th picnic.

Pete's head was throbbing when he left over two hours later. The last 30 minutes had been the worst. That's when Art insisted on brainstorming the article they were going to co-author, as he put it. He wasn't buying Pete's suggestion that he come up with some possible story angles for later discussion; it was evident he wanted full input from the very beginning. They wouldn't have to include all the names on his lists in their piece, he said with an earnest look, but they certainly would want to mention most of them. People were the community he said for about the tenth time.

• • •

Pete fed Art's lists into his small photocopy machine, waited impatiently as it ground away, and then settled in on his porch with the copies. He crossed off the names of people who'd died since moving to Millport, those who'd moved out of the area again, and those who were originally from the Millport area and had just returned to the place of their birth. Then he crossed off all women and the men who had moved to Millport before the time of the Oregon bombing. That left 64 names. He stared at the list and made an arbitrary decision to eliminate those who had moved to the area more than 10 years after the bombing.

He copied the remaining 27 names, in alphabetical order, on a legal pad. That was still a lot of people to check out. After thinking about it for a while, he dialed Art Norman's number, cringing at what he was letting himself in for. An hour later, his temples pounding again, he managed to disengage from Art's clutches with the information he was seeking: the approximate ages of the men on his pared-down list. The Oregon bombing had taken place 20 years ago, so to give himself a little tolerance, and allowing for misjudgments by Art, he focused on people between the ages of 35 and 45. Ted Corrigan would be 39 now so that should be a reasonable range. Norman was curious about why he wanted that information, but Pete adroitly deflected his questions and got him refocused on the article they were going to co-author.

He made a new list; it had 13 names. They ranged from a man who ran a seasonal fruit and vegetable store on the outskirts of Millport to one who worked at the lumber yard.

Pete studied the wanted poster and old photographs of Ted Corrigan that Stump had faxed to him. Corrigan was described as five-ten with a slender build, brown hair and brown eyes, and a fair complexion. His college identification card showed him with Afro-style hair. A man could change a lot in 20 years, but things that wouldn't change were his height, eyes and complexion. His build, assuming that meant bone structure, wouldn't change either, but weight could mask that structure.

The telephone jangled and interrupted his thoughts. His Caller ID showed it was Wayne Sable. He suspected he knew what the call was about and let it go to his voicemail. It seemed a little early in the day for the guy to be drunk, but with him you could never be sure. Besides, he had to get on the phone with the associate at his law firm who was working on the RyTech deal with him before he hightailed it out to see a certain lowlife who posed as an educator.

· · ·

Frank Diener had balked when Pete called and said he wanted to see him. He claimed to know nothing about the woman who drowned. Only when Pete told him her name used to be Cara Janicek, a former student of his, and that he was the attorney for her estate, did he finally relent. Pete could tell Diener knew exactly who she was from the very beginning; pleading ignorance was just a facade.

Pete entered through a side door of the school building as Diener had instructed and went directly to the second floor administrative offices. Diener must have been waiting for him to arrive because he was standing at the head of the stairs. No one else seemed to be around. He led Pete into his office and shut the door.

Diener slicked back his dark hair, which was graying at the temples, with the palm of his hand as he settled into his chair. There must be something about that affectation; he'd seen Deputy Richter do the same thing. Pete took a guest chair and glanced around the office. The walls were filled with framed photographs showing Diener attired in soccer and baseball uniforms when he was in high school and college. The *de rigueur* family photos covered the credenza behind his desk.

"Well, Mr. Thorsen," he said, showing a mouthful of perfect teeth that must have set his parents back a bundle for orthodontic work, "what's this all about? You said you're the attorney for Cara Janicek's estate."

"That's right. Did you have a chance to refresh your memory about Cara? You seemed to draw a blank when we spoke on the telephone."

Diener nodded and continued to show a lot of teeth. "Yes, I did. Boy, you've gone back a long time. It's been over 20 years since Cara was in school here. I was shocked to learn that she was the one who drowned."

Pete smiled back at him. "Yep, that was she. I understand you were a teacher here when she attended."

"Yes, I just completed my 25th year at the school."

"Impressive," Pete said. "But I assume Cara didn't come to see you when she was up here because you didn't recognize her name when I called."

"No," he said slowly, "I haven't seen Cara since she left our school."

"In addition to being one of her teachers, you were her soccer coach I understand."

"You've certainly done your homework," he said. "Yes, I was her soccer coach. She had some talent, as I recall."

"So you must have known her pretty well. Class, soccer practices, games."

A frown creased Diener's face. "Mr. Thorsen, what's the purpose of these questions?"

"Just curious, that's all. Are there other teachers on staff who were at the school when Cara was here?"

"A few, I think."

"Male or female?"

"Mr. Thorsen, I really am in a hurry and don't see where this is going."

"Bear with me a minute and then I'll explain."

"I don't have the personnel records here, but I think there are several women and two or three men."

Pete nodded. "Okay, I'll get to the point because I know you're busy. I assume you remember that Cara got pregnant when she was in school."

Diener nodded slowly. "Yes, it was very sad, as I remember." The guy was smooth, but Pete detected a hint of concern cloud his eyes when Pete mentioned Cara's pregnancy.

"Cara didn't leave a large estate," he continued, "but she did have a bank account in Chicago and some other assets. She didn't have a will and I've been researching who her lawful heirs might be. She wasn't married, and one of her heirs could be the child she put up for adoption." Pete wasn't an estate lawyer and had no idea whether what he'd just said was true, or for that matter the implications of the adoption, but it did take him where he wanted to go with Diener.

"I've been poking around trying to see if I can locate the child. Actually, she's in her 20s now. Anyway, I came up with some shocking information the other day. I learned that the father of Cara's baby might have been one of the teachers right here at your school. That just blew me away."

Diener steepled his hands and stared at Pete. His face looked a shade lighter.

"Have you ever heard rumors to that effect?" Pete continued. "I know it's ancient history, but I thought if I could identify the father, he might be able to steer me to the family that adopted the child."

"That's ridiculous," Diener said. He dropped his hands and began to fiddle with a pencil. "I've never heard anything about a member of our faculty being involved with one of our students."

"No? Do you mind if I call you Frank by the way? I'm not a very formal guy and you don't look like you are either."

"I'm absolutely sure," Diener said, ignoring Pete's attempt at informality. "It's defamatory to even make that suggestion."

"Humm," Pete said, "I guess that is a problem since we're talking about statutory rape and all, but I heard the story from two different sources and it kind of made me wonder."

"Wonder about what?"

"Wonder about whether Cara might have been up here to see the father of her child. Women can become pretty obsessed with finding a lost child, sometimes even after 20 or 30 years. A lot of things about Cara's death look suspicious and one scenario keeps banging around in my head: maybe Cara was one of those women who decided she had to find her daughter and she came up here and tried to enlist the father's help, but he has a family of his own now and is a pillar of society and didn't want to get involved, so she threatened to expose him and he panicked and killed her and dressed it up to look like a swimming accident. I know that sounds way out there, but that's what I'm thinking."

Diener rose from his chair, his mouth a thin line now. "That's absolutely preposterous. I'm sorry, I'm late for another meeting. I don't have any more time to listen to your twisted fairy tales."

Pete rose as well. "Well, I know it would come as a shock to everyone, but I'm going to talk to those people again and see if I can get something more specific. I have a feeling one of them knows who the father is but is reluctant to tell me."

He walked toward the door and then turned back to Diener. "Let's talk again in a couple of days, Frank. See if you remember anything."

Pete could feel Diener's eyes on his back as he walked down the corridor.

· · ·

When Pete got back to his cottage, he propped his feet up and watched the sun sink in the sky. The meeting with Diener had gone about as well as he could expect. He'd managed to keep his anger under control even though he knew he was sitting across from a child-molester. But even if Marian were right about Diener, that didn't mean he killed Cara or, for that matter, even knew she was at Clear Lake. He reminded himself again that he couldn't make the same mistake he'd made with Romer and automatically assume that just because Diener was a bad guy, he was guilty of everything. He needed to work Art Norman's skinnied-down list while keeping up the pressure on Diener.

He put a CD in the player, grabbed some iced tea from the refrigerator, and was staring at the 13 names on the list when his phone rang. He picked it up, knowing who it was.

"You sonofabitch, you just cut your own throat!" By the way Wayne Sable slurred his words, he definitely had been hitting the sauce again.

"Why don't you calm down, Wayne, and tell me what the problem is," Pete said, smiling to himself.

"I specifically told you that Julie couldn't come up to that cabin of yours." There was a pause and Pete could hear the rattle of ice cubes just like the first time he'd talked to him. "So what do I find out? Julie is at your cabin. My lawyer is going to take this before the judge, asshole, and get your visitation privileges revoked. The inter. . . the interests of the child are paramount in these cases." He pronounced the word "palamount."

"Let me explain a few things, Wayne. First, we don't call them cabins up here. Second, Julie is in fact at the lake, but she's staying with a friend whose parents are both there. And third, and most important, I have every right to have Julie up here, with or without your permission."

"You . . ."

"Shut up, Wayne. And here's something else you should know. We're going to be before the judge again, but it'll be when I file a motion to reopen the custody issue. You're nothing but a stinking drunk and totally unfit to be a parent."

"Listen . . ."

Pete slammed down the receiver so hard that the cradle skidded off the table and dropped to the floor. He stared at it for a few minutes and then picked it up. He was surprised to find there was still a dial tone.

Pete had been relaxed before the confrontation with Sable, but now he was wound tight as a banjo string again. The light was fading fast and it was too dark to take his bow out for practice. He pulled on a pair of trunks and headed for the lake. He splashed through the shallow water and then dove in and began to swim with a strong overhand stroke. He got into a rhythm and began to recite the names of the old Norwegian kings. *Harald Fairhair, Erik Bloodax, Hakon the Good, Harald Greycloak* . . .

TWENTY-EIGHT

Pete spent the morning visiting local business establishments. He fabricated reasons for asking people to point out the individuals he was trying to identify. He came up empty on his first seven stops. Too short. Too tall. Too swarthy. Eyes the wrong color.

Fred Beck, a local builder, was next on his list. When Pete called and said he was interested in remodeling his cottage, Beck suggested that he stop by his house at noon to shake hands and talk about his plans. When Pete arrived, Beck greeted him at the door and apologized while he finished chewing a bite of his sandwich.

Pete tried not to stare. Beck looked around 40, which would make him the right age, and was a shade under six feet with a wiry frame. His hair and eyes were brown, and while he was tan from working outdoors, his forehead had been shaded by the bill of his cap and showed a fair complexion. Shave off the neatly trimmed beard, change the hair and add some age, and the similarities to the young student in the wanted poster were striking.

"What do you have in mind, Mr. Thorsen?"

"Please, call me Pete. My place is on the west end of Clear Lake. It's 72 years old. Some work has been done on it, but it needs a lot of updating. A new kitchen and new bathrooms for sure, but I'm open to suggestions."

"Are you thinking about adding on?"

Pete shrugged, studying Beck's face without being too obvious about it. "I'm open, like I said."

"The reason I ask is that the permit process gets stickier if you change the footprint."

"I understand that. Is it possible to see some of the remodeling work you've done?"

"Sure," Beck said. "But I'd like to take a quick look at your place first. Based on that, I can show you one or two of the places I'm working on so you can visualize the possibilities. We can do it late this afternoon if you like."

"Gosh, I have a golf game this afternoon and then dinner." They settled on Friday evening after work.

Pete could feel his pulse race as he drove back to his cottage. It made so much sense. The fugitive from the Oregon bomb plot living in Millport under an assumed identity. Cara up here to meet with him for some reason. That fit with what Marian had told him, and what Father Joseph had implied, about Cara and her past.

But it also raised questions. How had Corrigan wound up in Millport, not far from Cara's place of birth, in the first place? How did Cara know he was there and why had she come to see him? Why had she acted so nervous that night? Had Cara threatened to expose Corrigan? Maybe out of vindictiveness because the rest of their old cell had done hard time and he'd skated? As Pete thought about those questions, he wondered how Diener fit into the picture. He was connected to her past, too.

He shook his head. Maybe he should just go to Sheriff Haskins with this new information and let him sort it out. Every time he acted on his own, something bad seemed to happen to him. But then he thought about Beck's wife and three kids and knew he couldn't go to

Haskins, at least not yet. He had to play it out for a while and see if he was right.

• • •

"Pete had the shot of the day," the Colonel said. "Four wood, right? I can't believe the way you curled that baby right in there."

"No time to warm up either," Pete said, grinning and sneaking a glance at Harry. He'd been late getting to the Arcadia Bluffs Golf Course due to his meeting with Beck and literally ran up as Harry and the Colonel were teeing off. All three of them duffed their tee shots, but Pete recovered and nailed that sweet four wood to within 12 feet.

"Of course then he blows his bird," Harry said with a disgusted look.

"Hey," Pete said, "I was just trying to take it easy on you guys. If I'd come out firing birdies, I knew you'd both fall to pieces. I wanted it to be a competitive round."

Harry shot him another dirty look.

They were sitting on the patio of the Colonel's Lake Michigan house, as he called it, just north of Arcadia. People in the area commonly called their seasonal homes "cottages" even if they were quite grand. No way the Colonel's stone and timber house could be called a cottage. A lake house, maybe, or a country house, but certainly not a cottage. He'd bought the house three years earlier from a Chicago commodities trader who became overextended and experienced a sharp reversal of fortunes.

Harry and the Colonel exchanged stories while Pete nursed his drink and thought about Beck. He was anxious to see him again, to size him up, to begin to probe. He wished he'd agreed to meet that evening as Beck had suggested. He would have had time if he'd limited himself to a quick drink with Harry and the Colonel after their round and then hustled back to Clear Lake. But they'd looked forward to getting together and he knew gulping down a drink and bolting would be unseemly.

The Colonel was fixing a new round of drinks. "See what I've got, Pete," he said, holding up a bottle of Thor's Hammer vodka. "I had to go to three different liquor stores to find it."

Pete grinned. "Sorry to put you to all the trouble."

"No trouble. I've got to keep my lawyer happy." He handed them fresh drinks. "Pete, I haven't talked to you since you and Mike went out to the Bridgeview plant. What do you think?"

"I'm sure Mike gave you a full report, but the environmental problems are more serious than I thought. I asked the consultant to give us some remediation options. We're going to have to negotiate the problem with RyTech. It always comes down to money."

The Colonel's eyebrows inched up. "I'm not going to give much on the money side. I told Mike that."

Pete nodded. "You may not have to. Let's see how it plays out."

"I mean it, Pete. They try to make me take a haircut and the deal's off."

That would be a mistake, Pete thought, in view of the price RyTech was offering. "Maybe they want the deal so badly you won't have to. As I said, let's see how it plays out."

The conversation turned to fishing. None of them had been to the AuSable since early the previous year. They agreed that they should take a couple of days and run over to the "Holy Waters," as they were called. That led to a conversation about whether the AuSable was open for fishing in September. Harry agreed to check it out and report back.

They sat quietly as the sun settled in the sky and agreed that it would be a nice sunset that evening. The Colonel was up and pouring again. Harry accepted graciously, but Pete begged off from another round. The Colonel fussed with the large umbrella to shade their eyes from the sun's glare.

"What's the latest on the drowning?" the Colonel asked.

Harry snuck a quick glance at Pete and said, "I haven't heard much lately. I understand that deputy and his detective friend are still investigating."

"He's a real loose canon from what I hear," the Colonel said. "Haskins told me at a fundraiser that he's going to wait until mid-September and then kill the investigation."

Harry looked at him. "I didn't realize you were that close to Haskins."

The Colonel chuckled. "I think he views me as a deep-pockets guy who will help fund his political ambitions. I've already helped him a little."

Pete thought about the Colonel's comments. Mid-September. He wondered if he could hold off reporting to his partners until then.

They sat quietly and watched as the sun sank lower in the sky.

"If Haskins engineers another drug bust like the one the other day," the Colonel said, grinning, "his party will probably slate him for governor."

Pete and Harry exchanged glances again. "Yeah, that was something," Harry said.

Hunger pains were beginning to gnaw at Pete's stomach and he volunteered to grill the steaks. The Colonel led Harry into the kitchen to whip up the rest of the meal. Knowing them, that would probably mean heating up a side dish or two in the microwave.

A half hour later, they settled in at the table. From the look of things, Pete wasn't the only one who was hungry. The boys in the kitchen had made a nice tossed salad and some *au gratin* potatoes that were out of this world.

"These are great," Pete said, "but I know you guys didn't make them. Where did they come from?"

Harry and the Colonel looked at each other, grinning like a couple of banshees.

"We had dinner at the Manitou a few weeks ago," Harry said. "We liked the potatoes so much we talked the chef into making a batch for us to take along and freeze. Zap them in the microwave and you're in business."

Harry got on one of his storytelling kicks and regaled them with his analysis of the dispute over construction of a new golf course along the lake. He went into detail on the battle between the environmentalists and the forces of development.

When he was finally done, the Colonel asked Pete, "How's your daughter enjoying her stay at the lake?"

"Okay, I think," Pete said. "But you know teenage girls. They get bored with anything after an hour."

The Colonel's face brightened. "I have an idea. Why don't I have Julie and that friend of hers out to Colcorp some afternoon? We have these new industrial robots I think they'd get a kick out of. Then we can take them horseback riding. Julie rides as I recall."

Pete nodded. "You'd have to watch them, but they've both been on a horse before. I think that's a great idea. I'll mention it to them."

They agreed to call it a night. On the way out, the Colonel asked Pete if he could stay for five minutes to talk about the RyTech deal.

"I got a call from their CEO yesterday," the Colonel said when Harry was gone. "He wanted to know where the draft Stock Purchase Agreement is."

Pete thought about the schedule they'd all agreed to when the letter of intent was signed. "That isn't due for another week."

"I know," the Colonel said, "but I've been pushing him hard to finish his due diligence ahead of schedule and he turned things around on me. He said the Stock Purchase Agreement would be out already if his lawyers were doing the drafting."

"Look, I'll meet any schedule you guys agree on," Pete said defensively, "but I don't think I should be held accountable when RyTech unilaterally changes a schedule we all just signed off on."

"Okay, okay, don't get your back up. I understand." The Colonel gave him a long look. "I mentioned in my office that day you seem a little distracted these days. I still get the same feeling."

"It's just that damn Wayne Sable," Pete said, scrambling for an excuse. "That's Julie's biological father. He's jacking me around again on visitation rights."

"That stuff can be a bitch," the Colonel said, continuing to look at him. "But just remember — we need to get this deal of mine closed. You need to clear the decks of everything else and take personal charge of things."

TWENTY-NINE

When Pete walked into the school the next morning, his conversation with the Colonel was still on his mind. He'd tried to keep his frustrations with his investigation into Cara Lane's death under wraps, but obviously hadn't been doing a very good job of it. Mostly, though, he was thinking about Frank Diener and how the guy dodged his calls. He climbed the stairs to the second floor administrative offices intent on having a more direct conversation with the principal.

Diener's door was closed. He knocked. No answer. He knocked again but there was still no answer. He walked down the hall to the school offices and asked to see Diener. A woman with short dark hair and green-rimmed glasses looked up from her desk and asked whether he had an appointment. When he lied and said yes, she got a puzzled look on her face and said the principal was out of town at a school administrators' conference and wouldn't be back until the following week.

• • •

Still smarting over the wasted drive to Hawkins, and under pressure to come up with entertainment for the girls, Pete called Bud Stephanopoulis and asked him to take Julie and Sarah tubing on his boat. Pete sat in the rear of the boat and acted as spotter and Bud took the controls. He started slow and then increased his speed as he went into a series of figure eights and other maneuvers. The girls skidded wildly across the water as centrifugal force took over. They shrieked and alternately asked him to slow down or go faster.

When they were finished, the girls thanked Bud and badgered him to take them out again before Julie had to leave. It didn't take much persuading; it was apparent he'd had as much fun as they had. Before going back to his cottage, Pete asked Bud about Gulf Investco. Even though he was retired, Bud was still connected in the financial community and hopefully would have some insights.

"Sure, I know them," Bud said. "That's a Middle Eastern sovereign investment company. We used to do work for Gulf. Are you trying to get some deal work from them?"

"No," Pete said, "I ran across the name recently. I was just wondering."

"Tough client to deal with. They're always trying to squeeze you on fees. I guess the managers feel that if they don't produce, they'll be in real trouble back home."

Pete thanked him and went back to his cottage with Julie and Sarah. While they waited for Beck, the girls amused themselves by playing Pete's CD collection. They would pop something into the player, hold their noses after a few seconds, and then try a different disc. Buddy Holly, to whom Julie had taken a fancy the day she arrived, and Bo Diddley were their clear favorites that day. They turned his porch into a karaoke club and sang along and practiced their moves.

Pete kept checking his watch, anxious to get another look at Beck and needed some photographs of him. He thought of the perfect way to get them without arousing suspicion. Since Julie would be leaving in a few days, he suggested that she take photographs of the cottage as it now existed as part of a "before" collection for a new cottage history album. He told her he was thinking of using Beck for the remodeling work and encouraged her to get a few shots of the builder as well.

When Pete saw Beck for the second time, it only reinforced his belief that Ted Corrigan was living right under their noses as Fred Beck. Julie tagged along as they toured the cottage and talked about possible upgrades. She seemed particularly interested in his ideas for her bedroom and took him back a second time for further consultation.

As they stood on the porch and discussed the next steps, Julie nudged her dad closer to Beck to position them for her shoot. She snapped pictures of them hunched over the notes Beck had taken and more important as far as Pete was concerned, from the front. Beck seemed uncomfortable when Julie zoomed in on his face but tried to be a good sport.

When they were finished, Pete walked Beck out to his red pickup.

"Fred," Pete said, "have we met before? You look familiar for some reason."

Pete thought Beck looked just a little uncomfortable, like when Julie had taken his picture.

"I don't think so," Beck said, reaching for his door handle.

Pete shrugged. "Funny, I thought maybe we'd run into each other somewhere."

After Beck left, Pete transferred Julie's pictures to his computer. The girls took their leave. Sarah's parents were taking them to dinner again and they didn't want to be late because there was a teen dance afterward at the Community Center. They were busy planning their entrance to attract maximum attention.

Pete printed out enlarged pictures of Beck and stared at his telephone for a while. He already had a date with Lynn on Saturday, but he didn't want to wait. After what he was about to ask her, though, he knew he might wind up having dinner with Harry instead.

• • •

When he called, Lynn kidded him about getting his dates mixed up. Pete denied his memory was faulty and explained that he had something he wanted to talk to her about. He cloaked it in mystery and after getting in some good-natured ribbing, she invited him over. He rapped on her door an hour later with a file folder in one hand and a chilled bottle of Terre di Tufi in the other. The Italian white wine, one of his favorites, was intended as a bribe.

"I only agreed to let you come over because you sounded so mysterious," she said. "I'm a sucker for mysteries. It's about your investigation, right?"

"There might be some connection," he said.

He stepped inside and looked around. A large fireplace made of native stone dominated the living room. The room was comfortably furnished with lots of color. Not floral prints, but Native American rugs and throw blankets and other adornments. Watercolors covered the walls.

"These are great," he said, walking around the room and looking at the paintings. He looked at her. "Would you do a piece for me?"

"Depends on whether we're still friends after I find out what the mystery is." She studied the label on the wine bottle. "Mmm, Tuscany. You're off to a good start."

She gave him a tour of the rest of the house. After the living room, the most spectacular room was her studio that provided a panoramic view of the area through a plate glass window.

Pete opened the wine, poured two glasses, and they sat in the living room on facing couches.

"Before you get me sloshed, I demand to know what this big mystery is."

Pete dug into his folder and pulled out the FBI wanted posters for Ted Corrigan and handed them to her.

She looked at the posters and cocked an eye. "It looks like you've been hanging around the post office."

"I got the posters from the lawyer in Oregon who represented Cara Lane at her criminal trial. I'm pretty sure this guy — he's still a fugitive — is living right here in our community."

Lynn stopped studying the posters and stared at him for a few moments. "You're kidding."

"No, I'm not. Can you keep this confidential?"

She continued to stare at him and finally nodded slowly.

Pete laid it all out, how Cara Lane had gotten pregnant while in high school and then became mixed up in a bomb plot while she was in college. A kid named Ted Corrigan, he told her, was involved in the plot as well, but fled and was never apprehended. Lynn flinched when he described the bombing and looked troubled when he told her about his conversations with Marian Janicek and Father Joseph.

"Everything points to the fact Cara was up here to see someone and it was serious enough to make her very nervous. At first, I thought it was that guy Romer, but when he got busted on drug charges . . ."

"That was you, too, wasn't it? I know Harry claimed he received an anonymous tip, but I had a feeling that was something the two of you cooked up. I saw those scratches on your face and somehow just knew."

Pete took another sip of wine. "Anyway, with Romer off the hook . . ."

"Am I right?" she asked.

"Let's just say Harry and I talked about it," Pete said, not meeting her eyes. "As I was saying, with Romer off the hook, I began to reevaluate things and concluded the connection to the 'old days' had to be one of two things. It involved either Cara's child whom she gave up for adoption or the people associated with that campus bomb plot 20 years ago."

"I can't believe that teacher is now the principal," she said. "God, that makes me sick. You must feel the same way."

He stared at the Navajo rug between the two sofas. "I do," he said. "I'm planning to see him again next week when he gets back in town." He went on to tell her how he'd gone about identifying Fred Beck.

"Why don't you take all of this to the sheriff? It seems to me you've got plenty."

"I'd like to," Pete said, looking troubled, "but I still could be wrong. Beck has a wife and three kids. I can't just go charging forward like I have him cold. I've already been wrong once," he said, thinking of Romer. He looked at her for a few moments. "I need your help."

"Why are you so nervous about this? I told you at your place that I overreacted and would be happy to act as a sounding board for you." She looked at him with a wary glint in her eyes. "Or did you want something more than brainstorming?"

"A little more," he said. He pointed at the Ted Corrigan wanted posters lying on the couch beside her. "I need someone with art skills to dummy-up a few of those."

She looked at the posters and then back at him. "Why don't you just copy them?"

"Because I need something called age-progression posters."

Lynn was silent for a minute or two. "I get it," she said without a trace of a smile. "You want me to forge FBI wanted posters to look like Fred Beck."

"Yes."

She continued to look at him. "Isn't that illegal?"

"It might be if we were going to show them to people, but I only plan to use them with Beck to rattle him."

"What if he takes the posters to the sheriff?"

"He won't," Pete said. "I'm convinced Beck is Ted Corrigan so the last thing he'll want to do is involve the law. And if by some chance he isn't Corrigan, he won't want to go to the sheriff anyway because word will trickle out that he might have been the one Cara met up here and that would cause problems at home."

She stared at the old picture of Beck. "How would I even do what you want? I don't know Beck and have no idea what he looks like."

Pete reached into his folder, plucked out the photographs Julie had taken, and handed them to her. "I've been considering engaging Mr. Beck to do some work on my cottage," he said.

When Lynn smiled and shook her head after studying the photographs, he knew he had a partner. She refilled their glasses and went to her studio. He watched as she began roughing out several sketches.

An hour later she said, "Would something like this work?"

He took a closer look. There were three sketches. One showed an older Beck with bushy hair and clean-shaven. Another showed him with longish hair and a neatly trimmed moustache. The third showed him with a carefully-trimmed beard and thinning hair.

"We can't just do one poster that looks exactly like Beck now," she explained, "or it will appear too suspicious. We need several variations that show how Corrigan might have aged over the years."

"Have you done this before?" he asked.

"No, why?"

"You seemed to know exactly what I wanted."

"I watch a lot of crime shows," she said, giving him a coy look. "Most age progression shots are done by computer today, but I doubt that a guy like Beck would know that." She took the posters back. "I'll do a better job when I'm sober."

Lynn put away the tools of her craft and they returned to the living room. She dribbled the last of the Terre di Tufi into their glasses and looked at the bottle.

"Empty. I guess we either have to go thirsty or break out my cheap stuff."

"Sit tight." He went out to his car and returned with a soft-sided cooler. He unzipped the top and pulled out another bottle of the wine.

She watched with a smile on her face. "Why didn't you bring in both bottles when you came?"

"Just planning for contingencies," he said as the cork popped. "If I wasn't able to talk you into helping, I was planning to take the second bottle to a beach somewhere and get very drunk."

She gave him a funny look. "I told you I'd help. Maybe it goes a little beyond brainstorming, but it's still behind the scenes."

He hesitated, then said sheepishly, "I thought this might be stretching things."

"Maybe it is, but I didn't bite your head off, did I?"

"No, you didn't." He was beginning to feel the effects of all the wine. By the way Lynn was looking at him, she was, too.

"Do you always sit across the room from women you date?"

"Not always," he said, moving to her sofa and taking a seat alongside her. She took his hand and kept looking at him with those eyes. Then she snuggled close and took another sip of her wine. He smelled the faint scent of her perfume and caressed her hair.

"Isn't this a lot better than some crummy old beach?" she asked as her lips brushed his neck.

"Much." He continued to stroke her hair, then pulled her close and kissed her. Softly at first, running his tongue over her lips, then more urgently. She kissed him back and they clung to each other for a long time. He slid his hand down and cupped her breast, not knowing what kind of reception he'd get. She gave a little moan and he began to fumble with her buttons. Either he was out of practice or the small volts that shot through his body each time she caressed his inner thigh were completely messing up his concentration. She helped him with the buttons and for the rest of the night, he forgot all about Cara Lane.

THIRTY

Pete arrived at the construction site early. The house Beck & Co. was rehabbing wasn't quite as grand as the Colonel's, but it did offer a similar splendid view of Lake Michigan. The site was the usual jumble of dumpsters, stacks of lumber, bales of roofing and other construction materials. The smell of fresh-cut wood hung in the air. Maybe some of Beck's crew had been working for a couple of hours even though it was Sunday.

He'd always enjoyed construction sites. Not the urban sites where heavy equipment pounded away and dust swirled and mud covered the sidewalk when it rained. More manageable sites where real wood was used and the sounds came from saws and hammers and the voices of workmen and maybe a portable radio blaring some Waylon.

He remembered tagging along with his father as a boy. Lars Thorsen didn't do nice houses like the one he was looking at; people didn't think of him that way. They came to him for small projects. A shed, maybe, or a pump house. But he brought the same craftsmanship to those projects as he would to the most imposing mansion. Pete remembered watching his father cut a two-by-four with his handsaw with absolute precision and dreamed of the day when L. Thorsen & Son would build the grandest homes in the county. It never happened, though. A man needs to know his limitations, the old line goes, and Lars Thorsen's limitations had been drummed into him for so long he just accepted them.

It had been quite a week. Seeing Julie made him realize how much he missed not having her around on a regular basis. And Lynn had stirred feelings in him he hadn't known since Doris died. He'd worried about how things would be after Friday night, but could have spared himself the concern. They were just fine.

He'd picked her up at two on Saturday, collected his wanted posters, and then headed for the Little River Casino just north of Manistee. The parking lot was packed, which surprised both of them. They joked about how decadent it was to spend a nice summer afternoon inside a gaming hall. They played the slots and wandered around and watched the people. Lynn insisted on playing blackjack, claiming to know a system from a friend. They blew right through the 100 bucks they'd budgeted, then matched that and blew through it as well. They had a good time trying to figure out what element of the system they'd gotten wrong.

After leaving the casino, they headed back north and did some shopping at McBeth in Onekama owned by friends of his. Lynn was in a good mood and he watched her stock up on M-22 coffee mugs and tee-shirts. That was only a start and they walked out of the marvelous little shop with two large, bulging shopping bags. They topped off the day by having a nice dinner and then spent the night at her place after he checked with Julie about her plans for the evening.

Beck clattered in right on time in his red Toyota pickup and gave Pete a tour of the site. He explained infrastructure issues and what they were doing in each room and how that might translate to Pete's cottage. Pete was anxious to get to the topic of the moment, but listened attentively because he really was thinking about making improvements to his place. When they finished, they went outside and sat on a pile of lumber and talked about things like scheduling. Pete decided it was time.

"Are you from Millport, Fred?"

"No," Beck said, seemingly surprised at the sudden shift in the conversation, "but I've been here for 18 years so I'm almost a native."

"Where were you born?" As Pete asked the question, he saw that look cloud Beck's eyes again.

"Southern Indiana. Small town. No one's ever heard of it."

"I'm from a small town myself," Pete said. "What's the name?"

The wheels seemed to grind in Beck's mind. He named the town and Pete made a mental note of it. Beck was right, though; he'd never heard of the place.

"How did a Hoosier boy wind up this far north?"

Beck seemed to be getting increasingly uncomfortable with the conversation and fidgeted with the lumber. He shrugged. "Our family used to vacation in the Traverse City area when I was a kid. I like it up here."

Pete nodded. "It's a great area. Very similar to where I grew up in Wisconsin. Funny thing. As a boy, I couldn't wait to escape and get to the big city to make my mark, and these days I get out of the city whenever I can." They both laughed at the irony.

"Pete," Beck said, "I've got to get home for dinner. Why don't you give me a week or so to sketch out some ideas and then we can get together again."

"Makes sense," Pete said. Then he stared at Beck for a few moments and shook his head. "Darn, Fred, I look at you and just know I've seen you somewhere. Where did you go to college?"

Now it looked like Beck's antennae were on maximum alert. "I took some courses at Northwestern Michigan College," he said after a moment. "Why?"

Pete ignored his question and did everything but scratch his head. "I did graduate work at the University of Oregon 20 years ago, before I went to law school. Did you have a reddish Afro in those days?"

The alarm bells clanging in Beck's head were almost loud enough for Pete to hear.

"No," Beck said, rising to his feet. "I never went to school in Oregon. You must be thinking of someone else."

Pete rose too and looked squarely at Beck. "I think your memory is a little faulty, Fred." He pulled out photocopies of the original FBI wanted poster and the age-progression fakes Lynn had prepared. "This is you, isn't it?" he said, pointing to the one that showed him with a beard. "You were Ted Corrigan in those days."

The color drained from Beck's face. He looked at the posters, then back at Pete. His jaw muscles twitched. "That's not me."

"It sure looks like you."

Beck stared at him, looking confused, like things were spinning out of control and he didn't have the faintest idea what to do about it. Pete's mind flashed back to his meeting with Diener. Maybe he should have taken a tougher line with him, too. It seemed to work.

He continued to bore in. "Cara Lane — you know, that woman who drowned? — came up here to see you, didn't she?"

"This is crazy!" Beck's fingers tightened on a piece of two-by-four. "I didn't even know Cara Lane!"

"Don't do it Fred," Pete said, pointing to the two-by-four. "You don't want another criminal charge to have to deal with."

Beck's hand continued to clutch the two-by-four in a white-knuckle grip. He glanced at it and then back at Pete.

"You knew Cara from the University of Oregon, didn't you?" Pete said. "You're the seventh member of the group that bombed that building. The one who was never caught."

"That's not true," Beck pleaded, shaking his head. "I told you, I didn't know Cara Lane."

"Well, there's one way to find out. I'll call Sheriff Haskins and we can go down to see him. The FBI has Ted Corrigan's fingerprints on file so it shouldn't take long to determine whether you're lying. Haskins can also get a team out to check your vehicles for hair and fibers and fingerprints and stuff. It's amazing what those forensics guys can do these days." He flipped open his cell phone and began to punch in a number.

Beck's eyes were riveted on the phone and his hands trembled like birch leaves in a stiff breeze. "Wait," he said, the resignation clear from his tone. "Please wait."

Pete stopped and stared at him. When Beck didn't say anything, Pete punched in several more digits.

"Please, I said stop. It's not like you said."

"Well you better tell me how it was then because I don't have any more time for your bullshit."

Beck's shoulders slumped and he sat down on the lumber pile again and dropped the two-by-four. "I knew Cara Lane, but not from the University of Oregon."

"Tell me, Fred."

He stared at the pile of lumber for a long time. "I met Cara when we were both at Northwestern Michigan College. I was working in Traverse City at the time. She'd just gotten out of prison and moved back to this area." He paused.

"And?"

"We became close friends. She told me about what happened in Oregon and her time in prison and everything."

"Why was she up here, Fred?"

He swallowed and wet his lips. "Some people were trying to involve her in something and she didn't want to go through with it. She wanted to talk it over with me."

"So you admit she came to see you."

"Yes, me and I think one of those people I mentioned. I picked her up at the airport and then saw her again Thursday night. That was the last time."

"What were these people trying to involve her in? Another bomb plot?"

"I don't know. They knew about her past."

"Who are 'they?' One of the militia groups?"

"She didn't tell me!" His voice was whiny, almost pleading.

"Alright, Fred, let's come at this from another direction. How did they get in contact with her in the first place?"

Beck's hands continued to shake. "There was some guy from around here who lived in Idaho when she was in college," he said, wetting his lips again. "A former army guy. One of those survivalists or whatever they called them in those days. He contacted her. I think she knew someone else associated with the group, too."

"Who?"

"I told you, I don't know! She didn't want to involve me so she didn't mention names."

"The Idaho guy trained her in the use of explosives. Why didn't he handle it himself? Why involve the pupil?"

Beck shrugged. "Cara said the government watches him like a hawk. That's all I know."

"Is he here or still in Idaho?"

"I'm not sure," Beck said weakly. "Cara said he was back here for a while, but I don't know where he is now."

Pete thought about what Marian had told him. "How about the child Cara had when she was in high school? Did she ever talk about that?"

Beck appeared to be counting the boards in the pile. "Sometimes," he mumbled.

"But her trip up here had nothing to do with that."

Beck continued to stare at the lumber. "She didn't say." Then he added, "I don't think so."

"And you have no idea who that other shadowy person is. The one she supposedly met after she had dinner with me."

Beck looked irritated. "I told you twice! I don't know!"

"I talked to the lawyer in Oregon who represented Cara. He said she carried around a lot of hate. He thought it had something to do with her unhappy family life. Do you know anything about that?"

Beck paused for a moment, as if trying to collect his thoughts. "Her dad lost his job when a foreign investor bought his company. She hated those people who ship jobs overseas."

Pete stared at him for a long time. "So what you're telling me, Fred, is that you're not the fugitive, but you were a close friend of Cara's and that's how you know all this stuff."

He licked his lips again. "Yes. We stayed in touch by telephone after she moved to Chicago. We talked every few weeks."

"Did you ever visit her in Chicago?"

Beck shook his head. "I've never even been to Chicago."

Pete stared at Beck for a long time and then said, "I think you're lying, Fred. I think you're the fugitive. I think Cara found out you were living up here under a false identity and threatened to expose you. It's not difficult to understand why she'd want to do that. She spent three years in a maximum security women's prison and little Teddy Corrigan just disappears and goes on to lead the good life in her old back yard. That would bring out the hate in anyone. And when you weren't able to talk her out of extorting you or blowing the whistle, you killed her and dressed it up as a swimming accident. That's what really happened, isn't it?"

"No! None of that is true!" He picked up the two-by-four again. Pete flinched and ducked back, but instead of swinging it at him, Beck smashed it into the pile of lumber. The sound echoed through the early evening air and Beck grabbed his right hand with the other.

Pete expelled air from his lungs. "If it's not true, then the best way to clear things up is for us to go down to the sheriff's office together so you can tell him what you've just told me. Assuming the fingerprint match comes up negative, you'll be in the clear."

"I can't," Beck said softly, continuing to hold his right hand. Pete could see blood, probably from a sliver.

"Can't or don't want to?"

He was close to tears. "I have a wife and three kids. This is a small town. If I'm dragged into this, it will come out that I've been in contact with another woman for years. I might as well be dead because everything will be over for me."

Pete stared at him again. "I'm going to give you one chance to prove you are who you say you are. Do you have a photocopy machine at home?"

Beck nodded meekly.

"Then you better meet me here at seven tomorrow morning with copies of everything you have that will help convince me that what you've just said is true. Birth certificate, driver's license, everything. And make it good."

THIRTY-ONE

Beck was already at the construction site when Pete arrived the next morning. He had a BandAid on his right hand. Pete took the large manila envelope from him and left without saying a word.

Back at his cottage, Pete ate breakfast and sorted through the contents of the envelope. There were copies of Beck's Indiana birth certificate, Michigan driver's license, Michigan marriage license, Social Security card and various credit cards. All in the name of Manfred T. Beck. He chuckled; he would have used the nickname "Fred" too.

There were bits and pieces of other documents. The items of greatest interest were a copy of a student identification card and two transcripts from Northwestern Michigan College. The other documents didn't prove much: an Eagle's Club card, a couple of awards from the Rotary, clippings from the *Sentinel* about his business.

On their face, the documents appeared to support Beck's claimed identity, but Pete was well aware that false identification documents were freely available for a price. Millions of illegal immigrants in the country knew that only too well. The cheap stuff rarely stood up to scrutiny, but if a person had the wherewithal, he could obtain documents that were damn near impenetrable.

Pete got on his laptop and Googled the southern Indiana town of Tennyson. He was pleasantly surprised to learn that the town had been named for the poet, Alfred Lord Tennyson. He clicked on some links and found no Becks in Tennyson, but did find several in neighboring towns. The absence of Becks in Tennyson didn't bother him. People moved around a lot in this country and the other towns weren't that far away.

He checked his watch; it was close to nine. He dialed Marian Janicek's number. She answered on the second ring.

"Is Hank gone?" he asked.

"Yes, Pete, I can talk. I was hoping to hear from you."

Pete gave her a sanitized update, skipping details like his meetings with Beck because he didn't want to falsely build up her expectations. Privately, though, he viewed Beck as his first real break in the case. In the past, everything had been supposition and, he realized now, his own efforts to force connections. But now, whether Beck was the fugitive or just a friend of Cara's as he claimed, Pete was more convinced than ever that his suspicions about Cara's death were correct.

"Marian, when Cara got out of prison, did she move to Chicago right away or did she come back up here?"

There was the kind of silence at the other end that always signaled she was dealing with something emotional, "Cara was hurting so bad when she got out of prison, Pete. She wanted to come home and live with her family. Hank wouldn't even talk about it, so she lived in Traverse City for a while. It wasn't home, but at least it was close. That's when she changed her name to Lane."

"Did she attend Northwestern Michigan College?"

"Yes, she took some courses there and worked as a waitress in town."

He thought about his conversation with Beck. "When would that have been, Marian?"

She thought about it a while and gave him some approximate dates. They coincided roughly with the dates on the transcripts Beck had given him. Maybe the guy was telling the truth after all. He hoped so in a way, because unlike Romer and Frank Diener, he didn't have a visceral dislike of Beck. What Marian had just told him made him think, though. If she hadn't said anything about Cara living in Traverse City, what else hadn't she told him?

"How are things around home?" he asked.

"I'm worried, Pete. Do you remember when Hank came in and got so mad and everything?"

"I do," Pete said, wondering how he could forget.

"We had a talk just like you said we should. He got real mad again. I told him I was going to Oregon to live with my sister. She has a room and everything and said I could come if I wanted."

"He left just like when he found out Cara was pregnant. I was afraid he was going to lose his job because nobody knew where he was." He could visualize Marian shaking her head the way she always did when she just couldn't understand something.

"But obviously he came back."

"He came back, but now we hardly ever talk. I saw him crying once, but he pretended he wasn't. Then one day I was with my quilting group and when I came home he was fixing Cara's swing. I didn't say nothing, though."

Pete thought about that. Maybe a little straight talk from his wife was exactly what the bitter old fool needed. Then he got an idea.

"Do you think he'd agree to meet with me, Marian?"

"To talk about Cara, you mean?" She sounded alarmed.

"Yes. We both believe Cara met with someone after she left me that night. I have a hunch the person she met might be part of a group that's planning something. Maybe another bombing. Hank may know things that would help me figure it out."

Silence again. "I don't know, Pete," she finally said with a wary tone in her voice, "he doesn't have many good things to say about you."

"Are you willing to ask him?"

"I guess so," she said slowly. "I just hope he doesn't get real mad again."

"It's your choice, Marian."

Another silence. "He's off target shooting or something. I suppose I could ask him when he gets back."

"As I said, it's up to you. But if you do ask him and he's agreeable, I'll stop by your house later today."

Then he got an idea. "Tell him I'm dropping off some of Cara's things. That's the main reason I'm going to be there."

Pete knew the position he'd just put Marian in, but he couldn't think of any other way to try to find out what Hank knew.

• • •

He went for a run and then took his longbow out for some practice. His side still hurt from what he'd been through in the past couple of weeks, but he was feeling a lot better. As he stood eyeing the targets, he thought of the nine names in Kral's memorandum. *Hal Ackerly, Freda Ellis, Stew Landers* . . . He focused on the hulking silhouette in the foliage 20 yards away. He nocked an arrow and drew the string back to his right jaw while raising the bow in a single, fluid motion, trying to emulate Lynn's form. He held the bow steady, sighting down the arrow, and saw Kral's face flash before him. He let the arrow go.

Thunk! The arrow ripped into the figure's torso. *That's for Hal.*

He nocked another arrow and raised his bow.

Thunk! The silhouette shuddered again. *That's for Freda.*

It was close to 11:00 a.m. when he finished with Kral, eight on the West Coast. When John Stump answered on the first ring, Pete couldn't help but wonder whether he'd be sitting around waiting for the phone to ring when he retired. He brought Stump up to date on what he'd been doing and asked whether he had any further thoughts on Cara's Idaho connection. In particular, he asked Stump if he knew his name. He didn't, but offered to make a call to a guy he knew, a retired ATF agent, and call back.

Pete spent the better part of the next two hours on the telephone with one of the associates at his law firm who was in the office working on a draft of the Stock Purchase Agreement for the RyTech deal. They discussed representations and warranties, indemnification provisions and other nuts-and-bolts terms of the Agreement. He hated to put pressure on her on a holiday weekend, but made her promise to email him a draft of the Agreement the following day. He didn't want to give the Colonel any more reason to complain that he was the one holding up the deal.

When he was off the phone, he thought about Marcus Vrba's death again. He couldn't get the timing coincidence out of his mind. He knew that the CTA had surveillance cameras at a lot of the stops. He assumed the authorities had reviewed the tapes thoroughly, but preferred to see for himself. He called Angie and got lucky and caught her in the office. He screwed up his courage and told her what he wanted, promising that it was his last request. She sighed loudly and said she'd see what she could do.

Marian called back shortly after one.

"I told Hank that you were dropping off Cara's clothes later today and you have some important things to discuss with him and me."

When she didn't continue, he asked, "What did he say?"

"He called you a bad name and said he doesn't want you in his house."

Pete thought about what Marian had said. "How did he act? Was he really angry or did you get the impression he just felt he had to say that?"

"I don't know, Pete." She sounded worried. "I don't know if he'll be here if you come."

Pete considered the options. He wanted to talk to the guy, but wasn't naïve enough to believe that Hank Janicek would suddenly turn into a model of civil behavior. On the other hand, he had to start giving

Marian some of the things he'd hauled up from Chicago to get them out of his cottage.

"I'm going to stop by at five, Marian, and see if he'll talk to me. But if he threatens me again, I'll have to leave."

"I understand, Pete. When I talk to you, I always think about what a nice life you and Cara could have had together."

He hadn't been prepared for that and cringed at the thought and said he'd see her later that day.

Stump had called back while he was on with Marian; Pete returned his call.

"I talked to my friend at home but wasn't able to find out a lot. The guy we've been talking about is named Clem Moffat. I'm told he left Idaho some time ago and reportedly moved back to your neck of the woods. He's definitely still on the fed's radar screen. My friend called a couple of his former colleagues at the ATF and they would barely talk to him about the guy."

• • •

Pete made something to eat and then thought about what John Stump had said. It pretty much coincided with what Beck had told him. It wasn't much, but he was still excited. He had another name now.

The gravel crunched in his driveway and he turned his head and saw a sheriff's department SUV pull in. It looked like the one Richter drove. He was right. The First Deputy got out; he was alone again. Pete rolled his eyes and went down to see what this latest visit was all about.

"Why didn't you come forward and claim credit for the Romer bust?" Richter asked.

Pete frowned, feigning ignorance. "What are you talking about?"

"You know what I'm talking about. You were there that night."

"Wrong, Deputy. I wasn't there. But what's this all about? Did you just drop by to talk about some slimeball meth dealer?"

Richter smirked and headed back to his SUV. Then he turned and eyed Pete. "We expect to have the results of our search any day now."

Pete stared at Richter as he pulled out of his driveway and back on M-22. *What a prick,* he thought.

THIRTY-TWO

When Pete arrived at the Janicek house, Hank's dusty old pickup was parked in the driveway. That was a good sign. Or maybe a bad sign depending on what happened when he walked in the door. He hoped he didn't find himself staring into the business end of Hank's shotgun.

Marian greeted him with a worried expression on her face. He didn't see Hank but was pretty sure he was in the house because he hadn't seen him outside. He took his usual seat and waited patiently while Marian looked through the bags of Cara's clothes he'd brought along. She pulled out a chocolate-brown knit dress and ran her fingers over it. Her eyes glistened with tears. Periodically she'd dab at her eyes and glance nervously toward the kitchen. Hank eventually stepped into the living room with the familiar pinched look on his face and glared at Pete.

"I thought I told you I don't want you here no more," he said.

Pete rose from the couch. "I brought Cara's clothes at Marian's request," he said, sticking to the script. "I told Marian that since I'm here, I believe it's in everyone's best interests for the three of us to talk."

"I ain't got nothin' to say to you."

"Hank!" Marian's voice was more a shriek than anything else and Hank looked at her, warily Pete thought. She'd gone from sobbing to a woman who looked angry. "I want to hear what Pete has to say!" she said. "You should, too!" She jabbed a finger in his direction. Hank just stared at them.

Pete decided to give it a try. "When Marian first called me," he said, "I thought Cara's death might be a swimming accident like everyone else. But the more I looked into it, the more I became convinced that someone had harmed her and tried to make it look like an accident."

The hostile expression on Hank's face hadn't softened and Pete decided on a tack he hadn't rehearsed. He painted a picture of Cara as a woman who was determined to get her life back in order. He told of Father Joseph's obvious affection for her and the commitment she'd shown to good works at his church. He told about the way she'd continued her education by taking courses at Roosevelt University while working two jobs to support herself. He told how Marcus Vrba and others valued her as a friend. He fuzzed up the edges along the way, but did his best to help redeem a daughter in the eyes of her judgmental father.

Hank didn't glow with love and tenderness, but he didn't scream and threaten and call her a whore and a criminal either. Pete thought that was a good sign. The downside was that he'd gotten Marian worked up into another emotional state and she kept wiping her eyes and sniffling.

"But in spite of Cara's determination to get her life straightened out," Pete continued, "there were people from her past who kept trying to drag her down. Some of those people live right here in your community. That's why she was up here. She came to tell them she wanted no part in their violent scheme. I think they killed her to keep her quiet."

Hank said nothing. Pete couldn't tell for sure, but he appeared to be thinking.

"Hank, do you know a man named Clem Moffat?" Pete asked him.

Hank's angry expression changed for just a second. It was clear he knew Moffat.

"Well?" Pete said.

Hank's eyes bored into him. "Why do you want to know about Clem?"

"He knew Cara. I'd like to talk to him."

Hank continued to glare at him. "Clem's a good man. He's a patriot and the friggin' government just won't leave the man alone."

Maybe, Pete thought, but he's also a purveyor of hate who trained your daughter in the use of explosives.

"All I want to do is talk to him," Pete said. "I have a feeling he might have some idea what happened to Cara."

"Hank," Marian said, "don't he live on the old Johnson farm now? That's what someone in my quilting group said."

Hank's eyes flicked between Pete and the floor.

"That's what . . ."

"Quiet woman!"

"Where's the Johnson farm?" Pete asked when no one spoke for a few moments.

Hank ignored Pete's question and his pinched face had a smirk on it now, like Pete didn't know what he was letting himself in for. "What are you planning to say to Clem?" he said like he was amused. "He ain't going to be very friendly to a smart-ass lawyer who comes pokin' around asking him a lot of Tom-fool questions."

"I just want to talk to him. How do I find his place?"

Hank shrugged. "Beats me." He still wore the smirk and started to go back to the kitchen.

Pete decided he could find out where the old Johnson farm was on his own and shifted gears. "Before you go, Hank, I have another question," he said. "You've lived in this area a long time. Have you heard anything about any of the antigovernment groups planning something?"

Hank turned to face Pete from the kitchen doorway. "Like what?" He spat out the words like a bitter seed and stood looking at Pete. The glare was back.

"I don't know," Pete said. "A bombing maybe?"

His eyes bore holes in Pete and he grunted derisively. "I ain't heard nothin' about no bombing."

Pete was out of questions and viewed the meeting as a success even though he hadn't learned much. He'd gotten Hank to talk without bull rushing him and maybe that would set the stage for a more constructive dialogue later on. He stood to leave and thanked the Janiceks. Hank just stared at him as he walked out. Marian followed him and as Hank returned to the kitchen, whispered in his ear that the Johnson farm was south of town off the county road.

• • •

Pete stopped at a gas station to get more specific directions to the Johnson farm. The man behind the cash register scratched his full beard and eyed him suspiciously, but gave him what passed for directions.

A half-dozen miles out of town, Pete came to an overgrown gravel two-track that reminded him of the one leading into Romer's meth lab. *No Trespassing* signs were posted everywhere. The overflow mail had been placed in a U.S. Postal Service bin. He got out of his Taurus and checked some of the mail. It was addressed to Clem Moffat.

Pete bumped along the two-track until he came to a dilapidated house with some outbuildings. An old tractor was parked in the tall grass and a rusted-out car without tires rested on a set of blocks. He pulled in alongside the car. There was no sign of activity.

He sat in the Taurus for a few minutes, eyeing the house, then got out and walked to the front door. He knocked several times, but got no answer. He went around to the side and peered in a window. The house appeared to be abandoned. He checked another window but saw nothing. He remembered Beck saying he wasn't sure whether Moffat was still in the area. He wasn't by the looks of things and apparently hadn't left a forwarding address.

When Pete reached the county road on his way out, he stopped near the mailbox again. He got out and flipped through the mail. Some of the postmarks went back to early June. Either Mr. Moffat had been very inattentive to his mail or he'd cleared out months ago.

As Pete headed back toward town, he wondered where Moffat had gone. The government might know, but based on what John Stump told him, it seemed unlikely they'd share that information if he inquired. It also seemed improbable that he had anything to do with Cara Lane's death even if he had been the original contact between Cara and the plot leaders. Still, if he knew who the plot leaders were, that would provide the link Pete needed. Assuming there were plot leaders. He still hadn't foreclosed the possibility that Beck was lying to him and Moffat's presence at the Johnson farm for some period of time was just coincidence.

Pete came to the center of town and saw Kelties. According to Marian, that was the other hangout favored by the "crazies." He was thirsty after his road trip out to the Johnson farm and decided to stop. He got out of his Taurus, confident he wouldn't be hassled this time on account of his vehicle, dusted himself off, and grabbed a cap to make sure he was properly attired.

The place was busy. He looked around and was surprised to see the two men sitting at the far end of the bar. One was none other than his old pal, Big Red. That wasn't particularly surprising, but the thing that really grabbed his attention was the man seated next to him. Unless he missed his guess, it was Mike Boehm. He considered going over to say hello, but then decided to pretend he hadn't seen them.

Pete walked to the opposite end of the bar, near the pool table, and found an empty stool and ordered a Miller Lite. He wasn't a big beer drinker anymore, but it tasted good and cut the dust from his throat. He was watching SportsCenter on the television behind the bar and wondering how Boehm and Big Red knew each other when he felt something hard poke him in his back. He turned to see Big Red looming over him with a cue stick in hand. The sight of the stick caused him to tense up but he relaxed when he saw the chalk in his other hand and realized that Big Red's turn at the pool table must have come up.

"Our lawyer friend from Illinois sure does get around," Big Red said in a voice that filled the room. "Hey lawyer, you still investigating me?" His face was as dark as that day at the Whitetail when he told Pete to leave the Janiceks alone.

"Investigating you. Now why would I do that?" Pete said, feigning surprise just as Big Red had done that day in the parking lot.

"He acts like he don't know what he's been doing, boys. Damn, ain't that just like a lawyer?" Laughter.

A man at the pool table said impatiently, "Red, your break."

Big Red ignored him and said to Pete, "The next time you ask around town about me, why don't you come right to the source? If you've got the guts, that is."

Pete was about to turn back to the bar and ignore the big oaf when he heard a familiar voice. "I see you two know each other." Mike Boehm slid between them. "Les," Boehm said, using his real name, "Pete here is the Colonel's lawyer."

Big Red looked at Pete and then at Boehm and then back at Pete. After a few moments, he regained his bravado. His beefy face broke into a grin and he said, "I thought he didn't look like no ordinary lawyer. Pete, Les Murton." He stuck out his hand.

Pete stared at him coldly and then accepted his hand. He squeezed as soon as he felt fingers and saw Big Red wince. It was a trick he'd learned from a client. When shaking hands, the guy never waited until the palms meshed. He simply grabbed a handful of fingers and squeezed like hell. When Pete got to know him better, he asked why he did that. He shrugged and said it was his way of asserting dominance right from the get-go. By the look on Big Red's face, it worked.

"Les, you're holding up the game."

Big Red flexed his right hand and glared at Pete, then walked over to the pool table. He broke with a vicious stroke. Three balls jumped off the table and he stood there surveying his handiwork. His playing companions snickered as he picked up the balls, re-racked and then broke again with a more civilized stroke.

Boehm had been watching Big Red, but now turned back to Pete. "Les is all right. He just gets a little carried away at times."

"I didn't realize the two of you were drinking buddies."

A faint smile crossed Boehm's face. "We're not, but around here, everybody knows everybody. What brings you out this way? Another meeting with the Colonel?"

"No," Pete said. "I had something else I had to do. I thought I'd stop for a beer."

Boehm nodded and watched the television for a few minutes. The Tigers game was on and the hitter had just bounced into a double play with the bases loaded. Boehm winced and turned back to Pete. "I met your daughter a couple of days ago. Nice girl."

Pete had nearly forgotten that Julie and Sarah had accepted the Colonel's invitation to visit Colcorp's facility, although with a healthy dose of skepticism. The Colonel had even sent a car for them so Sarah didn't have to risk her new license with the state and local law enforcement boys on M-115.

"Nice of you and the Colonel to entertain them. I hope they weren't any trouble."

Boehm had a habit of talking while staring at the bar or glancing up at the television. He shook his head and said, "No trouble at all. How about our deal. Do you think it's going to go?"

"Depends on whether the Colonel is willing to make a few concessions on the environmental issue."

"Concessions?" Boehm said. "The Colonel's not going to like that kind of talk."

Pete laughed. "I know. We've already had this conversation."

Boehm gave a little chuckle. "I should have warned you. He jumped all over me when I told him about the problems in Bridgeview."

They engaged in small talk for a while, then Pete said, "How long have you worked for the Colonel?"

"About three years."

"It looks like you landed in a pretty nice situation. What was the connection?"

Boehm shrugged. "When I got out of the army, I needed something to do and the Colonel was good enough to take me on. I just stayed with him."

"I thought you'd probably spent time in the military."

"Why's that?" he said, looking at Pete.

"You carry yourself like a military man. Is that where you got the tat?" he asked, pointing to the words "Never Forget" tattooed on Boehm's forearm.

He looked down at his arm and nodded.

"Is there some meaning behind it?"

He shrugged again. "Just words."

THIRTY-THREE

Angie and Steve Johnson called first thing on Tuesday to alert him to the latest missiles from the Kral group. Anger churned in his gut as soon as he heard Kral's name and all of the resentments he'd felt toward the guy bubbled to the surface again.

One memorandum, Steve said, attacked Pete and other members of management for the firm's recent sluggish financial performance and demanded several changes that would significantly reduce his authority as managing partner. Fortunately, they'd seen that coming the last time he was in Chicago and devised a rapid response that would do the best-run political campaign justice. They agreed Steve would get a memorandum out to the partners before the end of the day.

The other memorandum was more of a problem. The Kral group demanded that a partners meeting be scheduled for Friday of that week and that Pete be required to report on everything that had happened in the investigation into Cara Lane's death since their last meeting. That put Richter's search front and center which had been his concern all along. Lying about the search was not an option, and notwithstanding Richter's snide remark, he couldn't control when the lab results came back or when Haskins would make his swimming accident announcement. He'd have to see if he could push back the date. That might be possible since the Colonel had tentatively scheduled a meeting with RyTech for later that week. After he got off the phone with Angie and Steve, he put in a call to the Colonel to find out whether a meeting date had been set. The Colonel wasn't in and he left a message.

Then Harry called just to talk. It must have been a slow day around the newsroom because he recounted for about the tenth time Sheriff Haskins' news conference after they apprehended Kurt Romer and his partner.

"Christ, you should have seen him," Harry said, letting out a hoot. "You would have thought he'd just nabbed John Dillinger single-handedly. He invited all the Michigan media and handed out photographs of himself for reporters to use with their stories. One showed him kneeling and examining that padlock at the entrance to the two-track wearing latex gloves. Now he's trying to plant a feature in next Sunday's editions portraying himself as a crime-fighting lawman who's ready for higher office."

"And no credit to us."

"Not a word about that anonymous tip I received that was the linchpin for everything. He sounded like he'd been personally staking out Romer and his pal every night for the past year."

"Ingrate," Pete said.

"You bet," Harry said and he was off again.

When Pete got an opening, he asked, "Anything new at the sheriff's office?"

"Just more of the same. I guess Richter and Tessler continue to push for more search warrants, but Haskins has been holding them off."

"What do they want to search?"

"I'm not sure, but Cap implied it was someone's house. That made me think of you because that scumbag Romer now has an alibi. Richter apparently wants to search for drugs that might have been used to disable Cara Lane. Stuff like that. I guess Haskins put the kibosh on more searches, at least for the time being."

Pete thought about what Harry had just said. Richter was no fool; he seemed to be thinking along the same lines as he was — that someone had slipped Cara something to get her out to deep water and let her drown. He wondered why Haskins would drag his feet on search warrants. That seemed to be a change of heart since they searched his Range Rover and, apparently, Romer's pickup.

"It sounds like Haskins is counting down to his next press conference when he announces it was a swimming accident," Pete said.

"Yep, just like most of us have been saying."

They rehashed their golf game with the Colonel, and Harry talked like he'd shot red numbers that day. "By the way," he said, "what did the Colonel want to talk to you about the other night?"

"He accused me of holding up his deal."

Harry paused. "Are you? You've been spending a lot of time on your investigation."

"No, we're actually a little ahead of schedule."

"Then why's he so edgy about it?"

"He's eager to plow a chunk of the proceeds into that night vision business of his, I guess."

"It's important to our troops," Harry said

"Umm hmm."

After Harry let him off the phone, Pete made another pass at Cara Lane's non-clothing items he'd retained. He started with her calendar. The litany of church activities, work schedules, social events and political rallies was familiar to him by now. He studied each entry anew, searching for some clue, some pattern to her activities, some indication of the people she associated with.

When he came to June, his eyes fixed on an entry that read "Din M;" he couldn't read the last initial. He hadn't paid much attention to the entry before, assuming it just referred to a social engagement with a friend. He remembered seeing a similar entry later on. He turned to

July. This time the entry read "MB 7 pm." The "B" trailed off again, but if you studied it, you could see what it was. He flipped through the pages a second time. Those were the only two entries. He stared at the calendar for a long time. MB. Manfred Beck. They'd had dinner in Chicago at least twice that summer. *The sonofabitch had lied to him!*

He grabbed the phone and angrily punched in Beck's number. Then he stopped and checked his watch. It was just after 10:00 a.m. Some things were best handled face-to-face. He scribbled a note to Julie, who was leaving to return to school later that day, saying he'd be back shortly. Then he grabbed the calendar, jumped in his Taurus and headed for Beck's worksite.

• • •

When Pete pulled in, there were three other vehicles parked near Beck's truck. He didn't care. He intended to confront Beck and if he had to do it in front of his men, well that was tough shit.

"Fred," he called as Beck walked toward the house carrying an armload of molding. "I need to talk to you."

Beck looked at Pete standing near his Taurus, feet spread and arms folded across his chest, the calendar clutched in one hand and a scowl on his face.

Beck glanced nervously toward the house. "I'm right in the middle of something," he said in a low voice. "Can't this wait?"

"Now," Pete said.

Beck looked toward the house again. One of his workers was coming out the door. Beck mumbled something to the man and handed the molding to him. Then he turned and walked slowly toward Pete.

"What is it?" he asked, again in a low voice. "I gave you copies of all my identification."

"You're a damned liar Manfred. So you only talked to Cara occasionally on the telephone until she came up here, huh? That's bullshit. You met with her at least twice in Chicago in the past couple of months." He shoved the calendar in Beck's face and pointed to the two entries.

Beck stared at them.

"You were the one she was afraid of, weren't you? I want the truth, Manfred. No more bullshit."

"That's not me," he said, his voice trembling. "I swear."

"Sure it is. Manfred Beck. MB. It took me a while to piece it together until I discovered your name is Manfred. Or at least that's the name you've been using."

Beck's hands were shaking and his voice broke. "That's not me, I tell you. I've never been in Chicago. I was here in Millport every day this summer."

"You'll have a chance to explain everything to the FBI. I'm going directly to the sheriff's office when I leave here and he'll have agents out here in no time. You're a big fish, Manfred. A fugitive from a political bombing who's still on the most-wanted list. There's no statute of limitations for someone who fled like you did, either. Now you're going to have to deal with a murder rap, too."

"No, please. This is all wrong."

Let the sonofabitch plead, Pete thought. He didn't give a damn.

"MB must be the other guy she knew up here."

"You're a stinking liar," Pete said. He got into the Taurus and spun out of the site.

• • •

Pete's cell phone rang as he was driving back to his cottage. It was Beck. He let it go to voicemail and seethed about being dumb enough to half-believe his story in the first place. When he pulled into his driveway, he saw Julie's bicycle leaning against a birch. He got out of the Taurus and could hear music coming from his porch. Buddy Holly again. He smiled even though he was still mad as hell at almost having been handled by Beck or Corrigan or what the hell ever his name was.

"Hi, Dad. Got your note. I just made myself at home." She took a sip of Fuze.

His cell phone rang. It was Beck again. He let it go to voice mail for the second time and set the phone to vibrate.

"So how was your visit to Colcorp?" he said, trying to take his mind off Beck for a while.

"Cool. Did you ever see those robots? They can pick things up and carry things and put things together and everything. The Colonel said that in time robots will do all the work and there won't be any need for humans, except maybe one person to watch the computer." She pursed her lips and looked worried. "I don't know what young people like me are going to do for jobs."

Pete smiled. "I have higher aspirations for you than to work in a factory."

"I know, but I'm worried. I bet robots will replace lawyers, too."

"Oh, come on," he said. "Robots would get bored doing what lawyers do. Where did you have lunch?"

"We went to this really neat place in Cadillac. We ate outside. I had a wonderful pasta and shrimp dish."

"Then you went horseback riding, right?"

She nodded. "The Colonel is a great rider. Mike's good, too. Do you know Mike Boehm?" She gave a dreamy sigh. "He's sooooo hot."

Pete wanted to say Boehm was also almost three times her age, but held his tongue. "So you had a good time after all."

"I had a wonderful time. Are all of your clients that nice?"

Pete thought for a moment. "Some of them."

They talked for an hour, just the two of them. She told him about the courses she'd be taking in the fall term and her goals for cross country. They talked about going skiing in Colorado during semester break like they used to do when her mother was alive. Julie said that Mike Boehm was a good skier and spent two weeks in Colorado every winter. She wondered whether he would be there over school break when they hoped to schedule their trip. Pete became irritated again, but didn't say anything. They made plans for Pete to come to school for parents' weekend; she said she wasn't even going to tell Wayne about the event. It served him right, he thought.

"Dad," Julie said as she flipped through his CD collection looking for something else to put on, "do you like Lynn?"

"What kind of question is that?" he asked.

She studied his face carefully, searching for the answer. "Do you?"

Lynn had stopped over one afternoon when Julie was there and had given her an impromptu art lesson. Pete had watched the two of them drawing birds and felt good. There'd be no replacing her mother, but it was nice to see Julie bond with another woman who was beginning to occupy an important place in his life.

"She's very nice," he said.

"Dad, I *know* that. Do you *like* her."

"Isn't that my business, young lady?"

"It's okay," she said. "I thought she was great." She paused for a moment. "I'm going to spend a summer in Paris like she did and learn to paint."

He looked at her. She was so much more grown up when she was alone than when she was with Sarah or one of her other friends.

Julie looked at the clock on the wall. "Yikes, I need to get going, Dad. Sarah's parents are driving me back. They live in Bloomfield Hills, did you know that?"

"I did know that."

"This works out so good. Now I don't have to take the Hound or you don't have to drive me."

"It works out *well*."

She put a hand to her mouth and giggled. "Oops, I forgot I was around a lawyer." She nuzzled against him and kissed him on the cheek. She looked at the rental Taurus in the driveway. "When are you getting the Range Rover back?"

"Next week, I hope. They had to order more parts."

"Why don't you just buy a new car. That thing's old anyway."

"Hey," he protested, "I like my Range Rover."

She looked at him. "You never did tell me what happened."

"I had an accident."

"Okay, I knew *that*. But what happened?"

"I had dinner with Harry one night and was coming home on Prentice Road. This big pickup came up behind me and ran me off the road. The sheriff thinks the guy was either drunk or it was road rage." He didn't want to tell her the full story.

"Oooh, Dad. A fishing accident. Totaling your car. You need to be more careful."

"It's hard to be careful when someone runs you off the road," he said defensively.

"Sorry, Dad, I didn't mean it that way." She smiled at him. "Well, I guess I should go. I don't want to keep Sarah's parents waiting." She gave him a long goodbye hug. He told her he loved her and watched her ride off. She veered off the driveway and for a moment he thought she might have hit something and lost her balance. Not to worry; she was just tormenting a squirrel. He laughed and it took away some of the emptiness.

THIRTY-FOUR

Pete sat and stared at the phone while his printer cranked away. He'd been about to call the sheriff several times, but never placed the call. He walked across the porch and put some more paper in the feeder tray. The printer started grinding again and spewed out more of the attachments to Angie's email. She'd been unsuccessful in obtaining the surveillance tape, but her contact in the security department of the CTA had sent her the stills which she'd forwarded on to him. There were over 300 of them. He flipped through the stack of paper. He needed to have a closer look. Maybe he'd spot Beck on the platform and that would tie things up with a nice big bow.

He began the tedious task of reviewing the stills. They were grainy and he used a magnifying glass to get a better look. In the 73rd frame, he saw the figure of a slim man on the platform with his hair pulled back in a ponytail carrying a backpack. It looked like Vrba. He reviewed a few more frames and became convinced that's who it was. He was standing on the edge of the platform and in some of the stills looked in the direction of the approaching train. Pete marked those stills and drew red arrows to identify the man he thought was Vrba.

Another two dozen frames and he saw Vrba in most of them. He examined the figures around him, looking for someone who resembled Beck. He didn't see him. He put the photos aside to give his eyes a break for a while, then looked at more frames. The passengers on the platform close to Vrba hadn't changed much. A few men in suits, a man in glasses and a baseball cap, a woman with a firm grip on her child's hand, a group of teens.

He reviewed another 50 frames and the crowd on the platform had filled in. Ten more frames. A train was obviously approaching because most heads including Vrba's were swiveled to the left. As he reviewed the stills, he noticed that the man with the glasses and cap had changed his position so he was right behind Vrba. It didn't look like Beck, though. Beck had a beard and this man looked clean-shaven.

Pete knew the train that killed Vrba didn't stop at that station, which meant it would have been moving at high speed. Twenty frames more and Pete could see that Vrba was leaning toward the tracks. Or more precisely, falling toward the tracks. Pete skipped forward. Vrba had disappeared and the side of the train came into view. He winced at the thought of the train striking Vrba at high speed. He skipped forward a few more frames and saw how everyone on the platform had recoiled. He shook his head. He'd seen that reaction before.

He studied the frames again. The same people — all shrinking with horror — were there, but the man in glasses and the baseball cap was gone. He reviewed more frames and saw the man at the edge of three of them heading toward the escalator. Pete used his magnifying glass to get a better look. The cap was still clamped low on his head, but he no longer wore glasses. The man's face was more visible, too, and he could see that he was clean-shaven just as he thought. It definitely wasn't Beck. He zeroed in on the frame, trying to identify the man in the grainy photograph. The man looked vaguely familiar. He looked again, this time hunching over the still with his magnifying glass.

Pete sat back for a while, collecting his thoughts. Then he returned to the frames that showed Vrba starting to fall toward the tracks. The man with glasses and the baseball cap was close to Vrba and directly behind him, which Pete had noticed before, but he could see nothing to indicate he'd pushed him. He just stood there, clutching his soft-sided briefcase under his right arm. Pete returned to the stills of the escalator before the man disappeared from view and squinted through his magnifying glass again. He couldn't be sure — the cap obscured his face — but the man vaguely resembled Mike Boehm. As he stared at the frames, it hit him. Another man with the initials "MB."

Pete sat back for a while and rubbed his eyes and thought, then squinted through his magnifying glass again for a long time. He didn't change his view that the man, without glasses, looked like Mike Boehm. *What the hell was going on?* He reviewed in his mind what little he knew about Boehm. He was a former military man who visited Chicago on business and could have met with Cara while he was there. He was also in the city around the time that Vrba died. Maybe he'd come down early, contrary to what he told Pete. Maybe he was responsible for Vrba's death. *But why?* If Beck was the fugitive from the bomb plot, how did Boehm fit into the equation? He studied the stills again.

Beck called for the fifth or sixth time. He let the call go to voicemail one more time and then checked the messages he'd left. They were all the same. He repeated his claim that he hadn't been in Chicago and begged Pete to meet with him again before he went to the sheriff. Pete thought about it some more. He'd been convinced that Beck was lying to him, but now he didn't know what to think. If that really was Boehm on the platform . . . He needed more information on him, that was clear, but knew he couldn't ask the Colonel. The Colonel would never understand if he suddenly confessed to secretly carrying out his own investigation into Cara Lane's death and now pointed a finger at his number one man.

Pete got on his laptop and logged on one of several sites he'd seen that advertised access to everyone's military 201 records. Those records would be a starting point. Boehm was an army man, that much he knew, but he had no idea how long he'd been in the service or what he'd done or anything else. About all he knew was that he'd started to work for the Colonel three years ago. He selected the site that looked the most promising and punched into his credit card information to pay $39.95 for a trial subscription. Then he logged on and found that he needed the person's serial number or dates of service and army unit. He had none of that information for Boehm.

As he sat thinking about Manfred Beck and Mike Boehm and the initials on Cara Lane's calendar, the Caller ID on his phone flashed Lynn's number. That was a call he wanted to take and he immediately got the idea of inviting her for drinks to talk the whole mess through. What she had to say, though, left him with a dead feeling in the pit of his stomach.

"Rona is taking me to the Traverse City airport," she said. "I'm on my way to Seattle to see Melissa."

"Is everything okay?"

There was a long silence at the other end. "I don't know."

He wasn't sure what to say for a minute. "Did she call you?" he asked.

"No, my son called. He talked to her this morning." There was a pause at the other end. "She sounded suicidal."

Oh my God, Pete thought. "Is there anything I can do, Lynn?"

"No, thank you. I just need to get out there as fast as I can."

Pete could hear the distress in her voice. He expressed his concern in every way he knew how without actually being with her and made her promise to call him with a report.

The call from Lynn made him think about Julie again. It had only been hours, but he missed her already. Wayne Sable's challenge to her stay at the lake had fizzled like a cheap firecracker in the rain when Kyle Cummings hit his lawyer with a draft motion to reopen the custody issue. Pete hadn't discussed it with Kyle yet, but he was seriously considering filing the motion and the conversation with Lynn reinforced his resolve. Julie deserved better than Wayne Sable and he was sick of being jacked around by the guy.

Slowly his thoughts returned to Mike Boehm and how he could get background information on him. This wasn't something Angie could help him with, and besides, after all she'd done for him already, she'd probably shoot him on sight if he asked her for another favor. Then he remembered Bill Sullivan. Sullivan was a career army man who had been in the MP unit Pete was attached to. He hadn't spoken to him in 10 years. He was retired from the army, but had landed a job with the National Personnel Records Center in St. Louis and had worked his way up the chain. It was worth a try.

Two hours later Sullivan called him back and they spent a half-hour catching up. Sullivan, who was from Oklahoma, had become a dyed-in-the-wool St. Louis Cardinals fan. "The Cubbies have been slipping," he said, "and the Big Red's coming on. You better hold onto your seat." That led to more baseball talk.

"Well, what can I do for you, Pete? Or is this just a social call?"

"Part social, part business. Off the record?"

"Sure," Sullivan said, "off the record."

"I've been trying to check a man out. I tried one of those computer services that advertise access to 201 files, but I didn't have the basic information about the guy to get anywhere."

Sullivan laughed. "Those services are worthless anyway. By the time all of the useful information is redacted, which is what happens, you can't learn shit about a man through them. Who you trying to check out?"

"Guy by the name of Mike Boehm." He spelled it for him. "He's about 40, give or take. I'm not quite sure when he was in the army or for how long, but I believe he got out a few years ago."

"Let me run him through the computer. Is this urgent?"

"Kind of."

"Okay. Before I let you off the phone, the Cubs are playing the Cardinals in St. Louis in the middle of September. You want to come down? I can get us good tickets. Loser buys at Musial's."

"Just let me know. I'll be there."

Pete was studying the stills again when Sullivan called back later that afternoon.

"Boy, you picked a doozy. There are three things I think you'll find interesting. The first is that Boehm's military records are sealed. I had to go through a lot of hoops to get access to them. When I saw the file, I can see why. The upshot is I'm not supposed to tell you things two and three."

That wasn't what Pete wanted to hear.

"What do you want the information for?"

Pete told him about his personal investigation into the death of Cara Lane and his suspicions about Boehm.

"Interesting," Sullivan said. "Okay, this has to be strictly between you and me or I'll get my ass in a sling. Captain Michael Boehm — or I guess I should say former Captain Michael Boehm — was given a general discharge about three years ago. There's the honorable discharge, which good guys like you got. Then there's the dishonorable discharge for really bad dudes. Deserters and people like that. The general discharge is sandwiched in the middle.

"Okay," Sullivan said, using his favorite way of starting a sentence again, "here's the third thing, the meat as they say. Boehm pulled two tours in Afghanistan. He was in special ops and according to his file, had a rather unique aptitude for his job. One night three guys from his unit were out on patrol and their Afghan guide led them into a trap. All three of our guys were captured. The Taliban claimed credit and every day for the next week they issued a statement — kind of a press release, you might say — detailing where parts of their bodies could be found and saying the same thing would happen to all members of the allied forces if we didn't get out of their country. All three of our guys had been decapitated and their hands and feet were cut off. One guy looked like he'd been skinned while still alive."

Pete got a sick feeling. "Jesus," he said, shaking his head.

"Yeah, Jesus is right. Okay, two weeks later the bodies of the Afghan guide and his 14-year-old son, who reportedly was training to be a suicide bomber, were found skinned and dismembered in the same way as our special ops guys. Flyers written in Arabic were posted in their village describing where their body parts could be found. Some friggin' kind of vengeance, huh?"

"That's amazing. And Boehm was involved in that?"

"The brass thinks so according to the file. There was this big hush-hush investigation, but I guess they couldn't come up with any real evidence except the bodies. They did manage to keep it out of the media, though. There was a hell of a lot of sympathy for the guys under suspicion, but I guess that shouldn't come as any surprise. Extreme provocation and all that. No one was court-martialed, but I understand the mucky-mucks decided they couldn't let it go altogether so they came up with some kind of charges and that led to the general discharges of Boehm and the others."

Neither man said anything for a few moments.

Then Pete said, "We both spent time in the military. You a lot longer than I. Do you ever wonder what you might have done in those circumstances?"

"Sure, and I'm scared of the answer. You know what connected Boehm and the others?"

"No idea."

"After their buddies were killed, Boehm and three others went out and got these tattoos on their forearms. You know what they said?" Sullivan didn't wait for Pete to answer. "Two words: 'Never Forget.'"

When Pete got off the phone with Sullivan, he thought back to that day in Chicago when Boehm had driven his Hummer right at the two Muslim men in the crosswalk, eyes as hard as tempered steel, never flinching as they scattered for their lives. At the time, he'd attributed it to the stress of getting the deal done, but maybe there was more to it than that. The experience in Afghanistan could have affected Boehm more than appeared on the surface. It wouldn't be the first time.

He also thought about the books on terrorist tactics he'd seen in Cara's things. And he thought about the Arab-owned investment company that had bought the plant Hank Janicek worked for and promptly moved production offshore, beginning the downward spiral of the Janiceks' family life. Maybe John Stump was right and the anger in Cara ran deeper than it did with ideologues like Weisner. Maybe that anger is what linked Cara and Mike Boehm together.

But how would they have met? Cara hadn't lived in the area for years. Of course, Clem Moffat could have introduced them. That was a possibility. Maybe Boehm concocted some twisted plot against the Muslim community and it initially appealed to Cara, but as she thought about it some more, she backed out and Boehm killed her out of fear that she would blow the whistle. But what about Moffat? He knew about the plot, too, and wasn't going to participate and Boehm hadn't killed him. Or had he? The guy seemed to have disappeared from the face of the earth.

THIRTY-FIVE

Pete was still trying to sort it all out in his mind as he drove to the Janiceks for the second time in a couple of days. Beck and Boehm, Beck and Boehm. He kept going back and forth, weighing it all in his mind, trying to figure things out. Assuming Boehm was the killer and he was plotting some kind of strike against the Muslim community, what would be the target? He kept thinking about the maps of Millennium Park and the Chicago area shopping centers in Cara's things. They all had marks on them. But it made no sense to assume they were the targets because they had no more unique connection to Muslims than they did to Christians or Jews or Hindus.

And as much as the signs now pointed to Boehm, he had to face the facts: he had no evidence to link him to Cara. Or, for that matter, to Vrba's death other than his belief he was the man in the grainy video photos. He thought back to his conversation with Beck and wondered again how much of what the guy told him he could believe. What he said seemed to make sense, though, in view of what he'd just learned. Maybe another run at the Janiceks would reveal some answers.

• • •

Hank's pickup was in the driveway again. As he walked in the Janicek house, he handed Marian a box that contained more of Cara's things that he'd concluded had no relevance to his investigation. She ducked into the kitchen and returned with a glass of iced tea for him. Hank came out of a bedroom and fixed him with his usual hostile stare.

He looked at Hank. "I need to ask you again, Hank. Have you heard anything about some group in this area planning a strike against some target? Probably a Muslim target in Chicago. It could be the key to solving your daughter's death."

Hank stood there with a sullen look on his face. "I told you before, I ain't heard nothin' about no plot against nobody."

"Think about it," Pete said. "Maybe something that was part of a conversation at Kelties or the Whitetail. Maybe it didn't mean anything to you at the time, but it does now that you're able to put it in context."

Hank stood there with the pinched look on his face. "You hard of hearing or somethin'? I said I ain't heard nothin'."

The conversation was going nowhere. Then he thought of something. "Marian, could I see Cara's yearbook?"

She went upstairs and returned with the yearbook and handed it to him.

He paged through it. Hank watched him for a few minutes and then left the room. Pete continued to page through the yearbook. Then he found what he was looking for. There in the freshman class pictures was Mike Boehm. He'd been in high school with Cara and with a small student population, it was unlikely they wouldn't have known each other even though they were a class apart. There it was, the link he'd been looking for. His pulse raced as he stared at Boehm's picture, a scrawny teenager.

Hank returned. "Do you know a man named Mike Boehm?" Pete asked him. Like when he asked him about Clem Moffat, he could see the look of recognition on his sour face.

"Why are you asking me about all these people?"

Pete's response was hard and cold. "Do you know him?"

Hank stared at Pete for a few moments. "Mike's a war hero," he mumbled. "Served in Afghanistan two times."

"Are you aware of whether he knew Clem Moffat?"

Hank looked at Pete like he was the biggest fool to ever come down the pike. "Everyone from around here knew Clem. He was a hero to all the boys."

Pete softened his voice. "Here's why I'm asking. Like I said the last time we met, Cara was trying to get her life straightened out. But some people who knew about her skills with explosives — she learned those skills from Clem Moffat while he was in Idaho, by the way — just wouldn't leave her alone. I believe a group in this area is planning to bomb a Muslim target. I'm not sure where, but Chicago would be a good guess. They tried to recruit Moffat to help with the explosives. He begged off because the FBI and ATF people have him under close scrutiny. I believe Moffat told them to try Cara. That was an easy sell because Boehm is the leader of the group and he knew Cara from school. Plus he knew all about the Oregon plot. Are you with me, Hank?"

Hank's face looked more pinched than ever. He stared at the floor and said nothing.

"Cara was tempted — she knew it was an Arab-owned outfit that bought the company you used to work for and hated them for closing it down and throwing everyone out of their jobs — but in the end backed out. I'm not exactly sure why, but suspect she concluded she'd had enough violence in her life and didn't want to go down that road again. She had a friend in this area and came up to talk things over with him. That's why she was at Clear Lake. I believe she met Boehm after she left me at dinner that night and he killed her when she gave him her final answer. Boehm probably was afraid she'd blow the whistle on them or something. He was in special ops in the army and knew how to make it look like a swimming accident. I think Boehm also killed

Cara's roommate in Chicago because he feared she might have told him about the plot."

Hank was still staring at the floor as though traumatized. His face looked ashen and his gnarled hands opened and closed and his fingernails dug into his flesh. It was as though all the demons from the past had come to roost in his living room. Marian was sobbing and dabbing at her eyes.

"I'm going to take this to the sheriff. He'll have to coordinate with the authorities here in your county and down in Chicago, but when the dust settles, I expect Mike Boehm to be charged with murder."

Pete looked at the Janiceks. "Either of you want to say something before I go?"

Marian shook her head and dabbed at her eyes again. Hank just continued to stare at the floor.

"I'm really sorry," Pete said.

• • •

Pete needed something to eat. And time to think. He didn't want to stop at the Whitetail and risk running into Boehm or Big Red or someone else from that crowd so he got on M-115 and found a place in Mesick. He ordered a club sandwich and began to doodle with a pencil.

He knew he'd taken his investigation as far as he could. With Boehm's background, he'd be out of his mind to confront him directly as he had Diener and Beck. Or earlier, Kurt Romer. He had to go to Haskins. He knew he had a problem, though; much of his case against Boehm was circumstantial and he wasn't sure how Haskins would react. He'd just have to lay it all out and hope Haskins would pick up the ball. He suspected that a search of Boehm's home and vehicle would turn up evidence linking him to Cara. Maybe they'd even find the explosives he was planning to use in his bomb plot. And once the forensics people knew what to look for, they should be able to slice and dice the surveillance tape and pin Boehm to Vrba's death.

The question was what to do about Beck. His story had checked out, but that didn't mean he wasn't the fugitive. He still didn't completely buy the part of his explanation about having met Cara for the first time at Northwestern Michigan College even though the dates meshed. He finished his club sandwich and decided to go in and see Haskins in the morning. By then maybe he'd think of a way to deal with Beck. Thoughts of Beck's wife and three young daughters floated around in his mind.

Before he did anything else, though, he had to do something he wasn't looking forward to. He knew his relationship with the Colonel would be irreparably damaged if he simply accused his top lieutenant of serious crimes without at least alerting him first. And he had no idea how he was going to explain to the Colonel that he'd been spending much of his time on his private investigation into Cara Lane's death rather than concentrating on the RyTech deal.

THIRTY-SIX

It was almost dark when Pete pulled into the driveway of the Colonel's Lake Michigan house. His wife, Madelaine, said he was staying there because he had an early tee time at Arcadia Bluffs the next morning. The Colonel tried to pump Pete when he called, but he begged off, saying he preferred to talk about it in person.

The Colonel was alone. He met Pete at the door and led him into a spacious study off the entry hall. While the Colonel mixed drinks for them, Pete gazed out the large bay window facing the lake and wondered how to begin.

"Well, what's so urgent?" the Colonel asked as he dropped into a red leather arm chair, solving that problem for him.

Pete took a sip of his drink. "How well do you know Mike Boehm?"

"Mike?" The Colonel looked at him quizzically. "Pretty well I think. Why?"

Pete didn't know how to sugar-coat what he was about to say. "Are you aware of the allegations that he committed atrocities while serving in Afghanistan?"

The Colonel's eyes narrowed. "Who told you that?"

294

"A friend. I understand it involved revenge killings. Did he ever tell you about it?"

The Colonel shook his head slowly. "Not really. But why are you raising this stuff, Pete."

Pete locked eyes with the Colonel. "Because I believe he's planning a strike against the Muslim community and that he killed Cara Lane to keep her quiet."

The Colonel's face darkened. "Oh for crissakes, Pete. Have you been smoking something?" He shook his head in disgust.

"No, I haven't." He thought about it and knew it was time to come clean with the Colonel. He told him all about his personal investigation into the death of Cara Lane. By the time he'd finished, the Colonel was just staring at him.

"You lied to me," he said softly.

"I didn't lie to you," Pete said. "I just didn't tell you everything I was doing. There was something that kept gnawing at me about Cara Lane's death and I finally figured it out."

"You lied," the Colonel said, never taking his eyes off him. "My gut told me something was wrong. You flat-out lied to me."

"I'm sorry you feel that way."

The Colonel wiped his mouth with a napkin and placed his drink on the coffee table. "Excuse me for a minute. I've got to hit the john. Damned prostate."

He returned a few minutes later, "What evidence do you have that Mike is guilty of all those wild things you're accusing him of?"

"Unfortunately, I have a lot of evidence."

The Colonel stared at him again. Pete's cell phone rang. He checked; it was Marian Janicek. He let the call go to voicemail and switched the phone to vibrate.

He laid it all out for the Colonel, beginning with why he believed Cara had been murdered, Boehm's background and how he knew Cara from school, the Clem Moffat link, Boehm's dinners with Cara in Chicago. He added that when Cara gave Boehm her final "no," he killed her to protect the integrity of his mission, to use military terminology. The circumstances were perfect to make Cara's death look like an accident, Pete said: a steamy August night when it wouldn't be unusual for someone to go for a swim to cool off. Then, Pete said, Boehm killed Vrba out of fear that Cara might have told him about the plot. He tried to make that look like an accident, too, or possibly suicide. Pete didn't say anything about being run off the road. He still wasn't sure who was behind that.

The Colonel finally spoke. "I think you're forgetting one important thing in this crazy story of yours. The sheriff and the prosecuting attorney have basically concluded the Lane woman's death was a swimming accident. Like I told you after golf that night, Haskins himself told me they plan to make an announcement in the next week or two."

Pete hadn't anticipated debating the case with him, but said, "When they hear my story, I believe they're going to run more tests and find that Boehm either slipped Cara something or possibly immobilized her some way so he could get her out to deep water and let her drown. The M.E. is already questioning whether the cut on her head could have been caused by hitting her head on the raft. The angle is wrong."

The Colonel continued to stare in his direction without appearing to really see him. Pete's cell phone vibrated but he didn't check to see who was calling. He was at a critical point in his conversation with the Colonel and he could see the old soldier wasn't taking it well. Pete wound up by saying that the CTA surveillance tape showed a man he believed to be Boehm right behind Vrba just before he fell into the path of the oncoming train.

"That day I went with Boehm to visit the Bridgeview plant? I believe he came to Chicago a day or two early. That's when he killed Vrba."

The Colonel's eyes focused on him again. "I thought I knew you, Pete, but this amateurish investigation of yours seems to have addled your brain. I've been thinking about it while I've been listening to you and I've concluded it's time for me to get new legal counsel. You've really gone off the deep end this time."

Pete's cell phone vibrated again, but he ignored it as he'd done before.

The Colonel went to the bar again and freshened his drink. Pete declined and watched the Colonel rummage around in his desk drawers and pull out more cocktail napkins. Instead of returning to his chair, he took a seat behind the desk and stared at Pete.

Pete met his gaze. "I'm sorry, Colonel."

The expression on the Colonel's face was dark and brooding.

"Well," Pete said, "I'm going to head home. I'm sorry to have to give you this news, but I wanted to tell you personally. I'm going to see Haskins in the morning. I hope you'll reconsider your decision to change legal counsel. If not, I'll do everything I can to assure a smooth transition."

As he turned to leave, he heard an unsettling metallic sound behind him. He knew what it was even without looking and felt like he'd been kicked in the gut. The Colonel held a Colt Special Combat Government automatic in his right hand. The same .45 caliber weapon he'd watched the Colonel fire on his private range behind Colcorp's facility. Only now it was aimed squarely at him.

"Sit down, Pete," the Colonel said, sounding weary.

Pete eased back into his chair. All he could look at was the muzzle of the .45 aimed at his chest. When he got over the initial shock, he remembered that the Colonel's son had been killed in Afghanistan and he saw everything with a clarity that frightened him almost as much as the pistol. "You're involved in this, too, aren't you?" he said softly.

The Colonel stared at him with a hard-edged look Pete had never witnessed before. Like he were a complete stranger.

"You just couldn't leave this alone, could you?" the Colonel said. "I tried to send you every goddamned signal I could think of to get you to back off, but you had to keep poking your nose into things that don't concern you."

The Colt's bore looked like a drain pipe. Pete flinched involuntarily every time he looked at it. He'd grown up around guns and was familiar with a lot of different hardware from his army days, but he'd never looked into the business end of a loaded .45 before. Sweat trickled down his side and he struggled to keep his hands from shaking.

He took a deep breath and then said in a voice that he knew had a slight tremor, "Why, Colonel? You have everything."

The Colonel stared straight ahead for a long time, then muttered, "I have nothing."

Pete tried to think of what to say, how to reason with him. The Colonel was still staring into space.

"You've never lost your only son, have you?" he said after a while.

Pete slowly shook his head.

"You know what they did? They skinned his body while he was still alive. Next they cut off his hands and feet, one by one. After that they cut off his head and mounted it on a pike in one of their dogshit villages. Then every day for the next week they sent a communication to his unit telling them where to find a body part and saying the same thing would happen to all of them if we didn't get out of Afghanistan." It was the same grisly tale that Sullivan had told him.

Tears dribbled down the Colonel's face and his right hand, the one holding the pistol, shook. Pete knew better than to try something, though. He wouldn't stand a chance. His best option was to keep him talking, to show sympathy.

"Your son was in the same unit as Mike Boehm, wasn't he?"

The Colonel acted like he hadn't heard him. "A soldier knows the risks of dying in combat. There can be honor in that. But not what happened to Seth."

Pete felt empty inside. Then he said gently, "So Mike Boehm and the other special ops did the same thing to the Afghan guide and his son. It was retribution. I can understand how they must have felt."

The Colonel just sat there.

"But that wasn't enough," Pete said, "and you decided to make a strike against the Muslim community in this country. What was the target? A mosque?"

The Colonel laid the Colt on the desk, the muzzle facing Pete, and wiped his eyes with one of the napkins. Pete again thought about making a move. Lunge for the gun, maybe, and try to swat it away. He knew a struggle with the Colonel would follow even if he were successful, but at least he'd have a chance. Or maybe he could spin out of his chair and try to make it through the door and outside before the Colonel could get a clear shot at him. He knew the chances of that were slim, too; he'd seen the Colonel in action on the pistol range.

The Colonel must have been reading his mind because he said, "Don't try anything, Pete." His voice continued to sound weary, matter of fact. Pete felt his cell phone vibrate again.

"A mosque," the Colonel said, grunting in a way that made it sound like he was amused. "I don't think so."

"What, then?" Pete asked, fearing he knew the answer. His golf shirt was soaked with sweat, and he held one hand with the other to keep from shaking.

The Colonel just sat there for a few minutes, then said, "Bombing a mosque would only create sympathy for them. We need another 9/11 to create a backlash that will let us establish the right policy. We need to get the terrorist scum out of this country and then go after them in the holes where they live."

Pete thought of the maps of Millennium Park and the shopping centers in Cara Lane's things and cringed. The Colonel was taking a page out the book of experts who had long theorized that it was just a matter of time until terrorists began to focus on targets where Middle America lived and played and shopped rather than on trophy targets like the Twin Towers. Create terror among the people in their daily lives. That would trigger the backlash he wanted. It was sick, but it was exactly what was going on. He could see the Colonel kneeling at his son's grave, plotting his twisted revenge.

The Colonel used his thumb to punch in a number on his cell phone while he continued to keep his right hand near the Colt.

"*Shit*," the Colonel muttered when he apparently got no answer. "Where the hell are you?" he said. "I left a message that I need you here right away." He snapped the phone shut.

For the next half hour, Pete tried to keep the Colonel talking, desperately looking for a way out. His hopes sank with every passing minute. When Boehm arrived, he knew it was over.

The Colonel alternately picked up the Colt and trained it on Pete and then laid it back on the desk. He flexed his right hand, but it was never far from the pistol's grip.

A while later, Pete wasn't exactly sure how long because everything seemed so surreal, he saw headlights flash through the study window. His heart pounded. He had no options now, not even bad ones.

He heard the front door open. "In here, Mike," the Colonel said.

Pete heard footsteps and then saw the startled look on the Colonel's face. He turned his head and saw Hank Janicek standing in the door with his double-barreled shotgun pointed at the Colonel. From the odor, it had been fired recently.

"Your boy ain't coming, Colonel." Hank's gravelly voice sounded unemotional, almost calm.

"Hank. What the hell is this?" Pete saw the Colonel's hand inch toward the Colt.

"Take your hand away from that piece," Hank said softly.

The Colonel drew his hand back. Pete's eyes flicked between Hank and the Colonel. He was caught between two madmen, like a pawn in some larger deadly drama that was playing out right in front of him.

"You killed my girl." Hank said. His raspy voice was still so calm it was frightening. Pete had seen the hate on Hank's face when his anger had been directed at him. But he was different now. His pinched face was flushed and his eyes, black as the night, were fixed on the Colonel and looked dead.

"You're crazy, Hank," the Colonel said, clearly shaken by his sudden appearance. "Put that shotgun down and we can talk this out. This guy right here," he said, motioning toward Pete, "he's the one who killed your daughter. The sheriff is just waiting to come up with more evidence against him. Let's go down to the sheriff's office, Hank. We can go together."

The anger Pete felt when he heard the Colonel's words almost caused him to lose control and lunge at him. He wanted to choke the life out of the sonofabitch with his bare hands.

"You friggin' liar!" Hank's calm had vanished and like some wild, caged animal, the primal rage Pete had witnessed in him before surged to the fore. "Your boy told me all about it before I put him down! You killed my girl!"

Then the insane drama that was playing out around him exploded. Pete's cell phone vibrated yet again just as the Colonel grabbed for his Colt and Hank fired the first barrel. The sound rocked the room and was so deafening he could feel it ripple through his body with a lethal savagery. The Colonel sagged back in his chair and red mist floated through the air and slowly coated the wall and bay window. He saw Hank aim at the Colonel's slumping body again and could see his lips move in an angry snarl.

Pete lunged toward Hank. The second thunderclap exploded through the room just as Pete's left hand clamped down on the hot, oily barrel. He chopped down on Hank's arm as hard as he could with the edge of his right hand and could feel his grip on the shotgun loosen. Pete wrenched it from his hands. Hank's eyes were glassy and unfocused and he took a step toward him. Pete wielded the shotgun like a club and swung at Hank. Hank raised a hand in defense but he was too late. The stock caught him on the side of his head and he went down.

Pete stepped back. The acrid smell of cordite burned his nostrils and his ears rang like giant symbols were pounding in his head. He looked toward where the Colonel had been sitting just seconds before. The second blast had knocked him completely out of the chair. Blood was everywhere, splattering the wall and window with bright red. He stepped toward the desk and saw the Colonel's bleeding body. He closed his eyes and turned his head and stood there for a minute. He looked at the Colonel again but didn't see the Colt.

He felt nauseous. Hank was sprawled on the floor and blood seeped from a gash on his head. Pete prayed he hadn't killed him. He knelt and placed a finger on the inside of Hank's wrist. He could feel a pulse.

Pete backed out of the room, still holding the shotgun by the barrel. He couldn't stop shaking. Hank had left the outside door open and he went out. He kicked the door shut and stumbled down the steps. His heart was pounding like a jackhammer inside his chest cavity. He stood there, gulping in the cool night air, trying to steady himself.

After a few minutes, he threw the shotgun toward a patch of tall dune grass and walked to his car. He opened a door for light, keeping an eye on the house, and punched at the numbers on his cell phone. His placed one hand over the other to steady them. It took him three tries to get the sheriff's office number right. He gave his name and the Colonel's address. His voice sounded like it was coming from outside his body. He told the dispatcher to send officers to the scene as soon as possible. And an ambulance.

He took the keys from Hank's truck and flung them into the night. He looked at the house door. It was still closed. He checked the back of Hank's truck and found an iron bar and slid it through the handle to secure the door.

Then he flopped on the grass, still breathing hard. The scene from the Colonel's study burned in his mind. He stared up at the sky on another perfectly clear night, trying to stuff the images into that dark place in his consciousness reserved for unpleasant things. Tears clouded his eyes. He heard the sirens as he lay there feeling empty and sick and alone.

THIRTY-SEVEN

The October air was crisp under a cobalt blue sky, and a gentle breeze off the bay chased a handful of dry leaves across empty parking slots on Main Street. It was homecoming weekend at Millport High School and the street was blocked off for the morning parade that would kick off the day's festivities. Pete loafed along, enjoying the booster signs in the store windows and what color remained on the trees covering the Elberta bluffs across the water.

Harry's face crinkled into a broad smile when Pete stepped into the *Sentinel's* offices carrying the familiar bag from Ebba's Bakery. Pete opened the bag and slid it across the desk. Harry eyed the contents and plucked out one of his favorite blueberry muffins.

"I'm glad you emailed," Harry said. "I've got a nice day all planned out for us. In a little while, we'll go outside to watch the parade. Then around noon we'll head over to the Eagle's Club tailgate party and have brats and teriyaki chicken. That should give us time to make the kick-off. Both teams are undefeated so there's going to be a big crowd." He took a bite of muffin and grinned. "Fortunately, I have press credentials and should be able to get us in. Tonight we'll celebrate our victory with dinner at Rona's."

"Perfect."

Harry glanced out his window and got a faraway look in his eyes. "I was sitting here thinking before you came in. I still can't believe the Colonel was behind everything."

Pete pursed his lips and nodded. "He never got over his son's death. It wasn't enough that Boehm and his special ops buddies had already claimed their revenge. He was consumed by hate. Boehm, too."

"And the way they planned to do it. If they'd bombed busy parks and shopping malls and places like that, there could have been hundreds or even thousands of casualties."

"Collateral damage, to their way of thinking. They wanted to create enough terror within the country to drive the sort of policies against Muslims they favored."

"And that from a guy who raised more money for charity than anyone else in this area." Harry took another bite of his muffin. "He was even going to kill you."

Pete took a deep breath and expelled it. "He knew he couldn't let me walk away from his house that night. As far as that incident on Prentice Road, I'm not sure whether he was behind it or someone else. I still think it could have been Romer."

Harry shook his head.

"To the Colonel's credit," Pete said, "he did try to throw me off my investigation in non-lethal ways. He even created problems for me within my law firm to distract me."

"I thought Kral made that up."

"That's what I thought at the time, too. The thing that bothered me was I couldn't figure out how Kral discovered the Cara Lane situation in the first place and knew all the details. It never occurred to me that the Colonel was the only one with enough knowledge of the internal politics at our law firm to know where to plant the seed. It's all so obvious now, but it wasn't at the time."

"And he knew all along that you were poking around."

Pete nodded. "Since my first meeting with Mrs. Janicek. I'm not sure how he found out, but suspect it might have been from Big Red who was bragging around town that he'd run off a Chicago lawyer who was pestering the Janiceks. From that point on, he apparently knew about everything I was doing."

Harry shook his head.

"Things were trending the right way with Haskins who wanted to brand Cara's death a swimming accident for his own political reasons," Pete said, "and he felt that Richter would fall in line at the end. My investigation, though, made him nervous."

"Was Big Red involved?"

"I don't think so. You had him tabbed all along. He apparently was just an officious bully who couldn't keep his nose out of things. He was a useful source of information for the Colonel and Boehm, though."

Harry looked thoughtful. "It was interesting what the sheriff found when he searched Boehm's house."

"That's right. From what I heard, it looked like a Navy seal's supply chest. An inflatable rubber raft, night vision goggles, the whole works. After Boehm slipped Cara something, that's apparently how he got her out to deep water and let her drown."

Harry shook his head again. He looked out the window and then quickly turned back to Pete. "Oh Jesus, that was Art Norman. I think he might have seen you. He's been walking around town like a whipped puppy, complaining that you've never followed up on that article you promised to write with him."

Pete cringed. "Let's try to figure out something at dinner."

They sat quietly for a couple of minutes and finished their muffins.

"You know, I feel responsible for a lot of this," Pete said. "Two more people died because I wouldn't let the thing alone."

Harry stared at him with the look of a stern father. "You can't blame yourself. You did nothing wrong. You just wanted to see justice done."

He sighed. "Intellectually, I know you're right, but I still feel like I've ruined a lot of lives. The Colonel's family. The Janiceks."

"I told you, it's not your fault. The fault lies with the Colonel and Mike Boehm." He paused for a moment. "What's going to happen to Hank?"

Pete shrugged. "Don't know. He's up for two homicides. I've arranged for one of the best criminal lawyers in Chicago to represent him *pro bono*. We'll have to see."

"Insanity defense?"

Pete shrugged again. "I don't know."

They sat quietly again, each alone with his thoughts.

"Do you know what Hank was doing when Haskins' people got to the Colonel's house that night?" Pete said. "He was sitting against the wall with blood everywhere looking at an old picture of his daughter on a swing in their backyard."

Harry shook his head again. "So he loved her after all."

"I guess so. He also might have had some idea of what the Colonel's group was planning. He wasn't involved himself, but probably would have liked to have been. But he had no idea how Cara fit into the picture until it all came together that night when I was at his house."

"Then he exacted his own revenge."

Pete nodded.

"How about Mrs. Janicek?" said Harry.

"She wants to support Hank. Maybe she'll eventually go out to Oregon and live with her sister, I don't know." He paused and then added, "That's something else I blame myself for. If I'd taken her calls that night, maybe I would have been able to head off the Colonel's death."

"Maybe, but then you'd probably be dead yourself. No way the Colonel was just going to let you go."

He knew Harry was right.

"On the positive side, we had our big partners meeting on Tuesday and worked out a new strategic plan for the next five years." Pete couldn't hold back his grin. "But the best news is that Marty Kral will be leaving the firm at the end of the year by mutual agreement."

Harry reached for another muffin and raised it in a toast. "Congratulations. How did you pull that off?"

"He forced a vote on his proposal to merge into a larger firm and the partners rejected it. He'd hoped to leverage himself into a better position through a merger and most of the partners saw through him. I think I've also locked up a deal with a twelve-lawyer firm that will more than double the loss of revenue as a result of Kral leaving."

"So it's win-win," Harry said.

Pete nodded again. "As for yours truly . . ."

Harry cocked an eye at him. "You're not retiring."

"No, but I am going to retool so I can start doing some of the things I want to do while I'm still young enough to do them. We're reorganizing our management structure. I'm going to transition out of day-to-day firm management early next year and then we'll see."

"How do you plan to spend your extra free time?"

"Do some writing, spend more time up here, take on only those legal matters that really interest me, spend more time with Julie."

Harry looked out the window again, maybe to check on whether Art Norman was lurking outside. "Have you talked to Lynn?"

"Last week. I wanted to go out and see her but she discouraged me. Her daughter hasn't gotten better and she sounded exhausted."

"You miss her?"

He remained silent for a while, then said, "Yeah, I do."

Harry jumped up. "We need to get outside. I can hear the band." He handed Pete a copy of the *Sentinel's* Tuesday edition with a color picture of five pretty young girls on the cover. "Take this so you'll know who's who."

Main Street had come alive and people thronged both sides of the street. A block up, the high school band marched toward them four abreast, alternating between Millport High's fight song and John Philip Sousa numbers.

Pete glanced at the paper. The homecoming queen was a senior girl with long blonde hair. Her court consisted of one girl from each of the classes. The sophomore representative was Carrie Beck.

The band had saved their peppiest numbers for when they passed through the heavy part of the crowd. Tubas groaned and trombones wailed and cymbals clanged. Pete scanned the crowd. Across the street, in the middle of the block, he spotted Fred Beck standing with a woman he assumed was his wife and their other two young daughters. He stared at Beck for a few minutes, wondering, then resumed watching the parade.

A pair of vintage convertibles with tops down followed the floats. The queen and her oldest attendants were in the first car and the freshman and sophomore attendants brought up the rear. The Beck family clapped wildly and shrieked and pointed as the girls passed.

Carrie Beck perched on top of the back seat and waved and blew kisses and tossed candy to children along the parade route. As they passed, she made eye contact with Pete for one fleeting second and waved and smiled brightly. He smiled and waved back.

ABOUT THE AUTHOR

Robert Wangard splits his time between Chicago, where he practiced law, and northern Michigan. *Target* is his first novel, but he is the author of a half-dozen crime fiction short stories. He is a member of Mystery Writers of America, the Short Mystery Fiction Society, and various other writers' organizations.